THE EVIL THAT MEN DO

ROBERT GLEASON

A TOM DOHERTY ASSOCIATES BOOK
NEW YORK

THE EVIL THAT MEN DO

Copyright © 2018 by Robert Gleason

All rights reserved.

A Forge Book
Published by Tom Doherty Associates
175 Fifth Avenue
New York, NY 10010

www.tor-forge.com

Forge® is a registered trademark of Macmillan Publishing Group, LLC.

The Library of Congress Cataloging-in-Publication Data is available upon request.

ISBN 978-0-7653-3813-6 (hardcover)
ISBN 978-1-4668-3758-4 (ebook)

Our books may be purchased in bulk for promotional, educational, or business use. Please contact your local bookseller or the Macmillan Corporate and Premium Sales Department at 1-800-221-7945, extension 5442, or by email at MacmillanSpecialMarkets@macmillan.com.

First Edition: May 2018

Printed in the United States of America.

0 9 8 7 6 5 4 3 2 1

FOR TOM DOHERTY

SPECIAL THANKS

To Jerry Gibbs, for six decades of extraordinary friendship.

ACKNOWLEDGMENTS

To Sessalee Hensley and Christine Jaeger for their unflagging support.

To Linda Quinton, a true friend.

To Lucille Rettino, whose Herculean labors make us all look good.

To Jane Mayer, who deserves a Nobel Prize. Thank you so much for writing *Dark Money*.

To Bill Maher, who always makes me howl with laughter and whose satire deserves a Nobel Prize.

To Susan, to whom I owe basically . . . everything.

To George Noory and Lisa Lyon for always having my back.

To my editors, Eric Raab and Elayne Becker. You are both hydrogen on the atomic scale, the diamonds that cut diamonds.

To Masha Gessen, who risked her life to expose Putin's crimes. Thank you for writing *The Man Without a Face*.

To Karen Dawisha, whose book *Putin's Kleptocracy* is an astonishing account of Putin's atrocities and, for me, was a godsend.

To Maribel and Roberto Gutierrez—I will never forget.

To Mary Persic, for her clean well-lighted heart.

To Herb Alexander, 1910–1988—They threw away the mold.

There should exist among the citizens neither extreme poverty nor, again, excessive wealth, for both are productive of great evil...

—Plato, the *Laws*

Great men are almost always bad men...There is no worse heresy than [to say] that the office sanctifies the holder of it.

—Lord Acton, letter to Mandell Creighton, April 5, 1887

The love of money as a possession—as distinguished from the love of money as a means to the enjoyments and realities of life—will [one day] be recognized for what it is, a somewhat disgusting morbidity, one of those semi-criminal, semi-pathological propensities which one hands over with a shudder to the specialists in mental disease.

—John Maynard Keynes, as quoted by Robert Skidelsky in "Keynes and the Ethics of Capitalism"

Every age gets the monsters it deserves.

—Murray Kempton

PROLOGUE

Swift is the reckoning of Allah.
—The Koran

A woman stood along the edge of Riyadh's Deera Square. She wore a long white abaya robe, a matching niqab headdress and ultradark sunglasses. The square's grounds were covered with granite, its perimeter bordered with palm trees. Lined up under the shadows of the palm fronds were stone benches. Along the far edges of the square stood a huge L-shaped stone building, whose pillar-supported verandas faced the square.

She slowly walked toward the structure.

As she strolled across the park, she took out her encrypted cell phone and speed-dialed Kamal ad-Din, the head of the the "New United Islamist Front"—the recently created amalgam of ISIS, al Qaeda and Pakistan's TTP. A Saudi prince and a former intelligence minister, he had been a major leader and facilitator in the merger between the three terrorist groups. The most feared, most dangerous terrorist leader in the world, he was Raza Jabarti's wealthiest benefactor. He was currently living incognito in a lavish walled villa outside of Islamabad.

He picked up her call on the second ring.

"I received your email," Raza said. "You told me to call on our encrypted line. You said it was urgent."

"You must return to Pakistan."

"What?" Her voice was a soft but irate. She hated Pakistan.

"You know about Operation Fire and Sword?"

"I was one of the principal architects."

"You remember our friend Rashid al-Rahman?" Kamal asked.

"He was liaison between ourselves, ISIS, al Qaeda, and the TTP."

"He was the irreplaceable negotiator—one of the few people those maniacs would listen to."

"That's why we brought him in," Raza said.

"Three nights ago, we got word from one of our insiders at the Tower White House," Kamal said, "that Rashid was a double agent and that he ratted us and our plans out to his handlers at the CIA."

"The Agency knows about the operation?" Raza asked, shocked.

"Yes, but not to worry. Those people are idiots. The American president, J. T. Tower, claimed the story was Iranian disinformation and quashed it. Still we have to find out which other traitors belong to Rashid's network. I want you to interrogate Rashid personally."

"You have others who can do it," Raza said.

"We've had three of our best people working on him for three days and nights. They haven't gotten a peep out of him."

"But why me?"

"We're told he has issues with women. One theory is that he fears them. I think you'd split him wide open in one torturous night."

"I hate Pakistan."

"Don't we all, but you have no choice. This operation will not only bring the American foe to his knees, it will drive a sword of nuclear fire through the heart of the infidel world. For once and for all, they will know we can reach anyone, that no one in their world is safe from our revenge."

"But it's . . . *Pakistan*," Raza said, spitting out the word with disgust.

"Near the Afghan border in a Pashtun safe house. That region is more like Afghanistan than Pakistan."

"I hate Afghanistan too."

"Raza, this isn't a request."

"Very well," Raza said, acknowledging the inevitable. "Since you are being so mean, I shouldn't do this, but I have a small gift for you—something you will love and carry in your heart forever."

A miniature, customized, digital VidCam was concealed inside her sunglasses' thick black frames. She double-tapped one side, and his sardonically grinning face instantly appeared in the "Hangout Screen" inside the right half of her left lens. Her phone was now connected to her eyeglass camera and to his computer's Skype screen. Tapping the right side of her heavy frames two more times for a medium shot, she could now see he was lying on a huge circular bed with lavender satin sheets. Shockingly obese, he was dressed in a long white *thawb*, or robe.

Raza allowed herself a small scornful smile. Her favorite comic in all the world, Danny McMahon, delivered outrageous monologues on Kamal's behemoth body mass. Raza had a secret DVD stash of all of McMahon's routines, and whenever Raza was depressed, she put on a collection of McMahon's Kamal ad-Din weight jokes. They never failed to make her howl with hysterical hilarity.

On the bedside table, Kamal had a gold dish, on which sat a gold tin, and a sterling silver ice bucket in which a bottle of champagne was chilling.

A large crystal goblet of champagne was already in his hand, and he was chewing a toast point piled high with caviar.

Kamal clearly practiced his own version of Islam.

"What are you having for breakfast, my prince?"

"Champagne, caviar and dates, what else?"

"An exquisite Dom Perignon, I trust?" Raza asked.

"I trust not. Only you, my dear, would drink that goat piss. No, a very admirable Krug Clos d'Ambonnay 1995." He poured himself another gobletful.

"Any good?"

"At $4,000 a bottle, it better be," Kamal said.

He heaped more caviar onto a toast point with a small ivory spoon.

"Some excellent Beluga caviar to go with it?" Raza asked.

"You'd be wrong again, but then you always did have plebeian tastes."

"Okay, I give up. What is it?"

"The Iranian Almas caviar, which is haram—forbidden—in our kingdom. In fact, eating it is viewed as tantamount to treason."

"And punishable, my prince, by Allah knows how many lashes," Raza said.

"I know, I know," Kamal said. "I'm trading with our Persian enemy, but it's worth the risk. The Iranian Almas is undoubtedly the finest caviar on earth."

"Where do you find it?" Raza asked.

"I have it sent by private courier from Prunier's in Piccadilly. It comes in these little 24-karat gold tins at $25,000 apiece. But why not? We only go around our earthly dispensation once, yes?"

"Perhaps, but with hundreds of millions of pious Muslims worldwide living in abject poverty," she asked, feigning disapproval, "is it just—is it right—for you to spend so much money on what is merely grapes and fish eggs?"

She was, of course, being satiric. It was a game they periodically played. Raza would pretend to care about the starving masses. Kamal would dismiss her concern with patronizing disdain. In truth, Kamal knew that neither of them gave a shit about the eternal poor.

"What do you expect me to do?" Kamal asked. "Commiserate with them?"

"You could show some . . . *compassion*," Raza said.

Raza tried playing the part with a straight face, but she could barely contain her mirth. In fact, her eyes gave her away, glinting maliciously at the word, "compassion."

"Compassion?" Kamal asked. "Oh, my dear, the item's long out of stock."

Raza's guffaws shook Kamal's earpiece.

"Is that the only reason you called?" Kamal finally said, as her hilarity subsided. "To laugh at me?"

"Quite the contrary," Raza said, "I remembered two days ago you said you missed our many strolls in Deera Square. Well, because I'm a woman and forced to hide my face behind a niqab, I—unlike yourself—can roam our Saudi kingdom with impunity anytime I want."

That statement was only half true. Raza also required niqabs because she was wanted worldwide for her terrorist activities.

"Since I'm forced to wear this veil," Raza continued, "I can give you a digitized video tour of the square."

Raza was now halfway across the square. She could see a mother in a burqa, accompanied by a robed male guardian, walking her children around the park. *You must be insane,* Raza thought, staring at the woman and shaking her head. Near the stone building a sizable group of citizens was starting to collect.

"Why are you doing this?" Kamal asked.

"I worry about you, my prince." Raza said. "The state of our world—Dar al-Islam—must bother you to no end. I thought a pleasant stroll through the square might . . . lift your spirits."

"I doubt it," Prince Kamal said. "To tell you the truth, I don't see much in this life that's *uplifting.* For one thing, I fear that our Peaceable Saudi Kingdom is losing in its Cold War with Shia Iran," Kamal said evenly.

"But you have done a superb job of undermining Iran and blocking its entrance into the global economy."

"No more," Kamal said. "The Saudi leadership no longer finances those efforts. They've stopped putting their money where there mouth is. They plead . . . *poverty!*" He spat the last word out as if it were a curse. "They expect me to pay for everything, which is frankly insulting."

"Our Saudi leaders cry poor-mouth?" Raza asked, amazed.

"They say their U.S. oil revenues have tapered off to a trickle."

"Really?" Raza said.

"Oil prices sink, and our revenues shrink. Even the American president can't suppress the alternate energy movement, and their global lobbying power grows daily."

"Perhaps our struggle against Iran isn't that important," Raza suggested. "After all, it's unlikely they'll invade us."

"Short term, Iran's not a problem, but long term, they're a nightmare. They worship at the altar of modernity. They let their women ride bicycles, drive cars and take buses with men. Their women walk the streets in tight, provocative clothes instead of burqas. They wear skimpy silk scarfs instead of niqabs. Their women even wear pants! They blaspheme the Koran by dissecting its passages and debating its meaning as if it were a stupid speech by a *kaafir [infidel]* politician."

"The Iranian young people study real math, chemistry and physics, which our clerics denounce as 'sorcery,'" Raza said, agreeing.

"Half their science majors are women," Kamal said, "and they have a shockingly free press."

"Freer than that of any other Middle Eastern Muslim country," Raza had to admit. "The truth is that Iran has joined the Modern Age, and we haven't."

"Because of their modernity, Iran is acquiring all the military advantages of modernism as well," Kamal said, "which will include nuclear weapons and long-range missiles in the not-too-distant future—weapons which we have no defense against."

"Oh, we can defend ourselves against their nukes," Raza said. "Our clerics can chant Koranic verses at Iran's nuclear-tipped missiles, causing them to detonate on their launch pads."

Kamal's laughter boomed in her earpiece.

Finally, Kamal's laughter subsided. "On a more serious note, our enemies are, once again, maligning our beloved Kingdom. They say that if we Saudis had not spread our bloody brand of Islam throughout the Middle East," Raza said, "today that region would be Switzerland."

"Perhaps, but the United States helped advance our Wahhabist expansion as well. Between 1986 and 1982 the United States printed millions of schoolbooks for young Afghan children. Those American texts preached hatred, violence and death to the non-Muslim infidels such as the Russians. The United States then supplied us the money and weapons to fight the Russian infidel. They still finance our activities with their petrodollars and their high-tech weaponry."

"Policies which have won them the undying hatred of Muslims around the world," Raza said, laughing at the sheer stupidity of the strategy.

"No one ever said the Americans were very bright."

Hearing a plaintive wail, "In fact, take a look right here," Raza said. Raza fixed her gaze—and her customized video glasses—on a trembling, sobbing young girl. Less than a hundred feet away, she was dressed in a thin white lightweight muslin robe and a niqab. Two clerics were dragging her by the arms to a wooden post. They held her tightly while another man manacled her wrists to the heavy eyehook on the post's top.

"If this doesn't cheer you up, my prince, nothing will," Raza said. "You know the poor girl is only fourteen?"

"I am feeling cheerier already," Kamal said.

Nor was Kamal the only person who was eager to view the impending event. A growing crowd of onlookers was gathering. Some had brought their families—wives, grandparents, children. In fact, children now abounded—something that always sickened and astounded Raza. And more people were pouring in from all directions.

These people are crazy, she thought, staring out at the rapidly expanding throng.

One little girl had broken free from her family and was running around in circles, laughing. Another child tried to run up to the sobbing teenager and had to be restrained.

"What was the young girl's crime?" Kamal asked. "The one who's strung up and about to be flogged?"

"One of our religious police claims to have seen her winking and waving at a young boy on the street," Raza said.

"A girl after *your* own heart," Kamal said.

"Unfortunately, for her, our clerics view such licentiousness as one step away from adultery."

"Which means?"

"The flogging will be most severe."

Over the VidCam, Raza could both hear and watch Kamal breathing raggedly in short rasping gasps.

"If I could only be there in person," Kamal whispered.

"Were you spotted, you would not live out the day," Raza noted.

"Still we can watch it together?" he asked anxiously.

"But of course," Raza said. "I will record it and transmit it to your computer. Later you can stream it onto your 100-inch flat-screen TV and watch it as often as you wish in excruciating, close-up detail."

A black-robed man came forward with a stiff black four-foot leather-bound whip. The cleric turned to the crowd and announced:

"Inna lillaahi wa innaa ilayhi raaji'oon!" [*To Allah we belong and to Him we will return.*]

The group roared its approbation.

"La hawla wala quwata illa billah!" [*There is neither strength nor power except in Allah.*]

By now the cacophony was portentously powerful.

"SubhanAllahi azim wa bihamdi!" [*Glory be to Allah, most Great and Worthy of Praise.*]

The crowd's ovation was deafening, and the cleric had to order them to be still.

After which he pronounced the final and most important blessing:

"Rahimullah!" [*May Allah have mercy on her soul.*]

Now there was no holding the mob back. They bawled, bellowed, blustered, rumbled and clamored for the show. Even the small children cheered wildly.

The man began to flog the girl's back, his blows falling so hard and so rapidly Raza could barely discern the individual strokes. Raza was amazed the girl didn't howl like the mob, whose enthusiasm seemed boundless. Apparently, her pain was so unbearable it shocked her almost speechless. Breathless groans and violent paroxysms were her only reaction. Her body bounced reflexively up and down the pole.

"How many lashes will she get?" Kamal asked as the girl bucked and bobbed on the post like a deranged marionette jerked around by an insane puppet master.

"Relax," Raza whispered to him. "There's plenty more to watch. She's sentenced to 1,000 lashes, which are to be delivered 100 at a time."

A third of the way through the girl's ordeal, a commotion broke out a hundred feet to Raza's right. Instinctively, she turned to watch, automatically recording it. Two crowds were forming. She knew what had been scheduled for that time and quickly walked over to film those two exhibitions as well.

"No, don't stop," Kamal said, begging her not to take her camera-glasses off the flogging.

"No, my prince," Raza said. "This will be even better. You have to see it. This is one of your favorites."

"It's not—?" Kamal asked. "Is it—?"

"They don't call this place 'Chop Chop Square' for nothing, baby."

One black-robed man and a white-robed woman were being forced to their knees—one in front of a stone block, the other some twenty feet to his right.

Yes, it was happening.

Another black-robed torturer came forward wielding not a sword, but a terrifyingly sharp knife almost three feet in length.

The first victim's wrist was being shackled to a thick, heavy eyehook screwed into the block. Three men held the kneeling man by his arms and shoulders in front of the stone, his wrist now firmly fastened to the eyehook.

"What's his crime?" Kamal asked.

"The clerics said he was a thief," Raza said.

"Was he?" Kamal asked.

"Who knows?" Raza said with infinite hauteur. "They're clerics." Her imperious sneer spoke volumes.

The torturer was now repeating the four required invocations.

"Inna lillaahi wa innaa ilayhi raaji'oon!"

"La hawla wala quwata illa billah!"

"*SubhanAllahi azim wa bihamdi!*"

"*Rahimullah!*"

After each prayer, the crowd, which now numbered in the hundreds, responded with ecstatic screams.

The torturer then amputated the man's hand at the wrist with a swift, single blow.

While the crowd roared, he continued on to his next prisoner—twenty feet away—without looking back, and Raza followed him.

"This new and final prisoner is a seventeen-year-old girl," Raza explained.

"What was her crime?" Kamal asked.

"She was a servant, and she killed her employer."

"Did she give a reason?"

"He beat, raped and imprisoned her," Raza said, "all the while refusing to pay or release her."

"If she was a servant girl," Kamal said, "she was obviously not a Saudi."

"Of course not," Raza said scornfully. "She worked for a living."

Kamal laughed raucously at Raza's joke.

"She came from Jakarta," Raza added.

"Which means she has no rights here at all," Kamal said.

"Nor should it be otherwise," Raza said.

But now the presiding black-robed cleric was again offering up the same benisons that the previous prisoners had received.

"*Inna lillaahi wa innaa ilayhi raaji'oon!*"

"*La hawla wala quwata illa billah!*"

"*SubhanAllahi azim wa bihamdi!*"

"*Rahimullah!*"

The mob's excitation was ear-cracking.

The executioner's swing was level and exact.

The young woman's head tumbled from her shoulders and struck the granite square with a sickening *whommppp!*

Blood hemorrhaged from her severed neck as if out of a high-pressure hose.

In her camera-glasses' "Hangout Screen," Raza could see the prince sprawled supine on his bed, shrieking and howling as if all the damned souls in hell were inside of him, fighting to escape. His arms were buried under his robe, and his enormous porcine body shuddered spasmodically, almost seismically.

She dreaded to think what preposterous perversions incited his crazed convulsions.

PART I

Hot? You want hot? Raza's got a body that would make the Pope ... *butt-kick Mother Teresa through a stained-glass ten-story Vatican window!*

—Danny McMahon

1

"The show must go on . . ."
—Jules Meredith

Jules Meredith stood next to Danny McMahon in the wings of the 44th Street Theater. They were about to record his weekly TV talk show, in which his guests would discuss the week's major news stories, often with a comedic/satiric slant.

Catching her reflection in a backstage full-length free-standing mirror, Jules felt momentarily embarrassed by her black five-inch, shoot-the-wounded, take-no-prisoners spike heels, her matching minidress and her garishly crimson lipstick, all of which her publisher had emphatically insisted on.

"This is show business, Jules," her hard-nosed, terminally cynical publisher, David Williams, had explained to her on the phone. She had told him that she'd wanted something modest, but he had demurred, explaining exactly how the publicity department wanted her dressed and made up.

Publicity wanted Jules . . . *hot.*

"We want you looking hotter than the hinges of hell," the head of the company had told her. "We want you putting on that shiny carmine-crimson-vermillion lipstick that McMahon always tells his audience he loves so much."

Jules knew that to be a fact. Danny had said it to her once:

"I would love just to be there and watch you put it on . . . *slowly.* That would be so fucking hot!" He also once said to her: "Since you have the longest, most luscious, most lascivious legs I've ever seen on a living creature, you should always show them off to their maximal advantage. What are you anyway? Part giraffe? Your legs have legs. They start from your fucking armpits and go all the way to China, which, as we know, is a . . . long way down."

But her publisher was the one who'd dropped the hammer and forced her to look like a Hollywood harlot. Williams had ordered Danny's stylists to darken her eyes, racoon-style, then trowel on the mascara until her lashes looked like ebony rake prongs. The stylist also fluffed out Jules's jet-black hair, flung it over her right shoulder and halfway down her chest. To Jules's horror, her micromini and killer spikes screamed hooker chic. She looked as if she'd just finished hustling tricks on the Great White Way or in the midtown hotel bars.

"Consider your wardrobe and makeup 'the terms of your employment,'" her publisher had emphatically explained.

Ah hell, maybe he was right.

She was pitching her new book and had it fixed firmly under one arm. The publisher claimed he'd leveraged his firstborn to get her that extortionate mid-seven-figure advance her agent had insisted on, so Jules was determined to sell the hell out of it. She struggled to promote a stage smile, but in the mirror, it seemed to her more wolfish leer than grin.

She turned to study McMahon. He was meticulously attired in a tight-fitting black Savile Row suit, a white silk shirt with an Oxford collar and a dazzling silk tie, red as fresh-flowing blood.

The two friends wordlessly studied the audience. At least half of them were in their late teens and early twenties.

"You get a big college crowd, Danny," Jules finally said.

"I do a lot of stand-up at universities. They're my bread and butter."

"Those kids look angry though," Jules said.

"They have a lot to be angry about," Danny said.

"They're starting their careers with mid- to upper-five figures of college debt," Jules said, nodding her agreement. "And the jobs they're staring at are mostly boring as shit."

"Welcome to the real world, kids," McMahon said.

"You're a hard man, Danny."

"Yeah, I know. Makes you wonder why so many right-wingers do my show, doesn't it?"

"Why do they, anyway? You eviscerate them verbally, and that lynch mob you call an audience thunders hatred and insults at them at every turn."

"All the while brandishing torches, pitchforks, chicken feathers and boiling tar," Danny said, grinning.

"Your guests want their face time," Jules said, stating the obvious.

"You got it, kid," McMahon said, grinning. "Most of my guests will do anything to get on the tube. Even you."

"But I have a reason," Jules said. "I have a book to flog and a contract to honor."

"And a world to save?"

"That too."

"And you'll do anything to spend time with me."

"I love you, Danny, and that is no lie. I'll hang with you anytime you want. But if I didn't have a book to peddle, no power on this planet could get me on your show."

"You're different," McMahon said, "but most of the clowns that do my show would rather be abused than ignored."

Nodding her agreement, Jules studied the crowd. She estimated McMahon had 2,000 bodies out there tonight. There were some well-dressed suburbanites, but mostly they were rowdy college kids in outrageous T-shirts emblazoned with slogans insulting the rich, ridiculing the politically conservative or baiting the modest with shocking sexual taunts. One young busty girl in the front row had on a white T-shirt with a big sloppy taco on it and the caption in big black letters:

"IF GOD HADN'T MEANT MAN TO EAT PUSSY, HE WOULDN'T HAVE MADE IT LOOK LIKE A TACO."

Some wore T-shirts celebrating alcohol: "HELP ME. I FELL ON THE FLOOR AND CAN'T FIND MY BEER." "TEN REASONS WHY A BEER IS BETTER THAN A WOMAN." (The ten reasons, unfortunately, were too small for Jules to read.) "I FEAR NO BEER!"

One young woman, however, was not dressed like a rowdy collegiate. She looked to be of Middle Eastern descent and sat in the front row. She had a thick waist-length mane of jet-black hair and wore a short yellow dress that highlighted some astonishingly abundant décolletage. Her shapely legs were crossed, and her stiletto heels bobbed up and down. Her wide generous lips were colored a bright sinful scarlet—the exact shade Jules was wearing—the hue that Jules's publisher had ordered her to wear because McMahon claimed it drove him . . . *nuts.* The woman had dark wide-set eyes that glinted malevolently, and her lips seemed permanently curled into a wicked half sneer, half smile.

Jules glanced at her friend and noticed he was staring at her too.

"Well, Danny," Jules said, nodding toward the woman and paraphrasing the old Elvis Presley song, "*'if you're looking for trouble, you've come to the right place.'*"

"Have I ever. Any idea who she is?"

"All the hell and high water you've been looking for your whole life long," Jules said.

"And, thank you, God," McMahon said, "for bringing it to me."

"I'm not kidding," Jules said. "That one's trouble."

"Then trouble's my middle name."

"Watch it, boy," Jules said. "I've seen her face before. I just can't place it. I can't say where."

"And I tell you that face has 'I Want Big Bad Dan' written all over it."

"All my warning lights are blinking five-alarm fire-engine red with their sirens wailing and the rack lights flashing."

"So's Big Dan's Lust-o-meter."

"Okay, fine. But listen, Mr. Gonads-for-Brains, don't come crying to me when the shit hits the fan and you're bleeding from every pore."

"Never happen. I'm a TV celebrity. I got the power of the political/entertainment/media establishment backing me up."

"When you end up facedown—your dick in the dirt and your ass in the wind—just don't blame me."

"Big Dan is never out for the count," McMahon said. "I'm going to whale on that poor girl like she stole something."

"She looks like she could be Muslim."

"Then I'll convert her to the path of righteousness for my own name's sake," McMahon said.

"Which is?"

"Big Bad Dan."

"You're insane," Jules said.

"Only one thing could change my mind. You could take her place."

Jules treated her old friend to a hard sharp laugh. "Never happen."

"Why is it you won't give me a shot?"

"You're always buried alive under mountains of women. Why would I want to share you at the bottom of that pile?"

"'I'll change, I swear,'" McMahon said, quoting Dylan.

"You don't need me. You have women circling over you like flights stacked up over LaGuardia."

"Maybe they know something you don't know."

"I only know one thing: The show must go on, and they're cuing up the teleprompter for your monologue. Go get 'em, Danny Boy."

"To be continued."

Danny McMahon threw back his shoulders, pumped up his chest and swaggered out onto the stage—the baddest stud duck on the pond, the cockiest rooster in Chickentown.

2

"I hope Putilov drops daisy cutters on the UN."
—President J. T. Tower

Dark of night on the top floor of J. T. Tower's needle-thin skyscraper in New York City. At 59th Street and 2nd Avenue, one hundred stories up, the penthouse offered its owner, James T. Tower, also President of the United States, a 360-degree view of New York City. He was presently facing south and staring out over Midtown, the Village, Wall Street, even the new Freedom Tower—formerly the World Trade Center—as well as the tugs, barges and ferries plying New York Harbor. He could even discern the Statue of Liberty and Ellis Island in the dim distance. Like the boats and buildings, they too were brilliantly illuminated.

"Now you can't tell me this apartment doesn't have the best view in the whole goddamn world," Brenda Tower, J. T.'s older sister, said.

President Tower stared at her a long moment, then grunted:

"Jules Meredith, my eternal journalistic naysayer, probably can."

"Fuck Jules Meredith," his sister said.

Brenda Tower was seated in an overstuffed blond leather armchair directly across from her brother, who was slumped at the end of a matching couch. On her right was a circular polished oak end table upon which sat a liter bottle of Rémy 100-year-old Napoléon cognac, a square cut-glass ashtray and a large, hammered-silver cigarette holder—bearing the initials B. C. in black gothic type—containing two packs of Gauloises Blues. Alongside it was a matching initialed sterling-silver lighter. The woman was drinking brandy and smoking. She was always drinking brandy and smoking.

Decked out in a slinky black silk cocktail dress and ebony heels, she wore no jewelry. Slender of build, her thick shoulder-length hair was colored a tasteful lemon blond. Some of the most discreet, distinguished and exorbitantly expensive cosmetic surgeons on earth had artfully sculpted her exquisitely shaped facial features, most notably her high angular cheekbones. She consequently appeared at least fifteen years younger than her sixty-six years. Highly photogenic, she was routinely referred to by the fashion magazines as "a timeless beauty" and continually commented on her "patrician elegance." Most people, upon meeting her, confirmed that assessment.

Unless, of course, they looked into her eyes.

Granite-hard and glacier-cold, they discouraged intimacy, and she had few, if any, friends outside of her brother. Nor were the eyes misleading. Bitterly cynical, innately misanthropic, she neither sought nor wanted people's friendship; she mocked their opinions and cruelly spurned all but the most intrepid of lovers. Men often mistook her habitual disdain for all things male as presumptive evidence of lesbianism. In truth, Brenda Tower scorned most forms of physical and emotional contact regardless of gender.

"Jules Meredith says my needle towers are some kind of international criminal conspiracy," her brother said.

"Since when do you care what some hack reporter says?" Brenda asked with an indifferent shrug.

"That's what John D. Rockefeller said about Ida Tarbell, the so-called hack reporter whose *History of the Standard Oil Company* brought his business empire down around his ears."

"Jules Meredith isn't Ida Tarbell."

"Really?" Tower said. "Listen to what she wrote on the *New York Times* op-ed page this morning:"

*T*ower's last real estate development coup, which he had finalized just before his ascension to the U.S. presidency, was his erection of a half dozen one-hundred-story New York City needle towers. Each of them is a mere forty-six feet on edge, which, given their heights of over one thousand feet, makes them inherently unstable. These vertiginous, hideously dangerous eyesores are nothing more than another ugly example of J. T. Tower once again erecting monuments to his greed and hubris, a further flaunting of his ill-gotten riches and monstrous megalomania.

He calls these six eyesores "J. T.'s Towers of Power." He should have called them "Edifices of Avarice," since his company demands $40 million apiece for the condos, $150 million for the penthouses. Most purchases are made in cash, and virtually all of their purchasers buy them anonymously through shell companies. ISIS, al Qaeda, the New United Islamist Front and the Sinaloa drug cartels could be buying Tower's condos, and no one would know. Paying that much untraceable clandestine cash for real estate certainly suggests criminal activity. (Some would say such transactions are "presumptive evidence of criminal activity.") Otherwise why would his purchasers hide their identities and the source of their questionable currency? Tower's customers *are truly members of that disreputable elite that Theodore Roosevelt called "the criminal rich" and the "malefactors of great wealth."*

The people who buy Tower's condos and penthouses don't love New York City. They don't even live in it. They're just parking their foul-smelling lucre in J. T.'s odious abodes, so they can visit their money once every year or two and look down their noses at the rest of the city's inhabitants.

"Fuck her and the laptop she wrote that shit on," Brenda said. "She's just jealous she doesn't have a view like this."

"Times are changing, sis," J. T. said. "The world's metamorphosing all around us, and the ground is shifting under our feet. The country's madder than hornet-stung harpies at people like us. She could beat us."

"Are you saying that the UN's Anti-Inequality Initiative has a chance?" Brenda asked her brother.

"A better chance than it had a year ago," Tower said. "The Senate's Democratic majority is also pushing hard for the UN Anti-Inequality Resolution. They not only want to charge wealthy people like us with tax dodging, they want to expropriate half our offshore funds."

"At least the UN bill only wants to take a third of our offshore funds," Brenda said.

"You can't blame its supporters," Tower said. "It's a good deal for them— even though it's terrible for us."

Sighing wearily, President Tower glanced out over the city and caught his window reflection: a tall man—nearly six feet, four inches—casually attired in a black leather western-cut sport jacket, matching cowboy boots and pale blue jeans. He slowly nodded his approval. He liked the Wild West look. He thought it suited him. Then, however, his eyes drifted over to his face, and he winced. Heavily lined and hard-used, the face stared back at him, empty of affect or expression, its gaze pitiless as the sun. He was staring at a face that felt nothing, that cared for nothing, a face that neither asked nor gave with eyes cold as the grave. The face and eyes bothered even *him.*

No wonder you and your sister are so close, he thought. *You're two of a kind—raised by the same heartless old man.*

"I blame a lot of it on Jules Meredith," Tower said. "You ask me, she's a fucking Communist."

"And if she and the UN have their way," Brenda agreed, "Marx would finally win."

"It could happen," Tower conceded. "It's very hard for legislators to reject the will of their constituents."

"Then why don't you seem more concerned?" Brenda asked.

"Putilov says he's got something in the works," Tower said. "It's so hush-hush he won't tell me about it. He says it's because you and I need 'plausible deniability.' He also warned us not to go to that UN conference."

"Oh shit," Brenda said. "This could get ugly fast. Remember how Putilov consolidated his dictatorship?"

"Oh, yeah," Tower said.

"He blew up five Russian apartment complexes," Brenda said, "killing and injuring over thirteen hundred people. Blaming it on Chechen separatists, he declared martial law, invaded Chechnya and became Russia's dictator for life."

"Sheer fucking balls," Tower said, nodding appreciatively.

"Jimmy, it sounds like Putilov's going to hurt some people at the UN."

"Knowing Putilov," Tower said, "a lot of people will get hurt very bad."

"Very, very, very bad," his sister said. "And that doesn't bother you?"

"You mean because a bunch of pasty-faced, one-world, peace-creep ass-holes might get hurt," Tower asked, "I'm supposed to fucking care? Are you nuts? I hope Putilov drops daisy cutters on those UN cocksuckers."

3

"That dope could've... *made a glass eye weep and turned out a nun!*"

—Danny McMahon

Jules watched Danny McMahon's monologue from the wings while she waited to go on. She was going to be his final guest of the evening.

"This is the part of the show we call 'Get Real,'" McMahon said to his audience, "in which I give you my honest opinion on 'the state of play in the world today.' So far, we've had a lot of fun, but now this is showdown shit. In fact, I'm so serious, so intense, I wish I'd smoked .. *a great big fucking blunt before the show.* I could use something right now ... *to calm my nerves.*"

Instantly, hundreds of audience hands were raised, brandishing every type of cannabis, every type of cigarette paper and smoking appliance known to God and man.

"This is my kind of crowd. You people know how I occasionally enjoy a little Mary-*Jew*-Wanna."

The audience's guffaws were thunderous, but there were isolated shouts of: "Mary-*JEW*-Wanna?"

"What? I can say Mary-*JEW*-Wanna. I'm one-half Jew on my mother's side!"

Again, the audience roared.

"In fact, last night I enjoyed some hydroponic herb that was so mean—weed that was so wicked—"

"How mean was it?" the audience roared back at him. "*How wicked was it?*"

"Mean enough to murder Jesus! Wicked enough to kill a rock! That dope could've ... *made a glass eye weep and turned out a nun!* Where do they send ... *my corpse?*"

McMahon's audience exploded, and pandemonium reigned.

It took him a full minute to calm them down.

"But now we need to get serious. I want to talk about the Mideast's new Osama bin Laden, Kamal ad-Din. He claims to have merged al Qaeda and

ISIS with Pakistan's most formidable terrorist group, Tehrik-e-Taliban Pakistan, otherwise known as the TTP. He says he's liberating and uniting Muslims everywhere. That's bullshit, of course. Kamal has one goal and one goal only: To ride history's blood tide to its final apocalyptic end. To gain total power, absolute authority and to achieve complete dominion over that region. He calls himself 'the New Mohammed.' I would describe him as a cross between Mohammed crossed . . . *with Count Dracula times metastatic cancer!* He's the obese brain-damaged offspring of . . . *Josef Stalin and Chuckles the Clown! But then that's just me.*"

He then treated the audience to his infamously infectious smirk.

"Let's show the audience a picture of Kamal," McMahon said.

A close-up of Kamal flashed onto the screen. Decked out in a white robe, he had narrow, close-set beady eyes and a dark voluminous beard. His body was shockingly spheroid and spectacularly overweight.

"Wow!" McMahon said. "That is . . . *one fat motherfucker!*"

"How fat is he, Danny?" the audience roared.

"So fat it makes you wonder what his mother looked like. She must have won . . . *every Miss Goodyear Blimp Look-Alike Contest twenty years running!* To drop anything . . . *that intergalactically gross* . . . his mother must have been . . . *a human zeppelin!* She must have tipped the freight scale at least . . . *a half ton!*"

Again, the crowd's laughter rocked the huge theater.

"Look at Kamal's face." McMahon's pained grimace was agonizing to look at. "If I had a dog that ugly . . . *I'd shave its ass and make it walk backward!* . . . That's a face that would make . . . *a freight train take a dirt road and knock a buzzard off a shit wagon!* . . . Kamal's smile . . . *would make a pit bull drop a pork chop!* . . . I heard his mama had to hang a hunk of goat meat around his neck . . . *to get the dog to play with him!*

"That's not a man, that's . . . *a fucking dirigible*, that's the . . . *Muslim Moby Dick!!!!* . . . That's . . . *Kamal the Camel!!!* Who is his couturier anyway? *Omar the Circus Tent-Maker?*"

More thunderous laughter and applause.

"You know someone got a shot of Kamal sunning himself on a private beach? Put it up for the audience. This shot was taken surreptitiously through a telescopic lens from over 300 yards away.

"Wow! Now that is . . . *big!* That's not a Saudi prince. That's . . . *a living breathing garbage scow!* That's . . . *up-front, jump-the-shark, in-your-face, balls-ass, gag-me-with-a-spoon* . . . *ONE THOUSAND POUNDS OF BUTT-UGLY* . . . *FAT!* Talk about bringing the mountain to Mohammed. When it comes to this guy, this Mohammed . . . *is the fucking mountain!*

"Kamal, old buddy, you got more blubber on you than . . . *a Nantucket whaling ship!* Doesn't the Koran say anything about proper nutrition? I got five words for you, pal . . . *'the Bataan Death March Diet!'*

"Zoom in on that head. What is his hat size anyway? *Extra Watermelon?* I'd say: Fuck you and the horse you rode in on, Kamal, but the SPCA would have me for . . . *cruelty to animals!* Kamal's tonnage would . . . *kill a Clydesdale and drop a dromedary to its knees!*

"Surprisingly enough, I hear Kamal has an eye for the ladies." The crowd shouted out its skepticism, but McMahon lowered his hands and quieted them down. "He's got four wives, a dozen or more concubines, and I'm told he gets *beaucoup* hip-action. Can you imagine though what it's like having sex with him? Here's a shot of his first wife." She came up on the screen. She was as spherical in shape and almost as massive as Kamal. "That is one big girl. I hear after they have sex, she says: *'Thanks for the tip!'* "

The audience erupted in insane howls. Quieting them down, McMahon continued:

"I've heard he's a real hound dog too—that he'd fuck . . . *a crocodile if it didn't have teeth! . . . a goat with aftosa! . . .* a bear trap . . . *if someone glued hair on it!* A snake . . . *if somebody would hold it!*

"You know why Kamal wears . . . *robes?*" McMahon yowled at them at the top of his lungs.

"WHY???" the audience howled back.

"Because a camel can hear a zipper at fifty paces!!!"

More audience screams, more foot pounding.

"I know I make a lot of jokes, but now I want a moment of quiet. I want to be deadly serious. This may be the scientific discovery of the century. We know now with near-mathematical certainty where and how Kamal's genome came to be. NIH has studied his family history exhaustively and now has incontrovertible scientific proof that Kamal's earliest antecedents . . . *fucked monkeys!*"

The ovation went over forty-five seconds.

"Actually, I have heard that Kamal and his family are more than a little . . . *weird.* Do you know where Kamal goes to find . . . *dates with girls?*" McMahon finally asked.

"Where, Danny?" the audience bellowed.

"Family reunions!"

More hysterical howls.

"Ever seen his family tree?"

The audience brayed like an army of 2,000 feral mules, and McMahon bellowed his answer.

"It's a straight line!!!"

The audience thundered like Sturm, Drang und Götterdämmerung.

"I know, I know," McMahon said. "Some of my critics will point out that I too have a reputation as a ladies' man. They're going say, 'Hey, McMahon, who the hell are you to cast stones just because Kamal gets mucho pussy?' Well, I got a flash for you, sports fans. Unlike those trolls that Kamal flattens like a fifty-ton steamroller, my women get stoned . . . *before* . . . *they* . . . *fuck!!!*"

The crowd detonated for a full minute.

"I won't say Kamal's promiscuous, but I'm told his life's driving dream is . . . *to give HIV back to the monkeys!"*

The audience's laughter reverberated through the theater like a rolling artillery barrage in an echo chamber from hell.

"Look at that low, sloping forehead and the underslung, prognathic, Neanderthal jaw. God, does he look . . . *dumb."*

"How dumb is he?" the audience shouted.

"Dumber than . . . *a dump truck? Dumber than . . . a Dumpster? So dumb his friends have to water him like a potted plant! So stupid they hang jackets on him . . . like a coatrack!* Any dumber and . . . *pigeons would shit on him like a statue."*

The audience's laughter roared and soared.

"Then there's the Koran. The most tendentiously tedious . . . *crock of ground-up goat shit ever written.* I've read that book three times, and it just gets more absurdly imbecilic each time. I want to know why, if Allah is omniscient, omnipotent and could create us and this universe, why did he make himself . . . *such a shitty writer?* Forget Shakespeare and Homer. Why couldn't he write at least as well as, say . . . *Danielle Steel?"*

Again, McMahon had to calm the audience down.

"Still I have to add that I personally believe all followers of all faiths everywhere are dangerously self-deceiving. After all, why should anyone anywhere subscribe to any faith? Why does one group of people choose to worship Allah instead of Quetzalcoatl or prefer the Old Testament Jehovah over Shiva, the Hindu God of Creation and Destruction? As Sam Harris points out, worshippers do not come by their faith through rational choice but as an accident of birth. Ninety-nine percent of the time Christians believe in Jesus or Hindus adhere to Hinduism, it's because they were born into that faith. Their parents and their clerics inculcated it into them. The belief in one god over another has nothing to do with the superiority of one religion over another. Their religious belief was not a rational objective choice. These worshippers can't even prove any of their gods exist, let alone that one is superior to another.

"There is no more reason to follow the teachings of the Koran than to kneel at the fictitious feet of Olympus's capricious gods or to tremble before Odin in Valhalla's hallowed, mead-soaked, thunder-cracking halls. All faith in magical invisible beings is, by definition, detached from physical evidence. These votaries can never validate their deities' existence, so by definition such worshippers are . . . delusional—in other words . . . *psychotic.*

"You know who also admired Islam? Hitler was a ferocious fan. He desperately wanted Islam to be Germany's national religion. Under Allah's banner, he swore he could have conquered the whole fucking planet. Listen to what Der Führer said of Islam:

"*'It's been our misfortune to have the wrong religion. Islam would have been more compatible to us than Christianity. Why did it have to be Christianity with its meekness and flabbiness?*

"*'I can imagine people being enthusiastic about the paradise of Mohammed, but as for the insipid paradise of the Christians! Christianity is an invention of sick brains.*

"*'Had Charles Martel not been victorious at Poitiers, we would have been in all probability converted to Islam, that cult which glorifies heroism and which opens up the Seventh Heaven to the bold warrior alone. Then the Germanic races would have conquered the world. Christianity alone prevented them from doing so.*

"*'The only religion I respect is Islam. The only prophet I admire is the Prophet Mohammad.'*"

"And Kamal's followers call him the New Mohammed? That asshole is . . . *the idiot love child of Charles Manson and Pedro the Pederastic Clown!* He says his group is an alliance of al Qaeda, ISIS and the TTP? Bullshit. *It's an ululating horde of purple-ass mandrills, throwing shit with one hand and jacking off with the other!* Kamal isn't the Second Coming of the One True Prophet. He's just another brain-damaged terrorist . . . *from East Jack-Me-Off-a-Stan!* And his amanuensis and partner-in-crime, Raza Jabarti, has . . . *the soul of a cash register, the moral code of an Iron Maiden, the heart of a hard-trade whips-and-boots whore,* but I got to say she has . . . *a bodacious body that's hotter than all the fires of hell rolled up into one thermonuclear conflagration! Just look at her.*"

On the big wall-size screen behind him flashed shots of Raza on a nude Cannes beach and in a skimpy minidress in a Monte Carlo casino.

"Is there anyone here who wouldn't say Raza is . . . *hot?*" McMahon asked.

"*HOW HOT IS SHE, DANNY?*" The audience roared.

"Hot? You want hot? Raza's got a body that would make . . . *the Pope butt-kick Mother Teresa through a stained-glass ten-story Vatican window!*"

The audience guffawed, howled, war-whooped, rebel-yelled, ape-yiped and generally fell all over itself with comedic convulsions.

"But speaking of hot. I'd like you to meet our closing guest, the legendary author and war correspondent, the ravishingly lovely, deliciously delectable and mind-bogglingly brilliant Jules Meredith!"

Jules Meredith strolled across the stage toward him with a runway model's arrogant, I-don't-give-a-shit swagger, her smile sinfully sensuous and eyes filled with mockery, mischief and are-you-ready-for-the-good-times-to-come merriment.

PART II

Tower and his plutocratic pack are no ordinary band of psychopaths. They are men who have made their fortunes bilking entire nations out of trillions . . . men engaged in enterprises so preposterously profitable that there is no way they cannot be exploitative. For unlike the robber barons of the 19th century, Tower's billionaires produce almost nothing that is useful or socially redeeming. Instead they rip the public off with their Wall Street skim-scams, through fiscally destructive mergers— yes, 80 percent of mergers line the coffers of the key players but impoverish everyone else—through their predatory casinos, and, of course, through their debt-derivative con games that Warren Buffett has called "financial weapons of mass destruction." Theirs is an avarice so arrogant, a self-entitlement so maniacal and a hubris so soaringly grandiose that at some level these people have to be . . . deranged.

—Jules Meredith

1

"Then more's the pity."
—Elena Moreno

The Stockholm pub was all stainless steel, blond wood and matching leather. Sitting at its burnished hardwood bar, Elena sipped a glass of St. Emilion. It was 4:09 P.M.; the place had just opened. Near-empty, it was dimly lit.

Adara made her entrance. Decked out in black tights, a red half-sleeved designer T-shirt cut short just above her navel and dark, hand-tooled boots with three-inch heels, she strode toward Elena with long deliberate strides.

Glancing at her own reflection in the bar mirror, Elena saw a woman wearing black Levi's and a matching leather jacket, under which she a wore gray-black sweatshirt with the hood up. Even in the dimly lit bar she wore large Oakley sunglasses.

It was the reflection of a woman with something to hide.

Elena left the bar and took her drink to a circular table surrounded by a quartet of chrome stools with curved padded-leather backs and armrests. She took a deep breath. Whatever Adara had to say, it would not be good news. She wouldn't be here if it was good news, and neither of them wanted the bartender or customers listening in.

Adara grabbed up her double shot of Asbach Uralt brandy and Elena's bottle of Skol and took them to the table.

"How's it shaking, kid?" Adara asked. She was from Pakistan but had spent over a decade in the States. She'd spent a lot of time around Americans and spoke colloquial English.

Elena shrugged. "*'The highway's jammed with broken heroes.'*"

"*'On a last chance power drive,'*" Adara said, finishing the Springsteen lyric.

"But you're okay?" Elena asked.

"Still aboveground."

"Better than the alternative," Elena conceded.

"We have a friend who's not doing so well though."

"Let me guess," Elena said, shaking her head and rolling her eyes in dismay.

"I'll save you the trouble," Adara said. "It's Rashid."

"I thought he was dead."

"Everyone says that," Adara said.

"He's an asshole," Elena said.

"But he's *our* asshole," Adara said.

"*Your* asshole," Elena said.

"But he was *yours* when you needed him," Adara said.

"Which was in another life," Elena said.

"Oh, so now you're no longer part of this world, this life?" Adara asked.

"I'm not part of Rashid's life."

"Why? Because he's in trouble?"

"He's always been drawn to trouble."

"As the sparks fly upward," Adara conceded, "but he was there when we needed him, when no one else would stand up."

"No one else was dumb and desperate enough to do the ops we sent him on," Elena said.

Adara took a deep breath, struggling to compose herself.

"All right, Elena," Adara said. "Understood. Say all that's true, but it's me asking now."

"My palms bleed for you."

"I got him into it. I asked him to step up, to take the job."

"Then it's on you."

"But this one's big, and Rashid's the only one on the inside. The people who grabbed him—you know them better than anyone in the world."

"I'm out of that business, Adara."

"I can't bring him back without you. I'll probably need Jamie too. You're still with him, right?"

"Yeah, but what do you want Jamie for?"

"He's ex–Special Forces. He can handle himself in the field."

"You know several thousand guys who can handle themselves in the field."

"I heard he sold his computer security firm for $50 billion. I heard he walked off with half of that."

"So?"

"Someone's got to bankroll this op," Adara said.

Elena stared at her, speechless. Finally she got her voice back.

"You're too fucking much," she said.

"If you two don't help, these guys that have Rashid will torture him to death."

"You're breaking my heart."

"You owe him. You owe me."

"Name a figure. Anything. Jamie will pitch in too. No shit. It's yours."

"The people who have him," Adara said, "you have no idea how bad they are."

"He knew the gig when he signed up."

"Rashid doesn't deserve to go out this way."

"Cry me a river."

"You two are indispensable. I can't do it without you."

"The cemeteries are packed with indispensable people—from the bedrock's bottom to the roses on their graves." She continued. "Adara, let it go. You could never save him. He was always a runaway train on a downhill track."

"A runaway bullet train just screaming to jump the rail. But you still can't walk away."

"Why not?"

"The stuff he dug up, it's too fucking horrifying."

"What could possibly be that horrifying?" Elena asked.

"Remember when ISIS and al Qaeda merged with Tehrik-e-Taliban Pakistan, the TTP?"

"I know. Rashid brokered the deal."

"You also ran him."

"I ran the op. I was the op."

"And now those guys got him."

"I warned Rashid to stay off the grid. Jamie gave him enough money to retire. He should have listened."

"But he didn't. I got him back in, and it's killing me."

"You know what this is?" Elena's right index finger drew a circle on her left palm. "It's the world's smallest record player. Guess what it's playing?"

"I know."

"'My Heart Cries for You.'"

"But Rashid was doing some good. It was important."

Elena treated her friend to a small bitter smile and said, as gently as she could, "Adara, he was never very smart."

"He was dumber than chicken-fried horse shit," Adara said, "but there are other reasons you should do it."

"Like what? Your undying gratitude?"

Adara stared at her, silent.

Elena leaned in close. "I'm speaking as a friend. You're a bridge too far on this one. You watch your own six."

"Or?"

"You'll find yourself strung up next to your friend, electrodes hooked to your genitals."

"So that's it?" Adara said. "I ask you for help and you tell me to step the fuck back?"

"Tell you what: The drinks are on me. That's my best offer."

"Rashid was always there for you, for us. He never backed up, and he never backed down. I've seen him fight circle saws for both of us."

"There's a lesson in that."

"What?"

"Learn when to quit. Learn when to cut your losses."

"He never would have let you and me down. He'd have been there for us."

"Then more's the pity."

Adara ordered them another round.

2

"If you'd let me level St. Basil's Cathedral—right there on Red Square—I could fit both a Needle Tower Hotel and a really classy casino in that space."
—President J. T. Tower to Russian President
Mikhail Ivanovich Putilov

Mikhail Ivanovich Putilov carefully put the phone back in its holder. He hated Tower's phone calls. The man wasn't supposed to contact him unless it was absolutely necessary. Relations between their two countries were strained to the breaking point. Many world leaders viewed Russia as a rogue state and Putilov's administration an outlaw regime. Putilov was widely reviled as a despotic killer.

Most of the world was contemptuous of Tower too, for that matter. If Tower's calls became public knowledge, people would think that he and Putilov were plotting evil shit—which was, of course, true—and it would be bad for all concerned. Furthermore, Tower had no self-restraint. The calls were bound to come out.

But Putilov couldn't make Tower stop telephoning him. It was not widely known, but Putilov spoke good English—he even understood most American idioms—and the two men could converse fluently. As soon as Tower found that out, he began besieging Putilov. He had to talk—even though all Putilov got out of their interactions was a sick stomach, nerves on fire and a splitting head.

The calls consisted of Tower either bragging about how smart and tough he was or whining about how no one appreciated what he was going through or understood him. Oh, Putilov appreciated Tower, knew what he was going through and understood him perfectly. He understood he'd like to shove a double-barrel shotgun in Tower's mouth, ram it as hard as he could into the back of his throat, ear back the hammers and pull the twin triggers. After that, Tower's brain—assuming he had one—would be . . . *no more.*

The thought of splattering his office wall with Tower's gray matter almost brought a smile to Putilov's cruel lips.

Almost.

No, he was still too furious over Tower's call. Nothing he said or did could stop the cretin from calling, and tonight Putilov was so enraged he wanted to hurl the phone against the wall and shatter it like an egg. That infamous idiot had been telling him again about how they were so alike, how Putilov was the brother he'd never had, how he understood Putilov like no one else on earth and about how they would do great things together.

He'd then asked Putilov if, after he—Tower—retired from the presidency and went back into the private sector, he could build a "J. T.'s Needle Tower of Power Hotel" in Moscow. Tower told Putilov:

"If you'd let me level St. Basil's Cathedral—right there on Red Square—I could fit both a Needle Tower Hotel and a really classy casino in that space."

Demolish St. Basil's Cathedral in order to build a butt-ugly monstrosity, thereby defaming and disgracing the sacred ground that was Red Square? And Tower would further desecrate it with a fucking casino?

Putilov had pretended to seriously consider the man's demented request when, in truth, all he wanted to do was smash the phone in the imbecile's face.

Who did Tower think he was? Where did all his endless stream-of-consciousness macho bullshit come from? Where did he get his incessant horseshit about "rocks," "balls" and "stones" and how he and Putilov had had to have them to have been able to achieve what they had in their lives? What was this shit about *cojones* anyway? Tower didn't know the first thing about real courage, about taking serious life-death-or-thirty-years-in-a-Siberian-gulag risks. Tower knew nothing about the dangers he—Putilov—had faced and the ordeals Putilov had to endure to get to where he was. Tower had no idea what real *yaytsas* were.

That Putilov had survived the KGB during the Russian convulsions of the '80s and '90s took incredible brains and balls and was, in retrospect, a bona fide miracle. Tower had no idea what it was like to work as a double agent in Eastern Europe. Just learning all those tongue-twisting, jaw-busting, impossibly difficult languages had been a special kind of hell.

Tower had no idea how that agency functioned in those difficult times. It gained its own special power by leveraging those with real political and economic clout. Such influential people were best controlled through fear, and the KGB existed to teach people like them the meaning of fear. Working undercover, collecting incriminating information from people in the employ of highly placed politicians and highly influential plutocrats, agents—such as Putilov—could then use that dirt to force those big shots into turning on their friends and colleagues. But that was only the beginning. Putilov and his fellow agents would then force them to blackmail even more powerful big shots above them—and so on and so on, ad infinitum—until the KGB had an army of highly placed individuals who would do anything he told them to do. In Germany, through such operations, the KGB continually purloined invaluable Western technological secrets. The West's cyberindustrial industry and NATO's various defense ministries were immensely profitable targets. That kinds of coercion took balls beyond balls beyond balls.

Framing important people for sex crimes with trumped-up evidence and doctored photos, then threatening them with prison, exposure and disgrace—all that was standard operating procedure. Moreover, many of the people, whom they had frightened and strong-armed, were rich, powerful and politically connected. They hated the KGB with a blind rage, and they were influential people, eminently capable of retaliation. Consequently, an agent's life was in constant danger.

Tower knew nothing of real risks and real guts, but that did not stop him from acting like he did. He loved to brag to Putilov about how tough he was. The man even boasted that if push came to shove, he was probably tougher than Putilov. Really? Had Tower ever done anything even remotely . . . *difficult?* Anything . . . *truly terrifying?* Tower didn't know the meaning of the word "tough." If he had ever gone up against Putilov, the Russian president would have crushed Tower like a wet, soggy . . . *blintz.*

Putilov couldn't take it anymore. Standing up, he threw the phone against the wall as hard as he knew how and watched it detonate into slivers, shards and fragments before falling across his office floor.

3

Remembering Helena, Fahad shuddered.

Fahad al-Qadi stood by his bed in his Moscow safe house. His three-man team—Alexei Konstantin, Oleg Kuznetsov and Leonid Sokolov—were waiting for him. They were dressed in all black—suits, ties, even black shirts. Not that they were trying to make fashion statements—quite the opposite. After the op, while still in the car, they would strip off their clothes and throw them in a Dumpster. Their getaway attire was underneath—light T-shirts and thin cotton pants. They would then make their escape in the two vehicles they'd parked near the waste bin early that afternoon.

If the Russian police were searching for four black-suited hit men in a dark SUV, they'd be sorely disappointed. With any luck at all, they'd evade detection.

Fahad's men each had their standard-issue AK-47s packed in square metal suitcases, which they'd already stowed in the trunks of their SUV. Their Tokarev 7.62mm pistols were shoved inside their belts under their coats. Fahad's weapons and ammunition, however, were specially made, and he wanted to inspect them one last time. They were spread out on the bed in front of him, and he'd just finished testing the guns' firing mechanisms. He was now checking everything they needed on his equipment list.

The weapon on the bed nearest Fahad was a Saiga—a Taktika model 040. A semi-automatic military shotgun, it had a seventeen-inch barrel. Picking it up by the breech, he hefted it. It weighed just under eight pounds.

From its AK-74M folded-out pistol-grip polymer buttstock to the barrel's ventilated tip, it was less than two and a half feet long. Its box magazine held eight 12-gauge magnum shells. Every shell contained thirty-two small steel ball bearings, and its open iron sights came with a high post and a notched tangent at its rear.

So little weight, Fahad thought idly, *so much death.*

On the bed directly above the Saiga was Fahad's Dragunov SVD sniper rifle. It had a black folding polymer stock and a detachable cheek rest. Forty-four inches in length with the stock extended, its barrel was fitted with a slotted flash suppressor, a handcrafted silencer that Fahad had designed and built himself, and a PSO-1M2 scope effective for ranges well over 1,000 meters. Chambered for 7.62×54mmR rounds, it had a curved, removable magazine. The cartridges were double stacked in a zigzag pattern, and while it had a ten-shell capacity, Fahad never kept more than eight in one. He thought the spring was too weak for ten.

He loaded the Saiga and the Dragunov into their dark rectangular traveling cases. The bottoms came with custom-fitted slots designed to hold and lock the weapons and their accessories into place so that nothing would rattle around loose.

Fahad turned from the bed, entered the bedroom's walk-in closet, located a hidden lever and pulled back the false rear wall. He was facing a four-foot-tall Assa Abloy drill-proof, fire-resistant gun safe. After punching in the safe's lock codes, he swung open the door. He placed the encased Dragunov in the safe, standing it up on its end, buttstock toward the floor.

He'd be back for it later.

Locking the safe, he exited the closet and caught a glimpse of himself in the bedroom wall mirror. Women were always telling him he looked like that Egyptian actor who starred in the American movie *Doctor Zhivago*. An old girlfriend of his, Helena Katayev—a freelance flight attendant from St. Petersburg, whom he'd eventually recruited and still used from time to time for particularly horrifying assignments—had been especially adamant about it.

Remembering Helena, Fahad shuddered reflexively.

Jesus, she was one scary bitch.

Still he'd seen the actor once on the big screen, and he had to admit there was more than a fleeting resemblance. He just couldn't remember the guy's name.

Picking the Saiga's case up off the bed, he nodded silently to the team. They followed him out of the bedroom and toward the safe house's back door.

4

"Once you have the fissile highly enriched uranium, which isn't that hard to purchase on the black market, a high school student could cobble together a Hiroshima-style nuke. That's what Luis Alvarez, the inventor of the Hiroshima triggering mechanism, wrote."

—Jules Meredith

Danny McMahon escorted Jules Meredith to right-center stage. They each seated themselves on dark leather-and-steel armchairs and faced the applauding audience. When the ovation subsided, McMahon gestured to one of the cameramen, who then projected the photo of an extremely obese Middle Eastern man in a white thawb, or robe. He was standing in the desert in front of a tank. Beside him stood a slender, dark-haired, highly attractive Middle Eastern woman in camouflage fatigues and boots, the stock of an AK-47 cocked on her hip. Even in army issue she was . . . stunning.

"What do you think of this new global terrorist threat?" McMahon asked. "It's known as the 'New United Islamist Front,' and these two people there on the screen, Kamal ad-Din and his smoking-hot femme fatale sidekick, Raza Jabarti, are heading it up. According to your recent *Huffington Post* article, Kamal's bankrolling it. You wrote that Kamal and Raza have organized the strongest, most violent, most ruthless parts of al Qaeda, ISIS, and TTP into that new terrorist operation and that their goal is the nuclear destruction of the U.S. of A."

"Danny, after what those groups and their comrades have already done to Europe and the U.S., I will never discount the significance of their threat. And, yes, I do have sources who tell me that a nuclear attack is coming, that it's funded by wealthy Saudis and that President Tower is so deep in hock to them that he won't address this menace or even acknowledge it."

"I'm willing to believe all of that," McMahon said. "Look at President Tower's Muslim immigration ban. He claimed that there are people in those six countries—the ones whose people he prohibited from entering the U.S.—who would kill Americans on U.S. soil. No one from those nations has ever killed anyone on U.S. soil. Yet Saudi citizens and their Sunni allies have murdered Americans on U.S. soil by the thousands, and those nations aren't covered by the ban. Tower has clearly gone into the tank for the Saudis, their client states and for Mikhail Putilov."

"Tower is in willful nuclear denial," Jules said.

"How hard would it be for the New United Islamist Front to nuke a major U.S. city?" McMahon asked.

"Unfortunately," Jules said, "nuking a city doesn't take that much skill. If I drop a grapefruit-size chunk of bomb-grade highly enriched uranium on a same-size chunk from a height of six feet and hit it square, I could get 50 percent of the Hiroshima yield."

"But wouldn't making an actual bomb be seriously difficult?" McMahon asked.

"Not really," Jules said. "Once you have the fissile highly enriched uranium, which isn't that hard to purchase on the black market, a high school student could cobble together a Hiroshima-style nuke. That's what Luis Alvarez, the inventor of the Hiroshima triggering mechanism, wrote, which is why we have to kill this threat in the cradle and hunt down and eliminate its backers."

"And you've said the New United Islamist Front has the money to finance the building of a nuke and carry out the operation?"

"They get their money from a group of super-rich Saudis," Meredith said, "led by Kamal ad-Din, and I've also said that Kamal and his coven of billionaire killers are protected by Saudi Arabia and Pakistan. I have some evidence that they're in league with Putilov—and these are all Tower's allies."

"Can't we do anything to stop that funding?" McMahon asked.

"We won't even try," Meredith said. "Tower views Pakistan and the Saudis as allies and has declared their enemies our enemies."

"I see no difference between the Saudis and the New United Islamist Front," McMahon said. "From my point of view, Saudi Arabia is nothing but a New United Islamist Front that has made it."

"And has it made," Jules said. "The New United Islamist Front's caliphate *is* Saudi Arabia."

"Yet many on the left say we're too hard on Islam," McMahon said, "saying most Muslims are moderate and peace-loving."

"The truth is," Jules said, "Kamal and his kind pose a far graver danger to those moderate peace-loving Muslims than we do. Kamal and company hate Islamic moderates far more than they hate us. They consider peaceable Muslims to be apostates, and therefore far more dangerous than any possible heretics."

"And still," McMahon said, "many moderate Muslims view you and me as the enemy."

"Maybe," Jules said, "but when young girls are accused of violating Islam's so-called sacred laws, you and I don't stone them to death or cut off their hands or gouge their eyes. We don't clitorize and behead them. We don't sentence them to 10,000 lashes or incarcerate them in Middle Eastern hell-hole prisons until Gehenna freezes over."

"True, but they nonetheless accuse us of tarring all Muslims with the same terrorist brush." McMahon asked. "Our critics point out that most Western Muslims are law abiding."

"But we can't compare Islam in the West to the True Faith as practiced in the Mideast. Here, Islam is a small sect, a weak minority. As Sam Harris has written, the West's Muslims practice their faith in fetters. If they attempted violent insurrection, they'd be instantly crushed. If, however, Islam had the upper hand in the U.S. and Europe, who is to say they would not heed the clarion call of the jihadists in their midst? I've lived in that world for twenty years, and I deeply fear that if Islam held sway in the world today, we'd be witnessing a global jihad of thermonuclear proportions."

"Jules, I would love to discuss this further. We are short of time though, and I want you to talk about your new book. It's not about Islamist terrorism but about the depredations of the super-rich, focusing on our own president, J. T. Tower. I should tell the audience that you let me have a surprise look at a few chapters. You have come up with the best, most important, most terrifying reportage that I have ever laid eyes on. Anyone out there who doesn't buy and read Jules Meredith's book when it's released should be flogged, jailed, amputated and decapitated . . ." At that point, McMahon rose from his chair and roared as loud as he knew how: ". . . *LIKE A REBELLIOUS SAUDI WOMAN!*"

The audience exploded with shocked but tumultuous laughter while Jules stared at Danny, slowly shaking her head.

"And now I'm told you have a surprise announcement," Danny said.

Danny McMahon then sat down, and Jules stood.

"My friends," Jules began, "this week on my blog, www.TheJulesView .com, I'll be posting a series of articles for immediate release to the public and the media. In my new book, *Filthy Lucre: J. T.'s Tower of Financial Power*, I'm exposing President J. T. Tower—who is also the owner of a lethal petro-chemical empire, a dangerously deceptive consortium of Wall Street hedge funds, a chain of horrifyingly exploitative casinos and one of the most corrupt real estate development companies in the world—as the fascistic bastard that he is. With your permission, Danny, I'd like to read a segment of a new blog I will post tomorrow."

"Please do."
Jules Meredith began:

Three years after President Tower's election, we are now witnessing the rise of a J. T. Tower financial/political imperium run by Tower and a cadre of supercilious oligarchical billionaires. Profit and power are their sole raison d'être, and they destroy anything and anyone who gets in their way or even voices dissenting opinions. They view the U.S. Treasury as a cash hoard to be plundered, the federal regulatory agencies as enemies to be destroyed and the electorate as their lawful prey. Distrust and hatred of government is their rallying cry, and for a time they infected the Body Politic with that same anti-government rage.

It was not always thus. For decades the U.S. public feared big business more than they feared their government. The Great Depression and fear of the Wall Street fat cats who caused it—and who grew rich exploiting workers—made the American public skeptical of predatory plutocrats. Then the elites turned the public's hatred toward government; unfortunately for the public, government is the only entity capable of reining the plutocrats in.

But the American people are now awakening from their long dark night of anti-government paranoia and have taken the Senate back. After the American people witnessed repeated orgies of upper-bracket tax cuts, Wall Street deregulation and Bill of Rights infringements alongside the simultaneous rise of the new Tower Oligarchy, the electorate's fear of rapacious elites has returned with a vengeance.

Tower and his plutocratic pack are no ordinary band of psychopaths. They are men who have made their fortunes bilking entire nations out of trillions . . . men engaged in enterprises so preposterously profitable that there is no way they cannot be exploitative. For unlike the robber barons of the 19th century, Tower's billionaires produce almost nothing that is useful or socially redeeming. Instead they rip the public off with their Wall Street skim-scams, through fiscally destructive mergers—yes, 80 percent of mergers line the coffers of the key players but impoverish everyone else—through their predatory casinos and, of course, through their debt-derivative con games that Warren Buffett has called "financial weapons of mass destruction." Theirs is an avarice so arrogant, a self-entitlement so maniacal and a hubris so soaringly grandiose that at some level these people have to be . . . deranged.

They have to be stopped. The fate of this nation depends on it. We all have to stop them.

"So, J. T. Tower," Jules shouted, pointing her finger into the TV camera, "I'm coming after you. I got your name; I got your number; I know where you live. I'm fouling your nest and shitting where you eat and sleep. I'm dragging your dirty laundry into the streets and pissing on your grave. I'm going to make that UN global expropriation movement look like a trade union beer blast. I'm burning you down to bedrock and sowing your fields with salt like Carthage. And this is just the beginning, Jimmy Boy. When I'm done with you, there won't be enough left for the birds to carry away. When my book comes out, you're going read my words and weep. So give it up, bitch. Eat shit and die. You're going down hard."

Jules Meredith turned and walked off the proscenium, stage left.

For the first time in his professional life, Danny McMahon looked . . . *shaken.*

Clearing his throat, he finally rasped:

"And now for my closing remarks."

5

Putilov had made his gargantuan fortune the old-fashioned way: He'd stolen it.

Mikhail Ivanovich Putilov had just suffered through another one of Tower's secret, encrypted Skype calls. Try as hard as he could, Putilov couldn't make Tower stop phoning him. The prick had some perverse need for Putilov's approval, a sick compulsion to get Putilov on the phone and tell him how they were both the same, they were both . . . *self-made men.* He actually had the chutzpah to boast that he'd gotten nothing from his father but a small loan, which he'd parlayed into billions, that he was an up-by-the-bootstraps billionaire who had earned everything he had and that he'd gotten it all through hard work, guts, resilience, brains, self-reliance, resourcefulness and . . . *rugged individualism.*

Maybe Tower was genuinely psychotic. Putilov hadn't considered that contingency before—that Tower was, in fact, a dyed-in-the-wool lunatic who was incapable of telling truth from illusion and who believed the outrageous lies he was fabricating about his life and the mountains of mendacity he continually tried to pawn off on Putilov as "J. T.'s worldview" and "J. T.'s philosophy of life."

God, was Tower dumb.

What had that half-wit ever done except inherit a fortune in hard cash, a complex of lucrative petrochemical refineries, a gaggle of astronomically profitable hedge funds, a money-minting chain of casinos and a gargantuan group of global real estate development businesses from his filthy-rich father? That these concerns continue to make money has had nothing to do with Tower. The credit went to the legions of MBAs, tax lawyers, judges and pet politicians whom his father had already put in place. Those were the people who were responsible for Tower's operations. And even with all those advantages, Tower had almost bankrupted his real estate empire. Putilov and his army of pocket bankers had had to pump tens of billions of dollars into Tower properties and floundering construction projects to keep them afloat. Meanwhile, all Tower had ever done was attend big-money balls, appear at show-business awards ceremonies, play in pro-am golf tournaments and fuck avaricious supermodels.

Putilov, on the other hand, had started with nothing and now had a fortune that was so vast he wasn't sure how much he was worth. Knowledgeable Kremlin insiders estimated his worth to be well over $200 billion, which made Putilov far wealthier than Tower. In fact, it made him two and a half times richer than Bill Gates, who was, according to *Forbes*, the richest man on earth.

Furthermore, Putilov had made his gargantuan fortune the old-fashioned way: He'd stolen it.

Remembering those heady days of thievery, chicanery and murder-mostfoul brought a rare smile to Putilov's otherwise stern and wintry face.

Mikhail Ivanovich Putilov began his rise to wealth and power in the late '80s by putting together a junta of unrepentant, unreconstructed, revanchist, revisionist KGB officials, all passionately united by their hatred of Gorbachev's reforms. Putilov quickly allied them with a like-minded closeknit group of superwealthy, ultra-ruthless oligarchs, all of whom were in league with the Russian mafia. Soon he and his crew were liquidating the Communist Party's foreign coffers and funneling those funds into their own covert bank vaults overseas. This was no small bank heist. Over the decades, the Party—always sensitive to reversals of fortune—had secreted a clandestine hoard of foreign currency in the mid–nine figures, and within a few years Putilov had succeeded in stealing it . . . all.

If anyone objected to his myriad peculations, Putilov had them framed on phony evidence and sent to prison—or simply had them killed.

Putilov would later brag to his confederates that he had emptied the Party's cash trove—like he was "gutting a slaughterhouse pig"—and then plundered the rest of the nation as well. In the end, Putilov and his pals had walked off with the net worth of both their countries' corporations and the Russian Federation. Moreover, during these thefts, Putilov had proven himself the irreplaceable man—energetic, ingenious and utterly without fear.

While Putilov and his cohorts were acquiring great wealth and were brokering trade deals on behalf of cities and major Russian corporations, Putilov was also advancing his political career. As his power in the Russian government radically increased, his junta's power to transact those lucrative trade deals, many of which were international, likewise burgeoned. During that period, such deals in Russia were profitable but complicated. Since the ruble was not a globally recognized currency—and, in fact, had always been intrinsically worthless abroad—Russian cities and firms were uniquely dependent on foreign money whenever they wanted to do business overseas. Putilov quickly figured out how to exploit this dependency and how to pile up massive amounts of dollars, pounds, deutsche marks and eventually euros in secret foreign accounts.

He had a network of ex–Stasi agents who were active in the German banking system, one of whom rose through the ranks to become a top financial executive. He helped Putilov—who had been his former KGB case officer and was now a major St. Petersburg political leader—to broker these kinds of lucrative foreign business deals. Due to the ruble's weakness overseas, Putilov worked out barter transactions. For example, he would arrange for Russian cities or Russia firms to transport Russian commodities, such as gold, oil, coal, diamonds, gas or timber, to a foreign firm in exchange for whatever the city or Russian firm wanted. Since at that time computers were a hot item, Putilov did a lot of deals for foreign computers. The firm or city, which Putilov represented, would ship overseas the Russian commodities in anticipation of receiving high-tech computers.

Of course, those foreign goods would never arrive.

Instead of delivering the bartered goods, this ex–Stasi agent-turned-banker would pump huge amounts of foreign cash into the offshore tax haven bank accounts of Putilov and his cronies. When his clients pressed him for payment, Putilov would claim the computers had clearly disappeared in transit.

Due to their increased political clout, Putilov and his KGB-now-FSB-cohorts could guarantee asset protection for friendly oligarchs and ambitious plutocrats all over Russia. Well versed in the blackest of the old-school KGB arts, Putilov's asset-protection schemes quickly transmogrified into an outright extortion racket. Survival in Russia soon meant giving Putilov and his friends an exorbitant cut on anything and everything.

Many countries bragged of their folkloristic outlaws: America, for instance, took pride in the exploits of Dillinger and Pretty Boy Floyd. Late at night wealthy Saudis were known to boast sub rosa of the BCCI bank job, in which they and their Pakistani business partners had conned the world's top investors out of an estimated $18 billion. Putilov smiled when he read of such laughable attempts at larceny. He had pulled off the most spectacular financial shakedown in history, the expropriation of almost all of Russia's assets—the largest theft in world history.

He also became the wealthiest of the world's oligarchs.

And Russia's Boss of Bosses . . .

Putilov seldom consumed alcohol, but after he spoke with Tower, he found that his hands shook uncontrollably and that he invariably needed something to calm his nerves. When his chief of staff failed to come up with a palliative of sufficient strength, he remembered a drug his KGB interrogators sometimes gave people to calm them down, relax them, so they would lose their inhibitions and confess everything they knew. He immediately obtained a bottle of those pills for his Tower-phone-call anger attacks. In a state of hysterical rage, after each conversation, he unlocked his desk drawer and lunged for the bottle full of the super-potent pills. The tablets were called desomorphine. The street name was *krokodil*. After eight or nine of them entered his bloodstream, it was as if a two-hundred-pound sack of cement was lifted from his shoulders. Every fiber of his being, every nerve ending in his brain and body was at peace—something Putilov had never before known. The drug had come to him as . . . a blessing.

One of his bodyguards told him that the effects would be even more pronounced if Putilov ground the pills up between spoons, then chopped the granules up into fine powder with a razor blade. Dissolving them in high-octane alcohol, then adding splashes of ether and gasoline—just for an added kick—he could then heat the liquid in a bong over a lighter and smoke the fumes out of the bong's stem. By pure happenstance, Putilov owned such a bong—a souvenir he'd taken off a suspect he'd once tortured and killed. He'd never known why he had kept the man's bong. Now he knew why. He must have had an unconscious premonition that he would need it. Putilov truly believed that a large part of his genius was his "unconscious premonitions." He was in many respects a "gut player"—just as George W. Bush had once described himself to the Russian tyrant.

So this time when Putilov reached for the krok, instead of swallowing the tablets, he heated the powdered pills, vodka, ether, and gasoline in the dead man's bong and smoked the vapor.

He found the experience . . . exhilarating.

Of course, Putilov understood the dangers of addiction. Furthermore, he knew that desomorphine was eight times stronger than straight morphine. So he realized it was imperative that he only smoke it during emergencies—which were easy to define since they only occurred after Tower's phone calls.

But he also believed in his soul he could handle the krok. Putilov was a man possessed by an overwhelming will, by infinite resolve, and by indomitable self-possession. He would never allow himself to become addicted to anything, which was one of the reasons he so studiously eschewed alcohol or tobacco. He could handle the krok.

And he did need it.

God, how he hated Tower! How could a man like him be so moronic and yet get so far? Tower was terminally ignorant, devoid of even the tiniest iota of self-awareness and consumed by a grandiosity so ludicrously delusional, so monstrously megalomaniacal that he was truly beyond description or any form of psychiatric treatment. Tower's mental condition made a mockery out of the DSM's entire catalogue of psychiatric nomenclature and reduced even the most elemental attempts at serious analysis to stupid drooling absurdity.

And yet he was President of the United States.

To elect a man like that president, America had to indeed be a land of . . . *lunatics.*

PART III

"The fossil fuel energy and financial sectors gobble up over $6 trillion a year in global government subsidies. That corporate graft saps up over 8 percent of the planet's total GDP—so much that the World Bank has asked specifically to outlaw all energy subsidies everywhere."

—Jules Meredith

1

There are roads you do not go down.
There are rivers you do not cross.
There is ground you do not contest.
There are cities you do not strike.
There are orders from your ruler you do not obey.
—Sun Tzu, The Art of War

President Tower sat on the leather couch in his private New York penthouse and stared out over Lower Manhattan. He gazed on the skyline's grandeur with the same cerebral detachment that he might have felt staring at a rock pile or a garbage dump. Half-reclined on the long dark couch, he kicked his elaborately hand-tooled boots up onto the large oval walnut coffee table, looked at Brenda sitting across from him on an overstuffed leather armchair, and sighed deeply.

"Brenda," Tower said, "this UN expropriation movement—barring divine intervention—is likely to happen. The EU, the UK, Japan, even China and the U.S. Senate are on board. Our only hope of divine intervention is Putilov."

"So if he doesn't come through, we're fucked?" Brenda asked.

"Big-time," Tower said. "It's the perfect election platform for the Democrats. My only question is why did the country take so long to get behind it?"

"Because the country is packed to the rafters with mindless morons," Brenda said.

"True," Tower said, "but the morons are after us now."

"It's so surreal," Brenda said.

"Oh, it's real all right," Tower said. "Look what Europe is doing to Apple. They figured out how. The EU is raiding Apple's foreign accounts."

"Twice, even threatened to do it to Putilov's elites," Brenda said.

"At least twice," Tower said, "and the electorates everywhere are screaming for it."

"It's Revolt of the Masses the way Ortega y Gasset never imagined it," Brenda said.

Tower stared at her, nonplussed, unsure who the inestimable Ortega y Gassett was.

"Putilov's got a lot of incentive to fight this," Brenda said. "The UN's resolution would destroy him and his Russian partners."

"If it passes, even Putilov won't be able to stand up to it," Tower said. "Look what the Great Powers did to Iran when they tried to develop nuclear weapons."

"The U.S., the EU, Japan, Russia and Iran froze Iran out of the world banking system," Brenda recited as if by rote.

"Exactly," Tower said. "Iran could sell goods to foreign countries, specifically oil and gas, they just couldn't get paid. No bank would transfer funds into an Iranian bank."

"If the UN Anti-Poverty Resolution and that Senate bill pass," Brenda said, "and if we and our companies don't pay the fines and surtaxes on our revenues and on our offshore accounts, we could find ourselves kicked out of the world's most financially desirable markets."

"No foreign bank on the planet would be open to us," Tower said.

"And now there's going to be that big ugly meeting at the UN. Over five hundred of the world's richest billionaires will argue their case—with the whole planet howling for their hides."

"I know," Tower said. "We're putting them up in one of our Tower Hotels."

"So what are we supposed to do?" Brenda asked. "Lose gracefully?"

Her brother gave her a truly terrifying sneer. Brenda Tower knew that sneer. She did not like it. In fact, she feared it.

"Jim," Brenda said, "it's just money. You and I together, we possess one of the single largest fortunes on earth."

"Next to Putilov," her brother pointed out.

"Yes, and we don't need all this shit. We can walk away. Let's do it. Tell the world to go fuck itself."

"You know people always say I'm a my-way-or-the-highway kind of guy, that all I live for is kicking ass and taking names."

"That's the only Jim Tower I ever knew, and I've known you since you were born."

"But it's not true. If negotiating serves my interests better than coercion, I'll negotiate."

"Depends how vindictive you feel," Brenda said.

"I always feel vindictive," Tower said, "but I've negotiated through crises lots of times—as long as the other side leaves me room to maneuver. If the other guy paints me into a corner though and tries to force me into submission, he'll get something back he hadn't expected."

"You'll fry his balls like KFC and feed them to him for late-night snacks," Brenda concurred.

"But now Congress is trying to railroad me. You know what that means?"

"Yes," Brenda said, "and I also know that you and I can't fight the entire planet. Remember those lines from Sun Tzu I used to quote to you when I wanted to calm you down?"

"Not really," Tower said.

Brenda recited:

> There are roads you do not go down.
> There are rivers you do not cross.
> There is ground you do not contest.
> There are cities you do not strike.
> There are orders from your ruler you do not obey.

Tower looked at his sister and shrugged. "What's that got to do with me?"

"Maybe this is one war you cannot win," Brenda said.

"But I can make winning so painful for the other side," Tower said, "that the price will be unacceptable. I can make them forget about global expropriation and gladly give up."

"So the cure will be worse than the disease?" Brenda asked.

"If I have my way, the American public will never get its dirty hands on one cent of our money."

"Which is saturated with some of the most toxic petrochemical pollutants known to man."

"And worth every carcinogen of it," Tower said.

Brenda took a long pull on her balloon snifter, draining the cognac. She then freshened her drink, snubbed out her cigarette and lit another Gauloises Blue.

"Tomorrow night we're going to meet with the Saudi ambassador and Prince Waheed," Brenda said. "His CIA director, Billy Burke, is supposed to be there too."

"I wish you hadn't reminded me."

"They're two of the only allies we have in D.C."

"They're faithless friends and craven enemies," Tower said.

"So Big Jim is going to have to do it all himself," Brenda said.

"Hopefully with a little help from Putilov," Tower said.

"Does that mean we're going to the mattresses?" Brenda asked.

"War to the knife."

"All bets are off?

"Anything goes when the whistle blows."

"Sounds like it's going to be a pretty loud whistle," Brenda said.

"It's a screeching, shrieking blast of apocalyptic proportions," Tower said.

"Sounds like you've heard it before."

"Of course. I've even blown it myself. Hell, I own it."

2

Perhaps Nemerov should not have waved his bodyguards away...

Boris Nemerov and his fiancée casually strolled Red Square. They had just attended the Bolshoi Ballet, where they watched Natalia Osipova and Ivan Vasiliev in Prokofiev's *Romeo and Juliet*. The entire performance had been exhilarating, beginning to end, and afterward, Nemerov and Tatiana had a superb four-course meal at Café Pushkin. Since Russia's elites regarded it as one of the finest restaurants in the city, getting a table, even for Nemerov—who was one of Putilov's top presidential opponents—had almost taken an act of God. He'd had to book the reservation six weeks in advance, but it had been worth the effort.

Decorated in the style of a 19th-century aristocratic mansion, Café Pushkin's main room was graced with elaborately carved columns, and its wall shelves were filled with large leather-bound first editions of the great Russian classics. The tables and chairs were solid country furniture constructed of smooth curved oak. The atmosphere was intimate and old worldly. The staff's manners were impeccable and the cuisine exquisite—smoked salmon with caviar and sour cream piled on top of pieces of thinly sliced Russian blini; marinated lamb shashlik skewered with pork and onions had come next, followed by pelmeni meat dumplings with butter and sour cream along with crispy fried syrniki cheese patties with Nutella. Afterward came wedges of apple sharlotka. And, of course, no such repast would be complete without shots of freezing-cold Stolichnaya Elit and a bottle of Louis Roederer Cristal champagne chilling in an ice bucket.

When they finally left the restaurant, they were both happy, laughing and more than a little tipsy.

From Nemerov's point of view there was nothing like Moscow on a warm summer evening, and while as a presidential candidate, he was supposed to be continually surrounded by at least six bodyguards, tonight he had asked them to give him and Tatania some privacy. He understood he was putting himself in harm's way by keeping them at a distance. He was running for the presidency against Mikhail Putilov as a reform candidate and had been highly critical of his opponent's corruption—his plundering of the Russian economy and squirreling away of all that black money in offshore Western banks. He knew that Putilov had had people killed before for saying far milder things about him. He also knew the Russian people were hearing his message and were becoming increasingly inflamed. Nemerov was now a force to be reckoned with, and while he could not get his message out over the Putilov-controlled news media, Russia's "Dark Net" and had been on fire with his speeches, clandestine podcasts and exposés.

Nemerov was not alone in challenging the Russian strongman. The third presidential opponent, the great chess world champion and world-class political campaigner Borya Kazankov, had also been electrifying people on the internet and at large gatherings. He and Kazankov were giving Putilov his first serious challenge in twenty years, and Kremlin insiders hinted to him Putilov was in a blind rage. At the very least, he and Kazankov's incendiary campaign speeches were a constant source of aggravation to Putilov. Both of them blasted him nonstop for his criminal pillaging of the Russian Federation.

Perhaps Nemerov should not have waved his bodyguards away. Putilov was notorious for killing political opponents and muckraking reporters—anyone who embarrassed or menaced him—and Nemerov had done plenty of both. Still if he wasn't safe here, he couldn't be safe anywhere, and anyway at a moment like this, he needed to be alone with the woman he loved. Standing in the shadow of St. Basil's, he was about to ask Tatania—the most beautiful, most decent, smartest young woman he'd ever known—for her hand in marriage. This close to the Kremlin, Nemerov believed no one—not even that mass-murdering psychopathic bastard Putilov—would have the temerity to order a hit on him. Even Putilov would not desecrate the sacred ground in front of St. Basil's.

Stopping Tatania by a small park garden flower bed—overflowing with roses, gardenias and marigolds—Nemerov took both her hands and dropped to one knee. Taking the ring out of his vest pocket, he looked up at her. For a moment, he couldn't speak. Her beauty had struck him dumb on any number of occasions, and tonight was no exception. Her thick waist-length mane of hair, blond as summer wheat, her high angular cheekbones, her azure eyes, which, as usual, were carefree and smiling, once again took his breath away. She was so beautiful it sometimes made his soul ache.

"Tatania," he asked, holding up the 22-carat gold ring, surrounded by a cluster of three 3-carat diamonds, "will you accept this ring—and my hand in marriage?"

"Oh Boris," she said, her bright eyes suddenly moist, "I've wanted you since the first time I'd saw you—you and no one else. I'll marry you, live in sin with you, be your mate, partner, your friend, your mistress, anything, anytime, anyplace, for as long as you are foolish enough to have me."

Now Tatania's eyes were also tearing.

He put the ring on her wedding finger, then rose. Taking her in his arms, he kissed her in the view of the Great Kremlin Cathedral.

Suddenly, his bodyguards were screaming. A black SUV was pulling up next to them less than twenty feet away, and he knew that for anyone to be near him was to court death. Fearing for Tatania's safety, he pushed her away from him, sending her sprawling across the sidewalk. The man next to the driver was out of the car. He was holding what looked like a squat fat knockoff of an AK-47, and it was leveled at him. Nemerov suddenly realized he was staring into the muzzle, not of an AK-47, but of a semi-automatic 12-gauge military shotgun.

"Good move, Nemerov," the man with the shotgun said. "No reason for the girl to die."

Nemerov glanced at his bodyguards, who were already drawing their pistols, but they were not quick enough. Three other black-suited men, who had already rounded the SUV, were ripping his men to pieces with AK-47s. At the same time, the man with the shotgun was blasting a pair of 12-gauge magnum shells, each filled with double-0 steel buck, into Nemerov's midsection. Over sixty ball bearings, each the size of a .22 caliber bullet, shredded his Kevlar vest, turning it to bloody coleslaw. Then the man pumped a third shell into Nemerov's face—all three blasts hammering the politician as fast as the man could squeeze the trigger, detonating him head to thigh in less than three seconds.

Nemerov heard Tatania wailing, then he vaguely intuited her bending over him. But his vision was now so luridly crimson and badly blurred he couldn't honestly tell what was happening.

His mind was going too. His last fading thought, however, was not of the beautiful Tatania—whom he loved more than life itself—but of the stony-faced killer, the man with the shotgun. He'd looked to be an Arab and was remarkably handsome. He had Hollywood looks when you got right down to it.

In fact, Nemerov's last coherent thought was that his killer bore a striking resemblance to that Egyptian actor, the guy who'd co-starred in *Lawrence of Arabia*.

3

"We sold Pakistan its first nuclear reactors—i.e., their nuclear weapons' training wheels. We educated and prepped their nuclear scientists. We gave them enough money to make millions of bombs. We're responsible for Pakistan's nukes. We brought it on ourselves."

—Elena Moreno

The bartender issued last call. They had been drinking for eight straight hours, yet neither woman, to the bartender's amazement, seemed noticeably drunk.

"I honestly thought you'd died in Pakistan," Elena said, ordering a final round.

"For a while I thought I had too." Reaching across the table, she handed Elena a flash drive. "Sometimes I wish I had."

"That's a little extreme, Adara, even for you."

"Maybe, but you don't know what we're up against. It's going to get ugly."

"So?" Elena said. "You and I have seen lots of ugly, but we're still here."

"Nothing like this," Adara said. "Look at the stuff on this flash drive. I was hoping I wouldn't have to give it to you. This has to be strictly on the down low. It could get both of us killed, but it has everything you need to know."

Elena placed the memory stick on the table in front of Adara.

"Keep it, Adara. You and Rashid chose to go back to Pakistan. You wanted to be world-beaters and global heroes. I told you at the time you were nuts, and you didn't listen. Now you want me to bail Rashid out. Sorry. I've passed the torch. My days in the Special Ops salt mines are over."

"You still know Pakistan and their terrorist groups," Adara said, "better than any agent I ever knew."

"But I'm not into reckless risk anymore. Those days are over."

"Suppose I told you we had a chance to do some good—to make things better over there."

"What's life without a dream?"

Adara leaned toward Elena, placed the flash drive in her hand, and curled her fingers over it.

"I only got out," Adara said, "because Rashid covered my escape from that Pashtun hellhole. That's why I'm alive. He held the New United Islamist Front off with an M60 machine gun.

"That flash drive, did you try taking it to the Company? Or the FBI?"

"Why not just give it to Raza and Kamal?"

"You don't trust the Agency *or* the Bureau?" Elena said.

"Waheed, Putilov and Tower own them.

"How?" Elena asked.

"They're all in Putilov's trick bag, the Saudis included."

"So what am I supposed to do about it?"

"You can help me get Rashid out of Pakistan," Adara said. "He knows everything. He was in the middle of it, on the inside. You, Jules, Rashid and I can blow the whistle on the whole dirty mess. We can put them all away."

"Not possible. Tower, Putilov, Waheed—they're invulnerable to people like us. I know from experience."

"Rashid's got them nailed—dead-bang."

"Naw, they're wired too tight."

"Please. I'm begging you, Elena."

Adara's voice was starting to crack. Elena had never heard her voice break before. She was impressed. She also wondered if it was an act. She didn't think so. She took Adara's hand and held it.

"Nothing good comes out of the Mideast," Elena said. "It's the gift that never stops giving."

"Like the Hotel California."

"'*You can check out any time you like,*'" Elena said, quoting the old lyric, "'*but you can never leave.*'"

"Suppose I said there are people there ready to turn NYC into a nuclear necropolis?"

"I'd say what goes around, comes around," Elena said.

"The U.S. has done a lot of dumb things, and it's run by morons, but your country doesn't deserve to get nuked."

"Really?" Elena said. "We sold Pakistan its first nuclear reactors—their nuclear weapons' training wheels. We educated and prepped their nuclear scientists. We gave them enough money to make millions of bombs. We're responsible for Pakistan's nukes. We brought it on ourselves."

"You can tell that to New York's charred smoking corpses."

"It's not my fight anymore."

"There are Muslims, like Rashid and me, who want to do some good. We know people we can work with."

"Who?" Elena asked. "Your mythical Muslim moderates? You know the difference between Islamist extremists and Islamist moderates? The moderates are political opportunists and money-whores, while your ISIS soldiers and New United Islamist Front cretins are murderously messianic fanatics, but they're sincere in their paranoid beliefs and willing to die for their cause. Guess who wins?"

"Now that they have nukes they will definitely win," Adara said.

"Maybe that's what it will take before that region rids itself of the Islamist plague. Watch them nuke New York, and then watch the West obliterate the Mideast in a nuclear Armageddon. If that happens, it will be 'Goodbye, Islamist terrorists.'"

"That's nihilism talking."

"That's realism, girl," Elena said. "That's history. They have a barbarism there that goes back to ancient Babylonia. Did you ever look at any of those early Assyrian artworks? They depict a world, ghoulish and macabre, their trees trimmed with severed heads. It has not changed in 3,000 years. ISIS, al Qaeda, the TTP, the New Front, they decorate their electrical towers, lampposts and city squares with gibbeted corpses and decapitated craniums."

"Then do it for Rashid, do it for me."

"In God's name, why?" Elena fixed Adara with a hard stare—a stare so hard Adara looked away.

"Any time you needed Rashid and me, we were there," Adara finally said, the words choking in her mouth.

"That was in another world, another time, another life."

"Some things never change."

"I've changed."

"Then I need the old Elena back—one more time." Again, Adara crammed the flash drive into her old friend's palm and closed her fingers around it. "Here's everything you'll need to know. I'll help you assemble a team."

"That old Elena no longer exists. She's dead and in the ground."

"Then we'll resurrect her."

"I don't see why."

"Because Rashid was there when you were nabbed by the TPP and held in that desert hellhole. Rashid got you out."

"Jamie got me out."

"But Rashid found out where you were. Rashid choppered Jamie in and choppered both of you out when you were comatose on a stretcher."

"I guess I forget to thank him. 'Thanks, Rashid. Sorry you didn't have the brains to take my advice and walk away.'"

"We don't want your thanks. We want your help."

"I can't."

"Suppose I told you Putilov and Waheed are going after Jules next, that she's pissed them off too long, that they've heard about her new book and that Waheed, in particular, wants her taken out?"

"I'd say you're a lying bitch. I'd say you're using Jules to scam me into rescuing Rashid."

"Which is why I didn't want to say it. I knew you wouldn't believe me, but it's true. Talk to Jules. Find out what she has on them. She has . . . *everything,* and they know it. The only way to keep any of us safe is to stop those bastards in their tracks."

"Tell it to someone else," Elena said shaking her head.

"I'm telling it to you, and you can't say no. You owe me. You owe Rashid. You owe Jules."

Now Elena's own voice was starting to crack, but still she got it out:

"No good, no bueno. I can't. I don't do that shit anymore."

4

"We're crotch-deep in gasoline, and Meredith's about to light a match."
—President J. T. Tower

President Tower was in his Tower, Inc. New York headquarters with his sister, Brenda; Prince Waheed, the Saudi ambassador, and CIA Director Billy Burke. With a face like a basset hound, Burke had a thick paunch that almost popped the buttons on his tightly stretched shirt. He looked like a heart attack waiting to happen. Waheed, in contrast, was slender, athletic, and had a full head of thick jet-black hair and a dark bushy mustache. The two men were sitting on the long silk couch with Brenda, Tower on the big stuffed armchair. Spread out before them on a huge teak coffee table were an extra-large silver coffee carafe, white bone china cups and saucers.

"You wanted to talk about the UN Global Inequality Conference?" President Tower asked Waheed.

"How bad do you think it's going to get?" the Saudi ambassador, Wahid al-Waheed, asked. "It looks pretty bad back in the Kingdom."

"As you know, the General Assembly's on board," Tower said, "and most of the Security Council."

"Those new Jules Meredith exposés are inflaming the public even more," Brenda Tower said. "When her book comes out, there'll be real uproar. The TV, radio, internet will be on fire, 24/7, with her."

"So everyone says," CIA Director Burke confirmed, "except the publisher's embargoed it, and I can't find anyone with an advance copy. We really don't know how bad it's going to be."

"I have a source in her publishing house," President Tower said. "He can't get his hands on the actual manuscript, but he's seen reading reports on it. She's apparently got dirt on all of us."

"My source says her chapters on your charitable giving are real killers," Ambassador Waheed said.

"Meredith goes after you in that regard too," Brenda said to him. "She says in her articles you illegally funnel contributions to us and to the New United Islamist Front through phony charities."

"Unfortunately," CIA Director Burke said, "a lot of your Saudi princes do use charities to disguise their payments to terrorist groups, which makes it harder to deny Meredith's assertions."

"It's been money well spent," Ambassador Waheed said. "You don't see them blowing up Saudi cities, do you?"

"Europe could take a cue from you," Tower said.

"We also have enemies at home we have to deal with," Brenda said diplomatically.

"Look at all the money we spent, primarying our opposition," CIA Director Burke said. "Most of those bastards aren't around anymore."

"Ask any of those legislators who fucked with us," President Tower said.

"Where are Eric Cantor and Dick Lugar today?" Burke asked with a cynical grin.

"Giving Rotary Club speeches and sitting on local school boards," Tower said.

Again, the room exploded with mocking laughter.

"But I also know Meredith and the Democrats want to expose us," Brenda said, "and will do anything to take us down."

Burke got up, walked over to Tower, and put his arm around his shoulders.

"Fuck 'em," Burke said. "We can ride it out. People have written exposés about us before, and nothing happened."

"Meredith is different," Brenda said. "The times are different. We have the UN and the U.S. Congress on us as well."

"We're crotch-deep in gasoline, and Meredith's about to light a match," Tower said.

"She comes up with dirt on us we didn't even know existed," Ambassador Waheed said.

"What's most troubling is her sources," Director Burke said. "She knows everything we do. J. T., remember your last presidential election? She knew when, where, why and how Putilov fed me your opponent's campaign emails and precisely how he and I used them to embarrass the woman, skew the election's results and hand you the White House. It scares me that she knows so much about us, and no one knows where and how she gets that info."

"And you're the head of the CIA!" Brenda snorted.

"How does she get her info?" the president asked. "I think she's even managed to bug some of our meetings."

"All I know is she's got some big swinging *cojones* on her, fucking with you, Jim, and with us," Director Burke said.

"Most people think of Big Jim Tower," Brenda agreed, "and their nuts shrivel right up into their assholes."

"In deference to your sister," Ambassador Waheed said, clearing his throat, "I have to point out women don't have *cojones,* balls or testicles of any sort."

"Meredith may be one who tests that rule," Burke said.

"Even though she's hellfire-hot," Tower grumbled under his breath.

"Hot or not," Ambassador Waheed said, "she's still pissing where we eat."

"And defecating in our nest," Director Burke concurred.

"Jim," Ambassador Waheed said, "we have to find a way to stop her."

"I'm working on it," Tower said. "I intend to stop her cold."

5

Over the decades, Putilov had hunted his perceived enemies down and killed them no matter how far they fled...

Borya Kazankov sat at the large clear glass circular dining room table in his high-rise apartment. He was partial to that room. It had an extraordinary view of Moscow. In fact, he could see Red Square even though it was five miles from his building. He also knew that by now the square would be filling up with tens of thousands of his supporters.

The square better be filling up with his supporters, he thought grimly. *Running against Mikhail Ivanovich Putilov for the presidency, you'll need all the help you can get.*

Kazankov was a man of enormous wealth—not only from his tournament winnings but from his book sales, documentary residuals and superstar speaking fees—and it was a good thing. He needed money now—a lot of money. During the last two decades, he had found himself spending millions of dollars a year on personal security. He lived round-the-clock with five bodyguards and never traveled with less than nine. Moreover, they were his cooks as well as his protectors. They prepared and tasted everything he consumed. He hadn't eaten a meal out or had a drink in a bar in fifteen years.

To do so was to open oneself up to Putilov's army of professional poisoners. That murderous Russian president had had the beverages of countless reporters, activists and political opponents—including the former top FSB official, Alexander Litvinenko, and the fearless journalist-turned-antiwar-activist, Anna Politkovskaya—spiked with his insufferably agonizing yet almost impossible-to-trace toxins.

Nor was leaving Mother Russia a panacea. Kazankov was no safer on his trips abroad than he was on the Moscow streets. He'd been an implacable critic of Putilov's for far too long—since the man's earliest days—and Putilov, Kazankov knew only too well, forgave nothing, forgot even less, and his reach often seemed limitless, even universal. Over the decades, Putilov had hunted his perceived enemies down and killed them no matter how far they fled, tracking them to the most remote corners of the globe, often dispatching them on airliners in midflight. To provoke Putilov's rage was to invite never-ending peril—and a life spent on the run—but Kazankov had done it anyway. These last fifteen years Kazankov had done everything he could to shine a spotlight on the tyrant's crimes. He'd made it his life's work to expose that murderous maniac for what he was.

Tonight, his guards were dressed in white shirts and slacks, their dark suit coats hung on the backs of their dining room chairs. Two of them were bringing him his meal: coulibiac—a salmon loaf with rice, mushrooms, dill, and sliced-up hard-boiled eggs. On the side, they served him dressed herring, served diced on smothered carrots, beet roots, grated boiled vegetables, ground-up onions, and sour cream. They also brought two bottles of Ferenc Takler Reserve Syrah, one of his favorite Hungarian reds.

His guards always served him family style, placing the food on platters in the table's center. They spread plates, silverware, napkins and wineglasses, then helped themselves. Kazankov's security force always ate and drank first.

After a half minute, Kazankov decided it was safe to eat and tasted the coulibiac.

"Excellent," he said to his men.

"Boss," Vasily Fedorov, the rangy, raw-boned blond-haired captain of his contingent, said, "in forty-five minutes we have to take off for your Red Square rally. You have to allow time to get dressed and get there."

Kazankov shrugged, staring at his food.

"This is a big event," his second-in-command, Anatoly Baszrov, pointed out. "We have to allow for traffic."

"And we have to join other SUVs as well," Vasily said. "We're going in a caravan just in case anyone wants to intercept you along the way."

"It won't take me long to get ready," Kazankov said. "I have no appetite. We can reheat the coulibiac when we come back."

He got up and went back to his bedroom to get dressed.

6

"If you plan on pissing off Putilov," Elena said, "you'd better watch your ass."

Elena picked up her Skype phone. It was 7:00 P.M. Stockholm time, and Jules was on the other end. She turned on her computer's Skype screen and could see her friend's smiling face. Casually attired in gray workout sweats, Jules had her long ebony hair tied back in a ponytail.

"How's it going, Jules?" Elena asked. "Still saving the world? Still keeping it safe for democracy?"

"Save it?" Jules laughed. "I can't even get its attention. I can't even flag it down."

"Tell me about it," Elena said. "I just had Adara here, hounding me to play Crusader Rabbit. She wants me to go back with her to Pakistan on some harebrained rescue operation."

"She called me too," Jules said. "Unfortunately, we have a real problem over there."

"Not you too," Elena said, suddenly sounding tired.

"I'm not sure," Jules said, "which is what bothers me. You know my book on Tower's about to come out."

"The one that's so hush-hush. The one you wouldn't even let me or Jamie read."

"I've been pretty obsessed with it," Jules had to admit.

"So what did Adara want from you?" Elena asked.

"She wanted me to convince you to help her mount that rescue op in Pashtun."

"What's that got to do with you?"

"Rashid told her that Putilov is in a blind rage—as are Tower and Prince Waheed. Even worse, Putilov's convinced them that because of the UN Expropriation Resolution, they have to do something catastrophic. They plan to stop it even if they have to take out the entire city."

"So why did Adara think you could help?"

"She wanted to know what I have on Tower," Jules said. "Everyone seems to think I have enough to put them away."

"Do you?"

"I have enough to piss off half the planet and make the Putilov/Tower people pretty fucking miserable."

"If you plan on pissing off Putilov," Elena said, "you'd better watch your ass."

"And watch what I eat and drink," Jules said.

"Putilov kills reporters like you change your underwear."

There was a long pause. "Who says I wear underwear?" Jules said.

"Goddamn you," Elena said. "You have to take this seriously."

"I always take these assholes seriously," Jules said.

"Well, do they have a reason to want you dead?" Elena asked.

"Maybe."

"Then tell me why Tower's so scared and his two buddies are so pissed at you."

Jules punched up a PDF of her new book on her computer and began searching for passages to show her friend.

7

McMahon opened the door to his palatial hotel suite and entered his sitting room. He paused to study the long, rectangular, intricately carved ebony coffee table in the room's center, which was surrounded by a curving couch of vermillion velvet and overstuffed chairs of the same gaudy hue. Various other pieces of furniture, including the large ebony desk flush against the far wall, filled out the rest of the room, and a plush wall-to-wall crimson carpet covered the floor. McMahon loved this suite even though he derided its garish décor to friends—scarlet as sin—as "whorehouse red."

Still he was in a foul mood. He'd spent the evening desperately searching for the blisteringly hot, raven-haired Middle Eastern woman in the front row, the one in the short yellow dress and spike heels, whose come-fuck-me eyes had cock-teased him throughout his show. He'd told his producers and production assistants not to let her leave without him meeting her. Unfortunately, they'd returned empty-handed, saying she'd bolted out a side door and vanished without a trace. He'd wasted so much time yelling at his staff, drinking scotch, smoking his hyperpotent hydroponic weed, scrutinizing security camera footage, interrogating everyone around him in an insane attempt to track her down—to learn her name, get her contact info, anything—that before he realized it, it was too late to find another date. Anyway, he was too drunk and too hopelessly stoned to get laid. Wasted, horny, pissed off, miserable and exhausted, he'd finally returned to his hotel.

Throwing his suit coat on the couch, he momentarily glanced at the 96-inch flat-screen TV hanging on the wall. Too tired and grumpy to watch the tube, he trudged over to his bedroom, opened the door and walked in.

To his undying surprise, the mystery woman was in his bed, leaning against pillows, which were plumped up against the white padded-leather headboard. Scantily attired in a short black negligee with matching six-inch heels, she was pouring herself a goblet of Cristal, which had been chilling in a silver ice bucket.

"Mr. McMahon, I hope you don't think me too forward. In Saudi Arabia, where I grew up, my brothers and father would fill a box with rocks and line me up against the wall for what I'm about to do tonight."

"Luckily, I share none of your country's values, attitudes or beliefs."

She treated McMahon to a dazzlingly bright smile.

"Please, Mr. McMahon, make yourself comfortable."

With a nonchalant shrug, he began taking off his shoes, socks and pants.

She then poured him a goblet of champagne.

Stripped naked except for his white shirt, he sat down next to her, leaning back against the pillows. He sipped the champagne and groaned with pleasure.

"Allah never tasted anything better," McMahon said.

"Then Allah sold himself short. There are far better things in this life than a mere taste of the bubbly."

Unbuttoning his shirt, she leaned her chin on his chest and stared longingly into his eyes.

"I intend to bring you far more pleasure than a simple glass of fermented grape juice."

"Even though I say such terrible things about your faith, your country and your people?" McMahon asked.

"You just don't know us yet."

"I want to get to know *you* very much—every square centimeter of you," McMahon said.

"You're about to get to know me better than you think."

Seating herself on his lap, she placed her hands around the back of his head and pulled him toward her, artfully rimming the inside of his mouth and teeth with her licentious lips and dexterous tongue. She finally pulled away and stared searchingly into his eyes.

"Maybe you know me too well," McMahon said.

She kissed him again, long, hard, all the while rubbing his chest, stomach and thighs. Pulling way again, she said:

"Would you like to know me, our ways, our wicked, wicked ways . . . *far, far better*?" the woman asked.

"As long as it doesn't violate my religious principles?"

"Which are?"

"Anything that don't fly or have web feet."

"Do you see any feathered wings or webbed toes on me?"

"Not a one."

"Good, because I want you to not only know us but to see the world through our eyes. I want you to understand us down to the core of our being—our wants, needs, dreams and desires."

"You sure that doesn't involve sex acts with dromedaries?" McMahon said.

"No, but maybe it might involve some very unconventional congress with me," she said, "an erotic odyssey which will change you from your hairs' split ends to the bottom-most soles of your feet."

"Then I'm all yours," McMahon said. "I want to know everything about your world—you, in particular—down to the last microscopic detail."

"Then you must. You shall."

She turned away and poured him another glass. When she turned back to him, she had the champagne goblet in one hand and a big bulging doobie along with a box of wooden matches in the other.

"You speak continually of your love of the herb. I thought you might like to sample some of my country's hashish. It is utterly illegal in our kingdom, but some of our more adventurous citizens grow it in greenhouses and labs. They are quite scientific in their methods, and I am told it is the finest in the world."

McMahon immediately took it from her, struck a match on the box and fired it up.

Holding the smoke in a full half minute, he languorously let it out.

"Wow!" was all he could say.

"In my country, we are experts in fine herbs, Mr. McMahon," the woman explained. "*Hashish* is derived from the Arabic word *Hashashiyyin,* meaning 'hashish-eating assassin.' In this case, however, this herb will only assassinate your mind."

He immediately took another pull, held it in.

Then another.

Then another.

"Excuse me while I bogart this joint," McMahon said.

"Help yourself," the mystery woman said. "I've already indulged."

She poured him another goblet of champagne.

"There," the woman asked. "Are you now feeling better about our country, our way of life?"

"Am I ever."

"Even though you're a Muslim-hater and you view women as your rightful, lawful prey, as your own eminent domain—as mere disposable pleasures?"

"Yes, but I'm oh-so-lovable."

He took another long pull on the doobie.

"Maybe I can break down your oh-so-hard resistance," the woman said.

"I can be an awfully hard nut to crack."

"Consider me your personal nutcracker."

"But I am notoriously stubborn."

"Then I'll huff and I'll puff until I . . . *blow* . . . you down." She began massaging the insides of his thighs.

McMahon lay on his back and stared at the ceiling.

The room was slowly starting to sway, then revolve.

"Who are you anyway?" McMahon asked.

"The one who loves the pilgrim soul in you," the woman said.

"You'd have to find it first."

"Is it small?" the woman asked.

"Vanishingly minute."

"Really tiny?"

"Approaching nullity."

The room was now starting to spin, even as she continued her sensuous caresses.

"Suppose I told you, Mr. McMahon, doomsday looms. Suppose I told you that I fear for your immortal soul."

"Right now, I'm more concerned with my mortal flesh."

"Then let us tend to your trembling and tortured loins," the woman said.

She crawled down his body and turned around, until her head was directly over his crotch. Giving McMahon the most terrifyingly wicked smile he'd ever seen in his life, she lowered her eyes, her face, her mouth.

Suddenly, he was possessed with an all-consuming passion for the gorgeous Middle Eastern mystery woman, whom he'd believed he would never see again. Flipping her on her back, he threw himself onto her, wanting to devour her whole—body, mind and spirit—to touch and tongue every throbbing, palpitating inch of her, to drive her into fierce frenzies of insane excitation till there was nothing left to rub, caress or luxuriate over.

When neither of them could stand it any longer and they were both delirious with lust, he entered her. Racked by a heart-pounding, mind-cracking, hip-slamming fury, he was no longer a man but a trip-hammer from hell, going at her harder, harder, faster, faster, forcing her on a horrific hajj—that he seriously doubted she was prepared to make—a demented journey to the end of her soul's blackest night. Lost in the throes of their infernal fornication, they were fucking their brains out in a never-ending apocalypse of crazed cravings and criminal carnality.

Every time she came, she howled *"Daruba!"* and *"Haram!"* which he vaguely recollected as Islamic pleas for religious absolution. The realization that every one of her orgasms filled her with Islamic guilt and religious self-hate, combined with all the weed and alcohol he'd consumed, got him even hotter, turned him on even more, making him hopelessly, helplessly, hideously horny. He was employing every sick, dirty, kinky, perverted stratagem in his interminably twisted trick book of sexual turn-ons. Driving her to the furthest extremes of her most dangerous desires, McMahon kept her coming over and over and over again, her whole body crescendoing and climaxing into one final mind-blowing, pelvis-pounding, obscenity-screaming, genital-detonating roar of . . . *DA-RU-BA!!!!!*

Which McMahon loosely translated in his lust-mad, doped-up mind as:

"Allah, please forgive me for . . . COMING SO GODDAMN HARD WITH THIS OUT-OF-CONTROL INFIDEL . . . MO-THER-FUCKKK-ERRR!!!"

Then McMahon was exploding into a universe-generating Big Bang of lewdly libidinous proportions. It began with the creation of hydrogen, then helium, then stars, black holes, the heavy elements coalescing into solar systems, galaxies, the Milky Way, Earth, humankind. McMahon was born and lived his life right up through to this evening's show, right up through the entering of his hotel suite, finding the enigmatic creature in his bed, continuing right up to the point that they were making love, getting and giving head, fucking like maniacs, then coming over and over, the ecstatically electrifying spasms pumping out of him and her, through them both, again and again, a planet-killing Armageddon of voraciously voluptuous, luridly prurient convulsions.

Now, even worse, he was not the only thing going nuts. The room itself was vibrating, twitching, gyrating, ripping itself apart. It was as if his inner being, his mind's eye was free of his body, was drifting high overhead, floating above him along the ceiling, staring down on his trembling remains, spread-eagled on the bed. He was too weak to move; the mystery woman was now doing all the work, her head between his legs.

Then he was back in his body, watching her, her head still going up and down, up and down, in an eternal sequence of concupiscent collisions, merging into one single, white-hot, agonizing, insatiable, gargantuan . . . *Götterdämmerung.*

Then the room detonated too, blowing him out of the hotel, up above the city, through the stratosphere and into space. All by himself, naked, alone, soaring away from Earth, past Mars, Jupiter, he was picking his way through the shooting gallery of a million billion careening asteroids, then Saturn, Neptune, on and on, into the Edgeworth-Kuiper Belt, the circumstellar disc beyond Saturn, home to Neptune and Uranus, that remote realm where the planetoids lived, thrived and died. Cavorting with the comets, he bid the solar system a fond farewell, spun free of Sol's stern hold, and shot off into the everlasting vastness of the interstellar void.

And then suddenly everything around him was whirling out of control, a widening gyre that knew no stint, a burgeoning vortex of infinite infinitesimal bits, beyond time, beyond God, beyond madness, clarity and everything in between. Then the maelstrom was expanding exponentially, everywhere at once, ballooning into a massive ball of flame, and he was hurtling through it, plunging headlong into hell's deepest abyss. Down, down, downward to darkness he plummeted, until, in the end, all he wanted was surcease, all he wanted was for the terror to end. And then, to his surprise, his wish came true. Infinitude groaned, Eternity closed, the lights went out, and with a last gasping sob, Daniel McMahon gave up the ghost.

After that he knew no more.

PART IV

"You know what Danny McMahon calls our middle-class supporters?" President Tower said. "'The chickens that eat at Colonel Sanders.'"

1

Fahad planned to paint the air, the podium and Red Square itself with the chess champion's brains.

Fahad and his three friends were dressed in ebony leathers, matching boots and motorcycle helmets. All three had large black knapsacks on their backs. They pulled up behind the Tower of Ivan the Terrible on Red Square and parked their bikes on their kickstands. Putilov's FSB, formerly the KGB, had cleared the tower for Fahad, and Putilov himself had assured him he would encounter no interference in the course of his work—not on the way in or out.

"I'll be back when I'm back," Fahad said to the three men.

"See you then, brother," the tall one, named Dmitri, said. The other two nodded in silence.

Fahad climbed off his bike and entered the big unlocked door at the building's rear. He crossed the massive, empty, high-ceilinged stone hall in the back, reached the elevator bank, and punched in the top floor. Once out of the lift, he took the stone fire stairs to the top of the building. Putilov had seen to it the roof door was also unlocked. Fahad crossed the roof and walked up to the wall. Below he could see both Red Square and the Kremlin.

He shrugged the knapsack off his back and removed the case inside. Dropping to his knees, he clicked it open. It contained the scoped Dragunov—Fahad's noise- and flash-suppressed sniper rifle. He then allowed himself a quick glance over the top of the wall.

Three days before, Fahad had paced off the distance from the tower's base directly below to the speaker's stand on the edge of Red Square. Earlier this evening, he'd used that number to compute his firing plan's trigonometry and integral calculus. Taking out his calculator, he now factored in windage, which was blowing out of the north at eight nautical miles per hour. Done. Adjusting the scope, he bore-sighted the speaker's podium.

He was ready to go—as ready as he would ever be. Once the polymer stock and its pad were braced against his armpit, his eye would be clear and his hands would not tremble.

It was by any standard a difficult shot, but Fahad was undismayed. He'd

killed many men and women at greater distances and under far more difficult circumstances. Fahad had once put a round in a Chechen sniper's right
eye at 1,300 meters in a brisk wind—*downhill*. Now that one took some
doing.

Taking a deep breath, he once again peered over the wall. During the next
half hour, one of Putilov's sole surviving presidential opponents, the legendary Russian chess grandmaster and five-time world champion Borya
Kazankov, would enter Red Square and lead a major anti-Putilov rally.
People were up in arms over the brutal murder of Putilov's other rival, Boris
Nemerov, and Kazankov was getting serious traction. Putilov was in trouble in the polls, and the chess grandmaster could beat him.

Protected on the streets by a phalanx of nine devoted bodyguards, Kazankov had proven almost unkillable, so Putilov had finally brought in
Fahad—the man who never let him down.

For the first time in his life, however, Fahad had feared he might fail the
Russian dictator.

But then Kazankov had announced that he would address the rally in Red
Square. He would stand behind a bulletproof podium to give his speech,
and while Kazankov might protect his torso—even with body armor—his
head would be vulnerable. All Fahad needed was a high enough angle and
one good sniper round.

Then goodbye, Kazankov.

Fahad planned to paint the air, the podium and Red Square itself with
the chess champion's brains.

2

"These magnates write their political donations off their taxes, getting billions of dollars back from the IRS. Under the guise of charitable giving, they are fast transforming the U.S. from a democracy to an economic dictatorship. They perpetrate their pseudophilanthropic tax scams so relentlessly, so prolifically, that Warren Buffett has called their network the "Charitable-Industrial Complex."

—Jules Meredith

Brenda and Jim Tower were sitting at the breakfast table in his penthouse's kitchen area, drinking coffee and reading the papers. They had just returned from meeting with Tower's "Kitchen Cabinet" in the New York Oval Office the night before. From the beginning, he'd insisted on conducting almost all presidential business in New York City, but now it was getting harder and harder to make her brother attend even the most critically important meetings, even those with his Cabinet. He hated leaving his Tower of Power penthouse, and he could barely tolerate meeting people in his presidential offices in New York's Excelsior Hotel.

Brenda couldn't blame him. Their world was going to hell. All they got these days was bad news, worse news, and knock-me-down, drag-me-out, beat-me, fuck-me, shoot-me-now . . . *unbearable news.*

"She believes, I'm told, that 'writing is fighting,'" Tower said. "If so, she's about to get the fight of her life."

"I'd give this one a pass, Jim," Brenda said, shaking her head.

"Any particular reason?"

"You're blinded by rage and something else I can't define. You aren't thinking straight."

"So you're saying I should back down?"

"Remember what Twain said: 'Never pick fights with those who buy ink by the barrel.'"

"Meaning?"

"We eat the pitch. Take one for the team. We live to fight another day. Do that, and we can weather this storm."

"No can do, Brenda. That Meredith bitch has gotten to me."

"Jimmy, you're bigger than she is."

"Doesn't matter. I have to be there when Jules Meredith sees what we've pulled off, when she understands how painfully, horrifyingly and disastrously she's lost."

"Why do you have to be there?"

"To watch her get what's coming to her. Don't you just love that?"

"Not really," Brenda said. "I'm always afraid one day that person will be us."

"That's why we're meeting with the boys tomorrow—to see that that doesn't happen."

"I don't know, Jim. Maybe this time it's our turn in the barrel."

"You don't remember Big Jim's Third Law?" Tower said.

"What is it this time?"

"It's never Big Jim's turn in the barrel."

"Why not? We've spent decades ripping people off, and our daddy spent decades doing that before us. We pollute rivers and the air with a vengeance. Why not give something back just this one time?"

"It's not what we do."

"But no one's buying our bullshit anymore," Brenda said. "We've spent the last hundred years shitting on the entire planet. For a hundred years, we and our friends got all the tax breaks, all the tax loopholes, all the offshore accounts and all the supply-side, trickle-down economics our money could buy, while everyone else got austerity, shrinking wages and skyrocketing taxes. Well, those days are over. The people of Earth are hip to the scam, and there's no turning back the clock."

"Who says?"

"Wake up and smell the internet. It's on fire with stories of our profligacy, our trillions of dollars' worth of tax dodges and offshore funds. Bridging the Global Inequality Gap is the order of the day."

"And you think our reckoning is at hand?"

"The raven's croaking our name. The bill's come due."

"You see the UN resolution as some sort of karmic backlash?" Tower asked, his eyes filled with scorn and ridicule.

"Epic payback. There isn't enough fire in hell to burn our sins away."

"So we just let Jules Meredith pick us clean?"

"Just for the time being," Brenda said. "We'll come back at her later. We'll still be rich and powerful as God. We'll still own the politicians. We'll eventually roll the initiative back."

"This too shall pass?"

"If you let it."

"I got plans, sis, and Jules Meredith's not slowing me down."

"One world at a time, Jimmy, one world at a time."

"But you know how important this is to me."

"Which is why we have to hunker down, watch our butts and hang on to all those politicians."

"You mean our sock puppets?" Tower said, his eyes now merry with malevolence.

"They are idiots, aren't they?"

"Almost as dumb as the press," Tower said.

"They're all so stupid I sometimes wonder why we have to spend so much money on them anyway."

"We do it to promote the financial debaucheries of the super-rich, namely, us," Tower said.

"Our fiscal *and* physical debaucheries?"

"Yes, and then have the news media praise us for our crimes."

"That too."

J. T. poured himself another cup of black coffee.

"Goddamn, I feel good," Tower said. "I'm giving Putie a call."

"I'm sure Putilov will love it," Brenda said, voice toneless, her eyes empty of emotion.

Brenda was sure Putilov hated every second of his conversations with her brother. Why wouldn't he? She did.

She then lit another Gauloises Blue and poured herself her first morning snifter of Napoléon brandy.

3

"Did Tower actually think power meant . . . *pussy?*"
—Mikhail Putilov on U.S. President J. T. Tower

Putilov put down the phone. God, he hated Tower. He'd ducked the idiot's calls for as long as he could, but the man was relentless. It was like Tower was stalking Putilov, sniffing out his spoor, drooling on it like a puppy, fishing for the stupidest compliments. He practically licked Putilov's palms and feet, as if he had some sick masochistic need to get Putilov's approval when in truth, the only thing Putilov wanted to give Tower was his boot up his ass and a 12mm round between his goddamn eyes.

Putilov didn't know how much longer he could take dealing with him. Tonight, for example, the phone call from him had been a living hell. Tower had been unable to stop pontificating.

"You know, Comrade Putilov"—yes, the imbecile actually had the temerity to address him as "Comrade"!—*"what makes us so alike? We aren't motivated by the things that obsess most people. You and I recognize the preeminent importance of power in this world—its acquisition, its practices, its abuses and its uses."*

Power?

What the fuck did that cretin know about "power"?

One time Tower actually stopped talking long enough for Putilov to ask him what he meant by "power." Tower quickly warmed to the subject, telling him over and over and over again:

"Power means having anything you want—earning billions of dollars, owning monstrous McMansions, private airliners, expensive toys of every description and dimension, reaching high office if you want to, and getting that superstar super-head and sex-goddess pussy any time you want it."

Did Tower actually think power meant . . . *pussy?*

The man really was a moron.

Real power had nothing to do with sex or paltry possessions.

No, in Putilov's world, power had nothing to do with greed or lust. In Russia, where the courts and legislatures were inherently, irremediably corrupt and justice was always sold to the highest bidder, you had to have real leverage if you wanted to keep what you thought was yours—let alone acquire more. His was a world of apex predators who threatened those less powerful at every turn. Power meant having everything or nothing—being able to take whatever you wanted from whomever you wanted, including that person's life. Power meant not only your financial well-being but your physical survival and the destruction of those who opposed you. Without power, great wealth only made its possessor a gravely endangered species, a target with a great big fucking bull's-eye on the possessor's back. You not only needed more brains, more balls, more influence—more vlast, as he called it in Russian—than anyone else, you always had to be ready to defend what was yours, ready to hit and hit hard.

And if necessary, you had to be ready to kill.

In Putilov's case that meant the willingness to kill en masse.

No, mere political leverage and the acquisition of riches had only been his first step. Ultimate power, for Putilov, meant possessing the power of the State. Early on in his career at the KGB, he had realized that state power had to be vested, not in parliaments or in the business community or, heaven forbid, in the electorate but in an utterly ruthless ruler, namely himself. To achieve that end, he had to attack the very structure of the Russian government.

That opportunity had come not when Yeltsin succeeded Gorbachev, but after Yeltsin left office, drunk, sick and scandal-ridden. By then, Putilov had so enriched and empowered his junta of former KGB bosses, his superwealthy potentates and his coterie of ruthlessly rich mafiosi, he seemed to them a perfect choice for prime minister. Not only had he proven himself to be an effective, competent and talented leader but he had earned the trust of those around him, including many in the journalistic community. "He makes you feel as if he shares your opinions and has your interests at heart" was a common reaction to Putilov.

That he'd been born to poverty and was "a man of the people" further enhanced his political image.

He set about creating a personality cult that would one day rival Stalin's and reduce that of the tsars to absurd obscurity.

Glancing at the wall mirror to his right, he caught his reflection in it. He instantly forgot about Tower and allowed himself a rare arrogant smile.

God, you're a handsome devil—short light-blond hair, wicked blue eyes, that sly all-knowing grin. So what if your critics accuse you of narcissism? When you're as good-looking as you are, boy, you've got to flaunt it.

That was why he released that photo of himself bare-chested on a horse in a rugged wilderness. He wanted the people of the world to see him in all his guts and glory. Of course, his effete, weak-kneed, limp-wristed critics—particularly in the West—mocked him for his imposing and frankly amazing machismo. Those pathetic little creeps were so timid, so cowardly, so light-in-the-loafers they could not bear the sight of a real man—a man who was everything they weren't.

Looking away from his reflection, he—suddenly, inescapably, humiliatingly—flashed back to his last conversation with Tower, and once again he was consumed by blind fury. Where did Tower get off lecturing to Putilov about "the uses and abuses of power" and how he and Putilov were so similar and understood each other so completely? Tower had no idea what it had taken to seize power in Russia and become that nation's dictator. What did that idiot know about Putilov's life and his almost infinite capacity for inflicting violence and terror on those who opposed him?

Where did he get off thinking he could lecture Putilov on . . . *anything?*

His hatred of Tower was starting to drive him around the bend—so much so that three nights ago, after one of the man's ranting phone calls, he decided it was once again time to pay "the krok" a visit. God, that stuff was good. It relaxed him totally, and nothing ever relaxed Putilov. Sure, he knew it was addictive, but he also knew the krok could never conquer him. He'd make sure he never took it except in times of dire emergency. After all, he was Mikhail Ivanovich Putilov. He was an invincible avatar of iron discipline. He couldn't have gotten to where he was if he hadn't been.

He could handle a little desomorphine, and after a half hour on the phone with Tower, he definitely needed it. He had to have something that could put him to sleep. Otherwise, he didn't think he could take the stress of dealing with the man anymore.

It was quite possible that Tower was driving him insane.

4

The total amount of stolen taxpayer dollars residing in secret, numbered, offshore accounts equals over a third of the world's Gross Global Product.

—Jules Meredith

It was dawn when Elena finished her friend's book.

Well, she could see why Tower, Waheed, and that prick Putilov were pissed off. The book was a firebomb, and it was due to detonate just when it could hurt those three men the most.

Scrolling back up through the book, she reread a few of the passages Jules had tagged—only four passages out of hundreds.

> *Today eight billionaire oligarchs, six of whom are Americans, hold one-half of the world's wealth in their hands. These numbers are based on Oxfam, Forbes, the latest Global Wealth Report and studies by the Swiss bank Credit Suisse. President Tower and Russia's Prime Minister Mikhail Putilov missed the list only because most of their cash hoard is buried in offshore accounts so secretive they have not yet been located. But even their accounts will be penetrated in the near future. The UN and the U.S. Senate bills, if passed, will finally reveal once and for all how much illegal wealth the two men have amassed.*

In fact, Jules Meredith pointed out, *the total amount of stolen taxpayer money residing in secret, numbered, offshore accounts equals over one-third of the world's Gross Global Product.*

> *Mark Twain called the late 19th century America's "Gilded Age," but Twain did not foresee the half of it. Today's era is, indeed, the ne plus ultra of income inequality. Never in the history of the world have the upper-upper classes sucked so much wealth out of the global economy and pauperized so many people. Nor do they earn their wealth through manufacturing valuable products and creating jobs. They develop scams whereby they make money off money, all the while*

creating . . . nothing. Today, the U.S. financial sector vacuums up 50 percent of all non-farm corporate profits. According to recent studies, current trends will produce even more outrageously obscene economic disparities. Just five years from now, if the UN and U.S. Senate Anti-Inequality Expropriation measures aren't passed, three oligarchs will be worth more than one-half the world's population.

And democracy as we used to know it will vanish from the face of the earth.

Jules had even posted the billionaires' photos inside her article—then added the likenesses of Tower, Waheed and Putilov for good measure. The caption under those photos read: *"A Rogues' Gallery of the Criminal Rich."* Then she added:

The country needs a President Theodore Roosevelt. A leader who will break up this nation's power-grabbing billionaire oligarchy, not a predatory plutocrat like Tower whose best friends are Prince Waheed, a Saudi terrorist fund-raiser, and Mikhail Putilov, the genocidal maniac who is gutting Russia like a Christmas goose.

Elena continued scrolling up until she hit another tagged passage.

In the United States, the Oligarch Movement is headed by President J. T. Tower. The heart and soul of that movement are its 200 megadonors. He has organized them into a clandestine, rigorously disciplined political group he has nicknamed his "Killer Elite." Tightly coordinated at the grassroots level, this group is dedicated to steamrolling its opposition in state and local elections and radically gerrymandering Congressional districts in their favor. Active at the topmost levels of government as well, where it strong-arms legislators with primary threats, it is infinitely more powerful than any U.S. political group in history.

Its contributing members are a "Who's Who" of the world's biggest corporate welfare queens. In other words, they are the beneficiaries of some of the biggest, most outrageous government subsidies, tax breaks and outright patronage in history.

One example?

The fossil-fuel energy and financial sectors gobble up over $6 trillion a year in global government subsidies. That corporate graft saps up over 8 percent of the planet's total GDP—so much that the World

Bank has asked specifically to outlaw all such energy subsidies every-
where.

Another example of the energy industry's power?

According to military analysts, the U.S. has expended more blood
and treasure protecting Mideast oil for J. T. Tower and his associates
Elite than it did fighting the Cold War.

Then Jules took on Tower's political organization.

Furthermore, Tower and his cohorts continually lobby and coerce
America's politicians, pressuring them to weaken the country's tax
and environmental codes. At the state, local and federal level, Tower's
network of 200 billionaire investors—that Killer Elite also known as
"Murder, Inc."—spends more on elections than both parties spent on
their entire presidential campaigns a mere eight years earlier ...
combined. They represent an entirely new epoch in America. Tower
and his billionaire brethren are determined to seize power and turn
his presidency into the "Age of the Oligarchs."

At the industrial level, Tower's minions bankroll his Killer Elite at
the taxpayers' expense. These magnates write their political donations
off their taxes, getting billions of dollars back from the IRS. Under the
guise of charitable giving, they are fast transforming the U.S. from a
democracy to an economic dictatorship. They perpetrate their pseu-
dophilanthropic tax scams so relentlessly, so prolifically, that Warren
Buffett has called their network the "Charitable-Industrial Complex."

Tower and his billionaire allies have always been crackpots, but
their cracks have widened with age. They care about nothing save their
own personal wealth and power. No mere predators, they are veloci-
raptors of avarice, almost Luciferian in their hubris, and the war they
wage is not simply on the American people but against Life itself.
They are truly the Great American Greed Machine.

Then Jules went into Tower's poisoning of America's air, lakes, rivers, and
water table to say nothing of the populace itself.

Tower kills people en masse the way Putilov kills them with his
assassins and al-Waheed does through state-funded terrorism. In
fact, Tower probably kills more than both those other men put to-
gether. Because of his petrochemical avarice, one-half of the U.S. popu-
lation lives within ten miles of a toxic waste site. Those who live

nearby pay for these plants with both their lives and their tax dollars. Tower murders them with impunity, forcing these victims to eat the medical expenses generated by his cancer-inducing chemical plants, to pay for his decontamination costs when the EPA occasionally forces him to clean up one of his carcinogenic cesspools, which he continually creates, to pick up his IRS bills for him, reducing his tax burden to zero—to less than zero.

Instead of forcing Tower to pay taxes, the IRS gives him credits and refunds.

So Tower Enterprises continues to pour toxins into our water, air and earth; and the pipelines that they're constructing will poison us even more disastrously. Those conduits already leak like sieves. When Canadian oil companies proposed constructing the infamous Keystone Pipeline across the U.S. down to its Gulf ports, no one asked why they didn't build it across Canada and ship it out of Canada's Atlantic ports. You know why? The Canadian government and its people had declared that kind of highly destructive, carbon-dense oil too dangerous to pipe on or through Canadian soil. The shale and tarsand oil are too irreversibly corrosive and the pipelines too easily eroded and perforated. The Canadians know such systems would inevitably burst open and disgorge billions of gallons of highly toxic crude into Canada's soil and water systems, so Canada rejected the pipeline. Thus, Tower Enterprises proposed piping it across the U.S. Americans are more nonchalant about pipeline breaches and the ruination of America's aquifers and water table than their Canadian counterparts. So Tower, Inc. finally got the bill passed.

And now the jury's in. If Tower's idol, Putilov, has killed and poisoned people by the thousands, his protégé, Tower, has murdered them by the millions.

The whole book was one protracted attack on Tower and his coterie of oligarchs. Jules was calling them all out on their thefts and murders and on all the trillions of dollars these men and their pals had secreted offshore—the very thing the UN Resolution promised to expropriate.

But those chapters on Tower were only part of the book. The last third of it focused on Putilov. Elena had read it twice and still couldn't accept its implications. Jules exposed chapter and verse the horrors that Putilov had inflicted on the Russian citizenry—physically, financially and spiritually. Putilov had shattered that country's body politic in ways Hitler and Stalin never even dreamed of. Jules had concluded in an epilogue that Russia would never recover from Putilov's crimes against its populace.

Elena understood now that Adara was not exaggerating when she told her Jules was in serious trouble. Putilov had killed hundreds of reporters for far, far less. Furthermore, Tower and his Killer Elite would also see Jules as a terminal threat. Elena honestly believed that when Jules made those final Putilov chapters public, she would have to go into hiding.

Yet Jules had told her she planned to take her attacks public in less than a week.

Adara was right.

This shit was really going down.

Elena had to help Jules.

Reaching for an encrypted burner, she punched in Adara's number.

5

"Don't burn up that target-picture."
—Fahad al-Qadi

Red Square was filled with a howling crowd of at least 60,000 activists, all shouting "Down with Putilov!" "Fuck Putilov!" and "Give us Kazankov!"

For the most part, Fahad hid behind the walled roof at the top of the Tower of Ivan the Terrible—ignoring the crowd below—and kept a tiny non-glaring VidCam focused on Borya Kazankov's reserved spaces along the street nearest the speaker's stand. He studied those empty parking spaces on his iPad and waited for Kazankov to arrive.

Finally Kazankov's caravan of four black SUVs pulled up along that part of the square and parked in their reserved slots. A contingent of eighteen bodyguards climbed out of the four cars—nine more than usual.

Last but not least, Kazankov piled out of vehicle number three. To Fahad's horror the man was decked out in army camouflage and full body armor. He even wore an official army head protector.

Holy Shit, Fahad knew that helmet. The SSSh-94 Sfera-S. Inside of it there were sliding titanium plates configured to protect Kazankov's head as well as dampers to soften the round's impact on the helmet.

The prick was leaving nothing to chance.

Fahad had planned for such a possibility. He understood that Kazankov was smart—a five-time world chess champion—and he had to know Putilov wanted to kill him. Fahad had been afraid Kazankov might shield his skull.

One of the many reasons he brought the Dragunov—instead of a newer, fancier sniper rifle—was that the manufacturer machined the receiver for extra-heavy-gauge torsional strength.

And sometimes the op required a stronger, more durable firing chamber.

If his target was wearing bulletproof headgear—which was always a possibility—Fahad had to go for hot-loaded, detonating armor-piercing rounds. Such ammunition was volatile to say the least—almost as dangerous to the shooter as the enemy.

Still he had two of those titanium-jacketed shells—each now in its own padded box—hot-loaded with extra-high explosive. He'd also drilled a hole into each of the slug's curved sides and loaded these openings, just under their titanium tips, with fulminate of mercury. He'd then filled the rest of the apertures with cylindrical steel plugs that he meticulously shaped and assiduously filed to precisely fit the drilled-out holes.

He'd loaded and tested similar rounds many times in the past and was confident he could penetrate any helmet on the face of the earth with one of these shells. The bullet's hot load could, of course, destroy the rifle's firing chamber in the process—maybe the whole fucking breech, which had happened during a couple of his tests—but if he could hit him from 900 yards with a single shot, Kazankov would be a dead man.

Still he honestly hadn't believed the prick would show up wearing a helmet.

What the fuck? Stranger things had happened to Fahad, and over his two decades as a professional killer and saboteur, he'd learned to anticipate the unexpected.

Breathing deeply, he refocused the VidCam mounted on the top of the wall. On his iPad screen, he watched Kazankov stand at the podium, grip its edges, and wait for the roaring throng to quiet down.

Slowly the din subsided, and when Fahad saw that all eyes were fixed on Kazankov, the assassin ejected the Dragunov's magazine, pulled back the cocking hammer and slid a single exploding round into the receiver. Quickly, he stood. Placing a small sandbag on the parapet, Fahad hacked a groove in it with the edge of his hand. He swung the Dragunov down on top of the bag and into the slot.

Taking a deep breath, he allowed two decades of sniper training to take over. He then let the breath out and fixed his eye against the scope. In seconds, the crosshairs converged on the left-hand side of Kazankov's helmet.

The best look's your first look. Don't burn up that target-picture. You have him now—cold zero. Do it.

The big Dragunov jumped in his fists and kicked against his shoulder like a hammer blow. Flames shot out of the breech, half-blinding him, and he slipped back down behind the parapet, unable to see Kazankov and the result of his shot.

Somehow he had the presence of mind to drop the rifle at his feet, pick up his knapsack and race for the far side of the roof. Removing a rappelling line from the pack, he secured it to a nearby fire pump. The friction hitch, which would allow him to pay the rope out with maximal speed and minimal effort, was already attached to the line as was a black nylon climbing harness. Slipping into it, Fahad climbed over the edge of the wall and bounced down the side of the tower in long graceful leaps. He was on the sidewalk and next to his motorcycle in less than fifteen seconds.

Removing the rope and its waist-rig, he mounted his big bike and turned on the engine. He and his friends shot up the street. Each of the three identically dressed motorcycle riders immediately departed down a different street. It wasn't a foolproof strategy, but it improved the odds that he would escape and proceed to his next assignment.

Fahad further improved those odds by pulling up beside a small VW bug parked next to a Dumpster on the edge of an abandoned warehouse. He slipped out of his leathers and helmet, then threw them into the trash disposal bin. Laying the bike behind the big receptacle, he took a tarp out of the car's trunk and spread it over the bike.

The VW was fitted with a Porsche engine and would do 160 mph on the straightaways. He had plenty of cash and extra passports. If he could get out of Russia and get through his next series of ops, he'd be finished with Putilov, Raza and Waheed forever and never see any of them again.

Goddamn, he hated them all.

Turning on the ignition, he started up the street.

Suddenly, his burner phone was buzzing like a wasp against his thigh. Only one man had that number. His nemesis.

He took out the phone and put it to his ear.

"What did you load that round with?" Putilov roared. "TNT?"

Fahad did not want to tell him that the hot-loaded powder cartridge had almost blown up in his face. It had detonated so blindingly that he had neither seen nor known what happened.

"Just about," Fahad said, deliberately noncommittal.

"I'll say," Putilov enthused. "You blew his helmet, brains and skull all over the fucking Kremlin."

"I'm glad you're satisfied."

"Satisfied? I've never been happier in my life. Goddamn, you're good. Now finish the rest of it, and you'll be set for life!"

"Copy that," Fahad said softly.

Clicking off the phone, he headed toward the Moscow Ring, where he planned to get far away from Russia's capital and lost in traffic.

6

Danny McMahon had shaken his fist and thundered his name at the Everlasting Dark too many times for too many boisterous, blasphemous, drug-ridden, sexually possessed, obscenity-screaming years. Now the devil was shouting his name back at him and howling for his hide.

McMahon's mind was a jumble of drug-addled, sex-crazed memories. He recalled being back in his dressing room, smoking dope with a gorgeous Islamic woman. He was teasing her mercilessly, bombarding her with his most derisive anti-Islamic diatribes and one-liners. While he'd fucked her, he'd muttered one taunt repeatedly into her ear.

"*Haram!* . . . *Haram!* . . . *Haram!*" he'd grunted, reminding her over and over that her faith explicitly forbade what they were doing.

That zinger particularly enraged her. Had she not been coming so hard, she might have attacked him.

Then McMahon remembered becoming so aroused that he seemed to have been transmuted by his lust—no, transmogrified by it. He was going after her with everything he had, whaling on her not even like a human being but as if he were a banshee from the Underworld, a maniac of the libido, a demon of desire—banging her just as hard as he knew how.

He remembered her screaming more Arabic imprecations, begging Allah to forgive her for all the convulsive, uncontrollable, mind-blowing never-ending orgasms he was inflicting on her, sobbing, ululating, baying like a hydrophobic bitch-wolf deranged by moon-mad suffering. Every time she climaxed, her entire body, soul, astral being detonated deliriously, inspiring McMahon to go after her even harder, more furiously, until all he could remember was her howling hysterically amid her erotic eruptions even as he himself laughed raucously, uproariously, enraptured and enthralled by her agonizing ecstasy even as his own orgasms exploded out of him into soaring-roaring-horrifying madness.

But then at the height of his demented dreams and furious fever-fucking, his vision started to blur, and his voice began to slur.

Too late he realized she'd given him a drugged joint—and maybe drugged champagne as well.

"In my country, we are experts in fine herbs, Mr. McMahon," the woman had explained earlier. "*Hashish* is derived from the Arabic word *Hashashi-yyin*, meaning 'hashish-eating assassin.' In this case, however, this herb will only assassinate your mind."

He also vaguely recollected three men in dark well-cut suits and sunglasses entering his hotel room, gagging and blindfolding him. Securing his drug-heavy sluggish wrists behind his back with zip ties, they lashed together his ankles and knees, then stuffed him into a black, hugely outsized seaman's bag. Hanging the bag out the hotel window, they lowered him down on a rope to where some men waited in the alley below. From inside the bag, he felt himself being hustled into a van.

Then he knew no more until he came to. Still in the bag, his guards told him he was in a Saudi State Department jet. Bound, blindfolded and gagged, when he next came to, he found himself slumped over in front of a shipping container in the jet's baggage compartment.

A big ugly bear of a contractor, still dressed in a black business suit, removed the blindfold and said to him just as he shoved him through the shipping container door:

"Mr. McMahon, the next stop is Pakistan, so enjoy the flight."

"Yeah," another dark-suited handler said, "you're headed toward the worst place on earth. I wouldn't want to be you."

"You know," the other man said, "if you weren't such a miserable Muslim-hating infidel sonofabitch, I'd almost feel sorry for you."

"Almost," the other man said.

The two men both laughed, then slammed and locked the shipping container door.

His head throbbed. He felt dehydrated, and his joints ached from his restraints. Still he couldn't believe this was happening to him. Only gradually was he able to accept that he was in a dark, soundproofed steel box. Then slowly, surely, the utter horror of his situation began to sink in. This was no nightmare from which he'd awaken, frightened but relieved. No, he was in for his issue of big-time trouble. Danny McMahon had shaken his fist and thundered his name at the Everlasting Dark too many times for too many boisterous, blasphemous, drug-ridden, sexually possessed, obscenity-screaming years. Now the devil was shouting his name back at him and howling for his hide.

His deal was going down.

The vultures were coming home to roost.

This was all the trouble, he, Daniel James McMahon, had spent his life searching for.

Danny, you are finally, terminally, hopelessly . . . fucked.

7

"It didn't matter whether we called it 'supply-side finance' or 'trickle-down economics,' it always came down to the same thing, what David Stockwell called 'a Trojan Horse for upper-bracket tax cuts.' None of it ever reached the Great Unwashed. So why didn't they rise up before? They have to know it's never worked, at least for them."

—Brenda Tower

Later that night, Brenda sat up with her brother in his big New York penthouse overlooking New York, Long Island, Staten Island and New Jersey.

"Hey little brother, I see you've been wobbling a bit on immigration—on whether birth in the U.S. should guarantee babies citizenship. At least, when it comes to Russian babies, you're wobbling. You now say that it should?"

"You think I've turned softhearted in my old age?" He treated her to a smug smirk.

"No, I think you did the math."

"And which math was that?" he asked.

"The math that counts all the money you're making off your Russian birth-tourism business."

Tower allowed her another small smile of mean merriment. "We have made a few bucks off those Russian rug rats, haven't we?"

"A few bucks? Your tycoon buddies over there crank out hundreds of thousands of dollars every time they send one of their pregnant wives or mistresses to Miami. They pay us to put them up in our ultra-luxurious apartment complexes for three months or so. Their women-friends then drop their obnoxious tots here in the States. The mamas get to claim U.S. citizenship for the drooling, puking tykes, who, at the same time, keep their Russian citizenship. When the little ankle-biters turn twenty-one, their mega-rich parents can then apply for green cards under your 'family unification program,' all of it done through the good offices of J. T. Tower's lavish high-rises and your pals in the birth-tourism business."

"So I'm an astute but softhearted entrepreneur."

"One who also campaigned on the promise to send all those Mexican babies born in the U.S. back across the border, kicking and bawling and screaming."

"So?"

"Isn't that a little . . . *inconsistent*?"

"Consistency is the hobgoblin of little minds."

Brenda stared at him, shaking her head. "Do you have any idea at all who said that?"

"I did."

"Ever heard of Ralph Waldo Emerson?"

"He claims he said that?"

"He did say it."

"Then he can also suck my dick while he's saying it."

Brenda stared at him in frank astonishment. "Oh, my poor little brother," she finally said. "No one understands you, do they?"

"Obama and his attorney general, Eric Holder, understood me," Tower said to his sister, suddenly serious. "They knew that if they had sent the FBI after me and after Wall Street's top VPs in 2008, we'd have paid them back by crashing the global credit markets. We'd have eviscerated the international economy and bled it out like a butchered hog. We'd have flooded the streets with red ink and blood. We'd have proved once and for all who was really running things and that we were not only too big to fail, we were too big to jail."

Brenda stared at her brother a long hard minute, then sighed.

"Jimmy, why do we talk about money and power, violence and slaughter so much?" Brenda asked her brother. "Why don't we talk about something else?"

"You're not interested in my sex life," Tower said.

"What about love?" Brenda asked. "I'm told it makes the world go 'round."

"But filthy lucre oils the wheels."

"Is it possible that under all our cynicism and hardness that we've missed out on something?" Brenda asked. "I'm told it's okay to show the soft, sensitive side of our personalities to those whom we care about. Do you really think it's okay to love?"

Tower snorted with derision.

"You've never known love?" Brenda asked him.

"Oh, I get it. You think I've grown a paper asshole."

"You don't even believe love exists, do you?"

"Nada—only bills come due."

"Then, to you, collections are everything?"

"The only thing," Tower said. "Collecting what's yours is life's single-most important skill."

"The Jim Tower I know wants to collect not only what's his but half of everyone else's."

"You mean *all* of everyone else's."

"So love is just a promissory note."

"A quid pro quo," Tower said. "Nothing more."

"Like eye for an eye?"

"Fuck with me, it's a head for an eye."

"The poets say," Brenda said, "that love is a gift—one freely given and freely received."

"Nothing is free," Tower said, leaning toward her for emphasis. "Everything's bought and paid for."

"You talk like you hate love," Brenda said.

"How can I hate something that doesn't exist? What you call love's a snare, a scam, a fucking lie—pure and simple."

"How is it a lie if people believe it in their hearts, their souls, their minds?" Brenda asked.

"Because those people are liars," Tower said with a scathing sneer. "They begin by lying about love to themselves, then lying about it to each other, and then they end up lying about it to everyone else."

"Is making love to someone you care about also a lie?" Brenda asked.

"Sexual love might begin as a big, happy fun-fuck, but it always ends as a huge, ugly . . . *hate-fest.*"

"Does heaven—or hell—ever enter into your calculations?"

"I want both," her brother said.

"And what makes you think you'd like either?" Brenda asked.

"I want to visit heaven so I can see if peace, serenity and dreamful ease really exist."

"If they do, why would you want to go to hell?"

"For the nightlife," Tower said.

"You are your father's son."

"That I am, sis. That I am."

Tower looked away, strangely silent, distracted. Brenda could read his moods and saw he was morose.

"So what's wrong?"

"I don't understand any of it anymore."

"You mean why the people want to ransack our offshore bank accounts?" Brenda asked.

"That's not it," Tower said. "I understand why they want to close the inequality gap. From their point of view, it makes perfect sense. I'd try to shrink the wealth gap too if I were in their shoes. What I can't figure out is why the public has supported me for so long. They had to know I was going to rob them blind."

"We ripped off most of them," Brenda had to admit.

"Yes," Tower said, "and they willingly, adoringly gave their money to us and our friends."

"It didn't matter," Brenda said, "whether we called it 'supply-side finance' or 'trickle-down economics,' it always came down to the same thing, what David Stockwell called 'a Trojan Horse for upper-bracket tax cuts.' None of it ever reached the Great Unwashed. So why didn't they rise up before? They have to know it's never worked, at least for them."

"I understand why their representatives back us," Tower said. "We give money to them—to a lot of politicians to get them elected—and they fill our coffers many times over. Afterward, we all laugh on the way to the bank. But what about the ordinary people—the good, strong, hardworking men and women, in particular—who support us so slavishly? They have to know we're going to loot then piecemeal, and if we had our way, we'd take everything they had."

"Especially their Social Security, Medicare and Medicaid," Brenda said, nodding.

"They've always been at the top of our hit list," Tower agreed. "We've already grabbed up most of their corporate pension funds, so the voters have to know that their Social Security and their government retirement plans are next on the chopping block. Yet those assholes not only back me, I swear to God they actually *like* me."

"They *love* you, Jim. The crowds cheer for you like maniacs at your rallies. The women look and sound like they're having orgasms."

"You know what Danny McMahon calls our middle-class supporters?" President Tower said. "'The chickens that eat at Colonel Sanders.'"

"They are stupid, aren't they?"

"They're sheep bleating for our shears," Tower said.

"Is that why God made us?"

"Someone has to fleece them."

"So they, the Great Unwashed," Brenda said, "get nothing out of all this, even as we grow even richer than sin?"

"You and I give the Unwashed Masses the opportunity to work their asses off enriching those at the top, particularly you and me. It's not too much to ask."

"And you offer them nothing in return?" Brenda asked.

"The satisfaction of a hard job well done."

"In short, you offer them blood, sweat, toil and tears."

"Their blood, sweat, toil and tears—that's all the morons deserve," Tower said.

"Nothing else?" Brenda asked, amazed.

"They learn, if they're lucky, to kiss the whip—to willingly and gratefully sacrifice themselves for the financial betterment of . . . *us*."

"But I keep asking you, why *should* they do it?" Brenda asked.

"Because that's the way the world works," Tower said. "The strong prevail, the weak perish, and that is life."

"Ah, the situational ethics of the super-rich."

"I do see myself as a morally relative billionaire."

"Yeah, and if the Ignorant Masses ever found out how we live," Brenda said, "they'd set our world on fire."

"But they don't know," Tower said, "and anyway, it's all just laziness and envy on their part. If they wanted what we have, they'd simply work harder."

"Ah, Jimmy, the gap between us and them is unbridgeable. We travel in mega-yachts and on our own private jetliners. We own dozens of penthouses and McMansions, most of which sit empty year-round because we have so many of them. Our investment returns dwarf anything the Great Unwashed could ever imagine—in part, because they can't afford to buy politicians, dismiss regulators and cut their taxes. They don't have cross-border, wealth-management firms that stash their investments abroad in labyrinthine trusts, shell companies and in offshore, black-hole, black-money tax havens. Last year our businesses earned $129 billion combined in three small islands—the Virgin Islands, Bermuda and the Caymans. Those places have fewer than 150,000 inhabitants, so our profits would have come to almost $900,000 per islander had our firms actually done any real work over there."

"On the other hand, we're small potatoes compared to the Rothschild family," Tower pointed out, "which is worth upwards of $2 trillion and the Saudi Royal Family, which is worth $1.4 trillion."

"I heard the Saudi king recently bought a 500-foot yacht for $500 million."

"But what about the UN mandate, the anti-inequality bill," Brenda asked. "It sounds like the people of the world are finally rising up against us."

"A temporary setback," Tower said. "We'll turn them around quickly enough, bring them to heel, teach them what happens when they fuck with J. T. Tower and Mikhail Putilov."

"Jimmy, I don't know what Putilov has planned," Brenda said, "but knowing him, the solution could be . . . *unacceptable*."

"You're wrong, sis. This time it's for all the marbles, and the only thing that matters now is that we show no fear, we don't back down, we don't give an inch. This time it's total retaliation."

"So there are no ethical limits to our response?" Brenda asked.

"None at all."

"Does that explain our financial dealings with men like Putilov and Prince Waheed?" Brenda asked. "That the making of money recognizes no moral boundaries?"

"Money doesn't care where it comes from."

"But, Jimmy, those are dangerous men. We should be afraid of them."

"If Putilov and Waheed had any sense, they'd fear me."

"Really?" Brenda asked. "Suppose they turned New York into a nuclear necropolis. How would you justify your business transactions with those people then?"

"The cost of doing business."

"So it's prodigious wealth and moral relativism for people at the top, and serfdom for everyone else?"

"I couldn't have put it any better myself," Tower said.

"Is that why you insist on manufacturing benzene, the most carcinogenic chemical on earth? Jules Meredith calls you 'the Johnny Appleseed of metastatic cancer.' She says you've saturated the country's air and half its water table with carcinogens."

"So what's wrong with making a few bucks off benzene?" Tower asked.

"Meredith says it's fairly fucking disgusting."

"Fairly fucking lucrative, you mean, and anyway, why do you care? Our constituents wanted the pipeline. We called it 'a jobs creator.'"

"But they didn't want the terminal cancer, which the pipeline will eventually cause," Brenda said.

"No, but they want cars that'll go 160 miles an hour," Tower said. "They want supersonic airliners. They want high-performance war transport. I give them the fuel that'll get it done."

"But why are we doing business with the Saudis? We can get all the oil and gas we want in the U.S. and Canada. Do we really have to bankroll them? A cadre of Saudi royals underwrote the 9/11 attacks. They financed and created ISIS. They're behind the New United Islamist Front."

"Yeah, but the Saudis still have the cheapest oil on earth, and in this age of plummeting petro-profits, Saudi oil money, for us, is the difference between the red and the black, between fiscal prosperity and corporate collapse."

THE EVIL THAT MEN DO | 113

"I can't argue with that," Brenda said, emitting a long painful sigh.

"It's like I always say, Brenda, this life is a great big rock. You're either on top of it or under it."

"And that's all there is to it?" Brenda asked. "That's what it all comes down to?"

"You conquer the world or you're crucified by it," Tower said.

"With Jules Meredith hammering in the nails?" Brenda asked.

"She would if she could," Tower said, "but I intend to hammer her first, hammer her till she can't stand up—till she begs for mercy."

"Jimmy," Brenda said, her eyes widening in astonishment, "you aren't attracted to Jules Meredith, are you?"

"Am I ever."

"She's looking to you take down."

"I'm looking to take her down."

"You're kidding? You could have a thousand women as hot—or hotter—than her for a phone call."

"I've had them by the thousands. But, I don't know, sis, I've never known one like her. Hell, I even like listening to her talk, and I don't like listening to anyone talk. Now it's like I'm Captain Ahab, and she's my white whale. I can't stop thinking about her—about harpooning her." He rubbed his crotch.

"Maybe you've gone too long without a woman. Let me make some calls, set you up."

"Wouldn't do any good. I'm just not that interested in sex anymore. Nothing helps—porn, high-dollar hookers, Cialis."

"I hear you brag all the time to business friends, reporters and colleagues—even over the phone to Putilov—about what a stud you are," Brenda said, confused.

"It's all bullshit—just me trying to make myself feel better about myself," Tower said. "The truth is for the last five years I've been irreversibly impotent. Then one night about a year ago, I saw Jules Meredith trashing me on a talk show, and suddenly I was on fire for her. It's been that way ever since. One glimpse of Jules Meredith on a magazine jacket, anywhere, or if I just hear her voice on the radio, even when she's attacking me, and suddenly I'm crazy-mad for her. It's like I'm fifteen years old again—hammer-hard and jalapeno-hot—but she's the only one who does it for me. Otherwise, I'm deader than Kelsey's nuts down there."

"You have to get over this. That woman's uncut plutonium—pure poison. She could very well destroy you—us."

"And I have something I'd like to destroy her with." J. T. Tower again motioned toward his crotch.

"That's insane."

"Brenda, I have to see her. I'll go nuts if I don't. She's dying to interview me, you said."

"She's been trying to interview you for years," Brenda said.

"Then set it up."

"You're out of your mind."

"Just set it up. Call Jules Meredith. Tell her I'll meet her here—after midnight. Tell her I'm giving her that interview, but it's deep background. I tell you, Brenda, I have to see her—tonight at the latest. Tell her it's tonight or never."

PART V

"Tower's only patriotism, his only allegiance period, is to that country which allows him to pay the least amount of taxes, which frequently means paying no taxes at all."

—Jules Meredith on President J. T. Tower

1

"Rashid, your file also said you're a slave to drink; you have a weakness for drugs; and you are perpetually in hock to dealers, bookies and loan sharks. Are there no depths to which you won't sink? Is there nothing you won't do for money?"
—Raza Jabarti to Rashid al-Rahman

The woman's eyes flickered over the naked heavily scarred man. A two-foot rope bound his wrists tightly behind his back. Another line—affixed to a pulley and hanging from an unpainted eight-by-ten ceiling beam—ran inside his elbows. A third rope lashed his ankles, which were bent sharply behind him, bound to his wrists. He was hoisted a full foot above the raw plank floor. The stress on his elbows, shoulders, wrists and knee joints was excruciating.

Raza studied the man hanging from this crude simulacrum of a strappado—a specific form of torture sometimes known as the "Parrot's Perch"—clearly disdainful of his misery, but then her two-decade career as a professional killer and interrogator had inured her to most varieties of human suffering. In fact, her employers believed that her indifference to other people's terror and pain was, in large part, what made her such an indispensable asset.

She glanced around at her surroundings. The building was constructed out of concrete blocks, and the interrogation room looked to be fifteen by twenty feet across and a dozen feet high. In one corner was a draped-off toilet. Next to it was a dirty steel sink and an even dirtier steel worktable, on which rested an electric aluminum coffeepot. A single 100-watt bare bulb hung from center of the ceiling. It was one of the more bare-bones torture chambers the woman had worked in.

Raza turned around to look at Tariq al-Omari, who was sitting in a corner to her rear on a folding chair. He wore a white robe, or *thawb,* and rope sandals. His dark shoulder-length hair and goatee were meticulously trimmed. Smoking a black Turkish cigarette, he stared at Raza.

She walked up to him.

"I do not understand why Kamal insisted you interrogate this man," Tariq said with an angry scowl.

"Because your methods have become . . . *unsound*," Raza said softly so the prisoner couldn't hear. "You killed the last four suspects you interrogated. You tortured them to death, and we got nothing from them."

"They deserved no mercy," Tariq said sharply.

"Tariq," Raza sighed, "there's no point in arguing. I also wish Kamal had put you in charge. Do you think I want to be here? In the scorching heat of the Pashtun desert? We're practically on the Afghan border"

"I could have handled it myself," Tariq said.

"I'm sure you could have," Raza said placatingly, "but Kamal told me this man might be a double agent. We can't kill him, and we have to make him talk . . . *now*. You are not to go near Rashid unless Marika Madiha or me are there to supervise you."

"I know how to interrogate people," Tariq said.

"You are a legend in this business, my friend. You've become too . . . impatient though. Your anger is overruling your better judgment. Also Kamal thought that this man might have issues with women and wouldn't be able to tolerate being hurt by one. His file suggests that he liked dominating them, not the other way around. So Kamal wanted Marika and me to try. She should be arriving shortly. He hoped we might speed the process up. Kamal also thought I might enjoy breaking a big strong macho man. I would ordinarily, but not enough to come here—not to this torrid, arid Pashtun wilderness."

"He doesn't look that tough," Tariq said, staring at the hanging man and shrugging.

"Maybe he's not, but no one else has been able to get a peep out of him," Raza said. "So a woman's touch might be in order. I'm putting Marika in charge. She'll arrive later. If she needs help, I'll participate."

"And if you have trouble," Tariq asked, "you'll ask me to jump in?"

"With both hands and feet."

Directly across from the hanging man was a six-by-four-foot wall mirror. Looking over her shoulder, Raza noted Rashid's reflection in it—the contorted mask of agony that was now his face, and the intricate maze of ancient scars disfiguring his filth-streaked body. Those cicatrices bore mute witness to other interrogations in other nameless blood-splattered rooms, and they contrasted with the raw red complex of more recent cuts, burns and welts now dotting and crisscrossing his corpus.

This man had had a very thorough working over, and he hadn't given up one name.

This man was a pro—hard-core.

Raza stared absently at the mirror. Tariq had not hung it there by accident, and Raza understood its purpose. After over forty years of such interviews, Tariq had concluded that if the subject observed himself in a mirror, if he was forced to "visualize and internalize" the sheer horror of his situation—his abject humiliation, his incontrovertible helplessness, the utter hopelessness of his situation—he would give up and give them anything they wanted.

Over the years, that strategy had worked astonishingly well.

Until now.

Until Rashid.

Turning toward the prisoner, Raza caught a side glimpse of herself in the tarnished mirror. In contrast to the prisoner, she looked . . . *outstanding*. She'd learned decades ago that close-fitting Western clothing utterly unhinged devout Muslim men during interrogations. Abjuring traditional Islamic garb, she wore tight black Levi's, matching riding boots and a red T-shirt with the sleeves and midriff cut off. Her long ebony tresses hung down below her shoulder blades. Her high wide cheekbones and full generous lips framed her delicate nose. However, her eyes—flat as a snake's, hard sharp and pitch-black as obsidian—betrayed any semblance of conventional beauty. Her eyes told anyone and everyone precisely who and what she was. Her eyes froze Gorgons.

"Your shoulder and elbow joints must really smart," she said pleasantly to the hanging man, her voice lovingly melodious.

"Actually," Rashid said, "they feel . . . *marvelous*."

"No doubt. I've read your file, you know. It describes you as tough—as the archetypal mercenary with no theological or ideological beliefs. Is any of that true?"

"I have deep beliefs about some things."

"Such as?"

"Ever hear of money?" Rashid asked.

"Don't honor and high moral character have a role to play in your worldview?" Raza asked, smiling in spite of herself.

"Ever try spending honor and high moral character?"

"Point taken. Your file also says you have an eye for pretty ladies. An African-American mercenary you once worked and socialized with is quoted as describing you as a 'booty bandit,' 'some sheet-shaker' and 'a real pee-hole pirate.'"

"I've known a woman or two."

"Or maybe a thousand or two?"

"I can't help it if women like me"

"Rashid, your file also said you're a slave to drink; you have a weakness for drugs; and you are perpetually in hock to dealers, bookies and loan sharks. Are there no depths to which you won't sink? Is there nothing you won't do for money?"

"I'll do pretty near anything," Rashid had to admit.

Raza snorted disdainfully. "Are you even a Muslim? Do you know anything at all about the One True Faith?"

"I tried reading the Koran once," Rashid said, wincing.

"How did you like it?"

"Pretty slow going."

"Too many big words and long sentences?"

"Yes—also too many rules and regulations."

"Then why did you try reading it?"

"I guess I was looking for loopholes?" Rashid almost managed to shrug on a strappado.

"In your case, there aren't any. Allah disapproves of everything you've ever done throughout your whole disreputable life—past, present and future."

"So you claim," Rashid said, "but what do you really know of my life?"

"That your entire earthly existence has been dedicated to violence, drink, drugs, fornication and degenerate gambling. I also know Allah doesn't countenance any of those depraved activities."

"He's not exactly a god of fun, is He?" Rashid acknowledged.

"He's real big on work, worry and servile obedience."

"What else does my file say?"

"That you kill without compunction," Raza said, "that you lie just to keep in practice and that you positively eat betrayal."

"Sounds pretty bad."

"Actually, those are the good parts, but buck up. Where I come from you'd be considered a role model."

Rashid looked around the room. He spotted Tariq.

"That guy in the corner?" Rashid asked softly. "What's your take on him?"

"You definitely want to keep away from him."

"He seems harmless enough."

"He's one sick fuck," Raza said.

"You're trying to scare me, aren't you?"

"Remember when you told that merc that you were a 'booty bandit, some sheet-shaker, a real pee-hole pirate'?"

"Ye—e—e—e—s—s?" Rashid said with clear misgivings, drawing out the word into several syllables.

"Well you enjoy *les liaisons dangereuses*? Tariq enjoys collecting *kurtas* [*testicles*]."

"He has been staring at my crotch for quite some time," Rashid had to admit. "It's a little unnerving."

"He especially has it in for you. Our superiors are pissed at him. He kills too many prisoners prematurely during interrogations. He wants you to help him prove that he can still break men—totally. You're his last chance to prove himself."

"But you'll protect me from him?" Rashid asked.

"If you don't tell me what I want, I'll make Tariq look like the Holy Hajj."

"Suppose informing on my friends violated my religious convictions?" Rashid asked.

"Fine, but if you don't give me what I want, your religious convictions will experience an ass-whipping of apocalyptic proportions."

"Does it have to be either/or?" Rashid asked.

"Affirmative. A binary yes-or-no."

"You could try bribing me."

"Will you take a check?"

"I'll take checks, food stamps, IOUs, supermarket coupons, beads and wampum."

She wrote him an IOU for $100 trillion.

"Not enough."

"Suppose I were to give you a whole shithouse of hard cash," Raza said, laughing. "Would you even know what to do with it?"

"Absolutely," Rashid said.

"What would you spend it on?"

"What I always do—hard liquor, harder drugs, fast women and slow horses."

"And the rest you'd waste?"

"You just wrote my epitaph."

"Then I'll chisel it on your tombstone and piss my brains out on it," Raza said, smiling.

"Are you suggesting that I might not survive this little Love Boat?" Rashid asked.

"I believe we should all view each day as if it were our last," Raza said.

"Words to live by."

"Especially for you," Raza said, "given the life you've led. If you died right now, what would you leave to the world? What would your legacy be?"

"Besides cold graves and sobbing widows?"

"Exactly."

"I don't think about the Big Picture," Rashid said. "Not anymore. I just live for the day."

"Then today won't be one of your all-time greats," Raza said.

"But you could change all that."

"Maybe—if you give me what I want."

"Which is?"

"The truth, the whole truth and nothing but the truth."

Rashid shook his head glumly. "That's asking a lot."

She picked up a thick black device that looked like a flashlight and brandished it under his nose.

A cattle prod.

"So which is it?" Raza asked. "Will you tell me what I want to know or do I turn you over to Tariq?"

"What will he do?"

"He'll electrocute your genitals."

"So will you—so there's no difference."

Then Tariq opened his doctor's bag, removed a small leather bag and emptied it on the worktable. It had been filled with surgical instruments.

"There is one difference: My friend over there will geld you like a steer first."

Rashid watched in horror as Tariq began honing a scalpel on a whetstone.

2

"Our financial sectors have run up over $1.5 quadrillion of global derivative debt," President Tower said. "That's pure intrinsic uncollateralized...*debt*. When that market crashes, Washington will have to cover our losses—they'll have no choice—and they'll have to cut us more checks. We'll make a fortune. We'll own this country before it's over."

"We'll own...the *world*," CIA Director Billy Burke said.

It was almost 9:00 P.M. now, and Brenda had asked her brother's most trusted advisers, Ambassador Waheed and CIA Director Billy Burke, to come up to Tower's penthouse apartment. Relaxing on couches and stuffed chairs, they sat in their white shirtsleeves, their ties loosened, and stared out over New York City.

"You really think you can rein in Jules Meredith?" Brenda asked her brother.

"I'll have her bosses do it for me," Tower said. "My friends and I own a big piece of the news media. The people who run it aren't muckrakers; they're buck-*takers*."

Brenda smoked a Gauloises Blue and sipped brandy. She noticed that Waheed favored French reds, while Burke drank Macallan's single-malt neat. Tower sipped his ubiquitous black coffee.

"Jim," Director Burke said, "I hope you have them in your pocket. Our sources at her book publishing company say she's got the names and amounts of every one of your campaign contributors and contributions. She's also exposing all your offshore-tax-haven money."

"So what?" Tower said. "I'll simply announce to the world that she's vindictive because I wouldn't fuck her—or maybe because I stopped fucking her."

"None of that's true, Jim," Brenda said.

"I don't have to prove anything," Tower said. "All we have to do is vilify her character and cast doubt on her data."

"That's how we discredited the climate change scientists," Ambassador Waheed said, nodding and laughing. "And they were right on the facts."

"And in discrediting the climate change scientists, we proved facts don't matter," Tower said.

"In other words," Brenda said, pouring another snifter of brandy, "we lie."

"At the Agency, we call it disinformation," Burke said with a small smile.

"I prefer 'truthful hyperbole,'" Tower said.

"Someone once said no lie can live forever," Brenda said softly.

"And whoever said that had shit for brains," Burke said, shaking his head.

"Unfortunately for us," Brenda said, "Jules has the power of the press behind her."

"The press is not exactly filled with 'truth-tellers,'" Director Burke snorted contemptuously.

"'Truth-killers' is more accurate," Ambassador Waheed said.

"Mencken once described the American people as *Boobus Americanus*," Burke said.

"He also said no one ever lost money underestimating the intelligence of the American people," Brenda said.

"We sure as shit haven't," Ambassador Waheed said, sipping his drink.

"Look at how much money the public loses at our casinos," Brenda said, shaking her head, incredulous, "yet they keep coming back and throwing hundreds of millions more at us."

"And on all your derivative investment scams," Director Burke observed.

"What a country," Tower said. "Where else could we rob the public blind and get lionized for it?"

"Look what Romney did at Bain Capital and what Trump did with his bankrupt casinos," Director Burke said with smug smirk. "None of my Wall Street friends have done an honest day's work in over fifty years. They just pile up debt."

"Debt's the key," Brenda said. "Borrow enough money, and debt becomes currency. Milken proved that with junk bonds. Romney proved that with all those LBOs. They brag about it."

"Our financial sectors have run up over $1.5 quadrillion of global derivative debt," President Tower said. "That's pure intrinsic uncollateralized . . . *debt*. When that market crashes, Washington will have to cover our losses—they'll have no choice—and they'll have to cut us more checks. We'll make a fortune. We'll own this country before it's over."

"We'll own . . . the *world*," CIA Director Burke said.

They all nodded in silence.

"On our financial statements," Prince Waheed finally said, "we often list debt as assets."

"Exactly so," Tower said. "We can also convert all that debt into salable derivatives that no one understands, chop those instruments up into tiny fragments that are even more inscrutable, shuffle and combine those pieces into packages, and wait for the Wall Street firms to beat our doors down in a feeding frenzy just to be first in line to buy them."

"Isn't that better than making cars and trucks?" CIA Director Burke said.

"Romney sure as hell didn't go into his old man's auto business," Prince Waheed said. "He took over firms, looted them wholesale, then sold off the debt. Fucking brilliant!"

"Our bankers at Tower, Inc., do that all the time," Tower said. "They target firms for takeover, plunder their assets piecemeal, load them with debt and peddle them to unsuspecting pension-fund managers before all that debt goes comes due. We make a fortune."

"Those pension-fund managers," Burke said, "have to be the biggest chumps that ever lived."

"We take them every time," Tower agreed.

"Like Grant took Richmond," Director Burke said.

"Like Hitler seized power in Germany," Tower said, "and Lenin commandeered Russia."

"Putilov did it too," Director Burke said, "and made out like a bandit."

"I can't tell you how much I admire that man," Tower said. "You know, he and I have become good friends. Everyone else treats him with such fear and deference. I think he likes it when I treat him like 'one of the guys.' I call him 'Comrade' and 'Putie.' I believe I'm the only one who can speak to him as an equal—man-to-man."

"I'm sure he appreciates your candor," Ambassador Waheed said.

"In fact," Tower said, "I'm going to call him right now. You'll see how frank we are with each other."

"Great idea," Burke said.

Tower took out his digitally encrypted cell phone, put it on "speaker" and punched in Putilov's private number.

3

Still, in that last microsecond, balanced between truth and hallucination, between psychosis and reality, during that final hairtrigger eternity, Putilov heard a small voice asking him whether his hatred of Tower was driving him . . . *mad*.

Putilov said his good-byes to Tower and put down the Skype phone. He'd eluded the idiot's calls as long as he could, but this time Tower had told his assistant that the call was critically important—in fact, a crisis—so Putilov broke down and took it. The call, however, was about nothing at all, and he could tell Tower had his cell on speakerphone. Furthermore, his informants had told him earlier that Tower was meeting with CIA Director Burke, Ambassador Waheed and Tower's hard-drinking, chain-smoking sister. Putilov suspected that Tower had other people in the room and had only wanted to prove to them that he could get a direct line to Putilov any time he wanted.

Would the fool never give him any peace?

Putilov didn't know how much longer he could take dealing with him. Tonight's conversation had been especially distressing. Tower had been unable to stop bragging and lecturing.

Putilov poured ten desomorphine tablets onto his desk. Grinding the pills up between spoons, he chopped the granules up with a razor blade and dissolved them in 190-proof Everclear, ether and gasoline. He then boiled the solution in a Pyrex bong and sucked the fumes deep into his lungs, where he held them for a full half minute.

Smoking desomorphine radically heightened the pills' power.

Putilov and the bong went back a long way. He'd confiscated it from a suspect in Berlin and kept it as a souvenir. Breaking the man in a particularly brutal and bloodthirsty way, he had employed all the instruments of unendurable pain and perverse persuasion, including pliers, blowtorches and hot knives. He'd then handed the man his own bong, heated it and pumped him full of krokodil fumes, utterly robbing him of his sense and any final scintilla of resistance. In the end Putilov had not only tortured a flagrantly fallacious confession out of the man, he'd convinced the poor imbecile, that he, Putilov, was the man's best friend, that he had the man's best interests at heart. Putilov had so brainwashed the moron that the man had actually thanked him for the agonizing auto-da-fé. He had never achieved such total control over an individual in his entire life. It was as if he owned him—mind, body and soul. The man's eyes were filled with atonement and contrition; even when Putilov had finally granted him his release, his coup de grâce—a bullet between his appreciative puppy-dog eyes—the man was still murmuring his heartfelt gratitude.

At the time, that sense of godlike power had filled Putilov with the most amazing calm and serenity, something almost resembling . . . joy. Later, however, when he remembered the man's utter breakdown, his confession, thanksgiving and death, he had felt not mere satisfaction, fulfillment or even genuine happiness but a most special . . . arousal. Perhaps that feeling of excitation was the reason he'd never thrown away the man's bong. It reminded him of that very singular night.

Again Putilov put the bong's stem to his mouth and inhaled deeply. With an almost overpowering avidity, he waited for the drug to once more take hold of his senses, to vanquish his fears, doubts and anxieties, to hammer him like an express train, full-throttle and out of control. The krokodil never let him down. Still, at the last microsecond, balanced between truth and hallucination, between psychosis and reality, during that final hair-trigger eternity, Putilov heard a small voice asking him whether his hatred of Tower was driving him . . . *mad.*

PART VI

"I don't think J. T. Tower'll die until he's drawn, quartered, cremated...with a stake hammered through his ashes."

—Jules Meredith

1

Jules Meredith's cell phone rang a little after midnight. The caller was Brenda Tower.

"Well Jules," Brenda said, "you aren't going to believe this, but your wish has been granted. My brother is inviting you up to his New York penthouse."

"You know I've been asking him for an interview for three years," Jules said. "What made him change his mind?"

"Who knows? Who cares?" Brenda said. "Maybe your articles have so incensed the president that he finally feels compelled to set the record straight."

Jules showed up at Tower's penthouse a little after 1:00 A.M. The president let her in himself. Casually dressed in red sweatpants, a gray T-shirt and white Nike jogging shoes, he stood a good six four. Jules noted that his hair was colored—brownish-blond with a hint of red—but even so, it was, at age sixty-five, still full, piled thick and high on his head. His face was deeply but artificially tanned.

"At last, I meet the Troubler of my Peace," he said, shaking her hand.

Jules's attire was informal as well—pale bleached-out jeans, a navy blue silk blouse and ebony boots with three-inch heels. Her dense fluffed-out hair was, unlike Tower's, black as obsidian.

"Pleased to meet you, Mr. President. So this is your famous Tower of Power?"

"It's one of them. I also built five other needle towers in this town. They all have penthouses just like this."

"But you sold those penthouses to other billionaires."

"I have to sell something to someone. I can't own the world."

"But still you try."

"You ought to know," Tower said. "You seem bent on scrutinizing and publicizing every business I've ever run since, at age five, I set up a lemonade stand. I'd like to know why."

"May I speak plainly, Mr. President?"

"Please."

"I was born to bring you down."

"And to that end," Tower asked, "you've made exposing my business dealings your life's work?"

"Part of it."

"A big part of it," Tower responded. "You've unearthed stuff on me even I didn't know about."

"I'm a master of my craft."

"So murdering Jim Tower in the press is now a 'craft'?"

"Ah, Jimmy, no one can kill you."

"Why not?"

"You reanimate yourself nightly in your coffin."

"So now I'm a vampire."

"A very dangerous one," Jules said. "I don't think J. T. Tower'll die until he's drawn, quartered, cremated . . . with a stake hammered through his ashes."

"And you plan on driving the stake in yourself."

"Oh, do I ever."

Tower escorted Jules to the penthouse's center. Turning in a circle, she studied his luxurious lair and the world beyond. The living room, dining area and the partitioned-off study were a single open space and made up half the apartment. The bedrooms, bathrooms and kitchen took up the rest. With the bedrooms' and bathrooms' sliding doors open, Jules saw that she had a 360-degree view of Manhattan.

Resisting the impulse to gawk, Jules forced herself to focus on the décor. She wanted to remember the furnishings for future reference. Their conversation might be off the record, but Tower's penthouse wasn't. One day—perhaps soon—she would want to write about it.

Given that the apartment occupied the entire top floor, it wasn't as big as Jules had imagined—only forty-six feet long and forty-six feet wide—but then the building was a "needle tower." One hundred stories high, it was ultra-thin for a skyscraper, its square base also forty-six feet on edge, and each apartment occupied a whole floor.

The walls were almost entirely unobstructed glass, so the view of the city was 360 degrees. To the south, the penthouse overlooked Lower Manhattan all the way to Staten Island. The northern view included Central Park, Harlem and the Bronx. To the east lay Long Island, and to the west, New Jersey, but it appeared from the penthouse's point of view to be far more than two states. From her august vantage point, the entire country seemed to stretch before her in all directions.

Like a land of dreams.

The living room furniture was surprisingly simple—blond leather and blond wood. The large circular dining table was thick glass mounted on a chrome stand. The chairs were chrome with cream-colored leather seats and backs. The bar area and stools were also glass, chrome and leather.

Jules followed Tower into the living room. He motioned her toward an overstuffed leather chair, and he took the couch. A burnished oak end table sat between them. On it was a bottle of 100-year-old Rémy Martin Napoléon—his sister's favorite.

"I can get you anything else you want," Tower said, pouring a snifter.

"The Rémy is fine."

He poured three inches of cognac into each of two snifters and handed the first to Jules. She waited for Tower to take a healthy drink. She did not intend to partake of any bottle Tower did not sample first.

"I thought you never drank," Jules said.

"As a rule, I don't," Tower said, "but it seemed rude to suggest that you drink alone."

"Then a toast?" Jules asked.

"To the bitter end," he offered.

"That toast means you want us to do some serious drinking?"

"In vino veritas," Tower said, "and I want to find out what you really want from me and why."

"And you think liquor will loosen my tongue?" Jules asked.

"I'd prefer shooting you with scopolamine and sodium pentothal," Tower said, "but the law frowns on such techniques."

"You could always spirit me off to Guantanamo for physical coercion."

"Don't I wish."

"So liquor will have to do?"

"Liquor will have to do."

"And you know I won't get drunk if you don't join in."

"Yes," Tower said. "I expect you'll find the opportunity to loosen my tongue with liquor irresistible, and I plan on drinking you under the table."

"Let the games begin," Jules said.

She watched him drink off a good two inches of brandy.

She then decided the liquor wasn't drugged and took a drink herself.

2

"Don't give an inch. Don't whine or snivel. Laugh at them if you can. Make fun of them. Try to get them talking. Flirt with Raza. If Marika Madiha shows up, flirt with her too. Those women are vain about their looks, and they love the sound of their own voices. The more you can get those women to talk, the less time they'll have to torture you, and believe me, those maniacs love to do both. But don't ever whimper or beg. If they think you're starting to crack, they'll become rabid. Fear acts on them like catnip on cats. They sense it in you, and they'll hit you with everything—blowtorches, pliers, metal shears, hammers and nails."

—Rashid al-Rahman to Danny McMahon

When McMahon came to, he was in a small dark storage room lashed to a wooden bed frame. Moonlight filtered in through a high narrow window, and he could see he had a companion similarly secured to a second frame. The man was naked like himself, but his body was covered with long-forgotten knife and bullet scars as well as fresh burns and whip marks, all of the new ones a bright red.

"I'm in hell," McMahon whispered to his cell mate.

"No, just Pakistan," the man said.

"What's your name?" McMahon asked.

"Rashid."

"Why are you here?"

"They're interrogating me," Rashid said.

"What for?" McMahon asked.

"They want stuff I know."

"Okay, but what do they want from me? I don't know anything that could help them destroy the Infidel. I'm a comedian—a talk-show host."

"Yeah, I recognize you: Danny McMahon, the controversial American comic and political satirist. You're infamous in the Mideast for being one of Islam's most virulent critics."

"I have devoted fans everywhere," McMahon said dryly.

"Except the fans here would like to fry your balls for breakfast in a little garlic and olive oil," Rashid said.

"But I don't mock and ridicule ordinary Muslims, only Islamist terrorists."

"Unfortunately, the people holding you here are . . . *Islamist terrorists*."

"Okay, but I still don't understand why they abducted me," McMahon said. "I can't do anything for them. They didn't do it because they don't like my show, did they?"

"Oh, I get it: You want logic and reason from . . . *genocidal monsters*," Rashid said.

"Good point," McMahon said softly.

"On the other hand, you are a high-value target that will bring them a lot of publicity—maybe even a ton of ransom money."

"If that's the case, then they'd want to keep me healthy. They won't want to hurt me, right?"

"Were they only so rational. McMahon, you and I are both in for a whole world of hurt. We have Raza Jabarti and Tariq al-Omari handling our interrogations. They won't rest till we're begging them to kill us."

"Even if I don't know anything? Even if I've got nothing to tell them?"

"You think your stupid ignorance will stop them from torturing you?" Rashid actually burst into laughter.

"You're saying they'd torture me for no reason at all?"

"Is ice cold? Fire hot? Does camel shit stink?"

"So you're saying these people are sadistic psychopaths?"

"That's their good side."

"What's their bad side?"

"Nuking cities off the face of the earth."

"You've dealt with these people before?"

"I've worked with them, been around them my whole life long. I know everything about them."

"You speak awfully good English though," McMahon said.

"I spent a lot of time in the States, and I've freelanced for a lot of your defense and intelligence contractors—even the Agency."

"Any advice?"

Rashid turned his head and stared at McMahon, suddenly serious. "Don't give an inch. Don't whine or snivel. Laugh at them if you can. Make fun of them. Try to get them talking. Flirt with Raza. If Marika Madiha shows up, flirt with her too. Those women are vain about their looks, and they love the sound of their own voices. The more you can get those women to talk, the less time they'll have to torture you, and believe me, those maniacs love to do both. But don't ever whimper or beg. If they think you're starting to crack, they'll become rabid. Fear acts on them like catnip on cats. They sense it in you, and they'll hit you with everything—blowtorches, pliers, metal shears, hammers and nails."

"Never show the feather?"

"McMahon," Rashid said as earnestly as he knew how, "you're going to have to be all balls—no weakness whatsoever."

"But our situation seems so . . . hopeless."

"An hour ago, I'd have said yes. Now I don't know. You're famous and powerful. You've have connections. There are people in the States who care for you and want you back. Washington might try to rescue you. I personally see abducting you as a mistake. I don't know why they did it."

"There must be someone who wants to rescue you or would pay a ransom to get you back," McMahon said.

Rashid's laughter was painful to McMahon's ear. "Most of the people I know would pay these guys to torture and kill me."

"What about your friends? Won't they help?"

"Those people are my friends."

"You have no one?" McMahon asked in stunned disbelief.

"One person, and she's working on something," Rashid said. "She'll help if she can."

"Rashid, if anyone comes for me, I'm not leaving without you."

"Your people will want me. I know stuff the U.S. needs to know. Your country's survival is at stake."

"But in the meantime you and I are in for it, aren't we?"

"You better believe it," Rashid said. "Just don't crawl. Stand up to them. It's your only chance."

3

"In my doxology, there is no Higher Power, only the quick and the dead."

—President J. T. Tower to Jules Meredith

So what have you been up to?" Jules asked, sipping her Napoléon brandy.

"Besides scaling the Eiger and bow-hunting rhinos?" Tower asked.

"I thought chasing orphans across ice floes was more your style."

"I only do that in my spare time," Tower said.

"What do you do full-time?"

"Plot the downfall of Western civilization."

"And you're doing a bang-up job."

"So what's happening in Jules World?"

"You're happening, J. T." She gave him an infectious smile. "May I call you J. T.?"

"Of course—even though you don't feel that friendly toward me."

"You could tell?"

"You do have *me* in your crosshairs."

"Oh, do I ever—cold zero, dead center."

"Then it's lock and load?"

"Cocked and locked," Jules said.

"That doesn't sound good," Tower asked. "What would I have to do to convince you I was really all right?"

"Stop hurting people," Jules said. "Make the world a better place."

"There's not much money in that."

"Does everything have to have a price tag on it?" Jules asked.

"In Jim World it does."

"But you're already rich."

"No one can ever be rich enough."

"And what would you hope to get out of more money?"

"Anything and everything."

"In other words, in Jim World you get to play God."

"In Jim World, I am God."

"And the master of all you survey?"

"Not everything," he said, leaning toward her. "I've never mastered you."

"And never will, Jimmy."

"I'd like to change that."

"Say what?" Her face was suddenly filled with shocked skepticism.

"There has to be something I could do to improve your attitude toward me."

"Cure cancer. End poverty. Outlaw war."

"Isn't what I've already done enough?"

"What is it you've done with your life anyway?" Jules asked. "I'd really like to know."

"I created an empire out of nothing but my blood, brains, balls and my two bare hands."

Her laughter was loud and harsh. "J. T., I know all about your business career. Your father was a filthy-rich war criminal, and he started you out with $90 million of his ill-gotten gains."

"And I parlayed it into billions."

"Had you put it all into a Class-A New York City real estate fund fifty years ago, you'd have become ten times richer than you are now."

Jules knew those words would drive him nuts.

"I worked like a sonofabitch for everything I got," Tower said, his voice menacingly soft.

"I'll grant you're a sonofabitch, J. T.," Jules said, leaning toward him, giving Tower her brightest, most radiant smile, "and that you ran six of your largest businesses into the ground and put them into bankruptcy afterward. But tell me: Do you ever think about the contractors, suppliers and employees whose lives you destroyed while you deliberately eviscerated those enterprises?"

"Those people knew the deal when they signed up for it," Tower said.

"And what deal was that?" Jules said with a mocking smile. "Kill or be killed? Eat or be eaten?"

"Maybe you think the world's some fucking rose garden," Tower said, "but it's not. It's war to the knife, and I don't apologize for not laying down and letting it cut me to ribbons."

"Well then, what about that 'great big beautiful wall' you were going to build along our 1,500-mile Mexican border—the one Mexico was going to pay for? That was your number one campaign promise, but you couldn't even get your own Congress to go along with it—and your party dominated Congress. When they found out you needed $30 billion and three times the concrete that went into Hoover Dam, they told you to take the concrete and pour it up your butthole."

"They're mean-spirited, small-minded little men," Tower said, "with no vision."

"Or maybe they understood walls aren't the answer," Jules said.

"You know a better way to seal off our border?" Tower asked.

"Isaac Newton said we needed bridges not more walls," Jules said.

"Isaac Newton's been dead for 400 years," Tower said. "When I want advice, I'll ask someone who's still alive and understands what I'm up against."

"So much for Homer, Plato and Shakespeare," Jules said.

"Homer, Plato, Shakespeare and, yes, Newton, can suck my dick," Tower said.

"What about selling forty nuclear power plants to the Saudis and their neighbors? Your customers are the very people who bankrolled al Qaeda and ISIS, and those nuclear plants you're selling them are nothing less than starter kits for a nuclear weapons program. Once a nation has nuclear power they are 99 percent of the way toward building a bomb. Everything else is a low-tech, relatively simple operation."

"Hey, Eisenhower sold Iran and Pakistan their first reactors, and the Saudis bankrolled Pakistan's purchase. Why can't Jimbo and his friends get some of that M-O-N-E-Y?"

Shaking her head, Jules stared at him a long minute.

"Does honor have a place in your world?" she finally asked. "What about simple decency? Basic morality?"

"What's that got to do with Jimbo's bottom line?"

"So there is no right or wrong in Jim World," Jules said, "no categorical imperatives?"

"In my doxology, there is no Higher Power," the president said, "only the quick and the dead."

"And all that counts is that you're not the latter?" Jules asked.

"There are only two choices in this hard life," Tower said, now leaning toward Meredith, invading her space, staring at her fixedly. "Are you going to be the one on your knees, giving all those long, slow blowjobs—or the one getting them? What's it going to be, Jules?"

"That's the Fallacy of the False Choice, Jim Baby," Jules said. "Life is never black or white, either/or. And none of us ever gets it all."

"You mean we all fall down?"

"As Dylan says, 'we all serve somebody,'" Jules said.

"Then can I serve you?" He lifted the bottle and refilled both their glasses.

Jules paused to study J. T. He was pouring with a heavy hand. She had been told he never drank, but because she was a woman with less than half his body mass, he thought he could match her drink for drink and get her drunk.

That was a mistake.

No one had ever succeeded in matching Jules Meredith drink for drink— and stayed on their feet.

Tower had no idea what he was getting into.

PART VII

"Please, Mr. McMahon, do not understand me too quickly."

—Raza Jabarti

1

Over his two decades of service in the Mideast—including the Iraq War, followed by the Iraqi and Syrian civil wars—Fahad had not exactly grown used to violence. The truth was that violence had never particularly fazed him. His first assigned killing hadn't bothered him in the least, and professionals generally considered the first to be the most disturbing.

Fahad al-Qadi got off the plane at JFK and met his driver, Haddad al-Naqbi, at baggage claim. Both men wore black suits, white shirts, dark ties and sunglasses, but the resemblance ended there. The chauffeur wore a cheap, off-the-rack suit and a discount-store white shirt. A fake street-vendor Rolex adorned his wrist. Fahad's suit, on the other hand, was a Desmond Merrion bespoke custom-tailored for him in Dubai. A white silk D'Avino shirt and a Stefano Ricci tie of sheerest scarlet silk went with it. His Rolex platinum Submariner was studded with diamonds and rubies. Dita Grandmaster designer sunglasses completed the ensemble.

Most professional assassins sought anonymity. Fahad desired it as well. His problem was that as a dark-skinned Muslim male—especially one who had spent much of his life on utterly illegal missions, traveling through airports—he was subject to racial profiling, which could easily lead to search and seizure. Even worse, Interpol had his fingerprints, and he might very well be a suspect in those recent Moscow murders. After all, he'd done them.

Fahad had learned decades ago, however, that when he was expensively dressed, law enforcement officers tended to give him a pass, no doubt on the assumption that professional terrorists wouldn't dress like billionaire celebrities. Nor did they wish to provoke the ire of a man who appeared to be both wealthy and powerful. Also because of his expensive attire, people seldom looked at his face. They either glanced furtively at his wardrobe and accoutrements or gawked openly at them. They remembered the costly clothes, not the man's face.

And he liked haute couture.

As for facial anonymity, his ubiquitous sunglasses—combined with an ever-changing variety of haircuts, hair coloring and tinted contact lenses—further reduced the likelihood of facial identification.

The driver, Haddad, led him through the automatic glass doors, and Fahad followed him into the parking lot to the black Lincoln Town Car. He climbed in the backseat, taking his black Gucci shoulder bag with him.

"Is everything arranged?" Fahad asked.

"In the trunk, sir, *and* at the house."

"Excellent."

"Rush hour doesn't start for another hour, so we should make good time," the driver said.

Fahad sat back, loosened his tie and pondered his assignment. Over his two decades of service in the Mideast—including the Iraq War, followed by the Iraqi and Syrian civil wars—Fahad had not exactly grown used to violence. The truth was that violence had never particularly fazed him. His first assigned killing hadn't bothered him in the least, and professionals generally considered the first to be the most disturbing.

This op was different, however. Not only was he to cobble together a crude but powerful Hiroshima-style nuke and set it off in New York City, Putilov and that psycho, Kamal ad-Din, had added an extra, last-minute assignment. He was to take out a wealthy hedge fund manager whom Kamal and Putilov held personally responsible for artificially elevating Middle Eastern grain prices in seasons of drought, thereby precipitating famines in that region. The subsequently skyrocketing food prices had too often inspired people to take to the streets in protest. During the so-called Arab Spring, those protests had exponentiated to the point that Mubarak in Egypt and Qaddafi in Libya were thrown out of office and subsequently died ignominious deaths. Fahad had, at various times, plied his violent trade at the behest of Mubarak and Qaddafi as well, so ordinarily he wouldn't have minded killing the Wall Street titan out of simple loyalty to former employers who had once filled his personal coffers to overflowing. That fool had fucked with his current employers and caused the deaths of previous employers? That was good enough for Fahad. Fine. He'd be happy to put him down . . . *hard.*

But Kamal and Putilov had also involved that harpy from Gehenna, Raza Jabarti, and she even scared Fahad. He'd seen her do things to suspects during interrogations that still gave him the cold sweats, still kept him up nights and would haunt him to his grave. That whore was hell with the hide off. Raza gave a whole new meaning to the words "evil bitch."

Furthermore, both she and that satan from St. Petersburg, the Russian president Mikhail Ivanovich Putilov, had designed and defined how he was to kill the famine derivative . . . *creep.*

And now they were going to make him do something to that poor hedge fund bugger, which made him sick to his soul and scared him half to death—and nothing ever spooked Fahad. Raza and Putilov were paying him $5 million to put the guy through all the tortures of Dante's *Inferno*—and then some. Fahad did not know if he actually had the stomach to do it.

He took a deep breath. *You can handle it,* Fahad said to himself. *I know you fucking can. Just get a grip on yourself. You can make this happen.*

2

"If you and I were the last two people on earth, I'd try a bear."
—Jules Meredith to President J. T. Tower

Eyes locked and unblinking, they finished their brandies, and Tower went to the bar's liquor cabinet. Retrieving a liquor bottle, he poured some for each of them in rock glasses.

Over ice.

"What's that?" Jules asked.

"Nitroglycerine on the rocks."

He wasn't far off. He was pouring them Cruzan 151-proof rum.

So J. T. Tower really wanted to drink her under the table and was now swinging for the fences.

It's your funeral, buddy, Jules thought.

"Should we have another toast?" he asked.

"To the last one standing," Jules said and downed the 151-proof liquor.

"I like that," J. T. said, throwing back his rum.

"I knew you would," Jules said. "Everything to you is natural selection, isn't it?""

"Isn't that how you view your own craft."

"In what way?"

"You view writing as fighting," Tower said, "don't you?"

"Depends who I'm writing about."

"But you see me as your foe?"

"Oh, do I ever."

"But why?"

"You keep hurting people. Hell, your petrochemical wastes have murdered millions."

"That bothers you? A few faceless, nameless people die so the rest of us can enjoy the benefits of industrialization? It's called progress, Jules."

"It's called 'pathological.'"

"Profitable, you mean."

"Instead of killing and exploiting people, why don't you use your wealth to help them?"

"Why? Has hell frozen over yet?"

"Then you're right. You and I are in for a fight."

"I could make it worth your while to back off."

"What could you possibly offer?"

"Everyone has their price."

Jules laughed in his face. "Never happen, Tower."

"Too bad. We could have been friends."

"But only if I backed off?" Jules asked.

"Yes."

"That's not all there is though, right?" Jules asked. "That's not the only reason I'm here?"

Tower shrugged.

"What is it you want?" Jules asked.

"I only wish to propitiate a goddess."

Jules stared at him, speechless. "Did Pallas Athena just walk in?" she finally asked, incredulous.

"I don't want Pallas Athena. I want you."

Jules's laughter was harsh—a sardonic bark of scorn.

"J. T.," Jules said, "if you and I were the last two people on earth, I'd try a bear."

"If you really knew me, you'd like me."

"You mean I'd . . . *loathe you*," Jules said, still smiling but with eyes hard, dark, humorless and flat.

"We'd be good for each other. I know it."

"Tower, I wouldn't piss on you if you were on fire."

"You're making a mistake. You don't want to get me mad."

"Really?" Jules gave him her widest, brightest, most ingratiating smile—with just a hint of seduction in it. "Then let's have another drink. Where's that Cruzan bottle?"

3

"I can be anything you want me to be—as long as it is riddled with agony and fraught with death. I can be your Minotaur, your Nemesis, Satan freed from hell, the anvil on which all your hammers crack, the rack upon which all your foolish flesh finally breaks."

—Raza Jabarti to Danny McMahon

Danny McMahon finally came to. Blindfolded and stripped naked, he felt one of his captors remove the rag covering his eyes. McMahon was sorry to have it off. The brightness was agonizing.

His eyes took a long time adjusting to the light. When his vision had sufficiently cleared, he saw he was hanging by the wrists from a wooden overhead beam. He was in a concrete-block safe house, and his shoulder, wrist and elbow joints ached as if they'd been ripped out of their sockets. His feet were an inch or two above the floor.

His vision had now focused enough that he could see the woman sitting across from him on a straight-back chair. Her hair was long and lush, black as any crow's wing. A short red dress barely reached her thighs. Her legs were crossed, and she wore thigh-high ebony riding boots with four-inch heels and stainless-steel rowels. Boots and rowels were burnished to a mirror-gloss.

She had a riding crop under her arm.

Oh shit, he recognized her now. He was staring at Raza Jabarti—the terrorist femme fatale he'd made so many sick, sadistic jokes about.

Fuck me dead.

Then he remembered what Rashid had told him: *"Don't let them see you panic . . . Don't whimper or snivel . . . Fear acts on them like catnip on a cat."*

"How was your trip, Mr. McMahon?" Raza asked.

He struggled to promote a grin. "Splendid."

"You know we're big fans of yours here," Raza said. "I have all your DVDs and books. And I never miss one of your shows. I record them all."

"You have su-per-la-tive taste," he said, emphatically dragging out each of the word's syllables.

"Mr. McMahon, to tell the truth, you look sort of banged up. I hope your captors weren't too rough on you."

"I hope I wasn't too rough on them," McMahon said, struggling to promote an audacious sneer.

"Why? Did you hurt them?"

"I busted one fellow's foot with my kidneys. I think my nuts shattered some poor guy's kneecap. My nose split one man's knuckles wide open."

"You really showed them, Mr. McMahon," Raza said. *"Bravissimo!"*

"Yeah, they learned the hard way not to fuck with Danny McMahon," he said, mustering as much bravado as possible.

"You certainly are tough—a real cowboy," Raza said. "Where are you from anyway? What great American city do you hail from?"

She circled around behind him and was now out of sight.

"Blow Me, Idaho."

The riding crop whistled behind him, whipping him across his bare ass.

The pain was breathtaking. In fact, his eyes were watering involuntarily.

"Okay, I lied," he said, after he caught his breath.

"Then you better tell me the truth," she said cheerfully, her voice bright and melodious. "Where are you from?"

"Fuck You, Utah."

Again, the whistling crop.

Again, the blinding pain.

"I'm sorry," McMahon said, struggling to get his breath back. "I shouldn't put you on. I'll be truthful from now on."

"Excellent, Mr. McMahon. Now where are you from?"

"Down Syndrome, Indiana."

A dozen lashes seared McMahon's backside. Tears flooded his face, and he fought to choke back sobs. When he finally caught his breath, Raza was in front of him again, staring into his face, nose to nose with him, still smiling merrily.

"I know you pride yourself on your toughness, Mr. McMahon, but trust me. Toughness here buys you nothing. You're in the House of Pain now— the House that Pain Built—and I've wanted to get my curvaceous claws into you for quite some time. How do you like it so far?"

"I'm happy as a sissy in Boys Town."

"But you aren't in Boys Town, are you?"

"Tell you the truth, I don't know where I am."

"Oh, you're in the labyrinth's darkest heart."

"I thought a Minotaur was at that maze's center," McMahon said. "Instead I meet you."

"Le Minotaur, c'est moi."

"You don't look like a Minotaur."

"But I am. In fact, I can be anything you want me to be—as long as it is riddled with agony and fraught with death. I can be your Minotaur, your Nemesis, Satan freed from hell, the anvil on which all your hammers crack, the rack upon which all your foolish flesh finally breaks."

"Suppose I said I'm free in Christ. I've been to the mountain," McMahon said, attempting a feeble imitation of Martin Luther King, " 'I've seen the Promised Land, and while we may not get there together, I'm fearing no man, no woman, I am—' "

"Then I will be your Golgotha, your Hill of Skulls."

"Or maybe we can be friends."

"What a lovely thought, but no, Mr. McMahon, that is not possible."

"Pen pals? Bunk mates? Alter egos?"

Her trilling laughter tintinnabulated with derision.

"Mr. McMahon," Raza said, "I am the darkest night of your deplorably depraved soul."

Try to make them laugh, Rashid had counseled. *And, what the hell, she says she thinks you're funny.*

"Then I suppose blowing me is out of the question?" McMahon asked, struggling to promote his own pleasant smile.

"When I finish with you, Mr. McMahon," Raza said, "sex will be the last thing on your mind."

"But I was so looking forward to our little love-in."

"Mr. McMahon, when I am done with you, the rocks themselves shall sob, and the earth itself cry out from terror and despair—from your terror and your despair."

"Before you start can I first ask you a question?" McMahon asked.

"Ask away."

"Since you're a Muslim and a woman, why you aren't wearing a burqa or a niqab?"

"Because we are in my world now," Raza said, "and in my world, I do whatever I want."

"What if the men around you object to your freedom and power," McMahon asked, "what happens then?"

"They don't object long."

"Why?"

"My friends look out for me," Raza said. "You do not want to mess with my friends."

"I wish I had friends like that," McMahon said, his voice genuinely forlorn.

"Ah, but you don't."

"Sounds like I'm fucked."

"Fatally, terminally, inexorably, irreversibly screwed," Raza said. "But on the bright side, you have finally made the big time."

"I'll try not to let it go to my head."

"And I will do everything in my power to keep you humble. In fact, I will give you humble lessons that will make the gods themselves fall weeping to their knees."

She picked a thick black cylinder up off a nearby table. It looked like a thick black flashlight.

Oh shit.

An electric cattle prod.

"You're saying I'm in trouble?"

"I am all the trouble you've spent your whole wretched life looking for. I am your personal Day of Reckoning—all the bad parts in the Koran rolled up into one."

"But, you're oh so beautiful."

"In my country, we have a saying about great beauty. Do you know what that saying is?"

"That all great beauty is loving and giving?"

"Quite the contrary: That all great beauty is inarguably, unalterably . . . *bloodthirsty.*"

"But you're not like that—seriously," McMahon said. "I can feel it."

"Oh, Mr. McMahon," Raza said, shaking her head in dismay, "you are a stranger to our world. Please, please, do not understand me too quickly."

Flatter her, Rashid said. *Try to keep her talking. When Raza talks, she won't be hurting you.*

"No, really. I think underneath, you're actually quite . . . sweet."

"I hate to disabuse you of your illusions," Raza said, as she flexed the whip, bending it like a bow, "but perhaps a small demonstration is in order."

"May I ask why?"

"Think of me as all your karma coming home to roost."

"Suppose I said I don't believe in Eastern mysticism.

"Everyone believes in karma."

"Not me," McMahon said. "As I sometimes tell my audience, karma can suck my dick."

"Yes," Raza said, nodding her head vigorously, "but karma can also whip your ass like a rented Afghan mule."

In spite of himself, McMahon's eyes were now darting back and forth in reflexive panic.

"Maybe we can talk about this," McMahon said. "Come o-o-on? We can work something out, can't we?"

"No, Mr. McMahon, I'm afraid not."

"There must be something I can do."

"Not really," Raza said. "This time your ships are blazing in the harbor, and your bridges are burned all the way down to the river's bottom."

"You're saying a heartfelt apology will no longer suffice?"

"I am not a priest. I do not grant absolution."

Turning from McMahon, she took a deep breath and rotated her head, working kinks out of her neck and back.

"Look, I'm sorry," McMahon said, interrupting her exercises.

He was desperate now to divert her from the horsewhip. What was it Rashid had said?

Distract them. The more you talk and they talk, the less time they have to hurt you.

That's what Rashid had said.

Keep talking.

"I'm really am sorry for anything I might have said. I can be impulsive, irresponsible. I know that, and I'm trying to change. If I've offended you and your people and your faith in any way, let me make it up to you."

"Oh, we are going to settle up, Mr. McMahon. You can trust me on that account." Leaning forward, she gave him her biggest, brightest, most beautiful smile.

Encouraged by the gorgeous grin, McMahon took a deep breath and started to talk, not knowing what he was going to say but desperate to divert her from her torture plans.

"Maybe if we brought in my agent, Richie 'the Hammer' Hammerstein. He can work anything out. You don't have a problem with Jews, do you? Richie's really very moderate about Israel—and extremely open-minded about the Palestinian issue and the West Bank settlements. He can see both sides of it—really, he can. Now he's with William Morris Endeavor, and together they can fix . . . *anything.* They're working on a film deal for me right now. *The Danny McMahon Story.* There's a part in it for you if you're interested—a real reach and a stretch, as we say in Tinsel Town. It could be a major breakout role—if you play your cards right. I have to warn you though. Watch out for Richie. Don't fuck with him. He can be a nice guy, but deep down inside there's a shark in there. He makes studio heads and network bosses bawl like little girls when they mess with one of his clients. Let me call the Hammer, and he'll—"

The woman hit him off a pivot, getting her entire body weight behind the open-handed slap. Pivoting in the opposite direction, she struck him with the backhand. Changing hands after each pair of slaps, she hit McMahon over and over and over again, each blow across his face hard and loud as a pistol shot, forehand, backhand, forehand, backhand, over and over and over and over and over again until he lost count of the blows.

Still she continued.

When she stopped, his eyes were flooded with tears, and his face was on fire. Gradually, after the tears finally subsided, he could see both her hands were a brilliant crimson, front and back, even as his cheeks burned and his ears rang.

"When I want your opinion," she said cheerfully, "I'll bitch-slap it out of you."

His eyes were still teared-over, but he was still able to see that another woman had entered the room and was sitting behind Raza on a folding chair, pushed back against the wall. She was also attractive, disconcertingly so. She had long black hair and was attired in tight bleached-out cut-off jeans, a white tank top and gym shoes. She was smoking a thin black cigarette.

Shit. She was the woman who had seduced and drugged him in his hotel suite.

"Hey there," she said, grinning mischievously. "Long time no see. I love you forever, G.I., no fucking shit."

"Just tell me what you want me to do," McMahon said, his head still ringing, his words sounding distant and tinny in his ears.

"You don't know yet?" Raza asked. "You haven't figured it out?"

"It's very simple," Marika said.

"WHAT IS IT?" McMahon roared.

"Tell him, Raza," Marika said.

"We want to hear you scream," Raza said, cracking the crop against her riding boot.

"So let's get this show on the road," Marika said, walking toward McMahon, a pair of pliers in one hand, a cattle prod in the other.

McMahon's reverberating wails echoed through the night.

4

"I WANT MY FUCKING MONEY! GIVE ME MY FUCKING MONEY . . .
NOW!!!!"

—President J. T. Tower

Y ou want to take me down?" Tower asked. "Is that why you write such foul things about me?"

"I only hope to tell the truth and shame the devil," Jules said. "What's wrong with that?"

"Does your so-called 'truth crusade' give you the right to impugn my character and call me names?"

"Give me an example."

"That thing you blogged yesterday. You said I 'careen through life like a hurricane out of this inferno.' You described me, Jules, as 'swaggering through a hellworld of my own making with *Mein Kampf* in one hand and *Atlas Shrugged* in the other.'"

"I also described you as 'a depraved megalomaniac suffering from predatory greed, malignant narcissism, paranoid ideation and severe delusional thinking.'"

"That's only your opinion," Tower said. "My supporters call me a 'jobs creator.'"

"Except the world would be better off without the vile jobs and toxic products you poison it with," Jules said, "and without your heinous hedge funds and gargoyle-ugly needle towers."

"But what gives you the right to be judge, jury and executioner?"

"President Tower, I reported on some of your more disreputable deeds—stories that were all excruciatingly accurate—and then I summarized what they meant. What's wrong with that?"

"But do your summations have to be so hateful?"

"In your case, the truth has to hurt," Jules said. "You're a world-class psychopath with genocidal impulses and the world would be better off if you were dead."

Tower's cell rang. Grimacing, he said:

"Sorry, but my sister, Brenda, says I have to take this. It's the president of Mexico.

"Yes, President Rodriguez, very good to speak to you too. How's the family? . . . Excellent . . . Now, Señor President, I have people with me, and I'm a little pressed for time. If it's okay with you, I'm going to be blunt. I hope you don't take offense at my words, but you do owe me and Tower, Inc. . . . *money*. In fact, you and your entire nation are very seriously in arrears, and I and my company want our money . . . *now*."

There was a moment of silence during which Tower listened intently, his face reddening slowly.

"All right, I completely understand. Now let me tell you what my position is. I don't want to hear about how miserable and broke your people, taxpayers and businesses are or what a shithole of a country Mexico is. That is something I can do nothing about. Yes, I know you and your people are suffering. Well in my opinion you were all born to suffer. So no excuses or extenuations."

More silence, more grimaces and groans from Tower.

"Yes?" Tower finally said. "Yes? What do I want, you ask? . . . I WANT MY FUCKING MONEY! GIVE ME MY FUCKING MONEY . . . *NOW*!!!!"

There was a long silent pause, and Tower held the phone a full foot away from his ear, all the while smiling.

"Oh, you call me a '*bastardo*,'" Tower said. "Si, there are many *bastardos* in the world, and, *es verdad*, I am one of them. Some say we *bastardos* own the world, but in truth, we only run it. And you, *cabrón*, this time, you fucked with the wrong *bastardo*. This *bastardo*-gringo'll send some men down there who *will alter you surgically and set you up in a Tampico brothel as uno hombre-puto*. It will be a major comedown for a man of your machismo. Then I'll pimp out your mother, your sisters, your daughters. I'll destroy your credit rating in all the world's financial markets. I'll flood the market with dirt-cheap oil and drop its price so low you'll have to pay your customers just to take your petrol off your hands. When I'm done with you, you'll be *blacklisted from every bank, stock exchange and marketplace worldwide*. Forget about taking out loans or selling goods. The Mexican cartels will eat you alive and move to Colombia so you won't even have drugs to smuggle. You'll have to go to Bogotá to buy a joint. *Then I'll turn Mexico into a charnel house of horrors, a blood-splattered abattoir. There'll be enough left in your benighted land for the vultures to peck at. When I'm finished with you, you'll be so busted-out you won't be able to sell frijoles in an alley or peddle your fat ugly puto ass in the street.*

"In point of dull plain fact you have tried my patience long enough, so let me be just as plain as the balls on a tall dog. When I want to buy a woman . . . *I go to a whore.* When I want to buy a murder . . . *I go to a paid killer. And when I want to buy a squalid fifth-rate shit-stinking outhouse of a country and its brain-damaged IQ-30 pederastic president, I go to Mexico. I buy that country and that president lock, stock and barrel, and guess what? They stay bought. Your country stays bought. You stay bought. 'Cause if you don't, I'll nail your ass to the floorboards. I'll bring the whole U.S. Army, Navy and Air Force down on you. I'll then personally arm every peon, bandido, drug dealer and revolucionario in Mexico against you. When I'm done, you won't have enough money, property or credit to get jackrolled by your drunken, syphilitic* puta madre. *You'll be deader than refried* javelina *shit—deader than dead, dead as dead can be. Do you catch my drift? Is there any part of this you don't* comprendo? *Understand me now . . .* GREASER?"

Slamming the phone down, he looked up at Jules Meredith. "Now where were we?" President Tower asked with an amiable smile.

5

The thought of killing Tower brought a smile to Putilov's face.

Putilov woke from a stormy, anxiety-ridden sleep . . . *screaming*. Tower was not only devastating his days, he was plaguing his nights. Putilov couldn't stop dreaming—no, nightmaring—about the idiot.

In this last dream, the cretin was blathering on and on about what a great political genius he was, how he'd never held political office in his life, yet had beaten a seasoned pro, a New York senator, who'd served as Barack Obama's secretary of state. In the nightmare, he was bragging over and over again about his "great brain" and his "instinct for the political jugular."

Where did the fool get that shit? The truth was he, Putilov, had captured Democratic emails by the millions, ordered the FSB's "Disinformation Bureau" to fabricate and plant phony news stories under the names of reputable-sounding sources about Tower's Democratic opponent and his other rivals. Putilov had then rifled the U.S. election registration lists in key swing states and disqualified legitimate Democratic voters by the millions. Simultaneously, one of his plants was running the FBI and had also sub-poenaed and examined his opponent's political emails, handed out press releases filled with vague accusations and veiled attacks, ridiculous rumors and misleading innuendos—just enough stupid chump-bait to get the U.S. media blathering about how untrustworthy the poor woman-candidate was, how scandal-prone she was.

Did Tower understand at all the sheer size and scope of the cyberwar that Putilov had waged against his presidential rival? First, he'd hired a small army of Russian/Americans living in the U.S. He'd paid them through the Russian consulates there and then ordered them to set up hoax news sites. The little creeps had then bombarded the internet with thousands upon thousands of scurrilous ads, tweets and Facebook postings from those sites, linking them to phony news articles, which appeared to have been taken from serious outlets. These spurious stories savagely attacked Tower's presidential rival.

Putilov's cyber-goons also created thousands of bots for him—little ro-botic mischief-makers—which they then transmitted to right-wing online news sites and to social media everywhere, Facebook, Google, YouTube and Twitter in particular. These preprogrammed bots tracked all mentions of Tower's opponent's name, then inundated those internet locations with pro-Tower propaganda and with fictitious, utterly defamatory stories about his presidential rival, which nonetheless appeared to come from legitimate news organizations, engendering well over a billion viewings.

According to one estimate, over 25 percent of election tweets were generated by bots, many if not most of them created by Putilov and his ravening horde of Russian-American trolls. Former–FBI agent turned cyber-sleuth, Clinton Watts, had described Putilov's internet bombs as "bot cancers," which was exactly what they were.

Putilov had taken the American Social Media industry to the cleaners. He'd scammed 150 million Facebook users—well over half the electorate— with his specious advertising and spurious posts, his henchmen so brazen they bought many of their fake ads with . . . *rubles.* Twitter, he'd inundated with 1.4 million disinformation tweets, which had triggered 280 million viewings, burying Tower's rival for the presidency alive in denigrating lies. He'd also gone after Google and YouTube, pressing every conservative hate-button and driving America's right-wingers into frenzies of paranoid rage. The United States news media claimed Putilov's principal propaganda dispenser was *Russia Today,* aka RT.com. Its content was so electrifying that Google was soon designating it "a preferred outlet," guaranteeing that this online news service would be one of the most watched of the YouTube channels in the nation during that election cycle, scoring over 1 billion YouTube viewings. After the election, the United States Justice Department branded that outlet "an enemy agent," which pissed Putilov off. By then, however, Tower was firmly ensconced in the presidency, and in any event, Putilov never stopped—never even slowed—his incessant barrage of agitprop, which continually built up Tower and tore down his rivals. Why shouldn't he continue to hammer away? Most of America's social media refused to prohibit political dissembling, caring only about the "authenticity" of the sites releasing the ads and posts. The truthfulness of the attacks was irrelevant. America's social media industry viewed political lying as perfectly acceptable.

There was another reason, however, why those firms refused to scrutinize Putilov's propaganda. His cut-out investors had pumped billions upon billions of ad/investment dollars into those companies, so much money that the owners could not afford to probe too deeply into Putilov's activities on their sites, let alone block them. They did not want to look their gift rubles in the mouth.

The Saudis, like Russia, had also invested heavily in America's cyber communications companies and the fact that those digital dimwits had accepted all that corrupt cash still made Putilov shake his head in disbelief. Didn't they understand? Russia and the Saudis opposed everything the internet industries claimed to care about—all the messianic libertarian tripe about promoting free-market competition and the free flow of information everywhere, their pious platitudes about respecting all religions and points-of-view, giving everyone a voice and a platform, no matter how big, powerful or small the individual was. Putilov and the Saudis had proven that in the end the big internet media firms were just ... *money whores.* Tainted loot spent just as well as clean currency, and at the pinnacles of financial power that was all that mattered. In the case of Putilov, he and his pocket oligarchs were collecting their internet investments profits, then using them to finance their disinformation campaigns. Exploiting the weakness of the worldwide online community, they used social media to trumpet their anti-democratic, anti-free-market propaganda globally and to even subvert an American election. Nor did those firms' CEOs object. They were too intent on opposing Washington's attempts to regulate them, and nothing would divert these internet titans from their bottom-line monomania. Not even the fact that the Putilov gang and the Saudis intended to one day destroy the very freedoms these internet moguls swore fealty to. Nothing could stop these captains-of-internet-industry from snapping up Putilov's rubles and the Saudis' rivals. Nor did their ultra-wealthy high-tech firms need dirty money to survive and expand. Their business empires were among the most profitable on earth, and in the grand scheme of things the Russian-Saudi money wasn't that huge—all of which only made the unrelenting avarice of those social media chieftains even more appealing. They had betrayed their country for mere pennies, and Putilov knew why they did it. They took his ill-gotten lucre simply because it was ... *there.* For the truly greedy, too much was indeed never enough.

Putilov knew dictum for a fact.

It was a rule he lived by himself.

Bernie Sanders supporters' websites had been an especially target-rich environment for Putilov. Sanders's admirers were so angry at the American political process that Putilov was able to quickly and easily piss them off with sordid, bot-driven anecdotes about Sanders's primary opponent, now Tower's opposition. The Russian dictator had convinced them that Tower's rival was unacceptable and that if they disliked both candidates, they should stay home from the polls.

The American voters were so mind-numbingly dumb they actually went for all that shit! Putilov thought with smug satisfaction.

And shit it was. Putilov's cyber-trolls had confected and disseminated pseudo-news stories for him around the clock, accusing Tower's female opponent of everything from pornographic depravity to sadistic serial murders to gargantuan acts of larceny and fraud planetwide. They buried America's news outlets and social media sites alive in that dementedly derisive bullshit, drowning out all objective discourse. Putilov's salacious slanders proliferated exponentially in the social media echo chamber, the right-wing blogosphere and the conservative punditocracy, spreading like wildfire throughout the battleground states.

He had to admit that he found some of those phony news stories side-splittingly hilarious as well as shockingly effective. Perhaps, as Hitler had said, the voting public liked to believe big lies and outrageous fabrications. One prevarication was so insanely preposterous that it took the internet by storm and proved unstoppable. One of his malevolent little trolls had written that Tower's opponent was running a child sex-slave ring out of the basement of a D.C. pizzeria, and American voters by the millions gobbled it up. In fact, one of Tower's incensed acolytes went into a blind rage and shot the place to pieces . . . *with an assault weapon.*

Still Putilov had to admit he couldn't have done it without some help from that nitwit, Tower. He had to give credit where credit was due. The man's marketing team had assembled a mother lode of digitized demographic data on almost all of America's voters in the battleground states and had forwarded all those files to Putilov. That Mount Everest of electronic information had allowed him to target those swing voters relentlessly. Thanks to that inside intel, he had been able to deluge the American Idiocracy with specious news items and bot-generated Twitter/Facebook traffic, all of it disparaging Tower's opponent and praising Tower to the skies.

Of course, the FBI had also been of inestimable help. At one point an ex-MI6 operative had compiled a 35-page dossier on Tower, replete with evidence of both his libidinous perversions and his hideous history of global thievery. Those findings could have blown his election chances to Kingdom Come, but, thank God, FBI Director Conley had hidden that political bombshell from public scrutiny until more than a month after the election. Only after Senator John McCain handed a copy of it to the FBI had Conley been forced to acknowledge its existence. Even then, however, the director still managed to keep it quiet. Classifying it as an item of national security interest, he was able to drop a blanket of secrecy over it and keep it out of the news throughout his tenure at the Bureau—even as he continued to blast the shit out of Tower's political rival.

Furthermore, Putilov's "bot cancers" were still alive, well—and metasta-sizing worldwide like the malignancies they were. His army of cyber terrorists was still hammering innocent citizens across the globe with these malicious bots. Their goal was always the same—to carry out Putilov's grand strategy of dividing, confounding and demoralizing democracies everywhere with his fake hate-stories.

Of course, in the end, Putilov hadn't really needed all those fancy bots and cyber-trolls to defeat Tower's opponent. He'd waged those wars largely for the fun of it. The election itself had always been locked up and in the bag. No democracy could stand up to the kind of electronic campaign he'd visited upon the U.S. in that last election.

. . . Putilov had many reasons for despising democracies. First and foremost, it was too damn easy for men like himself to overturn their democratic elections. The stupid Americans had proven that point at a Las Vegas computer convention. At one exhibition, U.S. cyber-experts changed the voter tabulations on thirty different voting machines, turning thirty mock-election losers into winners. The experts changed those election outcomes in mere minutes. Furthermore, they left no trace, no evidence of their criminal manipulations.

Putilov had, of course, done the same thing during America's last presidential election. Unfortunately, Putilov's hackers weren't as good as the Vegas cyber-experts, and U.S. investigators were able to confirm that Russia had fooled with America's voting systems. To counter those charges, Putilov immediately launched a disinformation campaign. He ordered one of his stooges—that country's idiotic FBI director, Jonathan Conley—to issue a statement claiming that the U.S. voting system was too spread out, too diffuse and too diverse for hacking to succeed. That statement was of course a flagrant lie. The voting machines' software could be compromised in a heartbeat—as the Vegas conference had proved—and, anyway, the main tabulators, which counted the votes, were connected to the internet. The average smartphone had more anti-hacking protection in it than your typical voting machine, and the cyber-tools necessary for stealing elections—especially those needed to purge voter registration lists and to falsify absentee ballot requests—were readily available online. Consequently, Putilov could hack into the U.S. voting system at will and with a vengeance. Likewise, the systems' manufacturers and support technicians could plant vote-altering malware any time they wanted. Nor were the manufacturers interested in stopping Putilov's election hacking. When the Princeton Group began testing voting machines, one manufacturer threatened them with lawsuit, and when, in the documentary Hacking Democracy, *cyber-expert Bev Harris proved how vulnerable they were, the machines' manufacturers—instead of thanking her for tracking down the flaws in their equipment—had threatened to sue her.*

You got off lucky, bitch, Putilov thought to himself. *In my country, I'd have had you jailed, killed—or both!*

God, Putilov hated that documentary. He was sure that after it came out the Americans would build a cybersecurity firewall around their voting systems. In that film and on her website, www.BlackBoxVoting.org, Harris had described defect after defect after defect in America's voting systems. For instance, she showed how touch screens could be programmed to register one's vote for the opposite candidate. She laid out how incredibly simple it was to flip absentee and mail-in ballots and make them register as votes for a candidate's rival. She pointed out how in one district votes for Al Gore in Florida had been subtracted from Gore's final tally instead of being added to it. She demonstrated how—after voting systems had been hacked and the vote tabulations changed to elect the loser—forensic investigators lacked the technological means to detect and prove the system had been hacked and the outcome reversed . . . the same thing the Vegas experts had proved. She laid out for the world how hackable U.S. elections were.

But the moronic Americans did . . . nothing.

So Putilov had waged an all-out cyber-attack on America's last political race, and after more than twenty years of hacking elections—both in his country and in those of his neighbors—there was nothing Putilov and his experts did not know about rigging a country's electronic voting systems. So they penetrated and plundered every aspect of America's state, local and national elections, and those vote thefts had been as easy for them as stealing milk bottles from sick babies. In fact, they had faced no obstacles at all. The voting machine vendors refused to work with the anti-hacking experts, because they knew that they could be held liable, when their voting equipment was proven faulty and that their stock prices could very well plunge precipitously. The states, who had absolute control over all elections within their borders, also refused to let the Department of Homeland Security help to them insure the integrity of their elections. They had stonewalled them when they offered to help prevent election hacking. Many of those states were already in the business of rigging elections through voter suppression laws and voter registration purges, and they did not want the feds looking over their shoulders. The state politicians also feared that their ineptitude in the face of proven cyber-attacks would become a political issue. In the coming elections, their opponents would accuse them of gross incompetence, and their opponents would, of course, be right. Thus, the states, like the private firms, ignored almost all outside cybersecurity help. Putilov recalled how The New York Times had described in painful detail the states' refusal to cooperate with these federal anti-hacking experts. The Times reported that the states would not allow the cyber-cops—

both from within and without the U.S. government—to sort through voter databases, searching for vulnerabilities or attempts to phony up voter data, even though such intrusions had already been spotted in elections in over twenty-one states. Instead the states and the private companies rebuffed offers of almost all in-depth forensic investigations into their blatantly hacked elections. They had made sure that government couldn't probe and monitor U.S. elections and that there was almost no way to audit the vote tabulations afterward. Only two out of America's fifty states created systems that allowed for accurate vote recounts. Putilov and his allies could even kill many of their opponents' votes in the cradle before their ballots could be cast. Putilov and his U.S. allies could purge any and all voters who were ex-felons, who had the same names as other voters in the registry or who had failed to vote in recent elections.

Putilov allowed himself a small, malicious smile, as he recalled how he and his military spy agency, the GRU, had pillaged the providers of electronic election equipment and services and the anachronistic voting machines themselves as well as how he had exploited the states' laughably ludicrous recount procedures. Putilov and his henchmen had raided the private vendors and state-run voting systems in almost half of the country and reversed the nation's election results with breathtaking facility.

Of course, the GRU's manipulations did not go utterly undiscovered, but it did not matter. When cyber-irregularities were occasionally detected, Putilov's good buddies, J. T. Tower and Jonathan Conley, saw to it that his electoral sabotage was quickly debunked and deflected. Even before the election, when the FBI caught Putilov's people hacking into the Democratic National Committee (DNC), Conley saw to it that the Bureau bungled and delayed informing the DNC of the cyber-attacks. Consequently, Putilov had every file and email that he needed—with which to discredit the Democratic Party and its candidates—long before the DNC realized the seriousness of the breach.

Putilov's hackers now knew how to overturn any and all U.S. elections at the state, local and national level with impunity. There was nothing America could do about it. As Wired magazine had titled one of its articles, "America's Electronic Voting Machines Are Scarily Easy to Target."

The memory of those cyber-assaults forced the Russian dictator to laugh out loud. When North Korea had hacked the electronics/media firm, Sony, the U.S. had done more to punish the Hermit Kingdom than that country had done to Putilov, and he had overturned many of their last state, local and national elections. He had even made J. T. Tower the American president.

And now with the help of J. T. Tower and their Saudi allies, he and an elite cadre of global oligarchs were poised to purge the earth of all its so-called democracies. *The pernicious plague of "one person, one vote" would be flung down the planet's "memory hole" for all time to come.*

You can't help but love capitalism, can you? *Putilov thought, grinning. It had made him the richest man in the world, and now the Old Free Enterprise System was about to help him wipe all those reprehensible representative democracies off the face of the earth.*

Putilov couldn't wait to hack America's coming election. He would be even better at it next time. After that election his band of merry cyber-thieves would leave no evidence whatsoever.

Yes, Putilov thought, *he was the one who had made Tower president of the United States. That sleazy, weasily, cretinous geek had nothing to do with it, but all that pretentious retard could do was brag about his "great political brilliance."*

Putilov didn't know how much longer he could take it. Somehow he had to though. He had to endure Tower until he could stop the UN threat to expropriate his and his backers' clandestine offshore funds. He then had to consummate his seizure of the Baltic States and Ukraine, derail the Global Alternate Energy Movement and then, maybe then, just maybe, he could have Tower . . . *assassinated.*

The thought of killing Tower brought a smile to Putilov's face.

How would he have it done?

The image of Tower, writhing in blind agony, succumbing to a long, slow, infinitely torturous death, was the only thing anymore that brought Putilov anything resembling . . . peace. Maybe he'd have a marksman with a sniper rifle take Tower apart with exploding bullets a micrometer at a time, starting with the feet, inching his way up through the shins to his kneecaps, working his way up Tower's thighs, penis, scrotum, testicles, prostate, carefully hammering the shit out of the bladder, the colon, the small intestine, the kidneys and the stomach—shot after shot after shot after shot. He'd stop at the stomach. Any higher and the shooter might accidentally put Tower out of his misery.

And, Lord only knew, Putilov wanted the bastard to suffer.

Oh, did he ever want Tower to suffer.

Putilov went back to bed. He thought maybe now he might be able to get back to sleep.

But it was not to be.

Again, he sat up. He was too rattled. He decided he better smoke some more krokodil. The krok never failed to calm him down.

He fished an aspirin bottle of desomorphine tablets out of his bedside table drawer, dumped out ten tablets and began grinding them up. He got out the two tablespoons, the razor blade, the Everclear bottle, the ether squeeze can and gasoline flask, the bong and the lighter.

Razor-chopping the pills assiduously, he poured the powder into the bong and watched it dissolve in the super-potent liquor. He heated the solution with the lighter. Watching the fumes fill the bowl, he began to slowly suck them in.

He smiled with anticipation.

Putilov knew the krokodil was now the only thing in this world he could truly depend on. As he pulled the fumes deep into his lungs and held them there—greedily allowing the krok to seep into every cubic millimeter of his heart and body, soul and mind—his eyes rolled back in his head, and his jaw went slack.

The krok always knew what he needed.

The krok would always be there for him.

The krok would *never* let him down.

PART VIII

"But you, your relatives and your cronies could have made just as much money in legitimate businesses. Why did your father instead choose to traffic with devils like Hitler and Stalin? Why have you climbed into bed with the Saudis? You don't need them to make your billions. Does all their carnage—and the knowledge that you're backing and bankrolling their atrocities—turn you on?"

—Jules Meredith

1

"And what of the toxic waste your benzene refineries and your nuclear power plants generate? They flood America's earth, air and groundwater with some of the most carcinogenic toxins worldwide. Do you really believe you shouldn't stop the polluting and—if necessary—close those plants?"
—Jules Meredith

Jules studied Tower, who was staring out the east window of his Tower of Power penthouse apartment. Brenda had joined them, and she sat across from Jules, drinking and smoking.

"Do you realize," Jules asked Tower, "that during the last presidential elections cycle, you and your billionaire consortium contributed more money to Republican political campaigns than all the other contributors combined."

"And we got jack shit for it," Tower grumbled, refilling his and Jules's glasses.

He did not have to refill Brenda's. She had her own brandy bottle and poured her own drinks steadily and heavily.

"What did you expect from politicians?" Brenda asked. "Honor and loyalty?"

"No, but for the money we're paying out," J. T. said, "they should keep their word."

"Hell, yes," Brenda agreed, "we should . . . *own* D.C."

"Does doing what's good for the country ever factor into your calculus?" Jules asked.

Tower snorted his derision.

Brenda laughed in Jules's face.

"What's good for Big Jim," Tower said, "is good for the country—hell, for the world—or, at least, it ought to be. That's a truth I hold to be self-evident."

"You understand, Mr. President," Jules said evenly but her eyes scornful and insolent, "that most of your life you've grown rich off those needle towers of greed, off Wall Street confidence games, rigged casinos and toxic petrochemicals. Did it ever occur to you that your money could have been better spent?"

"Money knows no good or bad, no right or wrong," Tower said. "It doesn't care where it's come from or where it's going next. It comes and goes. It circulates."

"And in your world," Jules asked, "you strive to keep the money circulating. Good money, filthy money, it's all the same to you."

"Good for you," Tower said, clapping. "You finally got it. Money is indifferent to how it is utilized or where it came from—whether it's a force for ill or good. Dirty currency can do noble things, and moral money can bankroll terrorists. Money does what it does and doesn't worry about it. Money just . . . *is*. In Jim World money circulates perpetually. Hell, it's the Second Blood."

"So there's no such thing as filthy lucre?" Jules asked.

"Some of England's most prestigious families—the old-money aristocracy everyone genuflects before today—made their fortunes out of 'the Black Triangle,'" Tower said. "Starting out 400 years ago as ship captains, their dynastic forebears ran guns to Africa. After trading them for slaves, they swapped the human contraband in Jamaica for rum and molasses, which they brought back to England and sold at spectacular profits. After a decade in the Triangle, they—and their refined and sophisticated old-money descendants—were set for life."

"But does that justify your crooked casinos and your Wall Street derivative scams?" Jules said. "And what of the toxic waste your benzene refineries and your nuclear power plants generate? They flood America's earth, air and groundwater with some of the most carcinogenic toxins worldwide. Do you really believe you shouldn't stop the polluting and—if necessary—close those plants?"

"I don't see why," Tower said. "The Justice Department's not worried enough to shut those plants down."

"Okay," Jules said. "So you don't care about people or the planet. How about this? I called you something else: 'the Barbaric Billionaire.' Did you care about that?"

"That was low, even for you."

"Not at all. You've been married three times and slept with hundreds, perhaps thousands, of other women. Some of them accused you of sexual violence. One ex-wife said during a deposition that you pulled handfuls of hair out of her head while you raped her. Do you have anything to say about that one, Mr. President?"

Glaring angrily at Jules, he poured her and himself another large snifter of cognac.

Oh fuck, Jules thought. *This is going to get serious.*

2

"If you were any hotter, you'd spontaneously combust."
—Danny McMahon to Raza Tabarti

M cMahon came to. He was belly-down and stark naked, lying prone on a
flat wooden bench. His wrists and ankles were lashed to a windlass, his
arms and legs wrenched almost out of their sockets.

Fuck, he was stretched out on a rack.

Raza's whip welts, the cattle prod's scorch marks and the pliers' pinch
wounds covered his legs, arms and torso. Every square inch of his body felt
like it was on fire.

Looking up to his right, he spotted a 52-inch flat-screen TV monitor hanging on the wall. On the table beneath it was an open laptop.

What the hell is going on? McMahon wondered. *Were they streaming
Netflix? Checking their Facebook pages? Ordering more whips and cattle
prods online?*

Then, however, he saw Tariq and two goons in robes drag Rashid back to
the sleeping room. He was badly scarred, groaning in unconscious agony
and looked to have received a particularly ugly working over.

And now it was his turn.

The two women walked up to him, laughing, grinning.

"Did you have pleasant dreams?" Raza inquired.

"Yes, I wasn't here."

"Where were you?" Marika asked.

"At an Amnesty International fund-raiser."

"Raise much money?" Raza asked.

"A fortune," McMahon said. "I was their poster boy for illegal rendition
and enhanced interrogation."

Keep them talking . . . McMahon thought to himself, remembering
Rashid's advice. *Say anything . . . Flatter them . . . Tease them . . . If possible,
make them like you . . . Anything to keep them from hurting you.*

"Mr. McMahon," Marika said, "you only have yourself to blame."

McMahon looked away, silent.

Raza gently palpated McMahon's burns and scars.

"N-i-i-i-i-ce," she said, dividing the word into six syllables, purring them like a sleepy feline. "You told me earlier I was beautiful. Do you still feel that way?"

Flirt with them, Rashid had said. *They're vain about their looks.*

"I'm embarrassed to say so but, yes."

She was, in plain fact, very beautiful—frighteningly, breathtakingly gorgeous. He couldn't deny it.

"You always hit on your torturers?" Raza asked, still fingering his burns and welts.

"I never had one as attractive as you."

"You say that now, but will you love me in the morning?" Raza said, her smile scary yet still strangely enticing.

"You want to know the truth?" McMahon said. "I feel like we knew each other in another life."

Tease them . . . Keep them talking.

"Mr. McMahon," Raza said. "I hope you did not forget my warning?"

"Not to understand you too quickly?" McMahon asked.

"Bravo!" Raza said. "You are learning."

"Mr. McMahon, you're trying to convince us you're in love with your torturer," Marika said. "Do you even know the meaning of love? You ever have a serious relationship?"

"Only one."

"What happened?" Raza asked.

"She talked too much. I had to drop her."

"Really?"

"She'd talk me to death even while she was blowing me," McMahon said with a sad shrug.

Raza was now retrieving the cattle prod and riding crop from the steel worktable. She approached him with one in each hand.

"Do I talk too much?" Raza asked him.

"I want you to talk."

"Why?" Raza asked.

"When you talk, you aren't hurting me."

"What is it you like about me anyway?" Raza asked. "I haven't been all that nice to you."

"I love everything about you," McMahon said, "including your mind."

"What about my body?" Raza asked.

"If you were any hotter," McMahon said, "you'd spontaneously combust."

"You're just saying that because you're stretched out on a rack," Raza said, shaking her head with sardonic skepticism.

"That, and you have a fully charged cattle prod in your right hand," McMahon admitted.

"And a riding crop in my left," Raza said.

"Look, I give up," McMahon said. "Just tell me what you want me to say or do. I'll say or do anything you want."

"Who says we want you to say or do anything, Mr. McMahon?" Raza asked.

"Then why am I here?"

"I thought you knew," Marika said.

She relieved Raza of the riding crop, bent it in a perfect parabola and let it snap straight. It thrummed like a vibrating arrow in a target.

Marika then brought it down across his bare ass so hard it cracked like a rifle shot.

His eyes teared and all the breath whooshed out of his body. The pain was as intense as anything he'd experienced.

"Jesus, that smarts," Danny McMahon finally managed to say, struggling to blink back reflexive tears and catch his breath.

"As well it should, Mr. McMahon," Marika said.

"But . . . *why?*" McMahon asked, starting to lose it.

"Because we're trained professionals," Raza said.

McMahon's eyes rolled back.

"I mean why are you doing this?" he asked.

"Believe it or not, we're trying to get to know you," Marika said.

"As you say in the West, Mr. McMahon, we're just trying to 'relate,'" Raza said.

"We want you to finally understand us, our people, Islam," Marika said.

"Are the riding crop and the cattle prod part of my education?" McMahon asked.

"They are indispensable to it," Raza said.

"Do I have a choice in my curriculum?"

"Better us than the alternative," Marika said.

"Tariq?" McMahon asked.

"He doesn't like you," Raza whispered in his ear.

"He doesn't know me."

"Then he'd hate you," Marika said.

"I don't like me much myself," McMahon confessed glumly. "Why should anyone else?"

"But more to the point," Raza said, "do the words 'steer,' 'capon' and 'gelding' mean anything to you?"

"What do you want from me?" McMahon was becoming hysterical. "I said I'll do anything."

"Will you convert to the One True Faith?" Raza asked.

"Now you're laughing at me," McMahon said.

"Never," Raza said.

Her cell phone buzzed and she answered it.

"We have a friend who wants to meet you."

Kamal ad-Din appeared live on the monitor of a laptop computer. Raza quickly streamed the video transmission onto the 52-inch flat-screen wall monitor. Kamal was in a white robe, his gargantuan bulk taking up most of the vast circular bed on which he was sprawled. Three scantily clad prepubescent girls clung to his arms and legs. Their facial expressions seemed dazed, empty, opaque.

3

"What you did in the dark is coming to light."
—Jules Meredith on President J. T. Tower

Tower stared at Jules Meredith in silence while she studied the extraordinary eastern view of New York from the needle tower penthouse he called home.

"I asked you," Jules said, turning back to him, "what you thought of your ex-wife's allegations of physical battery and violently coerced sex."

"A tsunami of lies, which you and your fake-news commentators created out of your own sick minds."

"Facts aren't lies, and everything I charged you with is supported by hard verifiable evidence."

"You mean by smoke-and-mirrors gossip," President Tower said.

"Your divorce transcripts and your ex-wives' signed sworn depositions weren't smoke and mirrors. According to your first wife's divorce deposition, you raped her and ripped hair out of her head by the handfuls."

"Pure conjecture," Tower said, his eyes glazing over with alcohol.

"No more," Jules said. "What you did in the dark is coming to light."

"And every one of those fabrications came with a price tag on it," Tower said, "a bill from some bimbo looking to profit off my fortune, name and fame."

"Are you saying women only want you for your money?" Jules asked, baiting him.

"Especially you," Tower said, his chin drooping drunkenly. "You're making a shithouse full of money off me, pillorying me in the yellow press and parlaying those lies into seven-figure book contracts. You called me the 'Barbaric Billionaire.' All your stories came replete with banner headlines about tempestuous affairs, violence visited on girlfriends and wives, sometimes in the marriage bed."

"I documented all of it," Jules said.

"It wasn't my fault," Tower said, now slurring his words badly. "A good marriage counselor would have made all the difference in the world."

"Counseling wouldn't have worked," Jules said.

"What would have?" Tower asked, now very inebriated.

"Electroconvulsive therapy? A prefrontal lobotomy?"

"You're being cruel," Tower said, shaking his head. "A good counselor would have saved those marriages."

"Tower," Jules said, staring at him, incredulous, "you never needed a marriage counseler or even a shrink."

"What did I need?" he said, now barely able to hold his head up.

"An exorcist."

4

Instead Elena had dragged Jamie back into another Agency-fucked mission.

John C. "Jamie" Jameson lay in bed next to Elena but could not sleep. The room was pitch-dark, but still he stared at the ceiling, which he could barely make out.

Why the fuck was he going along with this shit?

The answer to that one was simple: Elena. She was going back to Pakistan again, and he couldn't let her go there on her own. He just couldn't. He didn't know how to turn his back on her even when walking away was obviously the smart move. It now seemed as if they'd been together forever, born joined at the hip, and he couldn't abandon her.

But he also knew that made no sense. He was a free man with free will. He did not have to walk into a buzz saw just because Elena was doing it.

So why are you doing it?

And where had it all started?

He knew where it had started—when he had met Elena in Pakistan. He had run some missions for the Agency, and she'd been his control. He'd even rescued her once from a Pakistani hellhole, after the TTP had abducted her.

They'd hit it off, one thing led to another, and they'd become lovers.

While in Pakistan, Elena had worked closely with the NSA to locate targets and enemy emplacements. She had introduced him to the NSA's world of cyberwarfare, showed him how it worked, and it turned out he had an instinctive affinity for it, a true gift for understanding and for maneuvering in that realm.

He was already putting in his fifth tour in Afghanistan, and when he came home, he was burned out on the whole Mideast. Resigning his marine corps commission, he took a job with a cyber-defense firm, and before long he was personally designing cybersecurity systems for them. His systems were astonishingly successful, and demand for them was heavy, globally. Elena had encouraged him to set up his own shop. She was still working for the Agency—still running the Pakistan desk—and had set him up with some top Agency and

NSA people, who hired him to set up systems for them. Soon clients from around the world were beating down his doors. Three of the systems he created revolutionized cybersecurity globally, and he held the patents on them.

In six years he was a billionaire, his firm designing and installing cybersecurity systems for half the countries on earth, particularly for their military and intelligence agencies as well as for the world's top transnational corporations.

Then he and Elena had stumbled onto a TTP plot to nuke D.C., and in their attempts to hunt down the terrorists, they, the hunters, had become the hunted. A corrupt White House and CIA Director had even issued shoot-to-kill orders on Elena, Jules, and himself.

They had eventually survived the attempts on their lives—in part by fleeing to Sweden—and they were eventually cleared of all wrongdoing; still all three of them had sworn never to return to the U.S. But now they had broken that vow, were heading home, and, boy, was he ever sorry. He'd made his fortune, and had wanted to kick back and enjoy it—and maybe find out if this life had any true serenity in it, any real happiness.

Instead Elena had dragged Jamie back into another Agency-fucked mission.

God, was he pissed.

Why the fuck couldn't he just tell her no? he asked himself.

Because there's no way you can stop her, and if you walked away and she got hurt, you'd never forgive yourself.

Because you love her more than life itself.

And so Jamie lay there, furious at himself, but not knowing what else to do. Staring at the dark, unseeable ceiling, he was still unable to sleep.

He waited for the gray of predawn to lighten the windows.

5

"Don't thank me till it's over."
—Fahad al-Qadi

F ahad's driver pulled the Lincoln Town Car into the garage of the filthy four-story, formerly white truck stop. It had been a truck stop up until a couple of years ago. Now it was essentially a big, dirty building that hadn't seen a coat of whitewash or paint in thirty years.

He got out of the car and entered the front door.

On the first floor was the machine shop, which was why the driver had taken a one-year lease out on it for Fahad. Haddad had also leased a dual-beam laser welder that could penetrate far deeper into ultrahard metals—such as titanium—as well as several other metal-cutting machines and other assorted pieces of machine shop equipment.

In Fahad's case, he had needed a custom-built, specially designed dual-beam laser that was capable of welding the two tamps into the ends of an old Civil War howitzer barrel. Fahad had bought the cannon from the estate of an old collector and had had it recommissioned. It was ready to go.

Two men dressed in white machinist's overalls walked up to Fahad. One wore a short beard, the other needed a shave and had a thick black mustache. Fahad shook both their hands. They were here to assist him in constructing the nuke.

"We've been cleaning up the shop," Mukhtar, the bearded man, said. "The owners had been unable to sell the place, so it hadn't been touched or taken care of for the last few years."

"We must have killed a hundred rats," Ramzi said. "A week ago, we brought in a couple of cats to help us. Now the rats are either dead, or the cats scared the bastards off."

"Excellent," Fahad asked, "and the dual-beam laser welder has arrived?"

"It's here," Mukhtar said, "ready and waiting."

"The howitzer barrel?" Fahad asked.

"It's under the tarp," Ramzi said.

"We have a forklift that can handle up to ten tons, and the shop has a hydraulic lift off to the side," Mukhtar said. "We'll have no difficulty machining the howitzer."

"And the medical supplies?" Fahad asked.

"They're all here—ready for you," Ramzi said. "We put the drugs in the mini-fridge in the corner."

"Great," Fahad said. "But now I'm going to have to take off for several days, and while I'm gone, I want you guys to thread the interior of the two ends of the howitzer barrel so that its grooves will match those of the two tamps. When I get back, we'll screw each of them in, then I'll weld the tamps tight."

"Will the weapon be powerful enough to do the job?" Ramzi asked.

"We only need one kiloton max," Fahad said. "The bomb will work fine."

"*Ta-Barruk-Allah*," Mukhtar said. *Praise be to Allah, our protector.* "We have waited for this moment all our lives."

"Thank you so much for allowing us to be part of your operation," Mukhtar said.

"Don't thank me till it's over," Fahad said. "We still have a lot to do. You can call me on one of my encrypted burner phones if you need anything. Remember to smash it afterward and scatter its pieces in the Hudson if you have to use it. You know not to say anything stupid that will expose what we're doing, right?"

"Of course," Mukhtar said.

"Then we're straight," Fahad said. "Haddad and I will spend the night here. First thing in the morning, we'll take off."

"I understand this will be hard," Ramzi said, "but I'm still grateful we've been granted a chance to retaliate against the Great Satan for what he has done to Iraq, Syria and Afghanistan."

"At last, we have the chance to hit his homeland—and to hit it hard," Mukhtar said.

"That is true," Fahad said. "I'll give you that. We will hit the Great Satan in a way the American people and the world never imagined possible—not in their darkest, wildest nightmares."

"*Ta-Barruk-Allah*," Mukhtar repeated.

"But in the meantime, I have some supplies to purchase," Fahad said. "I'll see you back here in a few hours and take off at first light."

6

**"We're the makers and shakers, not the losers and the mooch-
ers. Those Great Unwashed Assholes, otherwise known as the
American People, should be paying taxes to us, not Uncle Sam."
—President J. T. Tower**

Jules sat in Tower's penthouse, studying the southeastern view of the UN,
the East River and Brooklyn.

"Give me a hint of what's in your new book?" Tower asked.

"I discuss at length your penchant for prevarication," Jules said. "*The
Washington Post* and *New York Times* have now tabulated your total number of lies, since entering politics, as numbering over several thousand. *The
Wall Street Journal*—hardly a bastion of left-wing political discourse—has
complained on its editorial pages that you have set the political truth bar so
low that now half the country no longer believes anything politicians say or
what they read or hear in the news."

"I like to think of myself as being 'clearer than the truth,'" Tower said
with a self-satisfied smirk. "What else do you say about me?"

"Among other things, I describe at length how your father got his start
building weapons factories for Hitler and Stalin and that you admire him
for it."

"As did George W. Bush's granddad and many other good patriotic
American businessmen along with him," Tower said. "So what? They each
made a fortune, and, yes, I admire both of them for doing it."

"But your father was a petrochemical-munitions manufacturer, who
helped Hitler and Stalin build up their arms industries—specifically teaching them how to refine high-octane aviation fuel for their armies and air
forces. You profiteer off the Saudis. They are the chief financiers of Islamist
terrorism in the world today, yet you have offered to build forty nuclear
power plants for them and their Arab neighbors. Doesn't a willingness and
even a desire to profit off mass-murdering despots indicate a certain lack of
moral character?"

"Hell, no," Tower said, but his vision was starting to twitch and his tongue
was growing heavy. "My daddy and old George W.'s antecedents were real

men, not like those sissy bitches running companies today. They didn't stand on ceremony, decorum and red tape. They saw something they wanted, they went after it. It's always easier to apologize later than to ask permission. And all that ass they kicked and names they took, they did it all for the old U.S. of A. I tell you, they loved this land. Cut them old boys, Jules, and they bled red, white and blue."

"But you, your relatives and your cronies could have made just as much money in legitimate businesses," Jules pointed out. "Why did your father instead choose to traffic with devils like Hitler and Stalin? Why have you climbed into bed with the Saudis? So many people in your administration are making a fortune off Putilov's companies and off the Saudis. Are they patriots too?"

"Of course," Tower said. "And what's wrong with Putilov anyway?"

"He's a mass-murdering psychopath of global proportions for one thing."

"But he's also a hell of a businessman."

"Which in Jim World justifies everything?"

"You know 'Jim's Golden Rule'?" Tower asked.

"'He who has the gold, rules,'" Jules quoted numbly.

"You do understand me, don't you?" Tower said, smiling brightly.

Jules ignored his jibe. "And your support of the Saudis?" Jules asked.

"I suppose you hate them too."

"Hillary Clinton once described them as 'providing clandestine financial and logistical support to ISIS and other radical Sunni groups in the region.' Some people characterize their riches not as petrodollars but 'blood money.' Yet you do business with them."

"So do a lot of western businessmen," Tower said. "In fact, the Saudis just held a business conference in Riyadh, which I attended. They had 3,500 invitees—mostly from the western democracies—people, who in aggregate, controlled over $22 trillion. By my calculations that averages $611 billion per person. We all came to invest our dirty dinero in the disreputable Saudi Kingdom, and everyone kicked in. None of us had the moral hubris to reject their fantastically lucrative business offers."

"But you and your friends are super-rich. You don't need their blood-stained cash."

"Like I always say, Jules. Money doesn't care about its lineage or its future. It just . . . *is*. It flows through the earth's economic systems like the blood coursing through humanity's veins."

You don't need them to make your billions. Does all their carnage—and the knowledge that you're backing and bankrolling their atrocities—turn you on?"

"Suppose I said we do it for love of country."

"In other words, you're a patriot?" Jules said evenly, without emotion. "Before you ran for the presidency, you were quoted as saying you pledge allegiance not to the U.S. of A, but to the country with the biggest tax loopholes and the lowest tax rates."

"I once called that 'truthful hyperbole.'"

"But that does summarize your business philosophy?"

"When I'm in the private sector, my job is to maximize my profits and the government's job is to keep out of my way."

"But without laws we have anarchy."

"You've called me an anarchist before. In your last blog, you also called me 'an engine of entropy, a force multiplier for metastatic greed.'"

Jules did not like that he could recite passages of her articles by heart. She also did not like his glazed, drunken eyes and feral stare.

"But do you deny the charge?" Jules asked.

"Hell, yes, I deny it," Tower continued, but his speech was slowing down and his eyes were losing their focus. "We're the makers and shakers, not the losers and the moochers. Those Great Unwashed Assholes, otherwise known as the American People, should be paying taxes to us, not Uncle Sam."

"J. T.," Jules said, "as far as I can tell, on balance, you've paid practically nothing in taxes . . . ever. You're worth billions, yet most years you've run your companies at a loss."

"Were that true," Tower said, "I would take it as a compliment. I shouldn't have to pay taxes—not if I'm doing my job right."

"So in Jim World, no one should be allowed to rein you in?"

"Not that damn IRS or the FBI or the EPA or OSHA," Tower said, even though he was starting to sway, and his speech was erratic. "Fighting them is like fighting the Terminator, an army of ghosts, like waging war on the living dead. They keep coming at you, keep coming back to life despite all the mortal blows you hit them with. I beat back one ruling, they come after me with another and another, always with endless fines, which keep getting bigger."

Shit, Jules thought, *he's probably never been this drunk in his life.*

"You think you're cleaning out the Augean Stables?" Jules asked with mock irony.

"With a fucking Hydra," J. T. added, badly slurring his speech.

Reaching forward, he grabbed her knee. She quickly removed it.

Leaning forward, locking his eyes on hers, he grabbed her upper leg again, this time squeezing it as hard as he could until her thigh screamed in agony.

Jules bent his middle finger back and held it there, until he howled, dropped to his knees and fell onto his side.

"That's it, Tower. I'm in the archives. Even I can't stand you anymore. This is where the cowgirl rides away."

Standing, she spun on her heels and strode toward the door.

Tower attempted to stand but immediately became light-headed.

Fuck. He couldn't even get up off the floor. He was too drunk to go after her.

7

"Perhaps I was too judgmental," McMahon admitted sheepishly.

To what do I owe this pleasure, my prince?" McMahon asked nervously.

McMahon was still belly-down on the rack—his joints screaming with pain—and he had to crane his neck up in order to see the TV screen.

"You've been ridiculing my life and lifestyle for some time now," the portly terrorist financier, Kamal ad-Din, said. Lounging luxuriously on a big circular bed with red satin sheets, he was surrounded by the three embarrassingly young girls in skimpy negligees. "I thought it was time we met."

"I'm glad to meet you," McMahon said a little shakily.

"We'll see about that," Marika whispered under her breath.

The monitor filled with a prerecorded close-up of Danny McMahon. His grin was half leer, half sneer, and he was delivering a bitingly satiric TV monologue. Raza muted the sound, so the prince could comment on Danny's act.

"During one of your HBO Specials," Prince Kamal explained, "you said some very ugly things about me. You said, among other things, I'd 'fuck anything.'"

Raza turned the sound on, and on the screen Danny McMahon—with eyes blazing and grin glinting—was saying:

"*Prince Kamal'll fuck anything: Hair, hips, pits or lips. Eight to eighty, blind, crippled or crazy. He's fucked cops, firemen and Indian chiefs in war bonnets—the whole YMCA.*" The TV audience roared with laughter, and McMahon said after quieting them down: "*If America still made Model Ts and Stanley Steamers, he'd fuck them too.*"

"Then you made fun of Kamal's weight problem," Raza said, shaking her head with disapproval and freezing the screen. "Yes, he struggles with weight control, but that is not a laughing matter. It should be a cause for sympathy. Instead you called him '*a living, breathing dirigible*' and '*human hippo.*' You said he couldn't ride horses because he'd '*kill a Clydesdale.*' He'd even '*demolish a dromedary.*' You said his couturier was '*Omar the Circus-Tent Maker.*'"

"In one monologue, you said Kamal's hat size was '*extra watermelon*'!" Marika roared.

"You even ridiculed his mother's weight," Raza said

"You said she *'won the Miss Goodyear Blimp Look-Alike Contest twenty years running'*!" Marika shouted, outraged.

"The poor woman!" Raza said.

"Cr—u—u—u—e—l!!!" Marika said.

"Hurtful, Mr. McMahon," Raza said. "Your remarks were cutting, uncalled-for, unnecessary."

Marika ran another clip from one of McMahon's comic monologues. McMahon was saying:

"Their sainted Islamist leader and financier, Kamal ad-Din, has an idiot wind blowing through his brain from one end of Dar al-Islam to the other. He claims he's a Muslim, but in truth, he's their high priest of psychopathia sexualis. To that obese imbecile, floggings, stonings, amputations and decapitations aren't atrocities. They're Islamist foreplay! And as for the suicide bombers, whom Kamal so enthusiastically bankrolls with his ill-gotten billions, they are craven maniacs and sadistic halfwits just like Kamal himself . . . only not as fucking fat!"

"You called our beloved leader *Kamal the Camel!*" Raza fulminated.

"The *Muslim Moby Dick!!!*" Marika exploded.

"You once shouted at his photograph," Raza yelled at the top of her lungs, *"HEY, DUMBO, WHERE'S YOUR TRUNK???"*

"Your country, on the other hand, has spent the last two decades bulldozing its way through our Mideast," Marika said, serious and reasonable, "flattening everything in its path, yet you smirk and sneer at our culture, when, in fact, you have wreaked far more carnage and chaos here than ISIS, al Qaeda, the TTP and the old Soviet Union put together."

"Perhaps I was too judgmental," McMahon admitted sheepishly.

"Perhaps you were," Marika said, removing the riding crop from under her arm. Grabbing both ends, she again bent it over 250 degrees. Turning to Raza, she said. "And perhaps that is why we are here, Sister-Friend, to teach Mr. McMahon the error of his ways. But it's my turn now."

He caught the blur of motion just over his shoulder, and again the horsewhip whistled through the air and slashed his ass.

Through the fog of tears and pain, he could hear the raucous, booming guffaws of Prince Kamal; the demented wailing laughter of Tariq al-Omari, who'd just entered the room, clearly eager to watch the spectacle to come; Marika's high, tinkling, melodious chortles; and Raza's loud unwavering count as she announced in sequence the numbered strokes.

"ONE!"

Crack!

"TWO!"

Crack!

"THREE!"

Crack!

After the thirty-third blows he blacked out and gratefully lost count.

PART IX

This valley of dying stars.

—T. S. Eliot, "The Hollow Men"

1

_____

Promises had been made, and now Jonathan P. Conley was here to collect.

Former FBI director Jonathan Conley sat in a private waiting room outside J. T. Tower's New York presidential offices. It contained six red stuffed chairs, a matching couch, a coffee table piled with magazines and newspapers, wall shelves filled with books and a coffee station. The walls were adorned with Picasso prints. He was embarrassed to even be sitting in a room so ignorantly designed and disgustingly decorated.

It was all Tower's fault Conley was here. The president's deep-seated aversion to D.C. had inspired Tower to set up shop in the Big Apple, and he usually did business—if you could call it that—at his 59th Street Needle Tower penthouse or on the top floor of the Excelsior Hotel on 57th Street. Conley despised both places. In fact, just being in New York almost made him physically ill. He thought it the most depraved city in the world. A mere glimpse of its skyline made his flesh crawl. Deeply religious, Conley disparaged New York in private as "Sin City" and "Sodom by the Sea." He carried a small black King James Bible in his coat pocket, which, whenever he visited the city, he gripped in times of stress as if it were a charm against evil.

Tower was not only the biggest fucking asshole Conley had ever known, he was arguably the worst president in Conley's lifetime—perhaps in the history of the country. Furthermore, the man had no concept of loyalty. The idiot had actually had the chutzpah to fire Conley after Conley had risked going to prison to get him elected president. Tower claimed privately that Conley was disloyal because the FBI had agents investigating Putilov's hacking of the previous presidential election.

Of course the FBI had agents inquiring into Putilov's fixing of that election. The Democratically controlled Senate had forced Conley to assign agents to that case. Conley had no choice. But just because Conley had ordered agents to examine those election results didn't mean that, he, Conley, would let those numbskulls find anything—at least nothing incriminating. Couldn't Tower get it through his thick skull that Conley had his back?

And if that insult wasn't enough, now Tower had him waiting, cooling his heels for over an hour in the ugliest waiting room Conley had ever seen anywhere, and after an hour of sitting there he was getting both pissed and stiff. To loosen his tight sore muscles, he tried stretching, which was no simple task. Over six feet, seven inches tall, his body required floor exercises if he were to truly loosen it up. Still he did his best. His extended arms and legs, his suit sleeves and trousers now riding up on his wrists and ankles, reminding him that he was wearing his best, most expensive navy blue Brioni suit, a crisply starched white shirt and, he remembered, he'd also put on a red silk tie. God, suits made him hot—sweaty, in fact. He would have loved to take the coat off, loosen the power tie and roll up the sleeves of his white shirt. But this was an important meeting for him—the first time he'd be alone with President Tower—so he wanted to look important. He wanted to look like he was somebody.

Like he belonged.

Dress for the job you want, he'd always heard, *not the job you have.*

And why shouldn't he have something better than this bullshit former FBI director job? He deserved much, much more after all he'd done for Putilov and Tower. In fact, he'd been promised much, much more. After Putilov and the FSB had surreptitiously hacked the emails of Tower's Democratic presidential opponent, Obama's former female secretary of state, and disseminated them through WikiLeaks, they'd asked Conley to open an investigation of those leaked emails. They'd asked him to announce to the world that he was investigating her, to create the illusion she was guilty as sin of something, anything. Putilov and Tower had told Conley he had to convince the public she was untrustworthy. So he'd destroyed his own personal and professional reputation for Tower by leveling false accusations at Tower's Democratic rival, making it appear she was a crook and a liar.

Then when the emails came back empty and revealed nothing of substance, the two men had returned to him. Tower and Putilov wanted him to issue statements saying that the FBI was still investigating the woman and that she was still suspected of influence peddling, bribe taking and enriching herself at the public trough—anything, everything.

Conley had done all that as well—even though it was all a pack of lies.

And the ruse had worked.

Conley and Putilov had gotten Tower elected.

Conley had risked a treason trial and life in prison to get Tower elected.

Afterward, however, it started to get scary. The press found shocking evidence that Tower and Putilov had conspired to hack into the vote tabulations in key battleground states, that they had falsified the totals and thrown those battleground states to Tower, thereby cheating his opponent out of her rightful victory. The Democrats demanded a special prosecutor—his predecessor at the FBI, former director Ben Miller—and God only knew how far that bastard would take this thing.

So Tower and Putilov had begged Conley to personally take over the probe, to distract the Congressional investigators, to hide, deflect and if necessary destroy emails and electronic files, to stall and derail any and all inquiries no matter what the cost.

Conley had spent his whole life as a bureaucratic infighter, and he knew just how to throw sand in the bureaucracy's gears and tie up investigators in red tape.

He'd thwarted those investigations and throttled them to death.

The Democrats had objected, calling him a fanatical partisan infighter, but at that point in time Tower had still had control of both Houses, and fuck it, Conley's evangelical background and revivalist speechifying had convinced the religious right and the party's base that he was sincere.

And if you can fake sincerity, you can fake anything, he thought to himself with sardonic amusement.

During that last conference call with Tower and Putilov, however, when they were still begging him for his help, Conley had finally spoken up. He told the two men that he wanted something in return. A Texan by birth, he knew that that state's 87-year-old senior senator had a dicey ticker and would soon step down. Conley wanted Tower to make the Texas governor appoint him, Jonathan Conley, U.S. senator, and then when Tower ran for reelection, he wanted the number two spot. Jonathan P. Conley, Vice President.

Four years later, he believed in his soul that he, Jonathan Conley, could run and be President of the United States.

Tower and Putilov were so desperate for him to block the Putilov–Tower investigation, they had instantly agreed. They said they'd give him anything he wanted. They offered him the sun, the moon, the stars, if he could stop those goddamn inquiries.

So he had done everything the two men had asked. He'd defamed Tower's opponent, risked life in prison to get Tower elected, then protected them from criminal investigations for their hacking and falsifying of the election results. He'd sacrificed *everything* for Putilov and Tower. And then . . .

And then . . .

And then . . .

And then Tower . . . *had canned his fucking ass.*

Adding insult to injury, the two men had stopped answering Conley's phone calls and refused to even speak with him afterward.

They were giving him the middle finger.

But that shit was ending now. He was finally having it out with Tower. He deserved better. Promises had been made, and now Jonathan P. Conley was here to collect.

2

"We're harrowing hell for a lost soul, and we need some help."
—Elena Moreno

Eight men sat at a large, unpainted, heavily worn beer-soaked table in the upstairs room of a Belfast bar. They'd chosen to meet in Northern Ireland because Jamie, Elena and Adara had to hire a dozen mercs fast. So many soldiers of fortune lived in that city they'd have a broad assortment to pick from. Also meeting with so many hired guns wouldn't be that unusual in Belfast. Since contractors were everywhere—all over the city—their meetings would be less conspicuous in this city than in most.

The men were dressed in dark hooded sweatshirts, cut-off T-shirts, watch caps and baseball hats. One of them wore an old army surplus fatigue jacket, and most had unkempt beards. Only one man at the table was clean-shaven. Bottles of Bushmills, Dewar's and Hennessey, pitchers of beer and an assortment of mugs and glasses, were scattered across the table.

Adara and Elena entered, and Jamie followed, shutting the door behind him. Both women wore Levi's and T-shirts; Elena sported a short leather jacket with a black hooded sweatshirt under it as well and Adara a gray hooded sweatshirt. Jamie, who stood six feet, two inches, was beardless, his hair in a military buzz cut, and he had on a bush jacket. Adara kept a pistol in the small of her back under her skinny jeans and her hoodie. A subcompact slimline Glock 10mm, it held seven rounds plus one in the receiver. Elena kept the same weapon in a shoulder rig under her sweatshirt. She preferred shoulder holsters because they gave her quicker access to her pistol while sitting down. All three of them wore hip bags that held various weapons and extra magazines.

The introductions and hellos were minimal—waves, nods, brief greetings, no names. They had all worked together previously on different occasions.

"Well as I live and barely breathe," Elena finally said, as the two women sat down. "The dogs of war."

"Hydrophobic curs, you ask me," Adara said.

"Hey, you called us," Jonesy said. He was the one black merc, and if he had a first name, no one knew it. He had a thin curly beard and was dressed in a black shirt, matching Wranglers, cowboy boots and a leather sports jacket.

"And it was so nice of you to show up," Elena said.

"We came for the free drinks," the one called Andre said. He had a short blond beard and a ponytail. He wore a dark sweatshirt with the sleeves cut off. His cannonball biceps were covered with military tats. He had just finished field-stripping a .45 M1911 U.S. Army Colt. Disengaging the safety, he inserted a magazine and pulled back the slide. When he released it with a hard, sudden *snap!*, the action automatically chambered a round and cocked the hammer. Without thinking, he reengaged the safety—cocked and locked. He flashed Elena a cutthroat grin. Uncorking a liter Hennessey brandy bottle, he offered Elena and Adara glasses. They each nodded their thanks and took one.

"Where you been, *mon cher*?" Adara asked.

"On an existential quest for my identity," Andre said.

"Any luck?" Elena asked.

"Yeah, all of it bad," Andre said.

"Meaning, he found it," Adara said.

"*C'est tres vraiè*," Andre agreed, smiling. *That's very true.*

"*Viva le Morte [Long live death]*," Elena said, honoring Andre's years in the French Foreign Legion.

"*Viva le Guerre [Long live war]*," Adara said.

"*Viva Le Legionnaire [Long live the legionary]*," Andre said, finishing the ancient toast and his cognac.

"You still enjoy an occasional brandy?" Elena asked Andre cheerfully.

Andre was a notoriously heavy drinker.

"*Toujours*," he said.

"In this line of work," Stevie said, "you never turn down a drink or a bathroom, a meal or a piece of ass." A former IRA gunrunner with a short blond beard, he wore a black cable-knit seaman's sweater and a black watch cap.

"You never know when it's your last," Elena agreed, nodding and smiling.

Another man entered the room.

"What's this?" he asked. He was young, wearing a white shirt, dark blue suit, a striped tie and was looking for another party.

"Slide rule club," Stevie said.

"They have calculators now," the man pointed out.

"Same thing," Stevie said.

Noting the Colt .45 in Andre's fist, the man quickly turned and left, closing the door behind him.

"I thought you were dead," Elena said to the person sitting next to Stevie.

"I thought that too," Leon said, "for a while."

A short stocky man in a black Van Morrison T-shirt, Leon had a heavy overarching brow, dark hair and a carelessly trimmed beard. A deep jagged knife scar diagonally traversed his right cheek, and his long arms hung almost to his knees. When he walked, it was with a hint of a stoop, so everyone naturally called him Ape. But never to his face.

"Does anyone want to tell us why we're here?" Stevie asked.

"Besides 'Auld Lang Syne,'" Andre said.

"We're harrowing hell for a lost soul," Elena said, "and we need some help."

"Where's hell this time?" Stevie asked.

"The Pakistan–Afghan border country," Adara added.

"And we look like the SEAL Team Six?" Stevie asked.

"Seriously, we need to liberate a man from prison." Adara said.

"I spent too much time working them Abu Ghraib death cages," Leon said, shaking his head. "That's as close to a jail as I want to get ever again."

"That be a lock," Jonesy said, "and right now I don't feel like doin' nothin' sketchy."

"Last time I was in Pakistan," Stevie said, "the TTP kicked my butt till I almost choked to death on my colon. I'm not real eager to return."

"I wouldn't go back into Pakistan if I was free as a bird," Jonesy agreed.

"The pay will be proportional to the risk," Jamie said.

"Very proportional," Adara added.

"Up-front proportional," Elena said.

"All of it up-front proportional," Jamie said.

"The money would have to be very up-front proportional," Stevie said.

"The moment we take off, it has to be in my account," Andre said.

"The money's real as steel," Elena said. "We got us a bank."

"A billionaire bank," Adara said.

All their eyes turned to Jamie.

"You backin' this?" Jonesy asked.

Jamie nodded.

"Jamie's in on this," Stevie said, "it's real."

"And if Jamie's here," Jonesy said, "it's gotta be important. Jamie, you sure ain't in it for the money."

The men all nodded their agreement.

Another black merc, this one in an ebony turtleneck and a matching beret, entered the room. He shut the door behind him. Elena made him for at least six four, and he was built like a pro tackle. She knew him as Henry, and he was the second man who did not have a beard.

"And I definitely gotta git some flex," Henry said.

"It's cool," Jonesy said.

"Way past cool," Leon said.

The door opened right behind Henry, and the owner, Maurice, entered. He had red hair, an auburn beard and a fat belly. His pale chubby cheeks sported vividly purple grog blossoms. He cooked as well as supervised the help, and he wore an apron over a white kitchen uniform.

"We got us a problem," he said to Adara. "A couple of boys from the Or-gan-i-za-tion"—he pronounced it with a long *i*—"are beating the fockin' piss out of some boyo downstairs. I asked them to take it outside but they refused. They look like they might kill him, and I can't have no dyin' in my es-tab-lish-ment. I live in Belfast, if you know what I mean, but I also can't go up against the Or-gan-i-za-tion, no way, no how. But you'll be flyin' out pretty soon, right? And you don't live here."

"Want us to handle it?" Adara asked.

"I'd be in your debt," Maurice said, "but they be hard-looking lads—and there's five of them."

"No problem," Elena said.

"This won't take long," Adara said to the men with her.

"I assumed the men would handle it," Maurice said. "Jamie, won't you help out?"

"I don't fight with children," Jamie said, helping himself to a glass of Andre's Hennessey.

"Stevie?" Maurice asked.

"Wouldn't dirty me hands on them IRA bitches," Stevie said with a sly smile.

"We might off the muthafuckas," Jonesy explained, "and you said you don't want no one dyin' here."

"You wouldn't want that, would you?" Leon asked with a gruesome grin.

"Can you two really handle them?" Maurice said to the two women. "They're big men, hard men."

"Don't worry," Adara said. "We won't hurt them too badly."

"We'll reason with them," Elena said.

"Then we'll tuck them in for the night," Adara said.

"I think he's afraid you'll injure some of his repeat business," Stevie said.

"In that case," Elena said, "we won't hit them in their mouths."

"We know they need their mouths to drink," Adara said.

"But them buckos kneecap men for a livin'," Maurice said. "They're . . . *hard hitters*."

The two women got up from the table. They walked up to the door, and Adara slapped Maurice on the back.

"Never fear," Adara said. "We'll just kiss them good night for you."

Adara and Elena left the room.

"Want to go out on the balcony and watch?" Davey asked.

"Why not?" Stevie said.

The ten men rose and followed the two women out of the room. Taking their drinks to the balcony rail, they watched the women walk down the stairs and out onto the pub floor.

3

Oh no, Brenda thought. *Putilov's on board. Conley's in for it now.*

Tower sat in his Plaza Hotel offices on 5th Avenue and 59th Street. He stared at his sister, Brenda.

"Who the fuck booked that FBI asshole, Conley?"

"Your chief of staff, just before he quit and went to work for that Wall Street hedge fund guy, Benjamin Jowett. You know, the guy who pioneered 'famine derivatives.'"

"Yeah, I know the guy. He's a big contributor. But I said before I was never to be in the same room alone with Conley. Those were standing orders. He creeps me out."

"Understood," Brenda said. "On the other hand, you wouldn't be president if it hadn't been for Conley and Putilov. In fact, you'd be locked up if it wasn't for Conley. That man risked life in prison without hope of parole to make you president. Conley committed treason for you."

"So?"

"Jim, he also used to run the FBI—before you fucking fired him. He knows everything you've done wrong in your life since the first time you cheated at jacks. If he turned on you, he could make trouble for you."

"Yeah," Tower said, "and Putie and I could make trouble for him—big trouble."

Brenda sighed deeply in frustration. "But why should you? Just admit it. You owe him. It wouldn't hurt you to throw him a bone and get him off your back. He helped you out of two very big messes."

"That was then, this is now. What is he doing for me *now?*"

"You can't *not* see him. He's one guy you can't afford to piss off. He has too much on you and let me repeat . . . *he used to run the FBI.*"

Tower stared at his sister a long hard minute. "Okay. Send the asshole in."

Brenda punched the intercom and said:

"Send former director Conley in."

The door swung open and Conley walked in.

"Glad to see you, Mr. President," Conley said.

"You too, Jonathan. Hope you didn't wait too long. My door is always open to you. *Mi casa, su casa.* You know that. Coffee, a beer, a real drink?"

"I'm fine, Mr. President."

"That's great, Jon. I am a little rushed though, as Brenda explained to you, so can we get right to it? You can speak in front of Brenda. I tell her everything."

"Mr. President, unfortunately we do have a few problems to sort out, and there's not a lot of time."

"Which is why you're here," Tower said. "Let's get it fixed. Anything you want."

"To be frank, promises were made to me—by you and our mutual friend."

"Mutual friend? Could you refresh my memory?"

"You and Mikhail promised me that if I helped you two out of your legal problems, you'd launch me on my political career. Hank Pierson is retiring from his Senate seat at the end of the year. I'm also from Texas, and you said you'd see the Texas governor appointed me to Pierson's Senate seat. You then said that—when you make your reelection bid in two years—you'd make me your running mate. I want on the ticket."

"Must be old age, Jon. My memory's pretty fuzzy anymore. I honestly don't recall that conversation. Anyway, that Texas governor, Bryan Bunson, has a mind of his own. I can't order him around like he was a little kid. As for the VP spot, the Republican Convention has to ratify that, and I'm under a lot of pressure to nominate a sitting, Southern governor, maybe Will Parsons from Mississippi."

"And I've got a small army of Democratic senators and that special prosecutor, Ben Miller, a former FBI director himself, pressuring me to testify against you and Putilov for rigging that last election. They want you imprisoned for treason, and they've offered me immunity in exchange for my turning state's evidence. Get the picture, Jim? Anything you don't understand?"

So there it was. Tower stared at Conley a long hard minute.

"Jon, you make an excellent point. Truth is I never liked that redneck, Ole Miss cocksucker, Parsons, and I always liked you. And as Brenda was just reminding me, Putilov and I owe you—big-time. You'd make a superlative Texas senator and a spectacular VP. Let me make a few phone calls. I promise I'll get on that right now. In the meantime, let Brenda walk you to the door. I am busy, but you have my word that I will make those phone calls before you leave this building."

Brenda rose and walked Conley to the door. When she returned, her brother was already on the phone.

"Mikhail, thank you so much for picking up.... Yes, this one is a Code Red Emergency. We have a serious problem with that moron Conley. He's threatening to testify against us at those Senate hearings looking into the last presidential election, including your involvement in it. You remember? The Democrats want to prove we committed voter fraud? I don't think we can bullshit Conley any longer. He's madder than a hornet.... Really? You have a man that you're sending to help us out with those other problems? You say he's got a very reliable female operative he could hand this assignment off to, and that he's in New York right now? And you say she's truly terrifying, that she even scares ... *you?* Wow! She must be frightening as hell! I'm personally afraid of her already ... Yes, I can delay Conley and keep him in New York for the night. Excellent—and thank you for moving so quickly on this problem. I knew I could depend on you. Mikhail, I can't thank you enough ... Yes, same to you. You take care as well. Farewell, old friend."

He looked up at his sister and smiled.

Oh no, Brenda thought. *Putilov's on board. Conley's in for it now.*

4

When McMahon came to, he was again belly-down on his rack. Glancing around the room, he saw a chain saw resting on a wooden chair over in the corner.

A wave of horror swept through him.

God no, not a chain saw!

Looking over his shoulder, he saw Raza was still in the short red dress and rowelled riding boots. She was rubbing some kind of medicated ointment on his butt, which he could now see. He was sorry he could. To his eternal horror, it was a dense labyrinth of crimson welts. Every square inch of his body hurt hideously, especially his rear end, but the cooling balm felt like heaven.

He almost sobbed with relief.

And tried not to look at the chain saw.

"Feel better?" Raza asked, sounding strangely sympathetic. "Marika really let you have it, didn't she? Was she retaliating for something you did to her in New York? What went on in that hotel room anyway? You didn't take advantage of my friend, did you?"

"Never."

"What did you two do then?"

"We blessed the Prophet, read his holy Koran and prayed for world peace."

"You did not corrupt her pristine innocence, did you?" Raza asked, smiling.

"Not unless counting prayer beads and repeating Allah's ninety-nine names over and over again constitutes corruption."

"I'll bet that's all you did," Raza said, clearly dubious but still smiling, still amused. She then returned to rubbing the soothing ointment into his tortured backside. "There, does that feel better, Mr. Danny 'Allah Has Ninety-Nine Names' McMahon?"

"I think I'm in love," McMahon said in a half whisper.

"You may be feeling many things," Raza said, "but love isn't one of them."

"A man stretched on a rack will say anything to get in our good graces," Marika said, entering the room.

"If not love, what do you think he's feeling?" Raza asked.

"Sadoerotic possession," Marika said.

"Agreed," Raza said. "Why should we believe anything you say, Mr. McMahon?"

"Because my word is backed by my full faith and credit," McMahon explained, nodding sincerely.

"Marika, I think Mr. McMahon was making a joke," Raza said. "Do you think Mr. McMahon is poking fun at us?"

"Yes," Marika said, "and guess what? We have a few jokes too. Let's see how he likes our brand of humor."

The chain saw was sitting on a straight-back corner chair. Marika picked it up, pulled the cord, and it came to life, wailing like a scalded cat. Marika then took the chain saw to the wooden chair, cutting it up into dozens of detonating fragments. She walked up to McMahon and stuck the screaming blade between McMahon's legs, less than a foot from his crotch, edging it closer, closer, her eyes locked on McMahon's the whole time, utterly oblivious to the screeching, yowling blade now barely a quarter inch from his genitals.

"Why are you doing this?" McMahon shouted, hysterical with terror.

"Because you're a narcissistic bastard," Raza explained, "who hates everything he doesn't understand, who's utterly ignorant of our world."

"Who's out of touch with life," Marika said.

"And who can't accept the natural order of things," Raza threw in.

"So we're here to teach you a lesson, to shake you up, to wake you up," Marika said, "and to show you the way things are."

McMahon's eyes had rolled back into his head until only the whites showed. He was mouthing mute prayers.

"But you won't listen," Raza said. "Instead you attack us and defame our faith, our culture, even though you know nothing about us."

"Do you know anything about our world?" Marika asked. "Do you have any idea what it means to be an Arab . . . *man?*"

Joke with them, Rashid had said. *Try to make them laugh . . . Don't show fear.*

"I heard it has something to do with schtupping goats?" McMahon asked in a trembling voice.

"Is that supposed to be funny?" Raza asked.

"Actually, yes."

However, when he met her gaze, Raza wasn't laughing. She was glaring at him, her eyes empty and expressionless, the unnerving stare of a malevolent Mona Lisa.

McMahon instinctively looked away. Unfortunately, he was looking at Tariq, who stood in the corner by the worktable. He had taken a break from torturing Rashid to spend some time in McMahon's torture chamber. Once again Tariq was sharpening his scalpel.

Marika was standing near him, so McMahon asked her in a low voice:

"What's Tariq's problem?" McMahon asked.

"Tariq suffers from a psychopathic-paranoid-schizoid personality disorder," Marika half whispered back, "compounded by visual and auditory hallucinations, aggravated by a severe necrophilic-castration complex."

"Can you give it to me without the scientific jargon?" McMahon asked.

"He's stone-fucking-crazy-violent-nuts," Marika said.

"He also hates me," McMahon said, nodding glumly.

"Oh, Tariq'll turn you into a prom queen, if we let him," Raza said.

"Suppose I did convert to Islam," McMahon said, starting to panic. "Sincerely, with all my heart?"

"Do you know anything about our faith?" Marika asked, astonished. "Do you have any idea what makes one a good Muslim?"

Try to make them laugh, Rashid had told him the night before. *Raza said she has your DVDs and thinks you're funny.*

"Eating fifty falafels?" McMahon asked.

"I say we turn him over to Tariq," Marika said, "so his genes won't be passed on to future generations."

"Outstanding," Raza said.

"Why are you doing this?" McMahon asked, his voice rising despite Rashid's admonitions not to show fear or panic. "Why do you hate me? Why do you hate Americans so much?"

"Where do we start?" Raza said, suddenly serious.

5

"I'm just a humble former FBI director," Conley said.

Conley was still in New York, and he was furious. He'd been forced to stay overnight and attend some stupid worthless "emergency meeting" that Tower had foisted upon him. Then the private government jet that Tower had put him on had developed mechanical problems, and now he'd been stuck in that damn plane on the tarmac for five straight hours. Sitting in a bolted-down stuffed chair at a worktable in the main cabin, he'd been staring into a computer screen and answering bullshit emails for over three hours. He was now in a blind rage. He'd not only gotten the runaround from the asshole Tower and his drunken chain-smoking closet-dyke sister, he was now held up on the runway like he was flying commercial.

Like he was a fucking *citizen*.

He'd never had a private government jet held up for this long. This was unacceptable. He was the Former Director of the Fucking FBI. He felt like arresting that cretin of a captain and clapping his ass in Guantanamo just for pissing him off.

"Captain," Conley roared once again at the cockpit. "What the fuck is the holdup? Did the engine fall out of the plane?"

"No sir," the uniformed captain said, hurryng back to Conley's cabin. "I'm so sorry, but we have no flight attendants. Both of them are down with the stomach flu, and we can't fly without at least one. It's against FTC regulations."

"There's a lot of flu going around," Conley admitted grudgingly. "My stomach doesn't feel so well either. But goddamn it, can't you at least—"

Suddenly, a tall statuesque flight attendant opened the ramp-hatch and entered the plane. She had indigo eyes, her hair was long and lush—so incredibly light it looked almost platinum—and she had a smile like the end of the rainbow. Decked out in a short blue skirt, black high heels and black stockings, and with the top three buttons of her white blouse enticingly undone, she was showing enough cleavage and leg to take Conley's breath away.

But now she was strolling straight into his cabin, staring at him as if she owned him, as if she owned the whole plane, coming at him, her eyes un-wavering, unblinking, locked on him the whole time.

"I heard you say what you said about your stomach, Director Conley," she said. "Let me get you something for it."

She had a slight accent, which he couldn't place, and the name on her flight badge was Helena. He thought she might be Estonian.

"Scandinavian?" Conley asked.

"Further east."

"Finland?"

"Further."

"Russia?"

"St. Petersburg originally. But I'm American now through and through."

Conley gave her his best smile.

"We've been having some dealings with Putilov lately," Conley said, try-ing to sound serious, important. "Since you're Russian, you must have an opinion of him."

"He's a great man," she said simply.

"He and I are friends, you know," Conley said, smiling now, "close friends."

"Then you must be a very important man," she said.

"I'm just a humble former FBI director," Conley said.

"Which means you're someone very important, and I love big powerful important men. I find them so . . . *stimulating.*"

"Perhaps you could instruct me on how the Russian people view their leader."

"And I'm sure I could learn so, so much from you."

"Well I'm glad you two are hitting it off," said the captain, returning from the cockpit. "Even better, Helena has rounded out the crew and we're cleared for takeoff."

"Great news," Helena said. "Let's drink to it. Not you, Captain. You have to fly. But our friend, the director, could use a drink. He's been under so much stress with this endless wait. Mr. Director, you must have gotten tense, sitting on this runway. Maybe I could get you some good Russian vodka and untense you a little."

"I'll bet you could," Conley said, his voice growing thick.

"I can, and I will. But first a little drink. I have some orange-flavored vodka you'll never forget—Russian vodka." She rolled the *R* and pronounced the *v* as if it were a *w*. "I'll add a splash of OJ for good measure. When you finish that, maybe we can go into the rear cabin, get comfortable and have a nice private undisturbed conversation."

"I'd love nothing more."

"You would not know it but I've traveled widely. In my own way, I'm a real female Odysseus. I'll tell you the story of my travels."

"I can't wait," Conley said.

"I'll make you feel like you're traveling with me. I will make you experience every inch of my journeys."

"Any place special you want to take me?"

"Oh, I'm going to take you all the way . . . *around the world*. I will show you . . . *everything*."

Conley felt so hot he feared he might faint.

"But first let me get you that drink."

Turning, she walked over to the galley, swinging her ass like it was a diamond mine.

6

A second brief glimpse of Fahad's eyes expunged forever any further curiosity Haddad might have had about Fahad's assignment or the packages in the trunk. He contemplated instead hitting the road in search of another city and another job. But he was too afraid.

Fahad pulled up in front of U.S. Industrial Supplies, Inc., a massive warehouse of a building that sold heavy equipment to plants and factories. He walked up to Greg Mendes, the young fresh-faced cashier wearing dark gray coveralls. In his front pocket was a plastic holder filled with pens, Sharpies, pencils, scissors, a ruler and two box cutters. Next to it was pinned a black plastic employee ID that read U.S. INDUSTRIAL SUPPLIES, INC. and the name GREG. ASSIST. MANAGER.

It took Greg several seconds to recover from the shock of seeing a rather dark-skinned man, dressed in maybe $40,000 worth of clothes and jewelry, buying heavy-duty industrial supplies. Usually people came to Industrial Supplies looking like they just stepped out of a construction site or out of a steel mill.

"How can I help you, sir?" he finally asked.

"Greg," Fahad said, mustering a smile and as much good cheer as he knew how. "I need four fifty-five-gallon drums, a cold chisel, an extra-large plastic floor tarp, a heavy denim shirt and size twelve work boots. Throw in a pair of large gray coveralls like the pair you're wearing. A gray baseball-style work cap as well."

"Don't you want to pick the clothing out yourself, sir? Try some of that stuff on?"

"I trust your judgement," Fahad said. "Also they're for a friend, not me. Just tell me the amount."

The assistant manager did some calculations.

"Sir," Greg said, "it comes to $1,823.66."

Fahad removed an extra-large money clip containing a two-inch stack of $100 bills. He handed Greg twenty of them.

"Pickup or delivery?" Greg asked.

Fahad wrote out an address.

"I need them delivered at exactly 6:00 P.M. this Thursday. It's paramount they arrive precisely at 6:00. I'll have a $200 bonus for each man on the truck if they deliver it on time."

"Precisely 6:00?"

"Give or take fifteen minutes," Fahad said, struggling to produce a smile.

"Hell," Greg said, returning Fahad's fake grin, "for that kind of bonus, I'll deliver them myself."

"Then it's a $400 bonus. And I'm donating the change to the charity of your choice."

Greg quickly pocketed the change.

Fahad went back to the Lincoln Town Car and climbed into the backseat.

"Next stop," he said to Haddad, "is the nearest Home Depot."

Haddad went online and found one ten minutes away.

"What are you looking for?" Haddad asked, looking at Fahad in the rear-view mirror.

"Do you really want to know?"

"No sir," Haddad said quickly. "I don't know what we're doing, and you're right. I'm sorry I asked—very sorry."

"You weren't thinking, were you?" Fahad said.

"No sir," Haddad said. "I wasn't, but I won't make that mistake again. I'll stay focused. You can count on me."

Haddad turned around to look at Fahad when he said those words, and he was immediately sorry he had. One look at Fahad's eyes, and Haddad prayed to Allah to forgive him for opening his mouth.

Haddad quickly drove Fahad to a nearby Home Depot. Getting out, Fahad entered the store. An hour later Fahad walked out with a shopping cart filled with brown anonymous-looking mailing boxes. Haddad opened his door and got out to help.

"Stay behind the wheel and pop the trunk," Fahad said.

Haddad climbed back behind the wheel, and the trunk opened. Fahad filled it with the three brown boxes.

Fahad climbed into the backseat.

"Ready, sir?" Haddad asked.

"Take me to the machine shop," Fahad said.

Once more, Haddad sneaked a glance at Fahad. A second brief glimpse of Fahad's eyes expunged forever any further curiosity Haddad might have had about Fahad's assignment or the packages in the trunk. He contemplated instead hitting the road in search of another city and another job. But he was too afraid.

He knew in his soul he could never disobey the man in the backseat.

7

When Conley came to, he was on his stomach, hands bound behind his back and his mouth stuffed full of some foul-tasting gag. All the lights were out and the compartment was pitch-dark.

What the fuck had happened? Where was he?

Slowly it all came back to him . . .

He recalled taking the gorgeous Russian flight attendant back into the Executive Boudoir of his private jet. They had been sitting on the edge of the bed, Helena giving him a slow, erotic thigh-and-neck massage, interspersed with long, languid, sinfully sensual soul kisses.

In two seconds, she'd gotten him hornier than he'd ever been in his entire life.

He'd briefly felt a twinge or two of remorse—after all, he was a believing Christian, a married man and had eight children—but, strangely enough, he didn't feel all that guilty. The eight Screwdrivers Helena had pumped into him, the lurid massage, the libidinous kisses and the lascivious lap dances had sent his lust soaring somewhere north of Polaris, dispelling any doubts or hesitations as if they were dust in the wind.

His universe consisted of one thing and one thing only—the beautiful Russian woman gyrating her ass on his crotch and exploring his esophagus with her tongue.

And then suddenly, inexplicably his whole world had gone black.

Damn, he wished he could see something. He was trussed up so tight he couldn't move a muscle, and the bitch had not only stuffed his mouth with an excrement-reeking, piss-stinking rag, she'd shoved it halfway down his throat. He could barely breathe, let alone grunt.

Still he managed to squirm and emit a weak, mouse-like squeak, which apparently got someone's attention. He sensed another person getting up and approaching him.

"So you're awake now, right?"

He sensed Helena's vague form hovering over his bed.

"Hope the gag isn't too unpleasant, Director Conley. I didn't have much to work with and had to improvise."

All Conley could do was squirm helplessly.

"The only items I had at my disposal were your seriously soiled underwear and your foul-smelling socks. Really, Director Conley, doesn't anyone wash your clothes? You used to run the FBI. Good help can't be that hard to find, but we made do with what we had. It all worked out in the end."

Conley struggled unsuccessfully to force out a sound.

"In any event, I hope you enjoyed your Screwdrivers. Tasty beverages, weren't they? Of course, I added a little extra spice to yours. Comes from an only recently discovered flower found only in the Brazilian rain forest. One of our scientists discovered it down there. Wow, that extract we distilled from it is mean! That stuff does major-league damage to a person's insides. I can't tell you how excited President Putilov was when the man first told him about it. I heard he jumped up and down with excitement. In fact, our president immediately sent a small army of botanists down there to harvest the entire crop. Isn't that exciting?"

Suddenly, Conley felt an ominous cramping in the pit of his stomach.

Helena divined his discomfort.

"It's reaching your small intestines about now, isn't it? Right on time. You are feeling its effects, correct?"

Shit, he was. In fact, his duodenum was not only burning up, the flames were blazing a southern path, spreading lower, lower, hotter, hotter, more and more horrific, every inch of his digestive tract blazing with agony.

"And guess what, Director Conley, you're our first subject—other than a few experimental chimpanzees, that is. I saw the footage of those creatures' last few hours. God, those little simians suffered. They went through hell on earth, and you know the most amazing part of their ordeal?"

She had to put a hand over her mouth to muffle her giggles.

The former FBI director twisted and writhed in stone horror but could not force out a sound. Hysterical with panic, he shook helplessly from side to side.

What the fuck is happening! he muttered noiselessly to himself. *I thought Tower and Putilov were my friends. I made Tower president. Those two promised to make me a senator. They were going to make me Tower's VP. We had a deal! Promises were made!*

But now a flood of almost indescribable agony was tsunami-ing through his entrails like they were Fukushima at full flood. He could feel his eyes bulging and walling wildly, rolling back into his head, swelling with terror and rage until he feared they'd pop out of their sockets. It felt as if that big beautiful blond-haired blue-eyed Russian bitch had inundated his abdomen with molten lead instead of Screwdrivers. He wanted to scream, but Helena had shoved his dirty, stinking shorts and putrid socks so deep down his throat he could barely inhale, let alone roar.

And then, suddenly, he sensed Helena hovering over him and felt her remove the blindfold, the bright lights temporarily blinding him. Then he could smell her vodka breath and hear her soft clucking chuckles. His vision began to clear, and he could make out her face.

The slut was . . . *smiling.*

Aaaarrrgggggghhhhh! the former director soundlessly sobbed.

"So make yourself comfortable. I told the captain that you were meeting your wife and kids in Florida and that President Tower was putting you up at that big resort hotel of his on Isle Morado, so kick back. You're in for a really great trip—the flight of a lifetime."

Now Conley was uncontrollably hysterical. His back was arching hard enough to snap his spine, and his lips had pulled back in a feral snarl so terrifyingly taut that only the gag, teeth and gums showed, and all the while, Helena's chortling laughter burbled in his ears, and her scintillating smile glittered merrily in his tear-filled eyes.

"Look at it this way, Mr. Director: You wanted to run with the big dogs? Well guess what? Big dogs bite."

Then she was leaning over him, kissing his cheek, her treacherous tongue darting in and out of his ear, her breath rasping hoarsely.

Shit, the bitch was aroused.

"Think of it as a little like sexual assault, Mr. Director," she said, her breath heaving with depraved desire, kissing his neck and rubbing up against him. "Remember what macho boys like you, Putilov and Tower are always saying about forcible rape? When it's inevitable, just lay back and *enjoy the fuck out of it.*"

Suddenly she was on him, grinding her crotch against him, up and down, up and down, so close and clinging it felt as if she were him, and he were her. Then the only thing in his whole world were her groans, moans and her violently voluptuous orgasms.

Then she was gone, and he was lost and alone with only the firestorm below and the despair in his soul, racking his brain and inflaming his pain.

8

"This op would scare Hunter S. Thompson sober," Elena said, "clean and sober."

By the time, Elena and Adara had returned to the upstairs room, their friends were back at the table. They were drinking and talking—mostly about movies, soccer and women. The brawl hadn't been that interesting.

When the nine men reached the balcony rail, they saw five men below, dressed like themselves in jeans, T-shirts, sweatshirts, and work boots. They surrounded a man who lay prone on the floor. Red-faced with rage, the five men were kicking him half to death. The two women approached them from behind, one on each side of the group. Slipping saps out of their hip bags, each of the women walked up behind the five men and began rapping each of them carefully and precisely across their temples. They swung the saps—spring-loaded and weighted with double-0 buckshot—in quick wrist-flicking arcs, the snapping of the springs adding extra torque to their blows. Forehand, backhand, forehand, backhand, they hammered the men's heads as if they were banging speed bags, boxer-style. Instead, however, of hitting the men's temples with the back and front knuckles of a single fist, as boxers do when they work the bags, these women used the back and front of the weighted sap.

Before the men's knees could buckle, they were out cold on their feet, dropping where they stood like puppets unstrung. In less than eight seconds the violence was over, the five gang-stompers spread-eagled on the floor.

The two women helped the bloody, gang-stomped man to his feet and half walked, half dragged him over to seat at a nearby table. A waiter and cook took him back to the kitchen, where they could look after him and call an ambulance.

The two women sat down with their friends.

"Okay, but I only work with professionals," Stevie said.

"Who can hold their mud," Jonesy said, "and keep their shit."

"You think Adara, Jamie and I would be in this if it wasn't completely righteous?" Elena asked.

"We're going in with sixteen men in all," Jamie said.

"Who are the other players?" Andre asked.

Jamie rattled off eight more names.

"We saw them already," Elena said.

"That's a hell of a crew," Stevie said.

"When they found out who we were springing from that Pakistani hell-hole," Adara said, "they were in."

"Who is it?" Stevie asked.

"We didn't want to tell anyone until they were in," Elena said.

"It's Rashid al-Rahman," Adara said.

The men were silent a long moment.

"Why the fuck didn't you say so?" Stevie finally said. "Yeah, I'm in."

"*D'accord,*" Andre said. Of course.

"If the roles were reversed," Leon said, "he'd be there for us."

"He got me out of more shit than I care to remember," Jonesy said.

"Hell, yeah," Henry said.

"Just tell us the plan," Andre said.

"We come in in two Black Hawks," Adara said, "grab the guy and leave on one or both of the choppers."

"So one chopper's for backup?" Andre asked.

"In case we lose the other," Elena said.

"But what's the plan?" Stevie asked.

"That's it," Adara said. "We've all done extractions before."

"Shouldn't we have a rehearsal of some sort?" Leon asked.

"And leave it on the practice field?" Adara said.

"Or in the gym?" Elena said. "In the locker room?"

"So that be . . . *the plan?*" Jonesy asked.

"Uh huh," Elena said.

"So you got no plan," Leon said.

"Sure we do," Adara said. "We attack, kill, disrupt, improvise."

"We charge into that compound like Teddy Roosevelt at San Juan Hill," Elena said.

"That ain't a plan," Stevie said.

"It's some kind of horrible . . . *spasm,*" Leon said.

"That is embarrassingly true," Elena said.

Adara placed her leather shoulder bag on the table. She opened the flap and took out a manila envelope with folders in it. They were high-def aerial shots of what appeared to be a whitewashed blockhouse on the edge of a hill in the Pakistani desert.

"There's a TTP base maybe 250 meters due south," Elena said. "Otherwise the safe house is in the middle of nowhere."

"We chopper in from behind the hill," Adara said, "so we won't be visible to the base."

"We hit the safe house from behind the hill in the dead of night," Elena said. "We grab our target so fast and we're out of there so quickly they won't have time to react or call in for reinforcements."

"They'll never know what hit them," Adara said.

"You aren't serious, are you?" Andre asked.

"It worked in *Zero Dark Thirty,* didn't it?" Adara said.

"And *Rambo,*" Elena said.

"You left out *Apocalypse Now,*" Leon said.

"That too," Jamie said.

The eight men stared at the two women, silent.

"All feeling for Rashid aside," Stevie finally asked, "what's our end?"

"Besides the satisfaction of a job well done?" Adara asked.

No one laughed. The men's stares were hard enough to cut diamonds.

Jamie wrote a number.

"For real?" Jonesy asked.

"Half up front when you reach the chopper," Elena said.

"We'll put the second half straight into your numbered accounts after we lift off," Jamie said.

The men stared at them and slowly began to nod.

"Like it?" Adara asked.

"Love it," Stevie said.

"We go in strapped?" Leon asked.

"To the fuckin' nines," Adara said.

"Un'nerstan," Henry said, "Rashid or no Rashid, I gotta git paid."

"We said we got a bank," Elena said.

"Kind of bread you're promising," Henry said, "it better be Goldman Sachs."

Henry had come in late. He didn't know.

"I got it covered," Jamie said.

Henry emitted a soft, low whistle. "It be Goldman Sachs *and* J. P."

"Understood," Elena said. "We're all taking a risk."

"For sure," Leon said. "It's Pakistan."

"On the other hand," Elena said, smiling, "as someone once said, 'All of life is always six to five against.'"

They all nodded, silent.

"So you finally admit this is really dangerous?" Andre asked.

"This op would scare Hunter S. Thompson sober, "Elena said, "clean and sober."

"What are the odds of us actually succeeding?" Stevie asked.

"You want to live forever?" Elena asked.

"Fuck the odds," Leon said. "If I was afraid of chances, I'd have been an accountant."

"Fuck 'em all but six," Stevie said, "and save them for pallbearers. I wouldn't have it any other way,"

"Then let's burn this bitch down," Jonesy said, grinning.

"But we can't fuck this up," Stevie said, serious. "It's Rashid."

"Only the dead never fuck up," Leon said with a shrug.

"So we're righteous?" Elena asked.

"We're solid," Jonesy said.

"You couldn't find Johnny D. for this one?" Henry asked.

"You can find him at the Resurrection," Elena said.

"He got hisself aced?" Henry asked.

"Deader'n Elvis," Adara said.

"Deader'n a Kentucky Fried Rat," Elena confirmed.

"The poor *bebe*," Andre said.

"Just make sure," Adara said, "we don't join him."

"So we go in dark?" Jonesy asked.

"Like we were black holes," Adara said.

"Of course we go in dark," Elena said. "We're going in by fucking Black Hawk."

PART X

Well maybe you can't kill all your critics, but Litvinenko sure as hell won't bother you anymore. Neither will Anna Politkovskaya or Marina Salye. You killed those three deader than Dostoevsky's yaytsas [testicles].

—President Mikhail Putilov, looking back on enemies he'd had murdered

1

D o you really want to know why we hate Americans so much?" Raza asked McMahon, repeating his question.

McMahon, still belly-down on his rack, looked at Raza over his shoulder.

"Yes, I do," McMahon said. "We've had conflicts with other nations but afterward everyone gets over it. We all but obliterated Germany and Japan in World War II. We did the same to Vietnam as well, but now all those nations and the U.S. are best of friends. Their people love America. Not the countries in your region though. We've done relatively little harm to nations like Saudi Arabia, Egypt and Pakistan, yet everyone there hates us and would nuke us off the face of the earth, given the chance. Why?"

"Because deep down inside, what our people truly despise about you," Raza said, "is your devotion to science, your dedication to education and industry. Unfortunately, those things that we deem heretical are the very things that make you stronger and more advanced than us,"

"I don't understand," McMahon asked.

"You honor scientific advancement and intellectual achievement," Raza said. "We view those activities as Satanic, as overreaching the One True God. Yet those endeavors have also produced a military machine that dwarfs ours and reduces our attempts at self-defense to absurdity."

"What do you honor then," McMahon asked, "besides Allah and the Koran?"

"We honor the respect our men and women show one another," Marika said.

"The respect your women show to your men," McMahon said, "translates in our culture as slavish obedience."

"Since our men protect us," Marika explained, "we are obliged to show them our gratitude."

"But are you are obliged to let them tyrannize you?" McMahon asked. "To force you to suffer in chadors and chains?"

"Mr. McMahon," Marika said, "it is the way things are in our world. We don't expect you to understand."

"I understand your code of honor—your *ird,* your men call it," McMahon said, "but it holds women back. Your ird will keep you forever in the Dark Ages. No society that keeps its women—fifty percent of its assets, half its human capital—in bondage can compete in the world today, especially in this new digitized industrialized hyperscientific age."

"Mr. McMahon," Raza said, "you have it exactly right. But the world you have created and have attempted to force on our people is one of corruption and licentiousness, which is why our world can never accept yours."

"To do so," Marika said, "would offend our *ird,* which you so ignorantly disparage."

"And to adapt to your ways would be to blaspheme Allah," Raza said.

"But what about accepting modest reforms," McMahon said, "which would radically improve the lives of your people?"

"Mr. McMahon," Raza said, "there can be no truce with radical evil and no compromise with your hellish creed. Your country wages war not merely on us, but on life itself. We live in the Holocene, otherwise known as the Sixth Major Extinction Event, to which your country is the number one contributor and creator."

"Your own biologists estimate that by the end of the century," Marika said, "your digitized, industrialized world—through environmental degradation, through your poisoning of our atmosphere and waterways, by heating the planet to infernal levels—will extinguish half the species on land and in the sea."

"You created nuclear bombs and every kind of delivery system imaginable," Raza said, "then mass-manufactured them by the tens of thousands and retailed them promiscuously—not only to ourselves but to our most implacable enemies. You even proliferated the nuclear technology to those same nations so they could manufacture these superweapons themselves."

"And then you express dismay," Marika said, "when nations such as Pakistan, India and North Korea utilize that technology in order to master the black arts of nuclear annihilation, which you created and gave us."

"I cannot defend America's nuclear proliferating," McMahon said, "but nothing that America has done justifies your attacks on us—your suicide bombings and your own pursuit of terrorist nukes."

"Were that only true," Raza said, "but you created and proliferated the Arms of Armageddon. You threaten, intimidate and destabilize our Muslim brothers and sisters throughout Dar al-Islam with them. You invade

Iraq and Afghanistan, throwing half of the Mideast into anarchy, exile and civil war. We cannot attack you at home and do to you as you have done to us, because we fear your nuclear wrath. Therefore, we have no choice but to develop nuclear weapons of our own in hopes of deterring your future attacks. Then we can requite your violence against us with a true quid pro quo."

"Eye for an eye leaves both combatants blind," McMahon said.

"Yes, but it is also the way of our world—and yours. We all recognize only one unbreachable mandate—lex talionis, the Law of Retaliation. That is our sacred inviolable code of honor—the only commandment governing all people's lives—blood for blood, a life for a life."

"Is that also how your society justifies its barbaric abuse of women as well as its war against the infidel?" McMahon asked. "Lex talionis?"

"But of course," Marika said. "Throughout history, our men have feared that a woman's licentious nature inevitably compels her to resist her master's stern command. That our men gratuitously persecute their women for this alleged weakness is wrong, but that is the way things are. Our men avenge themselves on any and all people who do not bend to their will, be they women or infidels. Blood will have blood, and only blood vengeance can sate the rage of men. The strong rule, the weak obey—or suffer their wrath—and that is life. Our faith demands it, and to pretend otherwise is to deceive ourselves and to go against the natural order of things."

"So compassion has no place in your world?" McMahon asked.

"Of course, compassion has its place," Raza said, "but not in your sense of the word."

"To us," Marika said, "compassion does not mean feeling kindly toward one another. It means two souls sharing the same pain. It means literally 'to agonize with.'"

"And that is how you justify torture?" McMahon asked.

"Bravo, Mr. McMahon," Raza said. "You are finally starting to understand us. Yes, we are teaching you compassion."

"Think how compassionate you will be in the future," Marika said. "Henceforth, when you see people suffer, you will feel their pain, know their sense of hopelessness and you will care. We will have taught you to 'agonize' with them, and one day, if you survive this long dark night of your hideously sinful soul, you will see us as your mentors and your gurus. You will view us in a kinder, gentler light."

"I will see you as kinder, gentler psychopaths," McMahon muttered through gritted teeth, staring up at them from his rack.

"Perhaps," Marika said, "but you will also understand, at last, the natural order of things, the way the world really works."

"And I am so proud," Raza said, "that Marika and I could serve as your spirit guides."

2

"The phrase means 'Death-by-Fire' in your language," Putilov said. "It means I put a blowtorch to Conley's innards."

Russian President Mikhail Ivanovich Putilov had just gotten the autopsy report on that ex-FBI jerk, Jonathan Conley. His new poison had put that asshole through the tortures of the damned. Putilov was so pumped up he had to share his excitement with someone who would understand. For the first time in his life he felt the need to call Tower.

Tower was so shocked to get an unsolicited call from Putilov, he picked up immediately—even though it was the middle of the night in New York.

"You have to hear this," Putilov said. "For two decades I've sent my people all over hell's creation, researching the most obscure, most painful poisons on earth. I've had them comb the planet—from the frozen mountains of Tierra del Fuego to Uganda's sweltering jungles, from the Pacific Ring of Fire to the darkest depths of Chile's most noxious guano pits. I've had them tracking poisons for decades, and guess what? They've found a toxin down along Brazil's Rio Negro has to be the most diabolically depraved substance anyone's ever heard of."

"The Rio what—?" Tower asked, confused.

It was 3:37 A.M. Eastern Time in the States, he was half-asleep, and he had no idea what Putilov was talking about.

"We've extracted a hideously horrifying toxin from a deadly flower one of our botanists discovered in the Amazonian rain forest. It's an exceedingly rare blossom—found only on small, isolated, floating islands on the Rio Negro and—"

"No one calls black people 'negroes' anymore," Tower pointed out, yawning.

"Not negroes," Putilov shouted, incensed at the man's stupidity. "*Rio* means 'river' in Spanish. *Negro* means 'black.' It's a South American waterway called the Rio Negro—the River Negro. Get it?"

"Oh, I get it," Tower said quietly, still finding it hard to focus.

"This flower grows only on these floating islands on the Lower Rio Negro, a blackwater tributary to the Amazon, coursing through the heart of the Brazilian rain forest. The plant's extract incites the most agonizing death throes of any of my poisons yet. And best of all, no one will know what killed that asshole Conley."

"That's what you killed Conley with?" Now Tower was awake.

"Hell, yes," Putilov said. "We tested it on apes first, and they yiped and convulsed for hours on end like their insides were being incinerated. But even weirder was its etiology: We couldn't find any. No one could identify the cause of death. The apes' autopsy reports listed cause of death as nonidiopathic."

"Nonidiopathic?" Tower asked, repeating the word, confused.

"Don't you get it?" Putilov shouted. "I can kill anyone I want, and no one will know how I did it!"

"That's amazing," Tower said. "How did you say this poison works?"

"Didn't you read Conley's autopsy report?"

"No."

"Okay. Here, I'll show you. I just sent an email. Open the attachment."

Tower's bedroom laptop was at his desk and still on, so he got out of bed, crossed the room and went into his inbox. Clicking on Putilov's email, he opened the attachment. It read:

> GROSS ANATOMY: *The abdomen was markedly distended and contained feces, gas and approximately one liter of congealed blood. There was edema of both the small and large intestines obscuring the normal anatomic boundaries. The entire colon from the ileocecal valve to the anorectal junction appeared homogeneously black indicating intramural hemorrhage. A single large perforation was identified in the sigmoid colon that was associated with frank hemorrhage and extravasation of fecal material into the abdominal cavity. The lumen of the colon contained feces and approximately one liter of congealed blood. The greater and lesser omenta were edematous with patchy areas of hemorrhage, and the mesenteric lymph nodes were atrophic.*
>
> MICROSCOPIC ANATOMY: *Sections of multiple regions of both the small and large bowel were cut with a microtome, stained with hematoxylin and eosin and examined at both 10X and 100X magnification. There was complete effacement of the villi, denuding of the mucosa and transmural thickening (approximately 2-fold normal) in both the small intestine and colon. There was marked mucosal edema in the small bowel, and transmural hemorrhagic necrosis of the colon. The intima and adventitia of both the small*

and large bowel were diffusely infiltrated with inflammatory cells that appeared to be mostly neutrophils, macrophages and natural killer cells. Pneumatosis cystoides intestinalis was present in the sigmoid colon most prominently at the site of perforation. The greater and lesser omenta were diffusely inflamed and contained aggregates of acute inflammatory cells.

    IMPRESSION: *major blowout in the sigmoid colon due to toxin-induced hemorrhagic necrosis.*

"Sounds pretty bad," Tower had to admit. "What's all that jargon mean?"

"It means I fried the inside of Conley's intestines like they were kolbasa and eggs—for five straight hours," Putilov roared. "That autopsy means Conley died a thousand deaths!"

"Jesus," Tower muttered under his breath, clearly stunned.

"I thought you'd be pleased," Putilov said.

"I am," Tower said nervously. "It's just a little late here in the Big Apple. I'm still kind of groggy."

"Understood. I just wanted to share the good news with someone who'd appreciate it."

"And I do," Tower said. "Does this poison have a name?"

"Of course," Putilov said. "I named the toxin myself. I call it *Cмeptb-Ha-Koctpe.*"

"I don't speak Russian," Tower said.

"The phrase means 'Death-by-Fire' in your language," Putilov said. "It means I put a blowtorch to Conley's innards."

"That certainly sounds . . . intense," Tower said, not knowing what to say.

"People better take notice," Putilov said. "From now on, anyone who wants to fuck with Mikhail Ivanovich Putilov ought to think about what happened to Nemerov, Kazankov and Conley. They ought to think long and hard."

"I certainly would," Tower said with surprising sincerity.

Then Putilov's laughter brayed mule-like in Tower's ears until finally the Russian leader put down the phone.

Frozen in his chair, Tower stared at the autopsy report on his computer screen, aghast at the sheer horror and the unspeakable sadism of Putilov's revenge.

At the same time he couldn't help but be impressed. No one could doubt that Putilov was effective and knew what he was doing. In fact, Tower had a couple of people he'd like to settle up with, and Putilov was a dyed-in-the-wool expert on settling scores.

He wondered if Putilov would loan him a couple of vials of that poison.

3

"We can't ever understand. We just tourists."
—An anonymous merc

Elena sat in the first Black Hawk with eight of the men. They were on a Pakistani helipad outside of Peshawar.

Karim climbed into the chopper. He hadn't been in Belfast at the bar, but he was here now. He was dressed in black fatigues like the rest of them. He wore the white cap of a man who'd done the Mecca hajj and gazed on the Kaaba, the Black Rock, the holy of holies. He took it off, stuffed it into a cargo pocket on his right leg, pulled a black watch cap out of another cargo pocket and put it on his head. He sat down on one of the jump seats. He would serve as their translator if they needed one.

His white cap bothered Elena. They did not need someone who'd just found Allah.

"Glad you could make it," Elena said, "but you understand what we're doing?"

"An extraction," Karim said.

"And we may have to kill some people," Elena said, "getting Rashid out."

"What's your question?" Karim asked.

"Well," Elena said, "does Allah countenance the killing of Muslims?"

"If they're apostate motherfuckers he sure do," Jonesy said.

"That how you feel?" Elena asked Karim, ignoring Jonesy.

He nodded his agreement.

"So you can accept Muslim blood on your hands?" Elena said.

"Better than my blood on theirs," Karim said.

He buckled himself into the Black Hawk.

"Everyone's there?" Elena said into her wrist mike to Adara, who was with the men in the other Black Hawk.

"*Roger that,*" Adara answered in her earpiece from the other chopper.

"Then let's rock on out of here," Elena said.

The rotor turned, and her chopper lifted off. Despite the helicopter's deafening roar, Elena could hear the men talking around her. Only bits and pieces of the conversation came through, but still she listened to them absently, not really thinking or paying attention, not even trying to identify the speakers.

"*What a sorry bunch of assholes.*"

"*Sorry you signed on?*"

"*Sorry I ever heard about it.*"

"*Where's Johnny D.?*"

"*Choir practice?*"

"*Maybe he lost his way to the can.*"

"*Is Leon on board?*"

"*Sir, yes, sir!*"

"*We could all be killed.*"

"*Then I'll see your ass in hell.*"

"Humdililah." *Praise be to God.* Elena recognized Karim's voice.

"*What's that?*"

"*A prayer for the dying,*" someone said.

"*Have you made your peace with darkness?*"

"*Made my peace with your pussy ass.*" Sounded like Jonesy but she wasn't sure with the rotor.

"*I'm just twistin' the dials on you, sucka.*"

"*Twist this, bitch.*"

"*That's what I tell yo' mama when she suckin' my dick.*"

"*Why do they do this shit anyway?*"

"*You can't explain it. You gotta live it.*"

"*I don't wanna know why they did it, and I sure as shit don't wanna live it. I only wanna know why they do it now.*"

"*We can't ever understand. We just tourists.*"

"*You trip that shit?*"

"*High and hard.*"

"*How's it hangin', homes?*"

"*Bangin' hard, rollin' heavy, still beatin' the clock.*"

"*Ain't a wrong thang to put on your scorecard.*"

"*Just rattlin' the bars on your baboon cage.*"

"*I be sincere in my disinterest.*"

"*I'll be. A gen-u-wine swinging dick.*"

"*What did happen to Johnny D. anyway?*"

"*Got caught in the headlights.*"

"*Then there it is.*"

"*There it is, sports fans. There it is indeed.*"

The two Black Hawks roared through the night.

4

─────────

"How can the jihad end? To reach an end is to make a beginning."

—Fahad al-Qadi

Haddad was parked in the van in front of the machine shop when Fahad and the two machinists walked out of the shop and up to his car wearing dirty greasy coveralls and work boots. Both the machinists were clean, closely shaven and had their hair colored a light brown. Still Haddad knew they were from the Mideast.

He got out and opened a back door for Fahad, but when the two men walked to the car, Fahad didn't bother to get out. He talked to the men through the open window.

"With a little luck, I should see you two back here in four days." Fahad said. "You on top of everything?"

"We got it, boss," the taller of the two men, Mukhtar, said.

"See that the dual-beam laser welder is ready to go. We'll put the final touches on it Wednesday night."

"It's been a long time coming," Ramzi, the shorter one, said. "Do you think this could be the blow that rids our land of the Infidel forever?"

"The hard truth is," Fahad said, "the jihad never ends—not until the Final Day when Allah calls us all home. This attack will make a difference though, a major difference."

"But it won't end the Infidel Crusade?" Mukhtar asked Fahad.

"Perhaps not, but it may well mark the beginning of *our* New Crusade."

"Then the struggle never ends?" Ramzi asked.

"How can the jihad end?" Fahad explained. "To reach an end is to make a beginning."

"Then why do we do it?" Mukhtar asked.

"Because it is Allah's will and our way," Fahad said.

"Until Allah calls us home?" Ramzi asked.

"Until Allah calls us home," Fahad said.

"*La illahah illalah*," Mukhtar said. *Let us renew our faith in Allah.*

"*Bsimillah*," Ramzi said. *In the name of Allah.*

"Just remember," Fahad said, "when I come back, it'll be an all-night job. So get some sleep."

"I doubt that we can," Mukhtar said. "We've waited so long."

"This is so wonderful, my friend," Ramzi said, his eyes actually tearing over. "It's like a dream. I can't believe it's finally real."

"Oh, it's real," Fahad said, offering them a small dreamy smile.

"Thank you so much for letting us help," Mukhtar said.

"*Jazak Allahu khair,*" Fahad said. *May Allah reward you for your kind words.*

"*Fi Amanullah,*" Ramzi said. *May Allah protect you on your journey.*

Fahad climbed into the backseat.

"Where to?" Haddad asked.

"To the city," Fahad said.

Then to hell, Haddad thought to himself, almost shaking with fear and dread. Then another thought hit him, an injunction: *Don't do it. Drop Fahad off, then drive like a maniac as far from this nightmare horror show as your money will take you.*

But he couldn't. He wouldn't. One look at Fahad's eyes, and he could see that the man read his mind, his fear. Haddad also knew he could never run far enough or fast enough to escape Fahad's wrath.

He would have to carry this one out to the bitter end.

5

Putilov's hands shook as he hurled the phone at its rack. It bounced off its cradle and hit the floor with a resounding, rattling crash.

Tower had just been whining and sniveling to him, muttering:

"Putie, old comrade, the public will never know how lonely men like you and me are. They will never understand how difficult it is making 'the tough decisions.' Still we have to be brave, we have to bear up and brazen it out. We can't show the feather. We can't flinch or quiver."

What kind of "tough decisions" did that imbecile make in the course of his day? Whether to pay the whore for a straight lay, a half-and-half or cough up enough scratch for some knock-me-down, drag-me-out, scorchingly, howlingly hellish, mind-blowingly hot . . . *screaming skull*—the kind that made the recipient bay at the moon like a rabidly deranged dog? Those were the only decisions idiots like Tower worried about. That asshole knew nothing about truly "tough decisions."

Putilov sure did, and just thinking about some of the horrible things he'd had to do jangled his nervous system like it was an out-of-tune glockenspiel being pounded to pieces by a crazed ape. The only thing that calmed him down anymore was a bong full of desomorphine. He had one in his locked desk drawer, ready and waiting to be filled with Everclear, ether and gasoline and then fired up. He could see he was going to need it. He was now flashing back to what was arguably the most difficult and consequential decision of his entire life.

It had taken place eight years after the USSR had broken up. The economy was in the dumper after the banking crisis of 1998, and the whole country was a disaster area. The Afghan and Chechen wars had slaughtered, wounded and mentally maimed Russian soldiers by the hundreds of thousands. Furthermore, it had devastated the economy. That the people would be turning on the officials and politicians was only natural, and since he had been Yeltsin's prime minister, had replaced him and would now be running for President Yeltsin's vacated office, he was a target. His approval ratings sank to 2 percent. Even worse, he and his cohorts were clearly culpable for much of the country's economic deprivation and social unrest; there was no getting around it. He and his entourage had broken so many laws of God and man that if he was defeated in the election and if a reformist regime ever took over, he and his criminal cronies could all end up spending the rest of their days toiling in the Gulag Archipelago's slave-labor mines. Putilov's first term in office looked to be his last term ever, and he was fighting for his life. He was like one of the cornered rats he'd fought as a child, and he'd learned back then that cornered rats will leap at their opponents' eyes.

Now Putilov was looking for an eye to leap at.

Then late one night—while he was worried sick and couldn't sleep—he picked up a copy of Robert Waite's acclaimed study of Hitler, The Psychopathic God. At one point Waite described how Hitler—in order to seize dictatorial control of Germany—had contrived to set fire to the German Reichstag. Blaming it on the insurgent Communists, he convened the German parliament, surrounded them with his armed contingent of brown-shirted, jackbooted thugs, declared a national emergency and proclaimed himself military dictator of Germany and the German people.

Putilov realized he could do the same thing.

He called together his most trusted KGB—now the FSB—advisers and planned for the clandestine bombing of four square blocks of Russian apartment complexes in four major cities, including Moscow, and in three of the cities he'd succeeded.

He remembered again his demolition of those complexes: How his munitions experts strategically placed a third of a ton or more of RDX explosive under each of the buildings' most critical support beams so that their destruction would shatter the buildings' underpinnings and collapse . . . everything. He took down three city blocks of apartment buildings as if they were houses of cards.

It was an act of terrorism unique in the annals of history. Hitler, when he planned the Reichstag fire, had ordered it for a time when it was relatively empty; he killed or injured no one during that fire. Other tyrants, particularly in the Mideast, had ordered innocents murdered en masse during uprisings and civil conflicts, but those men were fighting in a time of war to stay in power. Putilov might have become the only despot in history who killed and injured over 1,300 innocent people simply to gain dictatorial power over a nation.

Of course, two vexing questions about Putilov's apartment bombings troubled Russia and the world. RDX explosive was manufactured only in a single, government-protected plant in Perm—how so much explosive could vanish undetected from that site was a question Putilov could never adequately answer. Critics suggested he couldn't explain the RDX's disappearance because he was the one who had stolen it.

The blasts hit Buynaksk, Moscow and Volgodonsk on 16 September. Another RDX device was found and defused in an apartment block in the Russian city of Ryazan around the same time.

Of course, the facts of the case were damning in the extreme. Any number of reporters, including Anna Politkovskaya and her editor, Yuri Shcheko-chikhim, wrote that Putilov was responsible for the bombings and that he set them off to divert the electorate from their economic woes. Even worse, police had captured a cadre of FSB officers in the act of sowing one of the apartment complexes with explosive devices. Putilov quickly fabricated a story that the men had been on "a training exercise."

To his eternal amazement, the vast majority of the Russian public never blamed him. The Russian people had bought his laughable lie, and he'd real-ized at that point that they were even stupider than he had believed. God, Putilov thought, looking back on those grim times, could the Russian people really be that dumb? He began referring to them in private as "credulous cretins" and "our teeming hordes of Russian retards." Still he had learned a valuable truth: He could make the vast majority of the Russian people believe anything.

The decades passed, but still the eyewitness testimony and evidence of FSB foul play would not go away. The charges against him came to a head when Al-exander Litvinenko, an FSB—formerly the KGB—defector became the first and the most credible of the top officials to accuse Putilov of organizing the apart-ment bombings, saying Putilov was personally responsible for the premeditated slaughter of 300 innocent Russians and the injuring over 1000 more. Lit-vinenko would even report and substantiate that Putilov also organized the Dubrovka Theater and the 2004 Beslan school assaults, again killing and injuring well over a thousand people, hundreds of them children.

Then that bitch Anna Politkovskaya had rounded up eyewitnesses impli-cating him in those three attacks, as had Marina Salye, who had been inves-tigating him for criminal activities since his days in St. Petersburg back in the '80s. What was with those women anyway? Even after he'd had them taken out, they still pissed him off. He'd had Anna Politkovskaya killed on his fifty-fourth birthday as a special present to himself, but he still couldn't get over his rage at her. Just hearing her name drove him around the bend. His hatred of

Marina Salye also knew no bounds; killing her had not alleviated his fury one iota.

Of course, there was no question that the en masse killings had been worth the flack he'd taken afterward. By blaming both incidents and the apartment bombings on Chechen separatists, Putilov had been able to announce a state of national emergency and demand dictatorial powers from the Russian parliament in order, he claimed, to protect Mother Russia from terrorism. He thereby solidified his grip on power—permanently.

But his role in the massacres had been exposed, and critics around the world raged that Putilov had orchestrated the bombings.

Well, Putilov said to himself, *maybe you can't kill all your critics, but Litvinenko sure as hell won't bother you anymore. Neither will Anna Politkovskaya or Marina Salye. You killed those three deader than Dostoevsky's yaytsas [testicles].*

He allowed himself a small hint of a smile. *Let J. T. Tower top that one,* Putilov thought wryly. *You want to tell me about your "tough decisions"? That's a hand I can call and raise.*

He decided it was time to get out that desk-drawer aspirin bottle of krokodil. In preparation, he'd already crushed and razor-chopped ten tablets into a fine powder and dumped them into the Pyrex bong. Pouring two shot glasses of 190-proof Everclear and two splashes of ether and gasoline over them, he began heating the solution with his gold lighter until it reached a rolling boil. He then put the lighter away and stared at the liquid, watching it cool.

Instead of putting the bong's stem to his mouth, however, he ignored the fumes, reached into the open desk drawer and removed a plastic bag containing a presterilized syringe. He'd put it in the drawer the day before, after a friend told him that the krok delivered an even bigger kick if one injected it into a vein.

Having injected many suspects with scopolamine and sodium pentothal, he knew how to use syringes. Rolling up his shirt sleeve, he took off his belt and wrapped it around his upper forearm. He then tied it off tight as a tourniquet. Large pulsing purple veins instantly popped up just beneath his elbow. He sterilized the needle and the largest of the distended veins with Everclear.

He paused before shooting up to ponder the implications of this moment—and to thank the Almighty that he was Mikhail Ivanovich Putilov—a man born with the indomitable fortitude and iron will to abjure addiction. He was truly one of those whom his idol, Friedrich Nietzsche, had dubbed *Die*

Übermenschen—the Supermen. No drugs—for that matter, no man or nation on earth—was powerful or cunning enough to make Mikhail Ivanovich Putilov do what he didn't want to do.

Slipping the needle into the distended vein, he pushed the plunger home and was instantly hit by a jolt of pure incandescent pleasure.

It's like kissing . . . God, he thought worshipfully.

Then his head fell forward, and his eyes rolled back until only the whites showed. His jaw dropped to his chest. Saliva slavered slowly out of the dictator's gaping mouth and rolled down his chin.

6

"We long for the End Times the way you lust after beautiful women. We do not fear death, and we laugh at extinction. We pray that we might vanish into the Final Fire. Nukes, to us, are not a deterrent but a temptation. That is the advantage we have on you, and I, for one, burn and yearn to unleash the nuclear lightning. Nothing, not even total nuclear retaliation, can stop us from erasing your major cities from the face of the earth."
—Marika Madiha

When McMahon came to, he was strung up by his wrists to the overhead beam, his feet dangling a half foot above the floor. Every inch of his naked body throbbed and burned with pain. His butt and joints felt like they were covered with flickering flames.

"But enough about us, Mr. McMahon," Raza said, "have you enjoyed our hospitality so far? How were your accommodations? Is this safe house up to your high architectural standards?"

"I'm not sure it's even a house," McMahon said.

"No?" Marika asked. "What does it look like to you?"

"Termites holding hands," McMahon said.

"That was hurtful, Mr. McMahon," Raza said.

"Utterly unnecessary," Marika agreed.

"More important though," Raza said, "is whether we have cracked your shell, whether you now understand the peace and comfort and commitment that over a billion and a half people worldwide find in Islam."

"I am concerned," Marika said, "that despite Raza's and my best efforts you are still critical of our faith."

"I don't care what religion anyone subscribes to," McMahon said. "I think they're all stupid. But I don't understand why yours is so violently stupid. I don't understand why you hate the non-Muslim world with such vengeance."

"And you never will," Raza said, shaking her head. "Mr. McMahon, you will never fathom the One True Faith. You will always look for multiple meanings and myriad motives. You will forever seek subtleties, nuances, complexities. You will always be a man of the West."

"Okay, but just out of curiosity," McMahon asked, "if Allah cares so much about his followers and their One True Faith, why are you people so backward? Why are you losing to us? If He's so powerful, why doesn't He kick some infidel ass Himself?"

"Allah has not vouchsafed our victory," Marika said with complete seriousness, "because we have let Him down. We've shown you *kaffirs* [*infidels*] too much soft compassion, too much Western-style weakness."

"But your faith in Him is undimmed," McMahon asked, "even though He has spurned you?"

"Yes. Always," Marika said.

"How?" McMahon asked. "Why?"

"Our faith unites our soul in action," Raza said.

"And in violence," Marika said.

"Some of us believe the Islamic soul is created in violence," Raza said.

"I don't understand," McMahon replied.

"Nor will you ever understand," Marika said, "not in your heart and soul, not in your bones and blood. You will never understand that our world—Dar al-Islam—is driven by a single primum mobile."

"And what is that?" McMahon asked.

"Surcease," Marika said.

"Death is our culture's sole determinant," Raza said. "It is all we know, see, hear and feel. It is the very air we breathe. Earth for us is hell, and Paradise is Allah's eternal peace. The best thing we can do is to die in such a way that Allah instantly sweeps us up into His Divine Everlasting. Striking a blow against the infidel accomplishes precisely that feat. Look in the eyes of our suicide bombers—in their smiling eyes."

"Dying for Allah may or may not get you into your Afterlife of Honey, Dates and Seventy-two Virgins," McMahon said, "which may or may not exist. The world around us, however, does exist, and martyring yourself for Islam definitely won't help you succeed in that world."

"Which is why our only hope of salvation lies in your utter obliteration," Marika said.

"In other words," Raza said, "in your nuclear obliteration."

"And you really think you can pull that off," McMahon said, "given our enormous advantage in high-tech nuclear weaponry and delivery systems? We might, in retaliation, turn your world into a thermonuclear parking lot."

"You forget the edge we have," Marika said. "There is no deterrence against a nuclear jihadist who desires one thing and one thing only—Armageddon—and that is our world in a nutshell. We long for the End Times the way you lust after beautiful women. We do not fear death, and we laugh at extinction. We pray that we might vanish into the Final Fire. Nukes, to us, are not a deterrent but a temptation. That is the advantage we have on you, and I, for one, burn and yearn to unleash the nuclear lightning. Nothing, not even total nuclear retaliation, can stop us from erasing your major cities from the face of the earth."

"Do you have any targets in mind?" McMahon asked. "Any auspicious time frames?"

"Oh, Mr. McMahon," Marika said, "let me assure you, your hometown, New York City, is numero uno on our hit parade, on any terrorist's nuclear list. And the time for its nuclear immolation is at hand."

"Why?" McMahon asked weakly.

"New York has so much to offer—Wall Street, the UN, Radio City, Jews."

"We don't call it *Jew York* for nothing!" Marika shouted.

"New York has more Jews than Jerusalem and Tel Aviv combined!" Raza pointed out. "It's the Jew capital of the world."

"And it is so Western," Marika said, "so decadent. Look what it represents: tolerance, togetherness, democracy, the melting pot—I especially hate the *fucking melting pot.*" Marika roared the last four words.

"Even our Muslim brothers and sisters," Raza said, "when they immigrate to New York, they *assimilate.*"

"They lose themselves in your *fucking melting pot,*" Marika growled.

"You know what else New York really represents, Mr. McMahon," Raza shouted. "Do you want to know the Big Apple's true bottom line?"

"What?" McMahon asked weakly.

"New York represents . . . *life!*" Raza shouted.

"I hate life!" Marika howled.

McMahon's mask of derisive stoicism suddenly cracked, and he grew visibly despondent.

"Look, Sister-Friend," Marika said. "The thought of nuking New York makes Mr. McMahon sad. You don't want us nuking New York, do you?"

"Not really," McMahon said.

"But I thought that you knew," Marika said, "that you'd figured it out. We've targeted Manhattan since the very beginning, and now we're going to do it. We're burning your beloved island down to bedrock, down below its waterline, till harbor and the rivers roll over it, converge, and New York is no more."

"There'll be nothing left of New York except salt water," Raza said.

"Is anything wrong with that?" Marika asked.

"Is anything 'right' in the nuking of New York?" McMahon asked. "Do you know anyone who wants mass slaughter on such a scale?"

"My world teems with such people," Raza said.

"Not mine," McMahon said. "The West abhors death."

"Perhaps," Marika said, "but yours is also a world steeped in blood, which has perfected torture and murder until they are a way of life. Your America is a world awash in nuclear weapons, insane with feral violence and blind greed, subsisting in death's teeth and avidly waiting for the nuclear hammer to fall, which is why your nation—your entire Western world—must go."

"Your world is in our rearview mirror," Raza said, "dimming, dwindling, disappearing into the vanishing point."

"New York most of all," Marika said.

"Come on, Mr. McMahon," Raza said. "New York's incineration won't be that bad."

"Were New York to go," McMahon said softly, "it would, to me, be as a death."

"So?" Marika asked. "What's wrong with death?"

"For that matter," Raza asked, "what's wrong with . . . *mass death?*"

"You're talking about doing what Herman Kahn called 'the Unthinkable,'" McMahon said.

"But not the undoable," Marika said. "Must I repeat? Your leaders for the last seventy-five years have worked 'round the clock to see that our world gets nuclear weapons, to make your own destruction not only possible but inevitable, and now we are about to give you what you've been asking for all this time."

"My friend is right," Raza said. "You sold us the original technology that got our nuclear weapons programs going. Did you really think we would not develop them? Well we did, and admit it: Deep down inside, you wanted us to use them on you. Your president Tower is trying to sell ourselves and our Muslim neighbors forty nuclear power plants, as we speak. Why else did you entrust us with your darkest secrets and most violent technology? Well guess what? We have those weapons now, and it's our turn to use them."

"Trust me, Mr. McMahon," Marika said, "we are going to use them on you."

"Mr. McMahon," Raza said, smiling, "You have my personal word on this. We will not let you down."

"Do you have any moral code at all?" McMahon asked.

"In the sense that you define it," Raza said, "remarkably little."

"Ever-approaching the nil point," Marika said.

"Asymptotically," Raza added.

"I've been told I personally have the ethical sense of an event horizon," Marika said.

"Which marks the maw of a black hole," Raza said, explaining the phrase.

"In my case a supermassive black hole," Marika said.

"So there is no right, no wrong in your universe?" McMahon asked.

"Wrong is whatever pisses me off," Raza said. "Right is whatever gets me aroused."

"And does the nuking of American cities turn you on?" McMahon asked.

"You betcha," Raza said.

"Why should anybody care about your country anyway?" Marika asked. "America is not so much a nation as a lunatic asylum packed to the rafters with self-righteous, pseudo-superior, apocalyptically violent, *me-me-me*, *what's-in-it-for-me, psychopathic narcissists!* Who cares if we blow that madhouse—particularly its nerve center, capital city, number one psycho ward, the Big Apple itself—into nuclear oblivion?"

Raza did a double take, then stared closely at McMahon's right cheek. A tear was rolling down it.

"Isn't that touching?" Raza said. "The poor boy is crying. He evidently likes New York."

"Oh, please," Marika squeaked with fake falsetto, pleading, "please don't hurt the Big Apple."

"But we must," Raza said, "or we abandon our faith, our honor, our sacred *ird,* and become infidel money-whores and deranged death merchants like yourselves."

"And in the process, abjure the One True God," Marika said.

"You know that any objective sanity inquiry would declare both of you psychotic?" McMahon said.

"Except in our godly realm what you call insanity is the accepted norm," Raza said, "and our people's ruling passion; therefore, it is in no way aberrant. It is in nature's course, the way of our world. Your dreams of love, of Christ's compassion and Isaiah's 'Peaceable Kingdom' we deem to be madness."

"So you reject 'Love your neighbor'?" McMahon asked. " 'Blessed are the peacemakers'? The Sermon on the Mount?"

"Your people did," Raza said. "You flogged Christ half to death, then nailed His body to a cross for three days and nights. And still each Sunday you cannibalize His flesh and drink His blood."

"Yet you call us mad," Marika said.

"Christians believe Christ died for their sins," McMahon said softly, for the first time in his life honestly identifying with Christ Crucified.

"Face it, Mr. McMahon," Raza said. "Your softheaded, softhearted, love-your-neighbor, blessed-are-the-peacemakers slave morality is the ultimate madness, and it has terminally corrupted your culture."

"How do you view the weak, the poor-of-spirit and the peacemakers of this world?" McMahon asked.

"In our world, the weak are irrevocably cursed," Marika said, "and the peacemakers are forever fucked."

"In our world, the poor-of-spirit strap explosives to their moronic bodies," Raza said, "and blow up your school buses and malls."

"Yours is the *only* culture that does such things," McMahon said.

"Want to know why?" Raza asked.

"Yes, please," McMahon asked.

"Because ours is the only culture that *gets it*," Raza said.

"Gets what?" McMahon whispered.

"The joke," Raza said. "I thought you got it too."

"What joke?" McMahon asked, against Rashid's exhortations, almost whimpering.

"The joke?" Raza said, smiling. "Tell him, Marika."

"That life sucks," Marika said. "That there is nothing in this vale of tears that is worth the awful misery it inflicts on us poor humans. Our existence is one huge horrible mistake, and we human beings have been made to suffer unbearably so the stars, planets, black matter, black holes, the infinite intergalactic void and, yes, the gods themselves, can look down at our pain and *laugh*. We'd all be better off dead, and Islam is the only religion that recognizes these fundamental hair-raising, irrefutable truths.

"Islam recognizes that life is inconsolable sorrow and that our only hope is in the Hereafter."

"Meaning: the grave," Raza said.

"Hope for this world sure as shit isn't in the *Mideast*," Marika snorted with hilarity.

But Raza was no longer smiling. Ignoring Marika's mirth, she said:

"Only Islam recognizes the harsh truth of our existence—that our lives aren't worth living," she said sternly, "and only Islam *revels in it.*"

"So you think that the poor should basically go fuck themselves?" McMahon asked.

"Actually, in our doxology, the poor should praise Allah and beg Him for an even quicker release from this mortal coil," Raza said.

"We are all supposed to view death as a gift," Marika said, "and we are all supposed to beg Allah daily to hurry our deliverance from this hellish dispensation."

McMahon could only stare at the two women in mute horror.

"Mr. McMahon," Raza finally said, "will you never understand? Mohammed conquered a kingdom for us. He departed this world ruling a triumphal empire, a grand and glorious imperium. At the time of His death, He was at the height of His powers and accomplishments. Christ, on the other hand, died in ghoulish agony, in shame and ignominy, betrayed by those who professed to love Him—and made His grave amid the wicked."

"Don't you like winners, Mr. McMahon?" Marika said. "Wouldn't you prefer Mohammed over Christ? The victor over the loser?"

"But you have to admit that Christ's religion," McMahon said, "teaches people a respect for learning, for philosophy and literature, for truth and logic, for evidence and facts—and for love. In the end the love of knowledge makes Christ's followers winners, and your hatred of knowledge makes you losers."

"Actually a contempt for learning may be Islam's greatest strength," Raza said.

"How?" McMahon asked.

"Because it allows us to define the truth any way we want," Marika said. "Which means we can shove industrial quantities of dromedary shit down the throats of our benighted masses and laugh about it afterward."

They roared heartily at the thought.

"You've created an Islamist *1984* the way Orwell never dreamed it," McMahon said softly, shaking his head.

"Georgie never knew the half of it," Raza said.

"And I suppose your Islamic *1984* justifies—indeed requires—torture?" McMahon asked.

"But of course," Raza said. "Torture has been de rigueur since time out of mind. In our land, it is a way a life, our heart's blood."

"What did Orwell say in *1984*?" Marika said. "'If you want a vision of the future, imagine a boot stamping on a human face—*forever.*'"

"Just as money is your 'Second Blood,'" Raza said, "I like to think of torture as ours."

"Our people believe in a loving God," McMahon whispered simply, not knowing what else to say.

"Yes, and we have a word for such people," Marika said.

"What word?" McMahon asked, his voice cracking.

"Idiots."

7

"Yeah, we all gotta get straight with the Man upstairs."
—Anonymous

The Black Hawks continued to roar through the Pakistani night. Adara listened listlessly to the conversation in her chopper. In the droning darkness, she couldn't tell who was saying what to whom.

"And the ball goes into the gutter."

"C'est la guerre."

"Vive le legionnaire."

"Stop taking the fun out of my day."

"Where's Johnny D.?"

"Got chalked."

"Dead?"

"Uh huh."

"Fuck him, man. He took the easy way out."

"This way's better?"

"Better the devil you know."

"Than the one fucking your brains out?"

"There you go."

"You can only do so much with duct tape and chicken wire."

"Or spit and chicken shit?"

"Whatever turns you on?"

"I get high on life."

"No shit?"

"And the Man upstairs."

"Yeah, we all gotta get straight with the Man upstairs."

"I hear He looks a lot like Hank Williams, Jr."

"Or Johnny Cash."

"The man in black."

"We go in looking for a way out."

"Righteous, but we don't back up. We don't back down."

"We hold our ground. We die hard."

"I makes the other muthafucka die hard."

"Outstanding."

"Out-fucking-standing."

"It always bid-ness."

"Always."

"I told them: 'The whole package never make it back to the station, cap'n.'"

"'It ain't my dope, Officer.'"

"Things got so bad we was stabbin' each other in the front."

"You wanna do them goat-ass muthafuckas?"

"So bad my dick hurt."

"My dick wanna bone itself some fine funky bitch."

"Bone your fist, you mean."

"You sayin' I ain't up for it?"

"You could mouth-bone a bitch maybe."

"Yeah, you got the mus'-snatch—I mean, mustache—to do it."

"Got to admit that be one fine poon broom."

"I hear your mama be a fine woman."

"Hard-hittin' woman."

"Fine funky woman. Easy-ridin' woman."

"A low-ridin' woman."

"With dead men in her eyes."

"Too much bitch for you, sucka."

"Don't you go pimpin' on my boy. He got him a fine pussy-pusher."

"Don't you give me that big-yard stare."

"What do you expect from me anyway?"

"A little love?"

"Can we keep it on the down low?"

"I said don't go pimpin' on my yard bitch."

"I ain't lyin', I ain't tryin'."

"When we get back?"

"In the fullness of time."

"That which does not kill me makes me dumber."

"You can't get no dumber."

"A natural-born fact."

"Slippin', slidin', easy ridin'."

"Let's shake and bake."

"I be your witness there."

"I be your witness there."

The Black Hawks continued on and on through the Pakistani night.

PART XI

"Let me put the pistols on the table, boy. Were you tappin' that ass?"

—President J. T. Tower to Mikhail Ivanovich Putilov

1

Putilov had whiled away many a lonely sleepless night studying those pathologically pornographic photos and watching DVDs of that cretin being humiliated in bed by leather-masked prostitutes of indeterminate gender, ethnicity and even species. Putilov had rollicked with laughter, his spirit soaring with pure transcendent delight, each time Tower abased himself in plain view of Putilov's hidden cameras . . .

Tower was unquestionably driving Putilov to distraction. In fact, Tower's last all-night Skype call to the Russian leader had nearly done Putilov in. He really didn't think he could tolerate the bastard anymore.

Where did that asshole, Tower, get off suggesting that he was in any way Putilov's equal—a brother-under-the-skin? What had Tower ever done except live off his inheritance and fuck predatory women who thought to exploit him for reasons of grasping avarice and personal advancement?

God, the man infuriated him. What Putilov really wanted to do was grab him by the shirt, slam him into a wall and shout in his face:

"*HOW MANY PEOPLE HAVE YOU KILLED??? WHAT THE FUCK DO YOU KNOW ABOUT ME AND MY LIFE???*"

Reflecting on all the people he'd murdered—or had murdered—always soothed Putilov's nerves. Sitting back in his easy chair, he stared out over the Black Sea, his personal fleet of yachts in the harbor, and he remembered the first time he had ever taken a life . . .

It went back to that tiny four-room St. Petersburg apartment, which had been home to his family and two others as well. Armies of ferocious brown rats—often ten inches in length, rump to nose—infested the apartments' inner and outer walls, savagely attacked the human inhabitants and had turned that building into a kind of Rat Battle of Stalingrad. They assaulted the apartments' occupants anytime, anywhere, devouring holes in the plaster and wood, the brick and Sheetrock—as well as in people. Putilov personally believed the little buggers liked the taste of that filthy shit.

Still he was ordered to stem the tide. When he wasn't at school, he had to spend his hours in the apartment, attempting to hunt and kill the invading rats. However, it was tough. Luring them into cages was unproductive. They were just too damn shrewd. Spring-powered traps they recognized and disdainfully ignored. Even placing arsenic-laced cheese in front of the holes did little good. The rats were too smart to devour it whole. They would test it first, nibbling a small bite or two, then waiting to see if it disagreed with them. If the bait did sicken them, they ignored the rest of it and told their comrades to do the same.

Sometimes though he could outfox the rats with a bait and switch. He'd feed them a good bait, say peanut butter, and convince them that it was safe to eat. He'd then slip some poisoned peanut butter in, watch them devour the entire portion and die. Sometimes Putilov would turn off the lights, leave a chunk of unpoisoned cheese or sausage or peanut butter in front of the rathole and hide behind a couch. He'd hide for hours, waiting for them to come out. Eventually they would enter the room, and Putilov would let them take their test-nibbles. When the rats were sure the food was edible, and they were alone, they dug in. Putilov had a small garden shovel in his hands, and when the rats were focused on and absorbed in their repast, he'd spring from his hiding place and hammer them to death.

He remembered the first time his parents had come home from work, and he'd presented them with his trophies. The five-year-old boy had killed three large rats.

His parents and the two other families living in the four-room apartment were ecstatic. They'd found a rat-killing prodigy.

Nor did his rat-battles end there. The apartment complex had a large, filthy, trash-strewn courtyard where all the children gathered and played. Whenever another kid got on Putilov's nerves, he didn't see a human at all but a rat, and he fought him the way rats fought. Clawing at the kid's eyes, he bit him savagely, ripped out clumps of his hair, kicked him in the shins, the balls and would not stop. Even when the kid gave up, and kids pulled Putilov off the youngster, he would only pretend to quit. As soon as he got his wind back, he would throw himself on the poor kid again, scratching, biting, crotch-kicking, pulling his hair.

In school, it was the same—so much so he was declared a hooligan. For several years he was denied entrance into the Young Pioneers—the much-honored USSR organization which was reserved only for good clean young Russian men.

Putilov was considered too unstable and too . . . psychopathic.

But he didn't care. He loved beating the hell out of people. Fighting, even killing, was as natural to him as breathing, as vital to his well-being as blood.

He not only fought his way through school, he would kill hundreds of rats before leaving that slum apartment. From his point of view, for the rest of his life, he'd never stop kicking the asses of kids who got in his way and killing rats—reporter rats, in particular. He'd killed those rats and tamed Russia's recalcitrant news media in a manner that would have impressed even his personal god, Uncle Joe. He wondered absently whether Stalin had exterminated as many of the press as he had? He honestly did not know. Possibly not.

The thought of all those murdered journalists and other political opponents brought an exceedingly rare smile to Putilov's lips. Their names rang in his ears like temple bells, like a paen of praise to his implacable will and unyielding resolve, a grim litany of deservedly dead enemies: Dmitry Kholodov, Ilya Zimin, Ilyas Shurpayev, Yury Shebalkin, Sergey Bogdanovsky, Dmitry Krikoryants, Sergei Dubov, Andrei Aizderdzis, Yury Soltys, Tatyana Zhuravlyova, Yelena Roshchina, Hussein Guzuyev, Gelani Charigov, Bilal Akhmadov, Vladimir Zhitarenko, Pyotr Novikov, Sultan Nuriyev, Jochen Piest, Valentin Yanus, Vyacheslav Rudnev—all of them he'd had killed outright . . . plus another two hundred journalists whose names he no longer remembered but whose deaths he would carry in his soul like a lover's sensuous caresses . . . until the day he died.

Remembering the men and women he'd murdered or imprisoned always brought him much pleasure. He had been especially eager to take care of the American multibillionaire hedge fund mogul who had invested so heavily in Putilov's Russia during the early years. The man had eventually become disillusioned with his regime's "financial practices," and he'd gone so far as to hire the tax attorney and financial auditor, Sergei Magnitsky, to investigate those activities. Sergei learned what happened to people who fucked with Putilov. He'd been imprisoned almost immediately, and Putilov had seen to it that, while in jail, he was starved, half-frozen and brutally beaten. Denied the medical care he had desperately needed, he had subsequently died.

Investigate me now, Sergei! *Putilov thought with a bitter snort.*

His employer, the hedge fund CEO, however, had proven himself an implacable and resourceful foe. He lobbied the U.S. Congress and convinced them to pass the Sergei Magnitsky Rule of Law Accountability Act and to impose economic sanctions on Russia. So far Putilov had had to kill five more people who were investigating him and his people for fraud and tax evasion under that act, including Valery Kurochkin, Oktay Gasanov and Alexander Perepilichny.

Putilov was especially proud of Perepilichny's killing. He'd ordered him done in with gelsemium, a poisonous extract taken from a rare plant found only in the Himalayas. Favored by Chinese assassins, the toxin was almost impossible to detect and verify medically. Still some supercilious coroner had managed to track it down, and Putilov had been furious. In fact, he'd almost ordered a hit on the asshole medical scientist just to teach him to mind his own business and keep out of Putilov's way. He still planned on doing something about the man in the future.

Then there was his former boss and mayor of St. Petersburg, Anatoly Sobchak. When Putilov had risen to power, the man had been vain enough to think he could prevail upon his past patronage of Putilov, talk to him friend-to-friend, even impose on their onetime friendship. He once even said to Putilov: "You know, I gave you your start. You had nothing until I hired you as my deputy." So Sobchak had to go. Putilov told his killers to paint his bedside lamp with an extremely painful, hard-to-trace poison, which, when the light was turned on, would heat up and emit ultralethal toxins that would kill anyone in the room.

You never saw it coming, did you, Anatoly? *Putilov thought with a cryptic trace if a grin.*

Thinking of Sobchak's demise brought back memories of Boris Berezovsky—the billionaire Russian TV mogul and owner of Russia's largest television news network, Channel One. More than anyone, he'd been responsible for making Putilov Yeltsin's prime minister, then forcing Yeltsin to retire and installing Putilov as interim president. Berezovsky had pilloried Putilov's presidential opponents on Channel One, falsely accusing them of scurrilous wrongdoing and malicious misdeeds. He'd so blackened their reputations that on election day, Putilov won easily.

Berezovsky, like Sobchak, thought he could remind Putilov how much he owed him.

Yeah, Boris, I owed you all right, and I've always settled my debts. When my hit team hanged you in England, you were paid in full . . . at the end of that fucking rope.

The Russian banker and Putilov critic Ivan K. Kivelidi he'd killed with the toxin cadmium. Human rights advocate Natalya Estemirova had been kidnapped and killed. Marina Salye had assiduously investigated his financial activities in St. Petersburg in the early '90s when he was first starting to steal fortunes for himself and friends. Before she'd been able to collect her evidence of his many killings, however, she'd seen the handwriting on the wall: She would not survive her inquiry. She'd gone into hiding and had wisely stayed undercover for twelve years. Then she returned to public life to resume her crusade against her longtime nemesis, knowing all the while that Putilov might have her killed. Despite the obvious threats on her life, she felt the tyrant had to be stopped.

Big mistake, Marina!

Instead of indicting Putilov, she died of a "massive coronary"—or so the coroner reported.

"Massive cornonary"? *Putilov thought, grinning.* Yeah, sure, Marina . . . pro—bab—ly!

He remembered how once in Belgium a French reporter had asked him to explain why he was using heavy artillery on Chechen civilians. He invited the man to come to Moscow, where he could explain Chechen terrorism to him more fully, in more detail and then have him . . . cas-trat-ed. "We have specialists in that," he'd told the reporter.

The look of horror on the man's face still made the Russian tyrant smile.

That was another journalist he planned on meeting again one day.

Perhaps Putilov's favorite hit of all had been his longtime political opponent and nemesis, Boris Nemtsov. Putilov had given him a fair warning. He'd jailed him several times, and Nemtsov's own mother had told him Putilov would kill him if he continued his crusade against the Russian president. The man wouldn't listen though. He was throwing large-scale political rallies and preparing to expose Putilov's invasion of Ukraine and seizure of Crimea for the war crimes they were. Well, those sorts of spotlights Putilov could not countenance. He'd had Nemtsov shot to death in front of his girlfriend under the shadow of St. Basil's Cathedral in the Kremlin.

What you put out, Boris, baby, *Putilov thought grimly,* you get back.

But while Putilov enjoyed reminiscing about all those enemies whom he had shuffled off this mortal coil, lately, Tower had taken to ruining even that small diversion for the Russian dictator. Whenever the idiot, Tower, heard about a Russian reporter or political opponent or human rights activist whom Putilov had had ingloriously eliminated, he'd call Putilov and congratulate him on "a job well done." Tower was even stupid enough to express on the phone his heartfelt wish that he, Tower, could "dispatch unfriendly journalists and opponents as expeditiously as you do, old friend."

"Why not announce on CNN that I killed all those people and you wish you could do the same?" Putilov had shouted at Tower. "Phones can be tapped you know? I tap them every day."

Tower had immediately apologized for his indiscretion and his lapse in judgment, but within a week he was, once again, on the Skype phone, complimenting Putilov on another journalist he'd "neutralized." Nothing Putilov said or did could make Tower shut up about it.

Human rights activists especially incensed Putilov—and he'd had any number of them eliminated—but Tower wouldn't even let him enjoy those murders in peace. The nitwit had been especially ecstatic at the murder of the beautiful and charismatic activist/reporter, Anna Polikovskaya. She was bent on exposing everything *Putilov had done. So he'd had her tea poisoned on an airline flight, and after she'd survived that attempt, he'd ordered her shot to death in the elevator of her apartment building two years later in 2006.* Some things, *he'd thought at the time,* you don't leave undone.

Tower had been insanely aroused over that one.

"Damn, Putie, that Anna P., she was some kind of gorgeous. *That bitch was* smoking-hot. *So right here I have to ask you a personal question. I mean, we're men. We both know about these things, right?*"

· "*What things?*" *Putilov asked, suddenly apprehensive.*

"Let me put the pistols on the table, boy. Were you tappin' that ass?"

A jolt of pure violent rage hit Putilov like nothing he'd ever felt in his life. It was as if he had a live volcano in his bowels, and it was welling upward through his abdomen, stomach, chest, esophagus, then hitting his brain like an explosion of molten boiling magma.

For a moment, Putilov blacked out and fell off his desk chair. When he came to, he was on his back, and he could hear Tower on the Skype's speaker phone, bellowing:

"Putie, where are you? Where did you go?"

Putilov might well have cracked and gone terminally insane at that very moment, but for the last week he'd been meeting with an anger management psychiatrist, who was helping him deal with his homicidal hatred of Tower. The man practiced something called "Eidetic Therapy." He'd taught Putilov to visualize himself and Tower in situations that reduced his rage and then concentrate on those images.

Well, the only images he had of Tower that gave him any relief were images of himself, Putilov, killing the imbecile . . . painfully, painstakingly.

Instantly, he pictured Tower standing there in his office. In his mind's eye, Putilov had an AK-47 in his hands and a bucket of plastique at his feet. Empting the AK's magazine into Tower's stomach and gonads—guaranteeing that his death would be horrifyingly slow, not quick and merciful—he then bent over him and shoved handfuls of plastique up his ass, into his groin and then his mouth. He inserted pre-wired blasting caps into the explosive, hid behind his desk, and with a smile on his face, big as St. Basil's, he pushed the detonator's plunger.

The blast was frighteningly loud, but it was worth the horrendous ringing in his ears.

For when he stood up, Tower was . . . gone.

Tower would never come back to haunt him.

The man would never bother Putilov again.

The realization brought tears of joy to his eyes.
Putilov was free! Free!

"Comrade," Tower was shouting into the speakerphone, "are you there? You disappeared."

Slowly picking himself up off the floor, he sat back down at his desk.

"Yes, I'm here. What was it you asked?"

"I asked if you were doin' Anna P.? Were you banging that booty? Man, she was scorchin'. You sure as shit should have gotten some of that before you had her hit. It's a code of honor with me. I never let good pussy to go to waste. Hell, I'd have thrown a fuck into her—just to give her something to remember me by—and then had her aced. She could have thought about that final hip action just as she was staring into her killer's ice-cold eyes and watching the hammer fall. I would have liked that. I would have wanted her last memory—just before the lights went out—to be of my *dick*. In fact, Putie, that thought is getting me turned on right now, even as we speak. Maybe I ought to go and, you know, as we say in the States: take care of business. Strike while the old branding iron is . . . hot. And, boy, Putie, the old Jim Iron is hotter than hellfire and brimstone right now."

Tower was truly unendurable, utterly relentless and would never let up. When Putilov had KGB General Oleg Erovinkin murdered, Tower would not stop with the calls. He never missed an opportunity to broadcast that one on his Skype, thundering his thanks and congratulations on a *fucking phone line!*

But then come to think of it, Erovinkin had pissed Putilov off as well . . .

Erovinkin had been in charge of discrediting Tower's political opponent during Tower's last presidential election, and the general had succeeded brilliantly. Even though the woman handily won the popular American presidential vote, Erovinkin had stolen the election from the former secretary of state in those swing states like a thief in the night.

Unfortunately for Putilov, the asshole general had gotten an attack of conscience and had ratted his boss's entire operation out to the English Secret Service. When the general had sent former MI6 agent Conrad Stillman an explosive dossier on Putilov's political disinformation campaign against Tower's female presidential opponent, he'd also thrown in shocking sexual materials—including photographs and DVDs—that Putilov had compiled on Tower during the moron's business/political trips to Moscow. In bed, Tower was a pervert of near-Hannibal Lecter proportions, and he'd had the deplorable judgment to indulge his insane tastes in Russian hotel suites with

Russian prostitutes . . . who worked for Putilov! Tower had, among other things, ordered leather-clad diesel dykes to ram his derrière with strap-ons, had paid hookers extra to treat him to face-first, open-mouthed "golden showers" and had participated in certain sadonecrophilic debaucheries that left Tower oinking like a pig and bleating like a sheep, bestial perversions so horrifyingly vile, so indescribably deranged, that even Putilov had never heard of them.

Putilov was still in shock. As a KGB operative, he thought he'd seen and heard of anything—everything that was disgustingly and sexually sick. But no one had ever heard of anyone anywhere who matched Tower for pure concentrated unmitigated degeneracy.

Well the good news was that Putilov had in his possession digitized audiovisual recordings of every twisted repulsive second of Tower's perverted sex acts.

Still Putilov was outraged that the general had gone public with the Russian president's own personal file on Tower. He had deemed Tower's sex file to be his own exclusive property and had grown attached to it. Putilov had whiled away many a lonely sleepless night studying those pathologically pornographic photos and watching DVDs of that cretin being humiliated in bed by leather-masked prostitutes of indeterminate gender, ethnicity and even species. Putilov had rollicked with laughter, his spirit soaring with pure transcendent delight, each time Tower abased himself in plain view of Putilov's hidden cameras. But an indispensable part of Putilov's thrill was the secret singularity of his experience. Putilov—and no one else—got to watch as Tower revealed himself to be the demented deviant and ludicrous lunatic that he truly was. Only Putilov knew the sheer excitation of seeing Tower so unmistakably unmasked and so grossly and grotesquely exposed.

He did not and would not ever, ever share it with the world.

But then the general double-crossed him—giving it to a retired MI6 spy who had leaked a description of the materials to the press.

That the cowardly London news organization reported only the substance of the story and refused to release the photos or DVD of Tower in full flagrante delicto in no way alleviated Putilov's rage. Putilov knew that because of Erovinkin, the truth would one day get out, and then everyone would know— not just Putilov.

When Putilov first learned of the general's betrayal, he had immediately had him killed and seen to it that he died a particularly painful death in the backseat of the general's own Lexus. Putilov had him killed with poisons so diabolically lethal, so awesomely agonizing, so impossibly difficult to detect that he doubted anyone would ever accurately determine the man's cause of death—only that the general had suffered hell's most hideous and terrifying tortures before he'd finally and gratefully succumbed.

Had Agent Stillman not immediately gone into hiding, Putilov would have taken care of him too, former MI6 agent or not. In fact, he was still committed to finalizing that piece of unfinished business. Some things you just don't let slide, Putilov thought to himself bitterly. In Putilov's line of work it was imperative that people knew no one was beyond his reach.

That asshole comic, Danny McMahon, was learning the hard way that fucking with Putilov and his good friends Kamal and Waheed was terminally . . . unwise.

And terminally was indeed the operative word.

He could not wait until the day came when he could take care of Tower too.

Putilov poured himself a cup of tea. It didn't help. His hands still shook, and he still ground his teeth in fury. Would he ever again know peace? No, J. T. Tower had robbed him of any bit of serenity he might have had, was filling him with an implacable anger that he could no longer contain, which was drastically distorting his judgment, finally forcing Putilov into the jaws of the krok. Desomorphine was the only thing that calmed his jangled nerves and soothed his savagely troubled soul.

At times like this, he actually wanted to kill Tower with his bare hands—strangle him and at the very end snap his neck or maybe just beat him to death with a shovel like he'd done so many times to those rats in that slum apartment.

But with Tower, he'd make the beating slower, more excruciating, more . . . unbearable.

Where did Tower get off with that know-it-all attitude? How could Tower ever comprehend what it was to be Mikhail Ivanovich Putilov?

Once again Putilov found himself returning to that small slum tenement overrun with its armies of rats. What could Tower ever know about fighting hordes of rodents in four crowded rooms? The endless hours spent stalking them, waiting for them, hitting them with shovels, cracking their necks with his bare hands? What could the spoiled rich kid J. T. Tower ever know about that kind of world, that kind of childhood, that kind of life? Tower would never understand one single thing about Mikhail Ivanovich Putilov.

Walking over to his desk, he took out a bottle of desomorphine tablets, two tablespoons, a razor blade, his bong and a lighter. He reached into the big bottom drawer and took out the gasoline flask, the ether can and a liter bottle of Everclear—the 190-proof corn liquor distilled by the American firm Luxco, and the strongest commercially made liquor in the world.

Damn, he'd developed a real fondness for the krok.

He was starting to dream about getting high off the beast.

Was that a bad sign? Putilov wondered.

He began crushing the pills two at a time between the tablespoons, then chopping up the granules with his razor blade. Filling the bong with the powder, he poured in the Everclear, added some ether, a splatter of gasoline for that extra jolt, and heated the mixture to a rolling boil.

Man, those fumes smelled good!

Putting the stem to his mouth, he sucked the steaming drug deep into his lungs.

Putilov's eyes rolled back into his head until only the whites showed.

2

I still don't understand why you hate the West so much," McMahon said to the two women. He was still lying belly-down, glancing up at them from his rack.

McMahon knew that Rashid was right when he said that the more time his interrogators spent talking, the less time they spent torturing him. And, Jesus, did they love to talk. They were chatty to the point of logorrhea and seemed to enjoy mocking him verbally as much as tormenting him physically.

"Besides despising your perverse worship of scientific evidence and proven facts?" Raza asked.

"Yes," McMahon said.

"I especially detest your pseudo-concern for the impoverished masses," Marika said.

"Indeed," Raza said.

"But your religion preaches tithing to the poor, the *zakat*," McMahon said. "It's one of the pillars of your faith."

"Yes, we toss the poor nickels and dimes, but we've never recommended piling up treasure in heaven instead of here in our earthly world. Our religion has never advocated 'to each according to his needs, from each according to his means.' We've never advocated a redistribution of wealth as your UN, the EU, Japan, China, Africa, Australia, Latin America, and the U.S. Senate are currently attempting to do."

"You would do nothing for those living in dire destitution?" McMahon asked.

"Oh, they have an important place in Dar-al-Islam," Marika said. "Our world could not exist without beasts of burden, without hewers of wood and drawers of water."

"But what happens when they are too old, sick or too tired to work?" McMahon asked.

"Why they die, Mr. McMahon." Marika said. "What do you think they do? Retire to the Costa de Sol and live off the fat of the land?"

"Why not make them suicide bombers?" McMahon asked, mocking his two tormentors. "You two probably view that occupation as a productive economic profession, no?"

"I see it as a splendid career opportunity . . . *for numbskulls*," Marika said.

"After all, even the stupendously stupid should have something productive to do," Raza said.

"Tariq," Marika asked, "we don't want to ignore you. What would you do about the world's malnourished masses?"

Tariq al-Omari looked up. He'd been assiduously honing a shiny, stainless steel scalpel with a whetstone.

"From my point of view," Tariq said, looking up from the blade, "the poor get what they deserve. They contribute nothing, so we owe them nothing. In fact, from my point of view, they should all eat shit and *die*. Were that infeasible, I'd at the very least castrate the morons like steers so they could not breed more morons." He resumed honing his scalpel, a small, contemplative smile forming on his lips.

"Fortunately, this is the 21st century, and people won't stand for it," McMahon said, his rage overwhelming his better judgement. "People want democracy, and they demand freedom."

"The people are told they want freedom and democracy," Raza said, "but deep down inside they hate it.

"So few Western leaders understand that simple fact," Marika said. "Throughout history, every time the people have been given freedom, they quickly and gladly surrender their democratic system of government at the first bump in the road. They turn their freedom over to their clerics, generals, political reactionaries and despots. The freedom, which democracy so unthinkingly forces on the ignorant masses, only serves to anger them. The people don't want choices. They want to be told what to do. They want us to give them something to believe in. Something, anything—a Cause, a God, a State, a strong leader. If nothing else a brutal, bloody, ugly *war*. In their hearts, the people seek not the freedom you torture them with, but what we give them. After all, Mr. McMahon, is not the translation of Islam 'submit' and 'surrender'?"

McMahon looked away, silent.

"Tariq?" Raza said. "Do you agree?"

Tariq stopped honing his gelding scalpel. "There is too much at stake for the people of earth to be free. If they choose badly, these Unbelievers will never know the bliss of Paradise; instead they will suffer the fires of hell perpetually. Therefore, we cannot allow people to risk misbelief or moderation, let alone to grant them 'freedom.' We must force the right choice on the world. It is better to burn in our cleansing fires here on earth—on the chance that the Unbeliever will convert—instead of burning eternally in Gehenna. Also torturing apostates to death serves as a deterrent to other would-be apostates."

"Do you really believe all that shit?" McMahon asked Raza in a half whisper, not wanting to provoke Tariq.

"God no," Raza whispered back, "but is it any dumber than subscribing to the Virgin Birth or Christ's walking on water? What about your savior's denunciations of M-O-N-E-Y? What do you think He'd say about your beloved 'democratic capitalism'? His contempt for filthy lucre and money lending wouldn't auger well for the free enterprise system. How does the Sermon on the Mount augment the gross global product, bolster the transnational corporate bottom line or put hard currency in my pocket?"

"But the religion you would force on the world is so violent, so terrifying," McMahon said, "people in my world fear it."

"True," Marika said, "Islam is an infinite fount of violence and terror, which is only one of the many things our people love about it."

"That's not a universally held position," McMahon pointed out.

"We're talking reality, Mr. McMahon," Raza said, "the natural order of things, the way the world works, not popular opinion. If history teaches us one thing it's that a leader's reluctance to employ violence and terror, to crush dissent with overwhelming force will inevitably doom a culture to unrest, rebellion, insurrection, revolution, overthrow and civilizational collapse. A lack of brutal and bloody resolve—of plain, iron-fisted, testicular fortitude—will doom a culture as thoroughly and as quickly as the K-T asteroid strike."

"So you feel it's better to reign in hell than to serve in heaven?" McMahon asked.

"Absolutely," Marika said. "We're in hell already, or haven't you heard? How is it you once described our movement? You said 'Islam is defending a bridgehead on the River Styx.' I rather liked that one, Mr. McMahon.

"When you talk like that, I sometimes think you do understand us," Marika said.

" 'A bridgehead on the River Styx,' " Raza repeated, half to herself. "I couldn't have put it better myself."

"Are you sure, Mr. McMahon," Marika said, "you aren't part Arab?"

PART XII

What was Life anyway? To Tower, it was nothing more than a knock-me-down, drag-me-out, beat-me, kill-me, make-me-write-bad-checks yet somehow sexy-as-hell whore, who seduced you into her bed, then took a straight razor to your balls... From Life's point of view, murder was infinitely preferable to impotence; natural selection was Her only iron law, and all moral values were empty as prayer and meaningless as a submongoloid's dreams... Death was a spectacularly stupid joke, worthy of only the darkest derision, an ignorant farce almost as ludicrous as Life Its Own Self... That being the case, Tower firmly believed nothing could be true, and everything was permitted. God— if there was a God—was an omnipotent idiot, and Tower couldn't believe God saw a dime's worth of difference between Adolf Hitler and Jesus Christ. Why should He? Tower didn't—and when Tower died (if he ever died!), he believed the universe would come to an abrupt and ugly end. In fact, the thought of all that infinite, starless, lifeless, ever-lasting void made Tower... hard.

—J. T. Tower, contemplating "Life"

1

"As flies to wanton boys, are we to the gods. They kill us for their sport."

—King Lear: IV, i, 36–37

J. T. Tower now sat in his penthouse apartment. Its eastern view overlooked the East River, Roosevelt Island, the Brooklyn and Manhattan bridges and Long Island as well, and if Tower did a slow circular turn, he could see the rest of New York's five boroughs. The view from one hundred stories up was, by any objective standard, overwhelming, and on entering any of his Tower penthouses, most people were awestruck. One man, on gazing out over the Apple, had told Tower he felt as if he "could touch the face of God."

Tower had asked the man to resist the impulse, saying that he "only liked being touched by beautiful women."

Many of the women he brought up allegedly found the Olympian view—combined with the financial power it represented—sexually stimulating. Tower bragged that women often became so erotically aroused at looking out over the city he bedded them within minutes of their arrival, including those with whom he'd never previously slept.

Whatever the case, anyone who walked into one of his Tower of Power penthouses and witnessed the 360-degree panorama of the city below had to be moved.

Everyone except Tower.

Tower alone looked out over the city and felt nothing.

It wasn't just that he was drunk. He'd never felt anything resembling empathy or awe. He understood that he was missing something—some milk of human kindness, that vast sympathy, common throughout the species, that was often described as a person's "basic humanity." That Tower was devoid of anything even remotely resembling "basic humanity" puzzled but in no way disturbed him. He could fake affection if the need arose—at a funeral or a disaster site, a wedding or a birthday party—but, in truth, he dismissed other people's compassion as a stupid weakness or a bullshit con.

His daddy had never fallen prey to such foolishness. J. J. Tower was the least sentimental man J. T. had ever known, and his son had respected him for it. That alone was something. J. T. respected almost no one. Of course, J. J. had taught his son that respect with his fists. In his youth, the old man had been a Texas state boxing champion, and when J. T. misbehaved, the old man took him down into the basement and gave his son an hour or so of "boxing instruction." When J. T. was a child, his father instructed him with open-handed slaps that left every square inch of his head, arms and torso covered with crimson finger welts. By the time J. T. was in high school, the old man was punching him with closed fists, focusing on his stomach and kidneys so as not to mark him too conspicuously but occasionally hammering the back and sides of his head, even bloodying his nose and working over his cheekbones and jaw.

From time to time, the old man would walk up behind J. T., reach back and give him a hard, roundhouse clout to the temple, knocking his son to his knees, the kid's ears ringing and eyes brimming.

"That's for . . . *nothing*," his father would say.

"When angered, my old man was the Wrath of God," Tower would occasionally reminisce. "He's the only man I ever feared, and he was the only person who could make me do his bidding."

Staring absently in the direction of the UN, he ignored the view and instead studied his reflection in the window—that of an aging angry man with reddish-brown-colored hair, a raptor's eyes and hatred in his heart.

Is there anything in the world that scares you? he wondered.

Probably not, although he had to admit that the U.S. government did occasionally worry him. With all its infinite power, all its investigative and prosecutorial agencies, it undoubtedly had the ability to put him in prison, and over the decades any number of officials and politicians had made ineffectual efforts in that direction. He did not consider such actions impossible or infeasible. Tower had done many things in his lifetime that could have put him in *durance vile* for the rest of his days. He'd always lived his life on the razor's edge and the hair trigger's trembling touch. Consequently, the impulse to watch his back, to cover his tracks and to protect himself from his enemies in DC and around the world was as instinctive in him as it was undeniably necessary.

He planned on neutralizing that threat soon though.

Only one obstacle stood in his way: that damn Meredith woman. During her decade-long investigations into his business dealings and his political machinations, Jules had uncovered and made public enough serious evidence to have put a less wealthy, less influential, less legally sophisticated and politically connected man in prison for the rest of his days. She had unearthed more dirt on him than the FBI, the SEC and the Treasury Department put together. Those agencies he would soon tame, rendering their attempts to expose him meaningless, but the Meredith woman he could not threaten or buy.

Well, Tower thought to himself, *Putilov had told you several times he'd close Meredith's account for you in one hot second. So, tonight, after she'd pushed you too far, you'd taken Putilov up on his offer.*

That interview he'd had with Meredith—during which she had so humiliatingly spurned his advances—was the last straw. She had to go. So he'd called the Russian president after she'd left and put the hit out on her. That he would finally be rid of her did not particularly bother him. Quite the contrary, what nagged at him was why he hadn't done it earlier. Over the years, he'd faced legions of enemies but none as dangerous and persistent as Jules Meredith. Of all his foes, she was far and away the most deserving of termination—termination with extreme prejudice. She had done more to jeopardize his business empire and his personal freedom than all his other enemies combined.

Why was *she still around? Years ago, he could have accepted Putilov's offers to eliminate her. Putilov would have done it if he'd been in Tower's shoes. Look how many hundreds of Russian reporters Putilov had had killed, and they were far less threatening to Putilov than the Meredith woman was to Tower. Why had Tower been so loath to order the hit?*

Tower did not want to contemplate the implications of his inaction. He hadn't grown soft; that was for sure. But there was something about that Meredith woman he couldn't put his finger on. For some reason, he could not give the order—until last night, after she had rejected his advances.

Aw, fuck it. It is what it is. That's the way it happens sometimes.

J. T. let his mind wander . . .

Yes, he thought to himself, the Meredith woman was a problem, but he had lots of problems. These were troubling times, no doubt about it. He had organized a select financial elite—superwealthy magnates who were willing to put their riches where their mouths were and change the world—into an unrivaled donor network. They had organized at the state and local level, and after a decade they had conquered most the state legislatures and commandeered the lion's share of the state governorships across the country. Those victories had given his organization the reins of real political control, the power to effectively disenfranchise minorities, college kids, single moms and the elderly—people who had a vested interest in opposing Tower's agenda. He'd also acquired the right to gerrymander voting districts to such a degree that he now controlled Congress as well, regardless of the national overall popular vote—which often, sometimes overwhelmingly, favored his opposition.

And then he'd finally staged the greatest coup of all: He had put himself in the Oval Office.

He wondered idly whether he shouldn't just imprison Jules Meredith.

Fuck it. It was more expeditious to kill her, and anyway the decision had been made, the order given.

He'd told Putlilov that he'd better do it soon. Times were tough, and he couldn't have her snooping around his finances any longer. He and his donor network were under siege as at no time before. Their enemies were all around them—college professors, crusading reporters, teachers, bureaucrats, scientists, unions, queers, blacks, Hispanics, Asians, Democrats anywhere and everywhere. Previously he'd thought his political organization—built on tax-deductible charitable donations, laundered through his political foundations—was impregnable. He'd always believed his control of the state houses and governorships was absolute, but he wasn't so sure anymore. It seemed to Tower that bleeding-heart pasty-faced peace-creeps were leeching the heart's blood out of this so-called republic. Of course, his father knew how to handle such agitators. When unions reared their ugly heads, he'd have his boys plant a half a key of heroin in the union leaders' lockers, then call in the cops. No need to break heads or pay them off. Let the cops do the dirty work for him. Ship a few union leaders off to prison on twenty-year sentences, and all those pesky labor complaints went away. The agitators found out what happens when you fuck with the Towers.

No more union problems now! his father would shout as he howled with laughter, as the union leaders were perp-walked off to prison.

By God, Tower Enterprises had come a long way since those difficult days. Back during his father's time, he and his ultra-right-wing plutocratic friends had been persona non grata. The politicians would barely talk to them and definitely wouldn't work with them. Oh, they'd take their money, but they wouldn't *do* anything in return. The whores wouldn't repeal Social Security, Medicare, Medicaid, SEC, EPA, OSHA or reduce the upper-bracket tax rates to fiscal absurdity. The politicians of the '60s and '70s had considered Tower and his network too extreme to climb into bed with.

That reluctance ended in the 1980s, when Ronald Reagan took office. Just thinking about those days made Tower smile. He was just starting to make a name for himself, and he'd found a true soul mate in the Gipper. They'd spent many a night together discussing their vision of the future.

*F*irst, the Gipper had explained, *I plan on abolishing the Fairness Doctrine. That will give an enterprising young man, such as yourself, an opportunity to create TV and talk radio networks dedicated to conservative doctrines and* *ideals, but which, in no way, will be required to let the other side state their opposing views. Communications satellites will proliferate such cable networks, and I'll see to it you get in on the ground floor. I can envision newspapers all over this land joining our crusade and spreading our gospel. I'm already in negotiations with the top TV evangelists. They've been politically neutral up to now, but I'm enlisting their services and television networks to join our cause and campaign as well. But I'm old, Jim, I can't do it all. Also as president, I'm under a microscope. The press watches my every move. You're in the private sector though, and you have the brains, balls and wherewithal to do it for me—covertly, anonymously. You can get this big conservative media ball rolling. When we get our operation up and running, the other side will never know what hit them."*

"Mr. President, J. T. had said, *I know what you mean, but I hate that word 'conservative.' It's so—so—"*

"Soft?"

"Exactly. We want a movement that's radical, that's revolutionary."

"And you'll scare the electorate into the arms of our enemies if you put it to them like that. You need to make us seem safe, steady, reasonable, reliable. You can't make them think we're plotting a right-wing plutocratic coup."

Tower nodded his agreement. The old man was obviously right.

"Just get that big media complex going," Ronnie said. *"The tax breaks and subsidies I'll give your petrochemical companies, investment banks, casinos and real estate development firms will more than fund it. We will also need conservative think tanks and foundations filled with scholars dedicated to writing the legislation and organizational plans necessary to our takeover. After we take control, we'll have all those bills and position papers locked and loaded, in the can, so we can make them the law of the land as soon as we have the power."*

"Won't the Washington elites try to block that legislation, Mr. President?"

"The Washington elites—including the Elite Media—will step in line. They're drawn to power like iron filings to a magnet. Mark my words, they'll come around to our side, and you know why?"

"Money talks and bullshit walks?"

"Hell, yes. They'll even come to believe in our Cause."

"They'll learn to 'love Big Brother.'"

"Just like Orwell wrote. They'll come around to our way of thinking."

"But with all due respect, we don't need more 'thinking,'" the young J. T. Tower had told the president. *"We need to turn things upside down and inside out. We have to shake this country up. Abolish Social Security, Medicare, all federal law enforcement, the goddamned IRS, the EPA, OSHA, the*

SEC. And we'll have to be strong, tough, decisive. We have to seize the flame. We can't show any weakness."

"We'll get there, Jimmy, we'll get there."

"But how, Mr. President? Through news networks, think tanks, words? We need action."

"Oh, we'll take action. How do you think Lenin came to power in Russia? How do you think Hitler took over Germany? Not through revolution. They were coupists, not a revolutionaries. Well, we'll do it quietly. Do the words 'silent coup' mean anything to you?"

Tower realized, of course, the old man was right.

"You're a wise man, Mr. President. I have much to learn from you."

"And you're a young, smart, strong and tough. You can be my sword, my shield. Together, we'll perform wonders."

"But we need to do some serious planning, Mr. President. This can't be a hit-or-miss, hit-and-run operation."

"You'll do it. I know you will. I won't live to see. You though—you could see it happen in your lifetime."

That day had come. Tower and his organization had put together a right-wing juggernaut of money, media, think tanks and lobbying groups that had taken Washington, D.C. and the state houses by storm.

If only a Wall Street meltdown hadn't hammered his first term and cost him the Senate, he'd have owned the country by now. Even so, Tower had been certain he'd get the Senate back during the next election, but now he was having doubts. It had all been going so well until Jules Meredith came out with that blistering series of articles. She was inflaming the electorate, and she was capable of taking him down the way Ida Tarbell had targeted and destroyed John D. Rockefeller's oil empire with a series of muckraking pieces, followed by her book, *The History of the Standard Oil Company*. The public outcry had been overwhelming, and within a few years, Theodore Roosevelt had rallied the Congress and forced the breakup of the Rockefeller empire.

Jules Meredith was whipping up public sentiment against him the same way, and if anything, he was more vulnerable than John D. had been. Tower's business dealings could not stand scrutiny, nor could those of his political/financial network. And now Jules Meredith was shining a spotlight on both those operations—a blinding spotlight.

She had to go—not only to stop her from probing into his business affairs but also to make it clear that *no one fucked with J. T. Tower.*

They were all conspiring to pauperize him and liquidate not only his fortune but everything he and his old man had worked for, robbing not just him but his children, grandchildren, great-grandchildren and their descendants to come as well. They wanted his head on a stake, his balls in a vise and every dime he ever made paid out in taxes, back taxes, penalties and fines. They wanted to bankrupt him *forever.*

And then imprison him.

Even worse, the prices of oil and gas, which had been on a decade-long decline, were now dropping like a rock. Tower had failed to foresee that new technologies such as fracking and the high-tech extraction technologies, which overnight had made unlimited amounts of gas, shale and tar sands oil readily available, would result in an inevitable drop in oil prices, which was now threatening his entire global empire.

A second mistake had been his failure to foresee that wind and solar would prove as practicable and economically competitive as they now were.

Hell, Walmart was now powering every one of its facilities with solar!

On top of everything, AI was rapidly rendering most employees obsolete, and the layoffs were pandemic. That downsizing and the stock market crash had so incensed the voters they had thrown the Senate incumbents out into the street, all but tar-and-feathering them. The electorate would be coming after him next with torches, pitchforks and noose knots.

All of them led by Jules Meredith. She was prying into his business and political operations the way Woodward and Bernstein had gone after Nixon.

But he wasn't Nixon.

J. T. Tower would not go gently.

Jules Meredith had no idea whom she was fucking with. J. T. Tower ate people like her for breakfast, and if he didn't, Putilov would. Maybe he should let Meredith know what he had done to that mistress of his, Juanita Juarez, who tried to leave him. She'd learned the hard way what happened to people who fuck with J. T. Tower. Last he heard, that Mexican drug cartel he'd paid to handle her had her hustling tricks in a Guadalajara *casa de puta.*

Hard-trade tricks.

It had been going so well. Everything was on track. What the fuck had happened?

His old man believed it all went wrong when that Jew, Roosevelt, was elected—him and his fucking New Deal—his "Jew Deal," his daddy used to call it. "Roosevelt and his fucking Jew York press," his daddy would thunder. He wondered what the old man would think if he were alive today. If his daddy needed any proof that the Democrats are all a bunch of depraved degenerates, the old man could just look at their former president, that Kenyan cocksucker, Barack Obama—case closed, end of story.

Tower's golden triumph had of course been Citizens United, the Supreme Court decision that nullified a century of campaign finance reform, clearly contradicting the will of the people, who wanted big money out of politics. That was supposed to fix everything. He and his hit team of 200 donors could spend any amount of tax-deductible dark money they wanted, privately, with utter anonymity. And they could write it off their 20 percent carried-interest taxes. Assuming they even paid that much.

Citizens United. It should have been called Oligarchs United, because that's what he was going to achieve, even if it killed him. The American people had proven themselves incapable of self-government, and now that the blacks and Hispanics were outbreeding the whites in this country, reproducing like Viagra-crazed lemmings on crack, he'd see to it that "one person, one vote" was a thing of the past. He'd piss all over their parade till his enemies thought they were getting swamped by a hurricane of stinking yellow urine.

Once more, he caught a glimpse of his aging face reflected in the window. Staring at it, he felt nothing. The more he thought about it, he wondered if he'd ever felt anything besides raw animal lust and a murderous urge to destroy anyone who got in his way or simply pissed him off.

Is that what everything came down to in the end? Is that all Life was—lust and destruction? Maybe that was all there was. Tower certainly knew what his life and his father's life had meant—and he did not see that Life itself was any different.

What was Life anyway? he wondered, staring absently at his reflection. *It was nothing more to him than a knock-me-down, drag-me-out, beat-me, kill-me, make-me-write-bad-checks yet somehow sexy-as-hell whore who seduced you into her bed then took a straight razor to your balls. Life was always ready to run a Georgia train up your ass, fill it with high-octane fuel and fire a flare gun into its fuming, gasoline-choked maw. From Life's point of view, murder was infinitely preferable to impotence; natural selection was Her only iron law, and all moral values were empty as prayer and meaningless as a submongoloid's dreams. Tower had glimpsed the skull beneath Life's skin, viewed Her death's-head stare and laughed at the cruelest hilarity of them all: that Death was a spectacularly stupid joke worthy of only the darkest derision, an ignorant farce almost as ludicrous as Life Its Own Self. That the joke was being played on as vain, vapid and self-deluding a species as the human race made the jest, in Tower's eyes, no less ridiculous. He'd once heard a friend quote a line from* King Lear *that he'd never found one reason to disagree with: "As flies to wanton boys are we to the gods: They kill us for their sport." That being the case, he firmly believed nothing could be true, and everything was permitted. God—if there was a God—was an omnipotent idiot, and Tower couldn't believe God saw a dime's worth of difference between Adolf Hitler and Jesus Christ. Why should He? Tower didn't—and when Tower died (if he ever died!), he believed the universe would come to an abrupt and ugly end. In fact, the thought of all that infinite, starless, lifeless, everlasting void made Tower . . . hard.*

Which got him thinking about Jules Meredith again—and again he found himself getting aroused. Maybe that was the reason he hadn't had Jules hit years ago: She was too goddamn hot.

And she was different. She was the only person on earth who had the guts to stand up to him, to tell him what she thought of him—to tell him he was full of shit, then prove it to him. And, then, of course, she was blazing-fucking-hot yet categorically refused to sleep with him, which only further inflamed his desire for her. That she wanted desperately to take him down only made her more dangerous, more exciting, more enticing.

Brenda had warned him once that he was drawn to self-destruction, that he was driven to touch the Luciferian flame, and that one day it would burn him alive.

Maybe that was Jules—his Luciferian flame.

So be it.

Still J. T. Tower had to have her. He was committed to it. He had to have her even if he hung for it.

Even if it brought down everything he'd worked for.

Even if it destroyed his whole goddamn world.

He swore on his balls and his eyes he would finally fucking have her.

And then he remembered he'd already put the hit out on her.

He wondered if he should call Putilov and rescind the order, but he feared Putilov wouldn't understand. He'd think Tower was soft, wishy-washy, couldn't make up his mind. And Tower couldn't allow that.

Also Tower sometimes worried that Putilov didn't like women.

Anyway, Putilov had probably already ordered the Meredith woman eliminated.

He was pretty efficient at that kind of thing.

Still Tower wondered if it was too late to call the murder off.

2

"God made the birds and sea creatures in three days.
Why can't we extract Rashid in, say, an hour or two?"
—Elena Moreno

The Black Hawk was now approaching the target. Given the brightness of the full moon and the starlit desert sky, the terrain was completely, amazingly visible from the chopper. As they came in for the landing and began setting down in the lee of the hill, the Black Hawk was surprisingly quiet.

"On the other side of that hill is Rashid's safe house," Elena told the men in her chopper.

"How will we recognize Rashid?" Eric asked. "I've never seen or worked with him." Eric had signed on at the last minute.

"He'll be wearing a keffiyeh and riding a dromedary," Eric said.

"Or he'll be ridin' a dromedary and readin' a Koran," Leon offered.

"I thought you knew him," Elena said. She showed Eric a photo of Rashid on her iPhone.

"Seriously," Kareem asked, "what's the plan?"

"We go in," Jamie said, "kill the men holding Rashid, and take him back to the chopper."

"That's the plan?" Kareem asked again.

"That's the plan," Elena said evenly with a small smile.

"Your plan is insane," Jonesy said.

"Oh, I get it," Jamie said. "Reality again."

"Kareem's got a point," Leon said. "You sure we can pull this thing off?"

"God made the birds and sea creatures in three days," Elena said. "Why can't we extract Rashid in, say, an hour or two?"

"Who these two ladies anyway?" Henry asked, looking at Jonesy.

"Fine funky bitches with dead men in their eyes," Jonesy said.

"Only thing that matters is . . . *are you ready*?" Elena asked.

"Ready as Freddy," Jamie said.

"Ready to punch in?" Elena asked.

"Rackin' and crackin'," Jonesy said.

"Are you ready to accept the plan God has for you?" Elena asked.

"Sir, yes, sir!" Jamie said.

"Then let's get that rubber on the road," Elena said.

"Give 'em that high hard one," Leon said.

Elena racked the slide on her .45 Magnum Desert Eagle, the most power-ful semi-automatic pistol made.

"Nice gun," Stevie said. "What's it for?"

"Killin' rhinoceroses," Leon said.

"Huntin' dinosaurs," Jonesy suggested.

"*Time to rock 'n' roll, ladies,*" Adara said in their earpieces.

"Anyone seen Junius?" Elena asked. "Where is he?"

"Checking his pecs in the restroom mirror," Leon said.

"*He's in this chopper with me,*" Adara said in their earpieces.

"Copy that," Stevie said.

"Anything else?" Elena asked.

"Can I detail your car?" Leon asked. "Do your income tax?"

"So we're ready," Elena said.

"Squared away," Jamie said.

"We good?" Jonesy asked.

"We're solid," Leon said.

"*Mais d'accord,*" Andre said in their earpieces. *But of course.*

"Big affirm," Elena said.

"Copy that," Jonesy said.

The two Black Hawks landed in the lee of the hill, and the people in their holds piled out.

3

To put the sum total of Putilov's thefts into perspective, consider that the U.S. GDP is $18 trillion and U.S. tax-free offshore accounts contain $2.1 trillion, or 12 percent of its GDP. The world's GDP is around $75 trillion, and the total amount of global black money buried abroad is around $26 trillion, or about 33 percent of the planet's GDP. As obscene as those percentages might be, they pale before those of Putilov's Russia. The $1.3 trillion that Putilov and his cronies have locked away in Western banks is more than 100 percent of Russia's GDP, which is only $1.26 trillion. In other words, Putilov and his wolf pack have devoured the equivalent of Russia's entire annual GDP!
 —Jules Meredith on Mikhail Ivanovich Putilov

Putilov stared into his computer screen, speechless with rage. Now he not only had that idiot Tower to deal with, Jules Meredith was on his case.

Ah hell, maybe it was *time for her to go.*

For the past year, he'd thought about having her hit. Waheed had been pushing for it. After all, she was major critic of Tower, himself and their whole Oligarch Movement. She was a troublemaker and a serious pain in the ass.

But she also drove Tower crazy, sent him into paroxysms of rage, and that was worth everything to Putilov.

In fact, two hours ago, when Tower had finally broken down and asked him to have Jules Meredith killed, Putilov had lied and said that he would, had yessed Tower to death, all the time fully intending not to do it. No one on the planet could aggravate Tower like Meredith, and tormenting Tower was all Putilov cared about nowadays. Hell, he'd have paid her any amount of money if she could piss Tower off even more. He'd have sent bodyguards to protect her—just to make sure she kept making that moron miserable.

That Tower had the hots for her physically and that she hated the ground he walked on pleased Putilov to no end. When Tower told him how, after he'd come on to Meredith, she'd said: "Tower, I wouldn't piss on you if you were on fire!" Putilov had wanted to toss hats in the air and do handsprings.

He'd wanted to kiss Jules Meredith himself. He counted hearing her response as one of the high points of his life.

But now Meredith had gone over to the other side. She had written and published a truly horrifying takedown piece on him—on Mikhail Ivanovich Putilov—and so she had to go. That Tower had changed his mind about Meredith and begged Putilov to call off the hit—claiming it was all a misunderstanding and that he wanted another shot at fucking her—was of no consequence. Putilov could not have cared less. Jules Meredith was finished—over and out. Like he'd done to so many other reporters before her, Putilov was turning out her lights.

It wasn't just that Meredith was now attacking Putilov in print. Lots of people had written articles and books on him and his myriad crimes: his wholesale plundering of the Russian State, the thousands of killings he'd ordered—especially all those pesky reporters and idealistic human rights activists he'd disposed of—the hundreds of thousands of people he'd had summarily incarcerated . . . most notably those free-market entrepreneurs who fell afoul of him or his supporters or who had naïvely thought they could do business in Russia without compensating the president for that privilege.

What was wrong with forcing businesspeople to pay those bribes anyway? In Mexico, such disbursements were called the *mordida*, in India the *baksheesh* and in Russia, the *blat*. The difference was, of course, that in his world, the *blat* was extortionately, excruciatingly expensive—magnitudes greater than it was in other countries—and those who refused to pony up found themselves facing imprisonment or even death.

But all those stories had been widely reported, were universally known, and had Meredith rehashed those old news items he might well have shrugged it off. Frankly he wanted people to know that in his country he ruled with an iron fist, and you paid to play. One more so-called exposé wouldn't be worth the effort of dropping that final life-ending . . . dime.

But Meredith's article did not stop with his crimes against so-called humanity. She took her attack on him to a whole other dimension. She concluded her piece by focusing on his crimes against the Russian people. In doing so, she tacitly encouraged them to rebel, and there was nothing Putilov feared more in all the world than popular rebellion.

He'd seen uncontrollable crowds of angry citizens before. After the Berlin Wall fell, and the German populace was rising up against their Russian masters, Putilov had witnessed a public insurrection in Dresden in front of the KGB headquarters. He'd been in charge there, and the headquarters had almost been overrun. He had seen what revolutionary violence could do. He believed it could happen in Russia as well—it had happened before—and he feared the Revolt of the Masses like hell itself. That was one of the reasons he was dealing so severely with that hedge fund bandit who, with his famine derivatives, had exacerbated the Mideast drought of 2012 and had driven the starving destitute people in that region to take up arms against their rulers. Putilov viewed such political uprisings as a threat against him and his country. He knew revolutions were quite capable of jumping borders and spreading long distances—even as far as Mother Russia herself.

Now that Jules Meredith was attempting to turn the Russian people against him with devastating reports of how he'd robbed them blind and stolen their hopes and dreams, he was determined to put her down hard.

He could not stop himself from masochistically rereading the end of her article:

> *What has Putilov's oligarchy done for him, and what has he done for his fellow citizens? In the late 1980s, he'd been thrown out of the KGB, and he was a nobody—just a busted-out intelligence agent who had drifted into politics. He had never been a lawyer, doctor, teacher, scientist or scholar—a manufacturer, a financier, or any kind of businessman. He was merely a KGB functionary who had created nothing of financial worth or socially redeeming value. Yet twenty-five years after entering politics, Putilov owned twenty official residences with 24/7 round-the-clock staffing. One of them—"Putilov's Palace"—cost his oligarchical supporters $1 billion. He is the proud possessor of four yachts—one of them worth $50 million—fifty-eight airplanes and almost $1 million worth of watches. One of his favorites is his $60,000 white-gold Patek Philippe Perpetual Calendar.*
>
> *Worth over $200 billion, Putilov is easily the wealthiest man on earth, with two and a half times as much money as the second-biggest billionaire, the legitimate businessman Bill Gates.*
>
> *How has he acquired such prodigious riches?*
>
> *In the 1970s the USSR had kept tens of millions of dollars' worth of foreign currency in secret accounts concealed in other countries—partly to fund operations abroad. Intelligence agencies worldwide had abundant evidence that Putilov and his brigands stole almost all of it. He then arranged for the theft of over 500 tons of bullion purloined from the old USSR's gold reserves. He and his ex-KGB associates also mastered the arcane minutiae of asset-stripping, the privatization of government properties, extortion of legitimate businessmen, outright thievery and the simple art of murdering anyone*

who got in their way. And of course, they exacted bribes on an almost cosmic scale. Even today, a simple meeting with President Putilov costs a Russian businessman $10 million. Some Russian businessmen privately grumble that the cost of doing major deals in Putilov's Russia is a 35 percent bribe to the new Czar.

A Spanish prosecutor who had successfully wiretapped many of Putilov's business partners while they were in Spain—building illicit villas with conscripted Russian military personnel—said the transcripts proved that Russia's mafiosi were an integral part of that scam and many of Putilov's other operations. In fact, over the decades Putilov and his coterie of oligarchs have found the Russian mafia to be invaluable allies. To this day they routinely employ them for brutal beatings, targeted killings and other acts of calculated terror, which assure the Putilov clique total domination over Russian politics and economic markets. All the while, he and his junta have reaped hundreds of billions of dollars.

Putilov has even managed to plunder his fellow brigands. Setting himself up as the ultimate crime boss, his form of government became known as Putilovism—a system in which all the players bow to his absolute authority and pay him tribute of almost incalculable proportions. In exchange Putilov confers on cronies the right to pillage those around them on a historically unprecedented level, and he has granted them utter immunity from legal punishment. As part of his protection racket, Putilov awards diplomatic counselorships to his most loyal followers, freeing them of domestic and foreign prosecution and most forms of intrusive surveillance.

Putilov has even co-opted the Western democracies. We assist Putilov and his people at every turn. After Putilov and his pirate crew lawlessly loot their own land, the Western world—with its strict adherence to law and order—sees to it that these freebooters' ill-gotten gains are safely and secretly secured. Under the aegis of these democratic privacy laws, Putilov has constructed for himself and his cohorts a seemingly impenetrable underground labyrinth of thousands upon thousands of hidden accounts.

To put the sum total of Putilov's thefts into perspective, consider that the U.S. GDP is $18 trillion and U.S. tax-free offshore accounts contain $2.1 trillion, or 12 percent of its GDP. The world's GDP is around $75 trillion, and the total amount of global black money buried abroad is around $26 trillion, or about 33 percent of the planet's GDP. As obscene as those percentages might be, they pale before *those of Putilov's Russia. The $1.3 trillion that Putilov and his cro-nies have locked away in Western banks is more than 100 percent of Russia's GDP, which is only $1.26 trillion. In other words, Putilov and his wolf pack have devoured the equivalent of Russia's entire annual GDP!*

So we know what Putilovism has done for Putilov and his billion-aire partners. It's made them all unimaginably rich, but what has it done to the Russian people? Theirs is a story of unremitting poverty and savage exploitation. Despite one statistically aberrant population spurt, that nation now faces a long-term population implosion—*not* explosion. *According to the Brookings Institution, by the century's end, Russia could well see its number of citizens drop from 143.5 mil-lion to 100 million people, its 1950 census level.*

Why the contraction?

Putilov's oligarchy has stretched his people to the breaking point. Instead of upgrading Russia's collapsing health care system, he has plundered those programs remorselessly and funneled the money into the pockets of himself and his wealthy friends. Consequently, the de-pressed and oppressed Russian people labor under some of the high-est rates of alcoholism, tobacco abuse and drug addiction on the face of the earth. Deaths from HIV/AIDS are rampant as are loss of life from heart disease, air/water pollution and suicide. Consequently, male longevity in Putilov's Russia is fifteen years lower than that of men in Germany, Italy and Sweden. The life expectancy of a fifteen-year-old boy in Russia is three years lower than that of a Haitian fifteen-year-old boy. Polish women live an average of six years longer than Russian women. In fact, each year, Russian men kill more women in their families than the Afghans killed Russian soldiers during that entire conflict.

Such long-term depopulation trends also spell economic disaster. A Yale University study says Russia has entered a "demographic per-fect storm." In thirty-five years, persons of worker-age in Russia will constitute less than 14 percent of the population. Moreover, the coun-try is witnessing a rapid decline in the educational and skill levels of its workers. All of these stressors will put profound pressure on the pension plans and health care providers servicing Russia's rapidly aging population.

Unsurprisingly, foreign firms are not eager to set up businesses and invest in Putilov's Russia. Among advanced nations, Russia under Putilov ranks number one for corruption and bribery; it rates last in legal, financial and political transparency. Moreover, doing business in Russia can be highly dangerous if you are not part of Putilov's in-group. In the last ten years Putilov's supporters in the business community have bribed cops, judges and prosecutors to imprison their competitors, putting over 300,000 innocent entrepreneurs behind bars. According to one estimate, such individuals represent 15 percent of Russia's prison population.

Putilov even refuses to build the minimal infrastructure business-people need to conduct business. While China during the last decade has built almost 4,500 miles of roadways, Putilov has yet to construct a single transnational highway. Because of corruption, pipelines in Russia cost 300 percent more than they do in the EU. Of the $50 billion Russia spent on the Sochi Olympics, over $25 billion went into the coffers of Putilov and his partners.

Each year, bribery, kickbacks and extortion under Putilov are estimated to drain 33 percent from its $1.26 trillion GDP.

The sad truth is that Putilov and his supporters are less interested in running Russia's businesses efficiently than they are in robbing the country's economic sector and hiding the money overseas. As we mentioned earlier, Putilov and his cadre of crooks have hidden over 100 percent of Russia's annual GDP abroad.

The effect that all this corruption has on the economic well-being of individual Russians is devastating. Credit Suisse estimates the median wealth of adults in Russian households to be $871. In other words, half of Russian adults have total household wealth of under $871. Under Putilov, median household wealth for a Russian adult was 85 percent of that for his or her counterpart in India, where that person was worth $1,040. In Brazil, median wealth is is $5,117; in China it is $8,023.

According to Credit Suisse, in the Land of Putilov, 111 people control 19 percent of that country's entire wealth, and the upper 10 percent possess 85 percent of the nation's money.

While the Russian people under Communist rule historically had a long tradition of literacy and academic achievement, and while they are still relatively well educated in math and science, they have embarrassingly limited job opportunities for their best-educated people, many of whom are brilliant, creative, ambitious and highly trained in these disciplines. The country produces shockingly little technological innovation or development. The state of Alabama produces more patents each year than Russia. Austria develops thirty-five times as

many. Employment opportunities are so dismal that one poll indi-
cated that almost two-thirds of the Russian population seriously con-
sider emigration.

Under Yeltsin, Russia had financial problems, but people and busi-
nesses enjoyed relative personal and financial freedom. Putilovism
changed all that. Russia's expanding free market system was turned
into an economic dictatorship with all major business decisions de-
pendent on the whims of a single ruler. To achieve this position of
total power, Putilov had to pauperize and subjugate the entirety of
the Russian people and rip successful Russian companies apart
piecemeal. As Karen Dawisha has written: "Massive companies that
had previously flourished in the private sector, like Mikhail Khodor-
kovsky's [oil company] Yukos, were raided and taken over by Kremlin
insiders."

Such tactics have driven most investors out of Russia. U.S. hedge
fund magnate William Browder is a classic case. He'd invested heavily
in Russia and had done well—until he rebelled against Russia's cor-
ruption and its lack of business transparency. Putilov responded by
arresting Browder's lawyer–auditor, Sergei Magnitskiy, and jailing
him. Viciously beaten in prison, Magnitskiy was also starved, sub-
jected to freezing cold and denied medical care. He subsequently died.

The United States under Barack Obama did fight back. Obama put
those responsible for Magnitskiy's death and for the illegal expro-
priation of Browder's assets on a visa-denial list and refused them
entrance into the U.S. Russia responded to these actions by trying
Browder in absentia and Magnitskiy posthumously—both for tax
evasion. After sentencing Browder, who by that time was living over-
seas, to a long prison term, Russia seized and gutted his Russian com-
panies, funneling hundreds of millions of dollars into Putilov's
private bank account and those of his jackal pack.

It was also the first time in history a legal system had tried a corpse.

Meanwhile, Russia's economy continues to fall apart. Not only has
their leader's ferocity frightened away foreign investors, it has scared
Russian businessmen into leaving Russia. Over 300,000 such busi-
nesspeople have moved to London, hoping to find a safer environ-
ment for themselves and their families. With macabre irony, some of
these émigrés have continued to work for their government, ransack-
ing the Russian economic sector. At the same time, however, they and
their families rely on law-abiding Londoners and that nation's respect-
for-the-law political system to provide peace and security for them-

selves and their loved ones. The hard painful truth is that the Western banks have acted as Putilov's willful enablers and fraudulent financiers.

There is light, however, at the end of this murky tunnel. Putilov's impenetrable financial labyrinth is impenetrable no more. Any cybersecurity system that can be built can be hacked, and the UN's, EU's and U.S. Senate's investigators have uncovered the locations and passwords for most of his and his partners' black money accounts. They will soon be in possession of them all.

Furthermore, such offshore accounts can be seized. In March 2014—after Putilov's illegal invasion of Crimea—Obama became Putilov's worst nightmare when he announced the U.S. was raiding the Western bank accounts of Putilov and his closest cronies. What followed was a race between the U.S., Putilov and his partners to see who could get to all that dark money first. The U.S. thereby created the technological paradigm and legal precedent for freezing and even seizing foreign funds after crimes have been committed internationally. Obama's people targeted one of Putilov's most lucrative business ventures with a particular vengeance, one in which all of his financial partners were heavily vested, on the grounds that the organization constituted an "outlaw bank."

The UN is now determined to go after not only Putilov's black assets but those of the world's other financial brigands and redistribute them to those more deserving.

The world's democracies are backing the UN's action.

Putilov, your deal's going down.

The Russian dictator stared at Meredith's column, his hands shaking even harder than before. He'd have Fahad handle Meredith. He was the best contractor Putilov had ever used, and he'd hired some spectacularly talented professionals over the years. As for Tower? Just a few more weeks—after Putilov had gotten rid of the UN's Global Expropriation Resolution once and for all—then he'd have Fahad deal with Tower. Putilov planned on doing Tower slow and hard.

Very slow.

Very hard.

He and that whore from hell, Raza Jabarti, had overseen the development of a brand-new, high-tech, scientifically sophisticated drug, and what it did to its victims was unspeakably gruesome. He sometimes described this new method to confidants as "killing men *the hard way.*"

It was a pun—an inside joke—and just thinking about it brought a vindictive smile to Putilov's lips.

Yes, the death he had planned for Tower was worth a celebration.

With trembling hands, he reached into his side drawer, took out his krok bottle and unscrewed the cap. Just staring at it got him aroused.

A small stream of spittle appeared in the left-hand corner of his mouth and rolled down his chin. It hung there a long moment before dropping onto the desk. More saliva appeared, then more and more and more.

Oblivious to the drool, now bubbling steadily out of the side of his mouth, Putilov began to grind and chop the pills.

PART XIII

"...it's time to blow this pop stand."

—Elena Moreno

1

It didn't matter how wicked the hedge fund bandit might be, what Raza and Putilov were forcing Fahad to do to him was pure, concentrated, unmitigated . . . *evil.*

Fahad's cab was stuck in gridlock on Manhattan's Second Avenue on the Upper East Side. Because of the UN's Anti-Inequality conferences and hearings, the entire East Side looked like a parking lot. He would have taken the new Second Avenue subway except he had a very large suitcase containing weapons and ammunition, which he did not want to tote around in public. He was an Arab; he didn't want people—or, even worse, some racial-profiling, compulsively curious cop—asking him about its contents.

Goddamn it, he was sick of this assignment. What the fuck was he doing here anyway? He didn't need the money that bad.

The job violated everything he had learned about personal and professional survival in his two decades as a paid mercenary. He should have turned Raza down ice-cold, gone to ground if necessary, and never looked back.

So why hadn't he rejected it? The answer to that one was easy. He'd never been short on guts, but even he didn't have the stones to say no to Raza, Marika and Kamal, not if he wanted to keep his balls in his nut sack.

He also did not want to get on Putilov's bad side, even though Putilov was dumping on him difficult, dangerous last-minute work. Putilov had ordered Fahad to hit a famous woman journalist, Jules Meredith, whom, even he, Fahad, knew about. Since she was notorious critic of Islam, he had no qualms about taking her out. A woman such as Jules Meredith, he was almost willing to kill for free.

Almost.

There was one obstacle. When Meredith exited her building in the morning, he wanted to shoot her from an apartment across the street. That way he'd have an easier time escaping. But first he had to gain access to one of those windows.

So Fahad had studied the occupants of the most strategically placed coops and finally settled on the one he wanted. The owner was a rather attractive woman, whom he'd shadowed and staked out for the last three nights. To-night, he planned to meet with the woman for the first time in a neighbor-hood bar, which she habitually frequented, convince her to take him home and then fuck his brains out.

For a man of Fahad's acumen, wiles and expertise, he knew her seduction would be no problem at all. He might even enjoy cajoling, enticing and screwing her.

One thing was sure: *That Muslim-hating bitch could die a thousand deaths for all he cared.*

He would definitely enjoy killing Jules Meredith afterward.

He understood intellectually and in the abstract that according to society's norms, taking the life of anyone was wrong, but he had no qualms about the laws of nations or the codes of men. He made his living murdering people, and afterward, he didn't apologize for it. It was what he did, who he was, what he'd always been.

So be it.

But what about the hedge fund guy? What he was going to do to him shook Fahad to his nonexistent soul. That was some truly monstrous shit. It didn't matter how wicked the hedge fund bandit might be, what Raza and Putilov were forcing Fahad to do to him was pure, concentrated, unmitigated *evil*.

Just take it one step, one minute at a time. Do it and don't look back. You can get through this.

But despite the pep talk he'd given himself, he wasn't sure he could carry it out. Even Fahad al-Qadi wasn't that cold.

Goddamn Raza and Putilov to hell!

They were two truly scary people.

2

"We're all monsters, but my brother's the worst."
—Brenda Tower

Jules sat in her apartment and stared out the window at the apartment building across the street. She was thinking about Brenda Tower. She hoped she was okay. Hard as it was to believe, she considered Brenda a friend.

Jules remembered the first time Brenda had suggested they get together. She had asked Jules to meet her late at night in a discreet hotel room after a charity event. Brenda believed she could ditch her bodyguards and surveillance team and that the two of them could meet privately. Jules had wondered why Tower's reclusive-billionaire sister wanted to meet someone so openly hostile to her family.

When Brenda informed her that she loved her articles on the Tower dynasty, Jules was frankly skeptical.

"No, I love your articles," Brenda had said.

"Why—y—y—y?" Jules had said, letting the word drag out.

"Largely because my brother loathes them. You really get under his skin."

"But you're part of the Tower clan too—a very influential part. My articles aren't kind to you."

"I don't disagree with anything you've written. We're all monsters, but my brother's the worst. He should have been jailed a long time ago."

"You aren't helpless," Jules said. "You don't have to look the other way and do nothing."

"True, but you also don't know what he's capable of. He's younger than I am, and I've been watching him, up close and personal, since he was born. I've seen him do horrifying things—things you can't even imagine. For me to directly challenge him—well, that's not a safe or even viable option."

"So you're saying your brother's even worse than what I've written. That he'd actually harm you? You're saying you—the person closer to him than anyone in the world—are terrified of him."

"I have reason to be afraid. You never knew our little brother, Ronnie. I saw what J. T. did to him, and I saw what J. T. did to the women in his life."

"He's reputed to be a rapist. The tabloids over the years have teemed with accusations of sexual predation."

"Until he sued those papers into submission," Brenda said.

"He is relentless. He's sued the papers I've worked for."

"Male or female," Brenda said, "he doesn't care, and I've never known anyone who could stand up to him."

"He's also the world's number one polluter. The carcinogens from your petrochemical plants are responsible for killing millions of people."

"And our casinos swindle millions more. He and I were talking about that last night. I asked him why he does it. What he hopes to get out of all these exploitative business dealings, all this death and destruction. Want to hear what he said?"

She took out a small digital recording device.

"What's that for?" Jules asked.

"He confides in me. I'm the only person he opens up to, and I've been taping him without his knowledge for years."

Shit, Jules thought. *J. T.'s sister—the only person in the world who he truly trusts—has been taping him surreptitiously. I may have hit the mother lode— or the sister lode.*

"And you invited me here," Jules asked, "because you want to help me to understand him?"

"Yes," Brenda said, pouring herself a rock glass of brandy. Jules accepted one herself.

Christ, it was 100-year-old Napoléon cognac.

"Why?"

"You may not believe me," Brenda asked, "but I actually like you. Maybe I see something of myself in you—something I could have been if I hadn't been born into the Tower clan."

"You understand that I'm committed to bringing down everything your family is, does and represents. Yet you want to help me?"

"I lack the courage to go up against Jim, but you're willing to do it. You aren't afraid. You'll never know how much that means to me."

"I'm not as fearless as you think," Jules said, shaking her head. "Now my friend Elena, she'd fight a circle saw. You should meet her."

"I expect I'd like her."

"I don't get it," Jules said. "You're saying you like me—after all I've written about your family—and you?"

"I admire the hell out of you," Brenda said. "You don't know it now, but you and I are going to be friends."

"But J. T. scares you?"

Brenda nodded. Twice.

"Then let's get him," Jules said.

Brenda turned on the recorder. The voices were unmistakably those of Brenda and her brother. Jules was entranced.

3

**"Jamie can shoot the balls off a runnin' buck at 800 yards,"
Jonesy said.**

Decked out in black fatigues, flak vests and watch caps, their faces darkened with camo paint, Elena, Adara, Jamie, Jonesy, Leon, Henry, Andre and Stevie crouched behind a truck-size boulder along the southern slope of the hill. They carried M7 machine guns, and their flak vests were festooned with flashbangs, fragmentation grenades, Ka-Bar combat knives and extra magazines. Pistols were holstered across their thighs. They each had extra ordnance in their packs. They could see through the windows that lights were on in the house, and the moon and desert stars were so bright they'd decided against night goggles.

The target was a cinder-block building, encircled by chain-link fence, which was surmounted by coiled razor wire. The blockhouse was flanked by a pair of Quonset huts. A watchtower rose above the far fence corner, manned by a solitary soldier. All around the compound, rocky outcroppings scarred its perimeter and the valley's arid slopes.

"Jamie, can you take out the man in the guard tower?" Elena asked.

"I can hit him from here," Jamie said.

"Jamie can shoot the balls off a runnin' buck at 800 yards," Jonesy said.

"No doubt," Adara said. "Still, move in a little closer. You have lots of rocks and escarpments to cover you."

"Affirmative."

Jamie slipped out from behind the big boulder and worked his way toward the gun tower, dogtrotting low to the ground from rock to rock, crawling when necessary, until he entered the shallow ravine that ran parallel to the front of the fence. He followed it in the direction of the tower on his hands and knees.

"When he takes out the guard," Adara said, "we'll make our way to the far side and open the fence with bolt cutters. Andre and Jonesy, you'll take teams with you and neutralize any troops in the Quonset huts, while Jamie, Jonesy and I will blast our way into the blockhouse with platter charges and flashbangs. We'll radio you if we need any help."

"We're in the middle of the Pakistan desert in a top-secret location," Elena agreed. "They have no reason to suspect anything."

"They'll all probably be asleep," Jonesy said.

"I'm more concerned with securing our two choppers," Adara said.

"It's a long walk out of here," Jonesy said, nodding.

"Which is why half the team is back protecting the choppers," Elena said.

"Tower guard down," Jamie said in their earpieces.

"You took him out?" Elena asked, double-checking.

"I thought it would improve his character," Jamie explained.

"And I bet he never even thanked you," Henry noted.

"Not one word," Jamie said.

"Then it's time to blow this pop stand," Elena said.

They split up into three groups and began working their way toward the fence, moving from rock to rock, from clump of brush to clump of brush.

PART XIV

"Your brother will come to grief with me."

—Jules Meredith to Brenda Tower

1

"J. T. Tower owns the FBI, the CIA, the SEC, the Treasury, the courts. Hell, that former FBI director, Conley, helped Putilov get my brother elected."
—Brenda Tower on her brother, the president

Jules Meredith couldn't believe Brenda had been taping her brother on the sly for the last ten years and was now playing the tapes for Jules.

She'd even said she was giving them to her.

The two of them listened to a small sample of Brenda's tapes—five hours' worth—and they were utterly mesmerizing in a macabre kind of way. Tower clearly proved in his own words that he was a psychopath of maniacal proportions.

The dawn sun was coming up over Manhattan, and the two women finally put the tapes and the recorder away. For a long moment, they stared at each other in silence.

"All of these recordings are yours," Brenda said. "Just promise me one thing: Somehow you'll make that bastard pay."

"Why is it so important to you to punish Tower now?" Jules asked. "After all these years?"

Brenda handed Jules a manila envelope. "Open it."

Jules perused it quickly. It was a recent medical report on Tower's sister, and its findings were unmistakable. The words "stage-four uterine cancer" jumped out at Jules.

"My condition is irreparable and beyond hopeless," Brenda said. "I've refused chemo and radiation."

"What does Jim say about this?"

"He doesn't know. He thinks I've been visiting Vegas for the drinking and gambling. I was, but I've also been seeing a cancer specialist secretly and incognito."

Jules put her hand on Brenda's arm, but Brenda gently removed it.

"Don't worry about me. I just want you to stop that sonofabitch. He can't go on doing these terrible things and profiting off them."

"Brenda, this is a very difficult undertaking, and you're ill."

"I can hold up my end, and I have dirt on him—in his own words—that will shake even you. We can put my brother away forever."

"I'm not sure I'm the one," Jules said. "He's the president of the United States. Really, the FBI would be better."

"J. T. Tower owns the FBI, the CIA, the SEC, the Treasury, the courts. Hell, that former FBI director, Conley, helped Putilov get my brother elected."

"All the more reason this won't work," Jules said.

"You're the only one who has any chance at all at nailing J. T."

"But this is too big—even for me."

"You have to do it, Jules. Please. You're the only one I trust. You're the only one I can turn to."

"Is the evidence you have on him really that incriminating?"

"I have stuff on him that would turn the heart to stone," Brenda said.

What am I going to do? Jules thought, looking away.

2

McMahon had mocked the faith of some of the most dangerous people on earth, and karma had finally come after him. And while he despised these people for what they were doing to him, he had to admit that, in part, he'd done it to himself. Like Odysseus, he'd chosen to howl at the Cyclops and shout his name at the gods.

Late at night, chained to a steel bed frame in a small locked room, McMahon stared at the ceiling. A narrow window just below the ceiling was filled with brilliant night stars.

Rashid, who was also shackled to a bed frame, lay a few feet from him. Tariq and Marika had been much harder on Rashid than Raza—than even Marika—had been on McMahon. This was, in part, because Rashid had information they truly needed. Also McMahon couldn't get over the feeling that Raza somehow found him . . . *entertaining.*

In fact, sometimes he wondered if she actually liked him.

What the fuck, he thought aimlessly. *That's how I make my living—entertaining people.*

"The stars in that window seem awfully bright," McMahon whispered to Rashid.

"We're in the desert. The stars are always brighter in the desert."

"I hate the desert," McMahon said.

"I'm told the desert is where we go to find God."

"If you think you can find God in Pakistan," McMahon said, "I have a great deal for you on reclaimed swampland in British Honduras."

"Finding God has never been part of my life's plan."

"Does your life's plan include being tortured to death by sadists? I'm worried about you, Rashid. I've got nothing these lunatics want. They just torture me for kicks, but they need what you know."

"My problem is if I tell them everything I know, I'm a dead man. So I'm better off holding out."

"You seem to be taking it pretty well," McMahon said.

"They aren't getting any cherry."

"Still you aren't giving them shit," McMahon said, "no matter what they do. I'm impressed."

"You aren't doing half-bad yourself. For a fucking TV comedian, you've surprised everyone. You got a pair of balls on you."

"You want to see balls, you should catch my act. Doing stand-up in front of an insane horde of stamping, shouting, drugged-out, crazy-fucking-PC college kids—now that takes balls."

"Still everyone's amazed. Danny McMahon—asshole Islamophobe celebrity—turns out to be a stand-up guy. Who would have guessed?"

McMahon closed his eyes. What was happening to him? He could finally understand why Raza and Tariq abducted him. They wanted spectacular terrorist attacks to frighten the West, and to convince the world no one was beyond their reach; that if they could abduct Danny McMahon, TV super-star, they could abduct anyone.

But now he was wondering not about them, but himself. In retrospect, he could see he'd been begging for something like this his whole life long. After all, what had driven him to write and perform monologues so insanely in-sulting, so outrageously inflammatory and conduct interviews so incendi-ary that they would inspire people halfway around the world to kidnap him and then smuggle him into Pakistan?

Why had he deliberately chosen to drive some of the most dangerous and demented people in the world into paroxysms of paranoid fury? What had caused him to fuck up so badly?

He did have a few ideas. In his student days, in classrooms, he'd always been a relentless provocateur. Once in college he'd run out of money and landed a job teaching eighth-, ninth- and twelfth-grade English. He'd in-stinctively set out to bait his classroom students.

When he taught the eighth-graders *Lassie Come Home*, he'd told them Lassie was a stupid hound who could never navigate hundreds of twisting, turning miles without help, guidance or direction and who was utterly, con-genitally, pathologically incapable of finding . . . her way home. He told his students that if he stuck one of them and their pet dog in a windowless room and locked the door from the outside, giving them only water and no food, within two weeks all that would be left of the student would be a glisteningly white skeleton and their pup, Fido, would be the only one left alive. He'd be licking his grinning, blood-flecked jaws, his belly bulging with their remains.

McMahon's tirades against man's best friend so angered the students that he got in trouble with their parents. The principal advised him to "stop at-tacking their dogs."

When he taught his ninth-grade pupils *The Old Man and the Sea*, he told them that the old fisherman, Santiago, was a self-destructive old fool who killed the big fish out of ignorant pride, broke the little kid's heart for no good reason and caused himself to have a heart attack. McMahon further argued that the novel's only winners, the only ones that knew what they were doing and had an honest productive mission in life, were the sharks, who stripped the big fish clean. They won; everyone else lost.

"If I had to be a character in that miserable story," McMahon had fumed at the class, "I'd want to be one of the sharks."

The kids screamed at him with blind hostility.

When he taught the twelfth-graders *Hamlet*, he argued that Hamlet was a psychopath who brought death and destruction to Denmark and was responsible, directly or indirectly, for killing everyone in the play. McMahon had then raged that the world would have been better off if Hamlet had killed himself in the "To be or not to be" scene. Or better yet the first act.

By the end of each of his classes he'd had the kids madder than hornets.

And he'd loved every second of it.

The truth was that's how he had always gotten his rocks off—antagonizing the mortal shit out of people all in the name of making them laugh and teaching them some sort of outrageous morality lesson.

Maybe in the end all he'd really wanted to do was piss them off.

Well, kid, you've pissed some people off big-time now.

Why had he always done shit like this? Once when he was out with Jules—and trying, unsuccessfully, to get into her pants—he had made the mistake of trying to match her drink for drink. He'd learned the hard way no one could drink Jules Meredith under the table.

Instead of screwing her, he'd gotten drunkenly maudlin and laid bare his soul. He'd told her about his childhood, about growing up in an Irish neighborhood in Brooklyn. His father had been born in County Cork, had encouraged him in sports and also bequeathed to him his dark, Irish wit and an inherent sense that the world was mad.

His mother was a librarian and a bookworm, who had instilled in him a love of literature, an obsessive interest in history and a burning sense of right and wrong. Her parents had survived Auschwitz by the skin of their teeth, and as a child she'd grown up listening to her relatives' Holocaust survival stories. When she entered school, she read all the Holocaust memoirs she could get her hands on. She was also, however, utterly irreligious. The Holocaust survivors' experiences had convinced his mother that there was no God.

McMahon had found nothing in his study of history or in his personal experiences to refute his mother's beliefs, and he had become an atheist at an early age. In fact, he was so passionate on the subject that atheism had quickly become his own Church Militant. By his early teens, he was already deriding people of faith as fools, knaves, charlatans or all of the above.

After that long drunken evening with Meredith, after she had listened half the night to stories of his Brooklyn childhood and after absorbing hour after hour of antireligious harangues, she asked why he was so iconoclastic, so eager to provoke and inflame.

"Because I believe in the things I say," he'd answered her glibly.

"I'm sure that's true," Jules said.

"But you think there's another reason?" he'd asked.

"Maybe." Jules shrugged. "For openers, you're the most deeply divided person I've even known. I've spent half my life listening to you fulminate against every form of wickedness and injustice—and that is all to the good— but most of the time it sounds like you're railing at yourself, as if the real war was inside of you."

"You think so?" he asked with wry mockery. "Then who's the enemy, and who's winning?"

"Oh, Danny, that's a war you can never win," Jules had said. "The half of Danny McMahon, which you got from your Jewish mother, hates the half of you that's a drunken, raving, hilariously funny Irish Catholic *asshole*. That half of you—the Irish Catholic asshole half—he despises the part your Jewish mother bequeathed you: namely, the somber intellectual activist who broods over injustice and will forever rage against the night. Each of your personalities has waged war on the other half for as long as I've known you, and as to either personality ever winning, that's not in the cards. Nor can you call a cease-fire, proclaim a separate peace or even declare a pox on both your houses and walk away. All you can do is fight, and that war will never end."

"It doesn't sound like you have a very high opinion of me," McMahon said.

"I think deep down inside of you is a really good man, and I hope one day you know in your soul how good a man you are, escape the self-hate that consumes you night and day, and feel the love, respect and admiration that all of your friends, including me, feel for you. I doubt that will happen, but still I hope. I am certain of one thing though: You may find love, but you'll never know peace."

McMahon had laughed long and hard at the time. He said he'd prefer getting "a piece of Jules" to "making peace with himself" any day of the week and then once again tried to get in her pants. She adroitly deflected his advances, eventually got them both into a cab and took him home.

He'd gotten up the next morning in his bed with a blinding hangover. Jules, who'd slept on his couch, was scrambling eggs and making coffee for him. She'd even fixed a Bloody Mary for his hangover. They talked all that morning about friends, their work, the fate of the earth and they laughed, but they never discussed what made Danny McMahon tick again.

In his own mind, he'd, of course, dismissed her analysis as "cheap-psych headshrinking" and "Julesbabble." Now, however, he had to wonder whether Jules had been right. Where had his iconoclasm and his contrarianism—most notably his war on religion—come from, and what had he hoped to accomplish with all his darkly comedic diatribes and funny-but-infuriating tirades? McMahon had mocked the faith of some of the most dangerous people on earth, and karma had finally come after him. And while he despised these people for what they were doing to him, he had to admit that, in part, he'd done it to himself. Like Odysseus, he'd chosen to howl at the Cyclops and shout his name at the gods.

Well the gods had had enough of his disrespect, his rank disdain and his insubordination. Their judgment had been rendered, and they were making their verdict known.

His day of reckoning was now at hand.

3

"My brother's planning shit with Putilov, the Saudis and the United Front that will make your story on them read like *Rebecca of Sunnybrook Farm*."

—Brenda Tower

Jules spent the next week listening to over one hundred hours of Brenda's most defamatory tapes. On them, her brother admitted and incriminated himself in scores of Class A felonies.

She had also given Jules all of her brother's offshore tax-evasive black-hole bank statements, including usernames, passwords and secret account numbers. Jules had enough evidence to put the president away for a hundred years. Sitting in their secret hotel room, Jules showed Brenda an annotated list of all the statutes her brother had violated and in what way.

"Are you sure you don't want to take this to the FBI or Treasury?" Jules asked.

"Too many of the directors and top officials are on his payroll. I know. I'm in on all of his business and legal meetings."

"And you're absolutely positive you want me to do it?" Jules asked. "You're about to cause a political earthquake."

"Yes, because I believe you'll see it through to the bloody end. I've seen you take on terrorists, the FBI, the White House, and you're still standing. I honestly think you'd stand up to a thermonuclear fireball, and I don't think you can be bought."

"Everyone has a price, and anyone can be scared," Jules said, shaking her head. "Also this would be no ordinary investigation. Other journalists have gone after J. T. Tower. They didn't keep their jobs. He doesn't tolerate reporters going through his dirty laundry."

"I will continue to lay everything out for you."

"Brenda, I've done some articles on him, and will continue to write articles. But frankly I'd wanted to get back to my book on the Saudis and the New United Islamist Front."

"He's part of that book. My brother's planning shit with Putilov, the Saudis and the United Front that will make your story on them read like *Rebecca of Sunnybrook Farm*."

"Jesus," Jules said, whistling softly, "I really am feeling . . . *inadequate*."

"Jules, he's genuinely diabolical. He's trying to sell the Saudis and their terrorist neighbors forty nuclear power plants."

Jules studied Brenda a long hard minute. Brenda's eyes were moist, and her hands were starting to tremble.

Jules finally let out a slow, deep sigh.

"Your brother will come to grief with me. I promise."

It happened just like that, and to Jules eternal surprise, their friendship was forged. It was not to be an easy friendship for either of them. Jules would force Brenda to relive some of the most horrifying episodes in her own life. In fact, once when Jules tried to commiserate with Brenda's cancer struggles, Brenda said:

"Uterine cancer's nothing compared to growing up with J. T."

Jules was relentless. Among other things, she wanted Brenda to tell her what J. T. was like when he first took over his father's company.

"At the time of Dad's death, J. T. had to have me around. He needed me, my support and my loyalty. He was already embroiled in divorce scandals. He eventually bought his ex-wives' silence, but at a very high price."

"I remember," Jules said. "He was mad at me for describing him as 'the Barbaric Billionaire.'"

"At first, a lot of reporters and talk-show comics ridiculed him," Brenda said, "but not for long. J. T. can pressure media CEOs like no one else."

"He can play a tune on people's heads," Jules said, "a real anvil chorus. I've seen him do it."

"In part," Brenda said, "because he's not afraid to make shit up. I've watched him blackmail politicians and CEOs with doctored photographs and fabricated emails. His scams were often bluffs, but they invariably worked. He always had crackpot media outlets ready to run with those stories. He always backed the big shots down."

"Most TV journalists are gossipmongers at heart," Jules said. "They'd have run with the stories and echoed them off each other to hell and back, whether they were true or not."

"You're the only one who's dug deep into his business dealings," Brenda said. "You and Danny McMahon are the only two that have stayed on his case."

"And now Danny's disappeared," Jules said.

"I hope J. T.'s not involved," Brenda said. "I wouldn't put it past him."

"The raw intelligence I've been able to gather on his disappearance," Jules said, taking Brenda's shaking hand, "has not been reassuring."

"If J. T.'s involved," Brenda said, "Danny McMahon is in for a whole world of hurt."

PART XV

"Oh, Mr. McMahon, we've only just begun your education."

—Raza Jabarti

1

"Will you walk with me out on the wire..."
—Bruce Springsteen

Fahad entered a dark, high-priced hotel lounge with a U-shaped mahogany bar—packed two- to three-deep behind a row of leather-padded stools. Three dozen high circular dark-wood tables with matching quartets of chairs accommodated the overflow. Art deco lamps were everywhere, and the walls featured large framed photos of the great actors and actresses of the '30s, '40s and '50s. The piped-in music was eclectic, ranging from the great jazz singers of those same decades—including Billie Holiday and Ella Fitzgerald—to the great rock stars of the '60s, '70s and '80s, artists such as Janis Joplin, CCR, the Stones, and the Boss.

Fahad squeezed in beside the tall, angularly slim woman seated at the bar. She had superlative bones and shoulder-length pale-blond hair. Her black, close-fitting Dior suit revealed a surprising amount of cleavage and thigh. Her slingback Jimmy Choo ebony pumps with five-inch heels completed the ensemble. He knew her name from her apartment building's directory and her Facebook page—Adrienne Harmon—and he also knew her to be a highly successful attorney-at-law.

He'd followed her for the last three nights, and her pattern seemed predictable. After work, no matter how late, she stopped off at this bar, her neighborhood watering hole, Ye Alde Pub. She always ordered the same: Jameson neat with a pint of Guinness backup. She was not averse to drinking several of each, and one of the three nights that he'd tailed her, she'd taken a gentleman home.

Tonight, he planned on going back to her apartment with her himself.

Fahad knew how to handle women, and he also knew she would like the way he looked. His whole life women had compared him to Omar Sharif, and he cultivated the actor's look assiduously. Shaving twice a day, he kept his five o'clock shadow to the barest minimum, and his mustache was always scrupulously trimmed. A high-priced haute-couture stylist cut his hair and darkened it to a deep ebony every other week. His wardrobe was always impeccably selected and meticulously maintained.

Since it was mandatory that he take Adrienne home, he was even more expensively attired than usual—an exquisitely tailored, black Armani suit, matching Gucci wingtips and a white silk Brooks Brothers shirt with a red Hermes tie. Holding the tie in place was a 4-carat diamond stickpin. He kept his left hand on the bar, so Adrienne could see that he wore no wedding ring but was sporting a platinum Rolex Submariner with emerald-cut, 3-carat diamonds.

Decades of close observation had taught him that women found the specter of great personal wealth—always implicit in ultraexpensive clothes and their costly bejeweled accoutrements—to be an all-but-irresistible aphrodisiac and that most women in bars were drawn to an attractive man with exorbitant riches like moths to a candle. He definitely had to draw this sensual moth into his licentious flame.

Springsteen was on the box, wailing "Born to Run." In raw, guttural tones he sang about a man offering a woman a chance to escape New Jersey and move, presumably, to the Big Apple.

> Won't you walk with me out on the wire,
> 'Cause, baby, I'm just a scared and lonely rider.

Fahad assumed that walking with him on the high wire was a euphemism for the two of them going to bed. Well, he needed to be in the woman's bed tonight.

"You ever feel like the guy in the song?" Fahad asked the woman. "Have you ever felt the urge to kick over the traces and run for the sun with someone you love and finally, forever, be . . . *free*?"

She turned to him, allowed him a quick perfunctory smile, then gave him a once-over. Pausing for a closer look, she gave him a twice-over. Blinking her eyes, she went for a brief, discreet . . . *thrice-over*. His incredible looks and awesome affluence were almost too much for her to absorb. Cranking her smile up all the way, she gave it every watt of candlepower at her disposal till the grin glittered and gleamed like all the lights on Broadway and all the stars in the heavenly firmament.

"With every second of my life," she said softly, "with every fiber of my being."

All the while her smile continued to scintillate, illuminating her eyes and crinkling the corners of her mouth. She was smiling at him with all her might, almost as if she were . . . *sincere*.

As if she . . . *cared*.

"You know," Fahad said casually, "sometimes I think I'd like to give it all up, donate everything I have to 'Save the Whales' and start out all over again, stone broke but without a care in the world."

"Having great wealth worries you?" Adrienne asked with an only slightly amused laugh.

"Always. I've never had the time to enjoy my money. It grinds away at me, like a heavy weight on the back of my neck, like a whetstone on my soul, and it weighs me down. My whole life has been nothing but work and worry. What's the point of it all, if you never have time to enjoy the fruits of your labor?"

"Maybe you need a womanfriend who could loosen you up, show you the time of your life and help you rid yourself of some of that burdensome . . . *loot*."

"Know of any volunteers?" Fahad asked, now giving her his widest smile, most of his thirty-two capped teeth, glinting like purest alabaster.

"What are friends for?" Adrienne said, putting a hand on his arm, turning to face him, leaning forward and gazing closely, intimately into his eyes.

Her smile was so infectious and so inviting that against his will he found himself liking her. In fact, he decided he would put some effort into this one. He'd make love to her that night like she'd never been made love to before. He would show her all the kingdoms of earth, the mountains of the moon and every kinky nether region in between, until the two of them had explored every infernal hellworld of her darkest, most diabolic desires.

He was determined to give her the fuck of her life, a fuck for the ages, a fuck that would rock the earth, stun the gods, till the stars themselves howled in shock and awe, till the galaxies screamed, and the angels on high trembled in envy, desire and disbelief.

Yes, Fahad al-Qadi would give her the hottest time of her hellacious young life—something special to remember him by. . .

Before he killed her.

2

"My brother's insane laughter rocked the room."
—Brenda Tower

Brenda had spent her whole life hoarding horrific stories of her brother, and now, late into the night, she was telling them to Jules. The tales seemed to rush out of her, as if they were river water thundering out of a detonated dam. The world would finally know the truth, and the truth did indeed appear to be setting Brenda free. Talking to Jules catharsized her.

The episodes were all shocking, but the one that really shook Jules and had haunted Brenda her entire life was how J. T. had driven their younger brother, Ronnie, to suicide.

"I suppose the worst period was when our father died," Brenda told her, "and Jim wanted the company all to himself. I wasn't a problem. I told him he could have my shares. I had more money than I could ever spend, and I didn't want to work that hard—hell, I never wanted to work at all. J. T. also knew I'd never stand up to him. Our little brother, Ronnie, though, had a lot of stock, and he also had a conscience. He staunchly opposed our petrochemical pollution operations, and he despised bilking people through crooked casino operations, through Wall Street scams and through predatory real estate projects and practices. He and J. T. were on a collision course, and after I saw what J. T. did to him on the last night of Ronnie's life, I knew I could never stand up to J. T. He was too scary."

"J. T. still tells everyone who'll listen that Ronnie was gay," Jules said.

"Ronnie was so reticent that none of us ever knew, and I never cared," Brenda said. "Daddy worried though, and J. T. constantly denounced Ronnie as 'queer' in front of anyone and everyone, especially the old man. I know it hurt Ronnie deeply."

"I heard rumors before that he'd made the kid's life a living hell in every respect," Jules said.

"You don't know the half of it. We had a horse farm in New Jersey near Saddle River, and Dad had invested in some very high priced Thoroughbreds, the most famous of which was the Derby winner Thundercrack. When Ronnie started hanging around the stables, he turned out to have a way with horses. He began getting press coverage for his work with them, which drove J. T. almost insane. He longed to be darling of the press, but Ronnie was getting all of the attention. The press had referred to Ronnie as Thundercrack's 'co-trainer,' which drove J. T. nuts."

"Your father had some other Derby winners," Jules said.

"Several," Brenda said, "but his most impressive Derby winner was Thundercrack, and Ronnie loved that horse. The kid was shy around people, but not those Thoroughbreds, particularly that one. The trainers were impressed with the way Ronnie handled him, and they encouraged him to exercise him."

"The trainers call it 'breezing' the horse," Jules said.

"Right," Brenda said. "Ronnie breezed Thundercrack all the time, but the horse wouldn't let J. T. near him. He'd buck and kick if J. T. tried to touch him and would even try biting him."

"Ronnie committed suicide in Thundercrack's stall if memory serves," Jules said.

"In an empty stall next to Thundercrack's," Brenda said. "A few days after the horse won the Derby, Ronnie was in Jersey, working with him. Late one night he was in his stall, rubbing him down and feeding him apples. Ronnie was the only person in the stable, and J. T. showed up in a total rage. He was bigger and stronger than Ronnie, and so he dragged him out of the stall by the hair. He called him a 'horsefucker' and a 'little queer.' He beat the living hell out of the kid, punching him, tearing out handfuls of hair—the same shit he'd do later to wives and girlfriends—repeatedly kicking him in the groin, shouting in his ear at the top of his lungs: 'I'm gonna beat the fucking queer out of you.'"

"The papers reported that Ronnie hanged himself in the stall that night from the overhead light fixture," Jules said.

"Or J. T. hanged him," Brenda said. "He wanted Ronnie's stock really bad, and the corporate bylaws stated that if one of us died, the siblings inherited the deceased's stock. Daddy had set it up and called it a 'tontine.' Since Daddy had just passed away and I'd already signed an irrevocable agreement, giving J. T. authorization to vote my stock, Ronnie's death effectively gave J. T. total, irreversible control of our father's company."

"How did you learn what J. T. did to his brother that night?" Jules asked.

"A few weeks after Ronnie's death, J. T. was sitting in his penthouse, late one night. He doesn't usually drink, but that night he indulged himself in a couple of snifters of my brandy. He was feeling effusive, boastful, and he told me most of the story, implying he'd killed him. He laughed about it. He was proud of what he'd done."

"He never showed any remorse?" Jules asked. "Ever?"

"No. In fact, a few weeks later I asked him, point-blank, if he was upset about Ronnie's death."

Brenda looked away.

"Did he answer you?" Jules finally asked after a long silence.

"'Hell no!' he shouted, his insane laughter rocking the room."

Jules sat with her a long time. Brenda cried quietly, and Jules held her hand.

Shortly before dawn, Brenda pulled herself together and left Jules's hotel room.

Jules went to the bathroom. Standing before the mirror, she made herself a promise:

"J. T.," she said softly. "I swear on my soul, on my sisters' souls and on my mother's, I am taking you down."

3

"We view Western women with awe and horror, referring to them as the 'Third Sex.' Their way of life is diametrically opposed to ours. We are ostracized physically and socially from early childhood on, trapped in a labyrinth of restrictions and regulations, most of which are brutally barbaric and utterly illegal under international law but which determine our lives as inexorably as birth and death. Who issues these edicts? Men. They serve Allah, but we serve them. Men dictate, and we obey."
—Raza Jabarti to Danny McMahon

McMahon lay on his back, stretched out on his rack. Moonlight filtered through the small high window, and he wondered idly whether he would ever see the open night sky again.

Raza wandered in and walked up to him. She pulled up a straight-back chair and sat beside him.

"Remember what I always told you?" she asked him.

"Not to understand you too quickly," McMahon recited dully.

"I wasn't kidding," she said. "I also told you you'd come out of this experience changed."

"You also said," McMahon repeated robotically, "I'd learn to love you in the daylight."

"Well, how are you doing so far?" Raza asked.

"I feel a new manic dynamism coming over me already," McMahon muttered under his breath.

"Joke, if you wish, but you do see us differently, don't you? Before, all you knew about our faith was words, but now you've experienced the harshness of Islam firsthand. Now you know precisely how the women in our world feel."

"You also break women on racks?" McMahon asked, harshly skeptical.

"Not that often, but we do flog and stone them. We clitorize them. You've been held captive several days, but our women are imprisoned their entire lives. We are Islam's real 'caste of untouchables.' Men can shake hands, walk hand in hand with one another, but for them to touch a woman anywhere in public is haram."

"How do your country's leaders justify their abuse of you?" McMahon asked. "What do they say when you ask them?"

"They tell us it is Allah's will," Raza said, "that Islam means submission. Just as men submitted to Allah, so, we were told, we women are forced to submit to men. Islam is the only justification our leaders feel they need."

"So the fact that Islam requires the enslavement of women makes it . . . *all right?*"

"Mr. McMahon, starting in childhood I was covered head to foot with those white sacks known as the abaya robes. My face was obscured by the matching niqab so that I looked like a dead sailor in a sailcloth shroud, just before his burial at sea. My sisters and I endured our endless Muslim prayers, or *salat,* in swelteringly hot burqas and chadors. School consisted of forced memorization of the Koran with the goal of having learned it all by heart at age fourteen. Lapses in memory were requited with the strap or the switch.

"Our walls at home featured no photos or portraits, no likenesses anywhere. Nor was music ever played—not once. All such pleasures were haram. We were to take our pleasure and enjoy our reward not in this life but in the Hereafter, though what form that heavenly pleasure would take for women was never spelled out, not even in the Koran.

"To be a Saudi woman is to endure a life of perpetual servitude, subjugation and surveillance. The family men can torment, even violate us with impunity and with a vengeance. Even the clerics have their way with us. On the streets, the all-seeing *mutawa'u*—the religious police—perpetually persecute us. In the mosque, the clerics routinely issue fatwas, mandating our makeup, fingernail polish, sexual activities. They even attempt to dictate when we may have our periods."

"Your life," McMahon said, "the lives of your daughters and sisters don't have to be that way. There are always choices. You can choose to resist."

"*Kaafir" [Infidel],*" Raza said, "you are naïve. We view Western women with awe and horror, referring to them as the 'Third Sex.' Their way of life is diametrically opposed to ours. We are ostracized physically and socially from early childhood on, trapped in a labyrinth of restrictions and regulations, most of which are brutally barbaric and utterly illegal under international law but which determine our lives as inexorably as birth and death. Who issues these edicts? Men. They serve Allah, but we serve them. Men dictate, and we obey."

"But not you?" McMahon asked.

"I am hard to subjugate," Raza said, smiling.

"But you now have power. You can help other women resist, change, be more like you," McMahon said.

"You do not know me, *kaafir*, and you do not know my world. Do not think for a moment I am like you."

"I know more than you think."

"You are a fool," Raza said with an angry frown. "You will never understand me, and you will never understand us . . . *at all*. Our lives are an enigma hidden in a paradox concealed in a conundrum. We live in what your poet Eliot called 'a wilderness of mirrors.' Our world is a maze of conflicting tribes, sects and factions, which our rulers tyrannize and suppress, controlling every aspect of our lives. Our paranoia is so intense we only trust blood of our blood, an obsessive reliance on family, which often requires the marriage of first cousins to first cousins. A tradition going back four thousand years to ancient Egypt, our attitude toward matrimony often mirrors those of the pharaohs, whose distrust of even their allies was so profound the kings married their sisters."

"Why not leave?" McMahon asked.

"Islam is in my bones and blood. I am not suited to your world."

"Why not?"

"You wear but one face? I wear a thousand: one for every time and place, person and mood. Only dogged duplicity allows any of us to survive. Without our lies and self-deceptions, we are nothing. I am nothing. They are all we have. They make us—sum us up. You fear death like the plague? I long for its cold, dark, everlasting embrace. The only peace I will ever know is the peace of the grave."

"Leave. You don't have to live like this." To McMahon's surprise his voice was breaking up and he found himself imploring her. "I can help you. I will help you."

To his shock and astonishment, he realized he was sincere.

"Mr. McMahon," Raza said, "that is so sweet. But, no, I am not cut out for your world or for mine. In point of fact, I am suited for one thing and one thing only—the fight."

"Come with me anyway," McMahon said, "till we find someplace safe. You can decide then what you want to do and then—"

"You think so?" Raza asked. "If my people, if your leaders—particularly Tower, the Agency and his FBI, which worked with Putilov to get Tower elected—find out you've been with us, they will assume you and I know too much about their own plans and operations. They will kill us both."

McMahon looked away. "Fuck them. You've told me nothing about whatever schemes they've hatched, and anyway we can still escape. I have friends, good friends, powerful friends. We can get away."

Raza laughed. "Run from people like Tower, Waheed and Putilov? You're naïve."

"We have to try."

"Danny, it is too late. Things are about to get bad—very bad." She touched his cheek, and her expression softened. "But when it happens, please do not judge me too harshly, too quickly. I am not the thing I seem. One day, you will understand."

"Really?"

"Mr. McMahon," Raza said, leaning over him till they were nose to nose, "Mark my words: I will surprise you before this is over."

"Then tell me why you're doing this? Who's your enemy? What do you fight against?"

"I believe that humanity's oldest and evilest enemy has always been filthy lucre and the power it commands. In our world, it is oil money, which shields our kingdom from ameliorating influences, strengthens our nation's tribalistic traditions, exacerbates our men's misogyny, allows them to subjugate the helpless Saudi women, bankroll terrorists and oppress Dar al-Islam."

"We suffer from the same sickness," McMahon said.

"Absolutely," Raza agreed. "Your world is haunted by 'the money curse' as well. Your immeasurable wealth has made your country our planet's premier nuclear proliferator and merchant of military death. The wealth and power of your politically rich plutocrats have been and will always be your country's and your people's eternal foe—arguably the focus of evil in the world today—and your predatory elites will inevitably bring you down. Quite possibly your country's politically rich will bring all of us down."

"So your war is ultimately against power and money?" McMahon asked.

"Now you're starting to understand me, Mr. McMahon. As your St. Paul wrote: 'We wrestle not against flesh and blood, but against powers, against principalities, against the rulers of the darkness of this world, against spiritual wickedness in high places.'"

"Well I'm glad you're opposed to 'wickedness in high places,' but you're not putting President Tower or Ambassador Waheed through hell. I'm the one you're breaking on a rack. So what do you have against me?"

"Nothing, Mr. McMahon," Raza said. "As I told you, I am your biggest fan. When I was young, I secretly collected your books and DVDs. I found them . . . *liberating*. I find *you* liberating. You've influenced and inspired me more than you can know."

"Is that why you kidnapped and tortured me?" McMahon asked, his eyes starting to roll back in horror. "To get to know me?"

Raza's laugh was not unkind. "In part, yes. I also wanted to repay the gift. I wanted to teach you something. You taught me about your world. I honestly wanted to show you what my world is all about."

"I admit you've taught me to howl like a feral hound, baying his brains out at a blood-mad moon, and you've taught me to the meaning of spine-freezing, nerve-fraying, hair-frying *terror*."

"True," Raza said, "but believe it or not, I want you to survive this ordeal, and I will do everything in my power to keep you alive. But live or die, win or lose, this I guarantee: You will be changed. I will change you."

"But not necessarily for the best."

"Perhaps," Raza said, "but I have benefitted immensely from our little tête-à-têtes. The truth be known, getting to know you, even under these extreme circumstances, has been the greatest thrill of my life. In my own way, Danny, I actually care about you. I always have."

"If this is caring," McMahon said, "I never want to feel your rage."

Raza stared at him a long minute. "You have been through a lot, and I must say, you've taken it remarkably well. Marika and I have been more than a little impressed. Even Tariq was surprised at your . . . endurance."

"You wouldn't know it from the way he hones that scalpel and stares at my testicles," McMahon said.

"We have been rather hard on you, haven't we?" Raza said.

"You've shocked me with cattle prods," McMahon said, "ripped my joints loose on a rack and a strappado, whipped me halfway to death with a riding crop, threatened to castrate me like a boar hog and pretty much made, parlayed and marmaladed my ass."

"You poor baby," Raza cooed, smiling.

"I've been blued, screwed and tattooed."

"Your watch is wound a little tight, isn't it?" Raza said.

"No fucking shit."

"Maybe I should loosen it for you—just a little bit?"

McMahon's face was an instant mask of paranoia. "It isn't going to breach my religious principles, is it? Or make me writhe in unbearable pain?"

"Oh, we shall certainly contravene my culture's beliefs," Raza said. "In my imperiously cruel world, a man may not touch a woman's hand. Such an act is strictly haram, strictly forbidden. Masturbation is even worse. It's a flogging offense. Want to go for . . . a twofer?"

McMahon stared at her, speechless.

"This isn't going to hurt, is it?" McMahon finally asked, his eyes darting back and forth nervously.

"Does this hurt?"

She was working him over with her eyes, then her hands, touching him all over, then she was on top of him, holding him so close it was almost like she was wearing him, reaching down, down, down.

"I'm going to make you shake and twitch like a baby goat passing olive pits," she whispered in McMahon's ear.

At which point she grabbed his lower extremities so hard a blazing bolt of white-hot fire shot through him, followed by a jolt of pure pleasure so dazzlingly incandescent that he almost passed out.

"That was worth at least a flogging, wasn't it?" Raza asked. "Now do you have the stones to go for the next level—and the serious possibility of a genuine Islamic stoning afterward?"

She raised herself up on her hands, hovering over him, pinning him with her black, blazing eyes. She began kissing him all over—his chest, stomach, neck, his—

For a second—but only for a second—McMahon blacked out, and when he came to, her head was at his hips, bobbing up and down, up and down. His entire being and body was now consumed by one ecstatic explosion after another, the orgasms blasting through him . . . like . . . like . . .

. . . *like the detonation of a suicide bomber's vest, like a dump truck full of C-4 blowing up a U.S. military barracks in Beruit and killing 231 marines, or truck bombers reducing two U.S. embassies in Kenya and Tanzania to rubble, the drivers' smiles serene, ethereal, all-knowing, or Raza dynamiting buses in Israel for the Hezbollah or with al Qaeda, beheading Syrians in Aleppo for ISIS, incinerating capital cities worldwide for the New United Islamist Front with a never-ending arsenal of terrorist nukes, or . . .*

And still the orgasms would not cease.

McMahon passed out a second time, and when he came to, Raza was sitting up over him, her short red dress gone but the riding boots still on. Magnificent in her nakedness, she appeared to him no mere woman, but a lioness of the species, an apotheosis of erotic apostasy, an Islamic avatar of lewd, lurid, licentious, lascivious . . . *lust.*

But he was spent. She had worn him out. McMahon could not go on.

"No more," he whimpered.

"Oh, Mr. McMahon," she said, suddenly growing stern, "we've only just begun your education, and I promise you I am the last woman in this world you will ever want to . . . *disappoint.*"

"Please. I can't."

"Want to bet?" Raza whispered, licking the interior of his ear, her steamy breath hotter than Hellmouth. "I'll make that phoenix rebear himself."

Reaching down with her left hand, she grabbed him violently between the legs, gripping his manhood with pit bull power. At the same time, leaning forward, she grabbed the rack's crank with her left hand and gave it two hard turns. The combination of the horrific pain in his separating joints and the electrifying agony in his genitals was unendurable. He roared like a dromedary in its death throes, gone mad with feral suffering.

But then as he groaned, sobbed and fought to catch his breath, to his utter shock he felt something stir, something wickedly libidinous, and then, to his undying horror, he realized he was coming back to life.

He looked up, and Raza was on top now, lowering herself on his hips, a supercilious smile twisting her mouth into a half grin, half grimace, her eyes glinting with sinful sensuality.

"What are you doing?" he groaned, terrified by her twisted sneer and her evil eyes.

"Oh, Mr. McMahon, I thought you knew. I'm going to hammer you like you were the last spike on the first Cairo-to-Baghdad railroad, and I was the fastest, hardest-hitting, most preternaturally powerful pile driver in history."

Then throwing her head back and wailing-barking like a hysterical hyena, she began banging him as if she were a jackhammer run amok, pummeling him like a rolling barrage of hellfire, damnation and apocalypse, like a bullet train rocketing down a steep mountain pass, jumping its rail and shattering into a billion trillion smithereens, as if all the banshees in Hades were raging inside of her, fighting to get out.

In the midst of his roaring pain and his raw, furious, burning hunger, McMahon was hit unexpectedly by the most frightening orgasm of his life—a demented detonation out of the abyss. It seemed to rip him in two like a thunderbolt. Against his will, screams ululated out of his lungs, shaking the room and careening through the desert wastes, like the screeching, shrieking, bloodcurdling howls of the damned, erupting out of hell's evilest, most infernal echo chambers. Harmonizing with his madly wanton wails was Raza's shrilling laughter, both of which soared, in eerie unison, through dark desert sky, the deranged duet ringing in McMahon's head like a death knell out of hell. But not even McMahon's heartrending, mind-cracking terror could prevent the prurient paroxysms from convulsing his gonads and pumping through his body, through his entire being, over and over and over again, until he feared the soul-searing, body-obliterating shocks would never stop.

On and on and on, the two of them climaxed, their carnal cries reverberating across the arid wastes and through the everlasting void. In a last fleeting barely lucid moment, McMahon wondered if the agony-in-ecstasy racking him would ever end, would ever set him free.

He prayed for oblivion, pleaded for release, begged for death, for anything that would make the relentless hammering cease and the Satanic spasms subside, but still Raza would not quit, would not let him go, and still the darkness would not come.

Only after the gray predawn tinted the torture chamber windows did the pit mercifully open into a black heartless hole of blind passion and eternal surcease, and McMahon finally fell in it. Where it would end, he did not know, but at last he was falling, falling, falling.

Into a night that knew no end.

PART XVI

"Remember General Tommy Franks's prophetic warning when he retired? He believed one nuclear terrorist attack on the U.S. and Congress would very likely hand its power over to a military-backed dictator."

—Elena Moreno

1

The memory of their meeting, drinking, seduction, lovemaking, garroting, her struggles and her death throes got Fahad . . . hot.

Fahad sat in a straight-back chair by Adrienne's living room window. The glass double doors in the front of Jules Meredith's apartment building were less than one hundred feet away, so he hadn't bothered with a high-power sniper rifle or even a scope. On his lap rested a scoped AR-15 set on semi-auto. It had a custom-made collapsible wire stock, flash and noise suppressors, and it would more than suffice. He could make that one-hundred-foot shot in his sleep, standing on his head, underwater, on sodium pentothal.

His main obstacle now was boredom. He'd been waiting for Jules Meredith to exit her apartment building for two hours, and he was getting restless. He willed himself to stay vigilant.

Still his mind drifted.

He remembered making love to Adrienne the night before. She was lithe, nimble and inventive in bed, but despite her many trysts, he knew she'd never experienced lovemaking with a man possessing Fahad's knowledge, talent and expertise. At one point, he'd made her scream with excitation, and after he'd finished, she'd sobbed like a little girl, thanking him over and over for taking her to sexual heights she'd never dreamed possible.

When at last he'd wrapped her thin leather belt around her neck, she had encouraged him. Sitting bolt upright, she told him she was all his and "ready for anything you want." The poor thing had thought he was teaching her a new weird trick, some sort of erotic asphyxiation game.

"This is so exciting!" she'd enthused.

So he'd encircled her neck with the belt. Wrapping the two ends around each of his wrists, he gripped them tightly in his fists and took a deep breath. He then yanked both ends crossways with all his strength. Her feet instantly shot up, kicking convulsively at the far wall and the ceiling. Her hands grabbed and clawed so furiously at his wrists it felt like he was battling an insane ape on a bucking bronco. Still he did not falter or flinch; he continued to pull as hard as he knew how, refusing to loosen his grip or relax the implacable tractor-pull of his arms.

She was stronger than most of his victims, and he had to fight her a full two minutes. Finally, however, her bladder discharged, and she died.

Fahad sighed. He would remember Adrienne. By Fahad's perversely outrageous standards, she had been exhilarating. In fact, the memory of their meeting, drinking, seduction, lovemaking, garroting, her struggles and her death throes got Fahad . . . hot.

All over again.

*F*ocus! he said to himself. He fixed on Jules Meredith's apartment's entrance, waiting for her car service to pull up and for Jules to exit her building's glass doors. Before she could step off the curb, he'd shoot her in the head.

Since the rifle barrel was flash- and sound-suppressed, no one would hear or see the shot. He was dressed in black, the rifle was dark as well, the window open, and his room would be unlit. He would not raise the rifle until the last second. No one would be able to tell where the shot came from.

All they would see was the woman drop, like a hammered steer, where she stood.

He would then take the fire stairs, three at a time, to the basement and depart by the service entrance along the side of the building.

This was going to work.

2

"I don't know if we've walked in on a United Front torture chamber or an S/M brothel."

—Elena Moreno

We've got company!" Marika yelled, bursting into McMahon's torture room, her shouts shocking him out of his demented delirium.

To her shock and confusion, Raza was stark naked and on top of McMahon, who had just come to and was clearly out of his mind. Both of them were in full flagrante delicto, mad with lust and concluding a final series of sobbing, howling climaxes.

"I thought you were torturing him," Marika said to Raza, stunned by the spectacle in front of her. "I thought those were screams of agony."

Raza wearily dragged herself off McMahon. Grabbing her short red dress off the floor, she threw it on.

"How many attackers did you spot?" Raza asked.

"At least ten," Marika said, unable to take her horrified eyes off the embarrassingly erect, supine man on the rack, "all armed to the teeth. They just killed everyone in the Quonset huts. We have to kill Rashid and McMahon and leave. Tariq's already split."

The soldiers outside began hammering the reinforced door with a battering ram.

"There's no time," Raza yelled, grabbing Marika and pushing her into the other room.

Through the open door, McMahon saw them lift a heavy trapdoor with a piece of carpet glued to the top of it. The women climbed down the steps into the escape tunnel below, lowered the trapdoor, and he heard them bolt it shut.

Raza was right. There was no time, and the two women barely made it. The second the trapdoor slammed, a platter charge blew the blockhouse door inward in an explosion of wooden slivers and shards. Elena was charging through the smoke and debris into the room with four mercs behind her, all of them dressed in black fatigues and watch caps, their faces darkened with camo paint, their MP7 H&Ks at the ready.

They quickly inspected the other two rooms, which were empty.

Coming back in, Elena cut the wrist and feet ropes with which his torturers had lashed him to the rack, shouting all the while:

"I heard you'd been kidnapped, Danny," Elena said, "but I never dreamed you'd be here."

McMahon was speechless. Relieved of the stress, his limbs and joints throbbed horrifically. All he could do was convulse with pain.

"What the fuck was going on?" Elena asked in horror.

His spasms slowly subsided, and McMahon looked up at Elena. She was staring at his crotch. In Raza's frantic effort to leave, she'd left her black laced panties coiled around his genitalia. Her undergarment was vividly stained with his lust and wet from Raza's exertions. His upper thighs were crisscrossed and crosshatched with scarlet lipstick smears.

"Where did everyone go?" Elena said, trying not to look at McMahon's still clearly aroused and hard-used loins.

"They escaped through a steel-lined trapdoor under that rug in the next room," McMahon gasped raggedly, barely able to get the words out, his ears aching, ringing and roaring from the platter charge's and flashbang's blasts. "I heard them bolt it shut behind them just before you blasted the door open and blew out my eardrums."

Elena could only stare at him, finally rendered speechless.

"What the hell is this?" Jonesy said, coming toward them out of the other room. He had an arm under Rashid's armpit and was half walking, half dragging him through the doorway. Coming to an abrupt halt, he stared slack-jawed at McMahon, who was still on his rack, the evidence of sexual activity glaringly, humiliatingly apparent.

"I don't know if we walked in on a United Front torture chamber," Elena said, still shaking her head, "or an S/M brothel."

"Or maybe both," Jonesy said, "Outside the door, we heard this boy here gittin' hisself some mean rocks. I don't know though. Him and Rashid both look like they gonna need some medical attention."

"Let's get them to the choppers," Elena said. "We can whip out the med kits and then get the fuck out of Dodge."

"Copy that," Henry said, standing in the front door. "There's a TTP base just over the rise, and they have to know we're here."

"Raza got to have hit an alarm button," Jonesy said.

"Time to adios, muthafuckas," Henry said.

Henry grabbed McMahon off his rack and threw him over his shoulder.

"We outta here," Jonesy said, throwing Rashid over his shoulder and carrying him out the door. "Gots to admit though, boy," Jonesy said to

McMahon, "you bangin' that pussy, stretched out on a muthafuckin' rack? You more man than me."

They all jogged out toward the rent in the fence.

They had to get around the hill and back to the choppers.

3

Yes, the chauffeur was definitely going down.
FOR BORING THE FUCKING SHIT OUT OF HIM!
—Fahad al-Qadi

Fahad watched Jules Meredith pause at the entrance to the building. The uniformed doorman looked like a banana republic general with thick shoulder pads, crimson epaulets, black braids and gold trim. He even wore a general's dress hat with a small ebony brim and more gold trim.

Fahad could shoot her where she stood, but the bullet would have to pass through the glass door, and he didn't trust the glass not to deflect the round. Forcing himself to be patient, he waited for her to move toward the open door, but Jules Meredith wasn't cooperating. Instead she stood there behind the glass, chatting with General Doorman. Fahad wondered what was taking them so long. There was no way the military-looking dork could be all that interesting.

Again, his concentration flagged, and his attention wandered. He thought he'd figured out why this last-minute hit had been ordered. All of Fahad's other New York targets were, in one way or another, enemies of the president and his allies, and Jules Meredith was writing a scathing series of exposés on President Tower. As long as the president was eliminating his adversaries, he probably thought he'd dispatch the Meredith woman too. In for a penny, in for a pound.

Oh well. Mine is not to reason why.

Still the woman continued to chat. Or listen. The old guy in the Third World general's uniform was talking up a storm, yakking as if his life depended on it. As for Jules Meredith, she just stood there, staring him dead in the eye and listening with rapt attention, as if she had all the time in the world, and he was the most fascinating motherfucker on the planet.

Well, Fahad was running out of patience fast. He had a whole city full of assholes he had to kill, and he didn't have time for this horseshit.

Maybe you should put a bullet in General Doorman's yapping mouth just for pissing you off.

A black Cadillac Escalade SUV pulled up in front of Meredith's apartment building. An ancient wizened gray-haired chauffeur in a navy blue suit, a white shirt and dark tie double-parked parallel to a white Ford Escort. The driver got out and limped up to the entrance of Meredith's building.

Still Jules continued listening to General Asshole Doorman like he was Moses come down from Mount Sinai with God's Word, blazing and smoking in two stone tablets. Every neuron in Fahad's nervous system wanted to shoot both of them through the glass door.

Calm down. Relax. Wait for your best shot.

The gray-haired chauffer-cretin opened the door and actually bowed before Meredith there in the doorway like she was Princess Di. When she moved toward the open doorway and paused, he'd kill all of them—the driver *and* doorman after he took out the bitch.

There. She was shaking hands with General Idiot. Now she was shaking hands with the chauffeur, and he was also telling Meredith the story of his life.

She was still behind the fucking glass!

Yes, the chauffeur was definitely going down.

FOR BORING THE FUCKING SHIT OUT OF HIM!

Fahad took a deep breath and willed himself to calm down.

Jules Meredith had stopped shaking hands with the driver and was waving goodbye to the doorman as she headed toward the open door.

He finally had her out in the open and dead in his sights.

4

"Someone was gibbering like a gibbon."
—Rashid al-Rahman

Seated in brown stuffed chairs around a bolted-down walnut table, Elena, Adara, Jamie, Jonesy and McMahon were flying over the Atlantic on one of Jamie's Gulfstream G650 jets. The five of them were wearing whatever civilian clothes they could find on the plane—jeans and slacks, polo shirts and jogging clothes. They were on course for a private New Jersey runway near New York City.

"Danny," Elena said, turning to McMahon, "We went there to rescue Rashid, and we find you. What the fuck were you doing there?"

McMahon stared at Elena a long moment. She was wearing khaki cargo pants and a black T-shirt. Even after a long hard op, forty-eight hours without sleep and with no makeup on, she looked terrific. He then caught his own reflection in a bulkhead mirror, and he couldn't say the same for himself. Decked out in a white T-shirt, tan cotton slacks, gym shoes and no socks, he was a mess. His eyes were red-rimmed, his face drawn and haggard, his brown hair dirty and unkempt, and he looked like he'd lost thirty pounds. A professional performer, he had always been scrupulous about his appearance; now he couldn't have cared less, which was weird. He wondered why he'd ever cared.

"You remember that show I did with Jules?" McMahon finally said, his voice hoarse and uncertain.

"Uh, yeah?" Elena said.

"Afterward, I found some crazy terrorist chick waiting for me in my hotel suite. She seduced and drugged me. Then three men in dark suits—partners of hers—kidnapped me out of my hotel room."

"You okay?" Adara asked.

"You wouldn't understand," he said softly.

He got up and headed toward the galley.

"Something wrong with Danny?" Jamie asked.

"I'll say," Elena said. "He won't even look at Adara or me, not even when we talk to him. I've tried flirting with him. Nada. It's like something's not there."

"Like he's been mind-snatched," Adara said.

"It's like talking to an abandoned house," Elena said.

"To a Dumpster," Adara agreed. "You get no affect, no connotation, nothing."

McMahon returned to the table. He had managed to liberate a water bottle.

"Where's Rashid?" McMahon, taking a deep drink.

"Lying down," Elena said. "You sure you don't want to rest?"

"I can't," McMahon said.

"What's wrong?" Adara asked.

"I keep seeing things I can't unsee," McMahon said.

"Wow," Adara said. "Raza flipped your switch, didn't she?"

"I never want to have sex again," McMahon said.

"That's not the Danny McMahon I know," Elena said.

"Me neither," Jonesy said. "We heard your ass outside the door. You was gittin' some hot-ticket booty in there."

"Hard-trade booty," Jamie said.

"You'll never know," McMahon said, shaking his head and looking away.

"We missed grabbing her by seconds," Jonesy said, "but we heard you and her going at it."

"That was one fever-driven fuckfest," Elena said.

"I heard you two in the other room," Rashid said, joining them at the table. He wore black jogging pants, a gray athletic T-shirt and running shoes. "It sounded like you were banging a gibbon."

"A gibbon?" McMahon asked, confused.

"Someone was gibbering like a gibbon," Rashid explained.

"More like a chimpanzee on crack," Adara said.

"What was all that yowling about?" Jamie asked. "You weren't mounting a mountain lion, were you?"

McMahon looked away, his eyes distant and unfocused.

"You sounded like a chain saw," Elena explained.

"It was like fucking Death," McMahon finally said, empty-eyed, emotionless.

Adara snapped her fingers in front of McMahon's eyes. They didn't blink.

"You really are an idiot," Adara said, studying McMahon intently.

"I hear a lot of that lately."

"What the hell did they do to you?" Elena asked.

McMahon just stared at her, unresponsive.

"And why did they do it?" Elena asked. "Why did they kidnap and torture you?"

"I'm starting to understand," McMahon said, "that there are people in this world who don't like me."

"My friend," Elena, said, patting his arm and giving him the kindest smile she could muster, "you are richly and widely reviled."

"But what brought you guys to the safe house, if you didn't know I was there?" McMahon asked. "What's going on?"

"Tell him," Jamie said. "Like it or not, we're all in this together."

"Why not?" Adara said. "After what you've gone through, maybe you deserve to know. Rashid, tell us what you said back in the chopper."

5

Jules was determined to give them bonuses they would never forget.

Jules said goodbye to the doorman. She and Niko had been friends for eighteen years, and his story of his daughter's divorce had been wrenching.

"Drugs and alcohol do terrible things to people," Niko had been telling Jules over and over again.

"That they do, Niko," was all she could think of to say. "That they do."

Well there was Jimmy, out of his car and entering the doorway. He was bowing before her as if she were the Second Coming of Christ. She had to find some way of breaking him of that habit.

Then he began telling her about the traffic jam.

"Ms. Meredith, that Anti-Economic Inequality Conference at the UN has traffic gridlocked here to the New Millennium. I'm not sure there's a good way to get you to your publisher's offices on time. It's too late to cut through Central Park. The West Side Highway—they now call the part we would want Jonathan DiMaggio Drive—is as far from the UN as you can get. Maybe if we took J. D. Drive down to Hell's Kitchen and cut over? Would that get us there? What do you think?"

Actually, Jules didn't care how they went. She did have to get there though. She had to tell them about the new series of exposés she was doing on President J. T. Tower and ask them whether there was any ethical way she could work any of her interviews with him into those pieces. She didn't think so. He'd been emphatic that conversations were on deep background and not for publication.

Still Jules wanted her publisher's input. She also need to discuss potential defamation of character suits. She thought they had the best libel lawyers in the news business, and she needed their input, given how wealthy and litigious Tower and his friends were.

"Jimmy, you know the streets and traffic better than I ever will. I trust your judgment. Let's take the route you think is best."

"I don't know, Ms. Meredith," the driver continued. "Maybe West End down to 10th Avenue and then cut over on—"

Jules was just stepping into the open doorway and onto the sidewalk when the screams rang out. Instinctively, she spun around and dived to the ground, off to the side, and away from the open door. A second later, Jimmy and Niko were throwing themselves on top of her.

Door glass was detonating throughout the apartment building's lobby and entranceway like shrapnel. Down the block people were screaming and horns honking and thankfully a siren began to wail.

Placing her hands over her head, she pressed herself as flat as she could on the lobby floor and hoped Jimmy and Niko, who were still spread-eagled on top of her, didn't get hurt.

Jules was determined to give them bonuses they would never forget.

6

"A one-kiloton terrorist nuke is the perfect weapon for a UN decapitation strike."
—Rashid al-Rahman

Rashid sat back in his airplane swivel chair and looked at his rescuers.

"I'd infiltrated the New Islamist United Front," Rashid explained to Danny McMahon and the people sitting around him on Jamie's plane. "Among other things, I learned the Front was plotting with Ambassador Waheed, President Putilov and with the full cooperation of the American president, to take out the UN with a one-kiloton terrorist nuke. They were fueling the nuke in the U.S. with bomb-grade highly enriched Pakistani uranium, which Putilov had smuggled in on a Russian transport plane under a diplomatic seal. They have an expert—our old friend, Fahad al-Qadi—assembling the nuke in a machine shop somewhere near or in the city. Kamal ad-Din and your old friend Raza Jabarti are involved in it too."

"You probably don't know Fahad," Elena said, "but he may be the most dangerous individual on the face of the earth."

"All of them are very bad news," Jamie told McMahon.

"But why nuke the UN?" McMahon asked.

"You know that Global Anti-Poverty Conference at the UN?" Elena said.

"Of course," McMahon said, nodding.

"The UN is voting on a plan to address global income inequality worldwide," Rashid said. "They've summoned the world's five hundred richest billionaires in an effort to convince them—coerce them if necessary—into donating a third of their gross annual revenues to the Anti-Poverty Initiative. Otherwise, the UN will mandate the expropriation of a third of all illicit funds held in the planet's biggest offshore tax-haven bank accounts."

"Which is nearly $10 trillion," Elena pointed out.

"The U.S. Senate, Japan, India, Australia, Brazil, Argentina, and the EU are all on board, which means it will happen," Jamie said. "The democracies of the world are demanding it. Even China's coming around, because they will receive on net far more money than their elites will have to pay out."

"And in the end," Elena added, "China's elites have other ways to funnel that money into their pockets."

"If you have a totalitarian state," Rashid said, "you can get away with all kinds of shit."

"On the other hand," Jamie continued, "the world's oil-centric megamoguls are about to lose a whole shithouse full of money. We believe the Saudis—who bankroll the New United Islamist Front—are joining Putilov, Fahad and Raza Jabari in this plan to obliterate the conference."

"Ambassador Waheed is central to this plot," Elena said. "Putilov and his Russian oligarchs are in it too. Russia used to be the biggest oil-exporting nation on earth, and plummeting oil prices are killing them. Furthermore, over 100 percent of Russia's GDP is squirreled away in foreign tax havens. The Saudis have 55 percent of their GOP hidden abroad. They'll have to give up one-third of those funds or face ostracism from the global economy in the same way Iran was banned after it attempted to accelerate its nuclear weapons program. Economic ostracism is no small threat; it almost bankrupted Iran. Still if you combine dropping oil prices and the planned expropriation of one-third of Russia's and the Saudis GDP, you're looking at the fiscal destruction of those countries. Either way, Russia, Putilov, his oligarchs, the Saudis and quite possibly our own president are terminally fucked. They see nuking the UN as their only way out of this mess. They'll do anything to stop the expropriation movement."

"You're convinced Tower is in on it too?" McMahon said.

"Putilov and the Saudis own his ass," Jamie said.

"Putilov, in particular," Elena said. "Tower wouldn't be president if Putilov hadn't fixed the last election for him."

"I must be hallucinating," McMahon said.

"Afraid not, Danny," Elena said. "It gets worse. Tell him, Rashid."

"When I let my CIA case officer know about an impending attack," Rashid said, "someone at the Agency tipped off the New United Islamist Front that I was a double agent. Raza and Marika told me about it while they were interrogating me. They were laughing about it. Marika even let it slip that the U.S. president, Putilov, his junta of billionaires and the New United Islamist Front were in on this operation. They were desperate to end all this offshore expropriation talk once and for all, and since all of their enemies will be gathered in a single location—namely, the UN—what better way to rid themselves of them than to nuke them all at once? They were trying to get me to identify my CIA handlers in Pakistan and to find out how much I'd told them about the plot when you arrived at the safe house."

"But if they nuke the UN," McMahon asked, "wouldn't they be nuking a lot of oligarchs too? They're attending the conference."

"They won't be at the UN," Elena pointed out. "They're staying at one of J. T.'s Tower of Power hotels. He's reserved the entire building for them."

McMahon could only stare blankly at Rashid and shake his head. "This isn't happening," he said quietly.

"Oh, but it is," Rashid said. "A one-kiloton terrorist nuke is the perfect weapon for a UN decapitation strike."

"And Tower and Putilov have plenty of fall guys to blame the attack on," Elena said, "an almost infinite assortment of Islamist terrorist groups."

"Also President Tower's hold on power's been slipping since that Wall Street crash last year," Jamie said. "The Democrats have control of the Senate, and they've threatened impeachment as well as expropriation. After a nuclear attack, Tower'd be able to scare the voters into rallying around him. The terrorist strike would consolidate his hold on power for the next two years of his second term."

"Remember General Tommy Franks's prophetic warning when he retired?" Elena said. "He believed one nuclear terrorist attack on the U.S. and Congress would very likely hand its power over to a military-backed dictator. Tower has close allies in both the FBI and CIA, so you can't count on the Bureau or the Agency to oppose a presidential coup."

"Remember that the former FBI director, Jonathan Conley," McMahon said, "joined forces with Putilov to hand Tower the election."

"After the nuclear attack," Jamie said, "Tower could easily stage a coup— if he had the backing of the FBI, the Agency, the military and Putilov. He could take the country over in a heartbeat."

"If we can't turn to the White House, the CIA, or the FBI," McMahon asked, "what are we supposed to do?"

"Somehow, Danny," Elena said, "we have to intercept that nuke before these guys can detonate it at the UN."

7

"I thought you cared for me. I thought we had something, that we felt something for each other. I thought there was...*a connection!*"
—Adrienne Harmon

Adrienne came out of the bathroom, screaming like a screech whistle, her hands, throat and torso covered with blood. Staring at Fahad, she pointed toward him with a fully extended right arm and an accusatory index finger, then started limping toward him painfully, haltingly.

"*Astaghfirullah,*" Fahad muttered under his breath. *Allah, help me.* He'd garroted her a full two minutes before her breathing stopped and her bladder voided. He'd then checked both her wrist and throat pulse. What was she? A fucking zombie? He'd killed her deader than deep-fried goat shit.

But the bitch had come back to life.

Now she was stumbling toward him, her hands reaching out in front of her like *Night of the Living Dead.*

Still he couldn't let her distract him. He had to do first things first. He had to take out the Meredith woman.

Raising the rifle, he sighted in on Jules, who was back behind the front door, and squeezed off three quick shots.

Door glass was exploding all over the lobby, and then the two old codgers were throwing themselves on top of Meredith.

Fuck it. Maybe he could fire into the mass of bodies and kill them all.

But before he could get off another round, Adrienne was on him, wrapping her legs around his waist, hammering him with her fists, scratching, kicking, biting and shrieking. In fact, she was now throttling him, spitting repeatedly in his face, tearing at the AR-15 and gasping-rasping wildly:

"I thought you cared for me," she yelled. "I thought we had something, that we felt something for each other. I thought there was . . . *a connection!*"

Shaking her loose, he grabbed a handful of hair along one side of her head. Rising to his feet, he pivoted and drove a forearm into her opposite temple, getting every ounce of his two hundred pounds into it. She collapsed like a rag doll with the stuffing ripped out.

Lowering the AR-15, he placed it over her chest and put two silenced rounds into her sternum. Taking a deep breath, he gave her forehead a third insurance tap, just above her left eye.

When he turned around, Meredith and the two old men were gone from the lobby, nowhere in sight, and sirens were wailing through New York's Upper West Side loud enough to wake the damned.

He took another long deep breath, paused to steady his nerves, and finally pulled himself together.

Well you have other targets on that list. You can settle with the Meredith bitch later.

He placed the AR-15 on the apartment floor, brushed himself off, and headed for the door.

He had to get to the fire stairs and make it to the service exit. Then get back to his Bronx safe house uptown.

PART XVII

"Do you want me to miss the story of a lifetime?"

—Jules Meredith

1

"Danny, can you get it through that reptilian brain of yours? You don't need to do this. You're paying tickets you don't owe."
—Elena Moreno

McMahon watched the team remove a diverse assortment of weapons from the three big duffle bags and spread them across the table. Elena's Desert Eagle was already in front of her. Adara had just taken a Mosby tactical 12-gauge six-rounder—with a wire fold-out stock and sawed off at the pump—from the bag. He saw four MP7 submachine guns and a variety of nines, including four Glocks and a Sig Sauer. Trijicon night sights. Nylon holsters. Extended magazines.

"What are the weapons for?" McMahon asked. "The Battle of the Apocalypse?"

"Just about," Elena said.

"Speaking of which, do we have a plan?" Rashid asked.

"Sure," Adara said, "we battle house to house, ditch to ditch, to the last person standing and the final fucking cartridge. Then we go to knives, rocks, sticks, feet, teeth and fists."

"In short," Rashid said, "we have no plan."

"I'm down anyway," McMahon said with an unemotional shrug. "After what you guys did for me, after what you've told me, you're the only people I trust."

"All due respect, Danny," Adara said, "none of us have time to babysit you once the shit hits the fan."

"I can handle firearms," McMahon said weakly.

His remark was greeted with a chorus of harsh, mocking horselaughs.

"I don't think our boy here knows an AK from a bucket of ribs," Jonesy said.

"Maybe," McMahon said, "but I am involved whether you like it or not, and I can contribute."

"How?" Elena asked.

She had the grace not to smile, but Jonesy was openly scornful.

"This ought to be good," Jonesy said with a sarcastic laugh.

"I have the biggest news-satire TV show worldwide, right?" McMahon asked.

"So?" Adara asked.

"I can be your embedded reporter," McMahon said.

"Now *I am* hallucinatin'," Jonesy said.

"Slow down, Jonesy," Adara said. "Danny may have something. We're on the verge of committing about nine thousand felonies against the richest, most powerful people on earth. If we survive this thing, they're going to come at us with a media firestorm, to say nothing of every law enforcement agency on the planet, to say nothing of the Russian and American armies. They'll claim we were the terrorists and issue orders to shoot us on sight. They can't say that about McMahon. He was captured and tortured by terrorists, and he's a super-famous, global celebrity TV star. He'd also be in a great position to argue our case in the court of public opinion, when this cruel war is over. It's not the worst idea in the world to have him with us."

"They'll say we kidnapped and brainwashed him like Patty Hearst," Jamie said.

"And I'll say bullshit," McMahon said.

"This is a joke, right?" Jonesy said, looking at the ceiling.

"I'll also get us the biggest, most lucrative book/TV/film deal in history," McMahon said. "We'll all split even."

"But it ain't about money with you," Jonesy said. "You already rich. You have one of them 'hidden agendas.'"

McMahon just stared at them, his eyes empty of expression, and shrugged.

"I was there," Rashid said, "and I know what you're thinking, Danny. You feel you got something to prove after what they did to you in that safe house."

"Something did happen," McMahon said, "something I can't explain. All I know is I have to see this through."

Adara slapped him softly on the shoulder. "Danny, you're all right."

"We'll see," Jamie said.

"Oh, hell, why shouldn't he come along?" Rashid asked. "I was with him. He stood up. I say his balls are as big as anyone's here."

"You got to understand though," Adara said to McMahon, "this isn't any TV talk show or comic monologue."

"We lightin' muthafuckas up," Jonesy said.

"Assuming they don't light us up first," Jamie said.

"Assuming we don't join Johnny D.," Adara said.

"And where's Johnny D.?" McMahon asked.

"Dead at the present time," Jonesy said.

"You have to understand," Elena said, "you roll with us, you roll all the way."

"Way out to the edge," Jonesy said.

"Tell him why," Elena said.

"It's the only place to win," Adara said.

"I'm in," McMahon said.

"Tell us what Raza's like," Jonesy asked, grinning.

"Enquiring minds want to know," Adara said, laughing.

"What do you think she's like?" McMahon asked.

"Hard-hittin' woman," Jonesy said.

"With dead worlds in her eyes," Rashid said.

"I think he misses her," Adara said, smiling. "Danny, you want to see her again, don't you?"

"In a cold-zero target picture," McMahon said.

"Damn," Jamie said, grinning, "you are down with guns."

"Danny," Jonesy asked, "you still say you know firearms?" Jonesy ejected the magazine from Elena's Desert Eagle, ejected a round from the chamber and handed it to him. "You want one of these?"

"I've owned bowling balls lighter than this," McMahon said, having to heft it with both hands. "What's it for?"

"In case Elena gotta shoot her way out of a Zombie Apocalypse," Jonesy said.

"Where's my gun?" Danny asked.

"Good question," Adara said. "What's Danny going to do, if we take him along?"

"Talk," Jamie said.

"He talks real good," Elena said, nodding.

"But he don't know shit about guns," Jonesy said.

"He wouldn't know a Desert Eagle from a Big Mac," Adara concurred.

"Danny, can you get it through that reptilian brain of yours?" Elena asked. "You don't need to do this. You're paying tickets you don't owe."

"But I do need to do this," McMahon said.

"Where we're headed, it won't be any comic monologue," Adara said.

"Where are we headed?" McMahon asked.

"The Eat-Shit-and-Die Hotel," Jonesy said.

"It can't be any worse than that safe house," McMahon said.

"He's got a point," Rashid said.

"Got any ideas about transport?" Adara asked.

"I think I can get us a news chopper," Elena said. "I have a friend who can get one."

"You're going to drag Jules into this?" McMahon asked, stunned.

"To get around Manhattan," Elena explained, "we'll need a helicopter, and Jules can get a news chopper."

"I don't want Jules coming either," Adara said, "but I do want that chopper."

"A van won't do it?" McMahon asked.

"The streets around the UN will be impassable, hopelessly jammed up," Elena said. "We'll never find Fahad and his crew."

"So we get Jules to commandeer a chopper?" McMahon asked.

"More or less," Elena said.

There was a long silence.

"Sounds like we gonna stack it up," Jonesy finally said to McMahon. "You sure you want in?"

"It's going to take balls," Adara said, staring at McMahon.

"Ride-it-into-the-wall balls," Jonesy said.

"Yeah, well, count me in," McMahon said. "Stuff happened back in that safe house, stuff I can't put behind me. I got to do this."

They stared at McMahon a long slow minute. Then Jonesy gave McMahon a wide, slow, surprisingly friendly grin. His smile gave the game away.

"Ah, hell, then, Danny," Jonesy said, extending his hand, "in that case, welcome the fuck aboard."

2

What you do in the dark will come to light, the Bible said, and Jules Meredith had descended on Benjamin Jowett like the Wrath of an Avenging God, shining the harsh spotlight of public scrutiny on all of his wicked ways and devious dealings.

Benjamin Jowett sat at his desk in the New World Trade Center and scowled. Here he was—fifty-eight years old, with a $3,500 haircut, a $50,000 dark blue, immaculately tailored Kiton K-5 suit, a $35,000 Hublot Big Bang Ferrari King Gold 45mm 18k Rose Gold Limited Edition watch. He was still handsome and still had all his hair, which was currently coiffed and colored a tasteful light blond. He still had perfectly capped teeth, which gave him a dazzlingly bright, movie-star smile. He was the proprietor of one of the largest privately owned hedge funds on earth, and yet despite all of his money, power, good looks and accoutrements, that muckraking bitch, Jules Meredith, could cut through his high-tech, anti-hacking security systems and his expensively produced, elaborately crafted gentlemanly façade like a chain saw screaming through steaming hot . . . *shit*. She could and was exposing all his most avaricious secrets to the mocking, sneering media, making him one of the most despised and derided billionaires in the world.

One of his more lucrative sidelines, for instance, was his so-called Weather Derivative Funds. In effect, it placed bets on the weather, which any outsider would have previously viewed as harmless, until, that is, Jules C. Meredith got her arching, needle-sharp talons into the story. She proved that he had his complex of subcompanies, whose sole job was to systematically buy and sell grain commodities during periods of acute water shortage, and thereby drive up the prices during commodity-market bidding wars. Jowett, thus, elevated food costs to heights far above anything that any protracted dry spell could have accomplished, all the while making him billions in derivative grain profits. An unfortunate by-product of their "business" was to put a subsistence diet beyond the reach of those already starving on the margins in Sub-Saharan Africa, the Mideast, South Asia, India, China, and Southeast Asia.

That Meredith bitch had described his financial instruments as "famine derivatives" and argued that Jowett was profiteering off the kinds of climate-change-inspired, famine-producing droughts that emaciated and murdered indigent peasants and Third World slum-dwellers by the hundreds of millions.

Many on Wall Street believed that his artificially induced price inflation of basic grains—and the famines that inflation aggravated—had in 2012 driven millions of people in the Mideast into the streets in protest of the skyrocketing food prices. These demonstrations led to the infamous "Arab Spring," a spate of revolutions that incited the overthrow of several authoritarian rulers. Most of these secular despots were replaced by fanatical Islamist tyrants who supported terrorism, fomented regional civil war, set the Mideast aflame and proved to be even more brutal and oppressive than their predecessors. Many economists held Jowett responsible for that Arab Spring and the pervasive anarchy that followed, a dubious achievement in which Benjamin privately took an almost narcissistic pride.

Not that he bragged about it in public. His "famine derivatives" were a highly profitable but dirty little secret he attempted to keep under wraps. He'd lavished scores of millions of dollars on PR firms all over the world over the last twenty years in an attempt to conceal that enterprise. And all the obfuscation and subterfuge had worked. He'd kept his grain-price manipulations below the media radar screen and had, in fact, successfully branded himself as a philanthropist, a patron of the arts and a commodities markets guru. He'd gone to New York's most celebrated charity balls, donated incalculable sums to Lincoln Center, PBS and the Metropolitan Museum of Art. For twenty years, he'd been there for every opening night at the Met opera and had been treated like a deity on the different financial networks, in newspaper and magazine interviews and on the national talk shows.

No more.

What you do in the dark will come to light, the Bible said, and Jules Meredith had descended on Benjamin Jowett like the Wrath of an Avenging God, shining the harsh spotlight of public scrutiny on all of his wicked ways and devious dealings.

She had sullied his reputation forever. Instead of referring to him as "a philanthropist, a patron of the arts and a commodities markets guru" she had renamed him "the Planet's Number One Famine Pimp" and "Our Preeminent Impresario of Global Malnuitrtion."

Then that madman, Danny McMahon, had taken to running news clips of his comings and goings, narrated by McMahon's own scathing commentary, in which he quoted Meredith or made up vicious attacks himself, denouncing Jowett as "America's Grand Panjandrum of Mass Famine" and "our Generalissimo of Genocidal, Baby-Murdering Greed," accusing him of "killing people with food deprivation the way Hitler killed them with gas chambers and Stalin killed them with hunger and cold in the Siberian death camps."

Damn it, he needed tonight's diversion, anything that would get his mind off that bitch Jules Meredith and her asshole friend, Danny McMahon. No less a personage than President J. T. Tower had called him up, saying that he'd been sickened by what Meredith and McMahon had been doing to Jowett, their friends and himself, announcing that he, J. T. Tower, was "settling Jules Meredith's and Danny McMahon's hash once and for all."

"As my number one campaign contributor, you deserve a celebration, Ben, instead of all that public ridicule," President Tower had said to him, *"and I am personally setting you up with the hottest young woman I have ever had the privilege to debauch, and you can take my erotic recommendations to J. P. Morgan Chase. I am the gold standard when it comes to bodaciously hot beauties. In fact, I picked this one out special for you. For years, you've told me about your fellatio fixation. Well, I too share that particular enthusiasm. I've had head all over the world—from the street girls of Rio to the sex goddesses of the Hollywood Hills, from Bangkok brothels to the supermodel penthouses of London and New York. I've had it in Hong Kong's royal palaces and in remote Sherpa villages high up in the Himalayas. When it comes to oral sex, I've been up, down and all around, here, there and back again, but I've never had anything remotely approaching what this young girl does. She could suck the chrome off an eighteen-wheel diesel-rig trailer hitch. I swear on my balls and my eyes she'll give you the wildest barracuda blowjob of your young life. Screaming skull? She'll give you a hummer that'll hammer your eyeballs right out of your head and send you shrieking like a banshee into the night. In fact, she'll do* anything! *Talk about having dollar signs for eyeballs, she'd let you burn her at the stake in a snuff flick if you laid enough scratch on her. And best of all, she's my personal gift to you, free and gratis."*

"J. T.," Jowett said, strangely and surprisingly moved. *"You're too kind, too generous. How can I ever thank you?"*

"No thanks necessary. We've all suffered hideously at the hands of Jules Meredith and Danny McMahon, but their reign of terror is about to come to an end. I have Mikhail Putilov's personal word on it, so let your own personal celebration begin tonight!"

"God bless Mikhail Putilov," Jowett said. *"I don't know what else to say."*

"*By the way, this young fellatrix may be* . . . underage. *I've never checked her ID. That's not a problem, is it?*"

Remembering his conversation with Tower, Jowett got so aroused he became light-headed. He had to walk to his bathroom and splash cold water on his face.

3

"We committed about nine thousand felonies, getting McMahon and Rashid out of Pakistan. You don't want to be accessoried to any of those crimes."
—Elena Moreno to Jules Meredith

Elena and her team met in the helipad hangar in New Jersey. Jules—decked out in jeans, a T-shirt and running shoes—was standing in front of the news chopper.

"This chopper any good?" Elena asked.

"It's a top-of-the-line Agusta with a camera on the fin and in the nose," Jules said, "which I will operate with a laptop and a joystick. I have a mini-cam as well. We have an EVS-1500 enhanced vision system. The auxillary transversal 132-gallon fuel tanks will let us stay up for five or six hours. Its lift is six tons, but I only have room for five of you."

"Jamie, Adara, Rashid and Danny are coming with us," Elena said. "Jamie will pilot."

"Danny?" Jules asked in stunned disbelief.

"He's earned it," Elena said. "Anyway, I may want him to contact Raza if we can get through to her. Believe it or not, she might actually talk to him."

"Why?" Jules asked McMahon, confused.

"We have a connection," McMahon explained.

"What is it?" Jules asked.

"Pelvic," Adara said.

"Are you sure we want him?" Jules asked, dubious.

"Danny's convinced me he can help," Elena said, "so he's coming. That's it."

The helicopter held exactly six of them, and Jamie was already in the pilot's seat, a duffel bag full of weapons on the deck.

They climbed into the aircraft and strapped themselves into their jump seats.

"I'm okay with McMahon," Elena said to Jules. "What I don't like is you coming along."

"Do you want me to miss the story of a lifetime?" Jules said. "The nuking of the UN?"

"We committed about nine thousand felonies," Elena said, "getting McMahon and Rashid out of that Pakistani torture chamber. You don't want to be accessoried to any of those crimes."

"Also if Tower learns we're in the Apple," Jamie said, "he'll order the goddamned U.S. Air Force to shoot us out of the sky."

"We won't be hard to spot," Elena said. "There won't be a lot of choppers checking out the UN. Jules, I really don't want you with us."

"You need me," Jules said. "When we're in that TV news chopper and over Manhattan, if the cops radio us, I can talk to them. I'm the only one with press credentials, and I'm well known. I can bluff my way past most law enforcement."

"How long did you say this crate will stay up?" Adara asked.

"Five or six hours," Jamie said.

"And it's got a cruising speed of two hundred miles per hour," Jules said. "If you want to get to the UN in time for the Secretary General's address to the General Assembly on the Anti-Inequality Expropriation Bill, we better haul ass. The clock is ticking."

"Copy that," Jamie said.

"Let's hit it," Rashid said, slapping a magazine into a Barrett M83 .50 caliber anti-transport sniper rifle. "I'm door gunner in case we run into any violent opposition. This Barrett'll take down planes, choppers, tanks and battleships at sea. Jules, you got your tail-, nose- and mini-cams set up?"

"They're ready to go," Jules said, "locked and cocked."

"Then let's get this bird in the air," Jamie said.

The rotor turned, and the din was deafening.

4

"Think of yourself as Paolo, in Dante's Second Circle of Hell. He and Francesca whirl together for all eternity in an agony of lust, which they can never satisfy or consummate. Except yours will be more agony than lust."
—Fahad al-Qadi to Benjamin Jowett

When Benjamin Jowett came to, he was in a suite in one of J. T.'s Needle Tower hotels. To the south he could see Wall Street and to the west, the vast expanses of New Jersey. It was night, and New York and the Garden State were bathed with brilliant luminescence.

He suddenly realized he was spread-eagled naked on an ultra-king-size bed atop purple satin sheets. His wrists and ankles were lashed to the bed frame's legs, and he was tightly gagged. Adding to the weirdness and the terror, a translucent bag filled with a clear liquid dripped slowly into a needle inserted into his arm.

How the fuck had he gotten here?

Slowly, it all came back to him.

He'd come up to the room, just as President Tower had told him to do, and the president's young woman was waiting for him in a white negligee and matching high heels, ready and eager but at the same time strangely shy, appealingly innocent. On the bedside tables were sterling silver dishes overflowing with pure cocaine, beluga caviar, toast points and Cialis. On both sides of the bed were sterling silver ice buckets of Dom Pérignon.

After fortifying himself with the refreshments, including the Cialis, he lay back and let her undress him. Working her way around every square inch of his body—stomach, back, arms and hands, legs and feet—she gave him the most incredible world tour of his life. Finally wending her way up his knees and thighs, she paused at the immensity of his . . .

Tower was right. She was soon giving him the greatest barracuda blowjob he'd ever known. Part of her skill was to take him to the edge of ecstasy but then pull him back, return him to the brink and then yank him away from it again, then again, then again, over and over, until he was begging her to finish, to let him come, every ounce of his coke-addled, Cialis-fueled lust driven mad by his criminally carnal, odiously obscene cravings.

"No," she said, stopping to look up at him with her large, amazingly expressive eyes and to grin sensuously. "First, a fresh glass of champagne, and then I will give you the greatest, grandest finale of your life, followed by much, much much more."

So she poured two glasses and insisted that they each drink one in a single gulp. At that point, she'd done everything so perfectly Jowett was ready to go along with anything she said.

But as soon as he drank the champagne he felt light-headed.

The room was moving, lurching.

He was growing weak, faint, dizzy.

Then he was spinning—down, down, downward to darkness, into a bleak bottomless abyss of blackest night.

And then he knew no more.

He suddenly saw the young woman walk out of the boudoir's bathroom.

She was smiling, the grin no longer sweet and demure but filled with conceited condescension and venomous contempt.

Then a Middle Eastern man in a black expensively tailored suit and a platinum Rolex with emerald-cut diamonds was standing beside her. He bore a startling resemblance to Omar Sharif.

The man loosened the gag.

"Any questions?" he asked.

"Yeah," Jowett asked. "What the fuck is going on?"

"We understand that you are exquisitely sensitive to Viagra and Cialis, both of which create in your genitals a rare condition called 'pathological priapism.' Furthermore, your affliction has grown worse as you've grown older. During the last year, by our count, you made six trips to the hospital to reverse this condition. Nonetheless, you still insist on fooling around with anti–erectile dysfunction drugs, otherwise known as AEDs. Your abuse of AEDs and your addiction to shockingly hard-core porn have made an already dangerous disorder much, much worse."

"Well," the woman said, "we now have something even more powerful than Viagra and Cialis for you to amuse yourself with. It's totally illegal, of course. One of America's drug companies developed it and spent millions trying to market it, but could not get it through the FDA. When it was tested on rats, they either died of what doctors call 'expiration by erection' or, if female rats were available, the males simply . . . *fucked them to death*. You, I'm afraid, won't have this option. During your last hours, you'll be all alone, spread-eagled and gagged on this bed, in this hotel penthouse, watching nonstop porn starring . . . *moi*."

"So get ready," the man said. "The drug company called their original version Verpusarrigas, and it's the drug currently entering your brachial artery through this intra-arterial drip. It will induce terminal tumescence. Eventually producing a thrombus in your corpus cavernosum, this drug will incite penile ischemia, necrosis, infection and gangrene, all of which will seed your bloodstream with pathogens so lethal they will inevitably engender a fiercely fatal sepsis. Your genitals will experience unimaginable suffering, which will lead to your long interminable utterly unendurable *demise*."

"You aren't really going to do this," Jowett said, "are you?"

"But we are," the woman said. "In fact, this version of the medication is even more powerful than what your drug companies had originally attempted to create and market," the man said. "Mikhail Putilov had his scientists take a crack at it, and they have now made it truly . . . *excruciating*."

"That is true," the man said. "In the past Putilov had ordered me to kill a number of people with polonium-210, a poison that caused its victim to suffer several days of unbearable pain. It felt as if the polonium was setting fire to the recipient's stomach and intestines."

"Unfortunately," the woman said, "Russia was the only nation that manufactured polonium-210, and the toxin had become inextricably identified with Putilov. Anytime he had someone killed with it, everyone knew instantly who had ordered the hit. Much to his chagrin, Putilov had to stop using it."

"So guess what?" the man said. "You will go down in history—as the first man to be tortured to death by this landmark drug."

"But I thought we had a thing!" Jowett shouted at the young woman. "I thought we felt something. I felt something."

"You felt lust. I felt nausea."

"But you can't do this," Jowett said, shaken, unbelieving.

"Oh, we can do it all right," the man said. "Unfortunately, what we can't do is stay and watch. We both have other pressing matters to attend to."

"I can, however, offer you a surrogate me," the young woman said. She pointed to the 100-inch flat TV screen. She clicked it on with a remote. On the screen a young, spectacularly gorgeous hooker—namely, herself—was giving him head.

She then wheeled in five more 100-inch flat screens. The same porn video was playing on all of them.

"The sedative and painkiller should be wearing off by now," the man said. "Do you feel . . . uncomfortable?"

He was suddenly aware that he was *very uncomfortable*. In fact, he was currently experiencing a firestorm down below. He stared down at his luridly livid, grotesquely engorged member. Christ, it felt like a thermonuclear conflagration was engulfing his crotch.

The young woman was laughing at him now, mocking him with childish giggles.

"Big tough macho Wall Street big shot," she was saying, barely able to contain her hilarity. "I want our little encounter to be a night for you to remember. I want you to watch us on the TV screen for as long as you *live*."

"Think of yourself as Paolo in Dante's Second Circle of Hell," Fahad said to him. "He and Francesca whirl together for all eternity in an agony of lust, which they can never satisfy or consummate. Except yours will be more 'agony' than 'lust.'"

"You can't!" Jowett howled.

"Oh, but we can," Fahad said, "and we shall. If it's any consolation though, you won't die unsung. You will, in fact, die in a blaze of infamy and notoriety."

"We'll see to it that a digital copy of you, me and your final hours is sent to Jules Meredith and Danny McMahon," the young woman said. "Mr. Jowett, we're going to make you a superstar of porn."

"Albeit snuff-flick porn," Fahad said.

"With you our snuffed star!" the young woman enthused.

The man held Benjamin's nose, and when his jaw opened, he inserted a hard black rubber ball in his mouth. The ball was affixed to a leather strap that he tied tightly around Benjamin's head.

"Here, let him listen to some music," the woman said.

"Excellent idea," Fahad said. "It will drown out his groans and sobs."

"Not that anyone would hear him anyway."

The girl then cranked up the surround sound stereo, and the sensuously melodious, extravagantly erotic lyrics of "Pillow-Talkin' Time" filled the penthouse.

The two left laughing, congratulating each other with high fives and back-slaps.

To Benjamin's eternal horror, he could not take his eyes off the six TV screens and their prodigiousy libidinous, erotically arousing images of the young woman wailing dementedly on his . . . *thrill hammer.*

Even when the conflagration in his groin became insupportable, even then he could not take his eyes off her.

Damn, that bitch was good!

At last, though, the fire-down-below got the better of him, and slowly, ineptly, Benjamin C. Jowett attempted to scream. But the rubber ball, crammed and strapped deeply into his mouth, and the music blaring over wall-to-wall surround sound speakers, blocked and drowned out any protest he could utter.

The best he could summon up was a low, soft, choking, wrenching, pain-racked sob.

But through it all, try as he might, he could not take his eyes of the TV screens and all he could think was:

Damn, that bitch is hot . . .

PART XVIII

"Oxfam—in conjunction with *Forbes* and Credit Suisse—has published a rigorously researched and painstakingly documented study that proves that eight men, six of whom are Americans, now possess more wealth than one-half of the world's population. These figures probably understate our fiscal crisis. Some economists now argue that the top seven oligarchs are richer than half of the planet's populace."

—UN Secretary General Jean Paul Renault

1

Putilov sat in his office at his big, sprawling, polished oak desk, reading his daily intelligence briefing, when an encrypted Skype call rang on his computer. He turned on his Skype phone and both Kamal ad-Din and Ambassador Waheed appeared on his computer screen.

"My friends," Putilov said with a beaming smile, "how nice to hear from you."

"Everything is going as planned," Prince Waheed said. "Raza and her associates have landed in New York, and 'Operation UN' is about to commence."

"Excellent," Putilov said. "I also see you have taken the time to dispose of a few loose ends."

"I thought you'd appreciate the job we did on Jowett," Raza said.

"A work of art," Putilov said. "I just got a digital link to it. It made my polonium-210 assassinations look amateurish by comparison."

"We didn't tell Tower about our plans for Jowett," Kamal said.

"We were under the impression he liked Jowett," Waheed said.

"Tower's an idiot," Putilov said with disgust.

"It didn't matter what Tower wanted," Waheed said. "Jowett had to go."

"Absolutely," Raza said. "Jowett almost single-handedly provoked the Arab Spring riots that toppled Mubarak and Qaddafi."

"I was running the Dresden KGB offices when the Berlin Wall came down," Putilov said, "and we were nearly overrun by rampaging mobs, screaming 'Revolution!' You'll never know how much I hate uprisings like the ones that fool Jowett incited in the Mideast."

"Those insurrections could have spread to our Saudi Kingdom," Ambassador Waheed said.

"Even worse, another drought is about to hit your region," Putilov pointed out, "and Jowett's famine derivatives would have made the cost of grain soar—just as they did before Arab Spring. We couldn't afford to have that whole area go up in flames. This time the mob uprisings might very well have spread to your esteemed Saudi Kingdom—even Mother Russia."

"Jowett was a lunging live wire in our region, wayward and dangerous," Ambassador Waheed agreed. "His man-made famines had the potential to destroy all of us."

"Fahad performed admirably," Raza said. "It would have been a perfect op, if he hadn't missed that Meredith woman."

"He said he couldn't get a clear shot," Ambassador Waheed explained.

"And he's never failed us before," Kamal said.

"I guess there's a first time for everything," Waheed said.

"That had to be a disappointment for Tower as well," Putilov said. "Jules Meredith has spent the last decade all but crucifying him."

"Yes," Waheed said, "but Tower did not hear about Fahad's missed shot from us. As per our discussions, we kept Tower out of the loop."

"Tower talks like he's a tough guy," Putilov said, "but I always thought he was soft."

"And stupid," Kamal said.

"Which is a major problem," Putilov said. "If there's one thing I've learned during my sixty-plus years on this earth, it's that you can't trust *stupid*."

"Agreed," Ambassador Waheed said. "Stupidity is always the most deplorable of all human follies."

"But everything else is well on your end, Raza?" Putilov asked.

"Fahad is bringing the package to the chopper," Raza said. "It's heavy but cylindrical in shape. We'll be rolling it down a steel ramp with a hydraulic lift and then onto the top of the UN tower. We'll have a timer set, but we can also trigger it with a radio detonator as well."

"The ambassadors to the United Nations will have to expropriate our offshore wealth in the Afterlife," Waheed said, laughing.

"I take it you won't be joining them for a vote on the Anti-Inequality Resolution?" Raza asked Ambassador Waheed.

Waheed roared with hilarity, and his friends joined in the mirth.

"Those UN agitators," Putilov said, "will have a hot time in the Big Apple tonight."

"A very hot time," Prince Waheed agreed.

2

. . . Yet from hell's flames
No light, but rather darkness visible.
—Milton, *Paradise Lost*

Fahad sat in the South Bronx machine shop, which he'd had Haddad lease several months earlier. It took up the entire basement floor of a onetime truck repair shop, and it contained everything he'd needed—metal lathes, screw machines, laser-beam welding equipment, acetylene welding units, drill presses, tool and die sets, power vises, forklifts, hydraulic lifts—anything he'd required to cobble together the crude but highly effective one-kiloton bomb.

The UN's much-vaunted Global Anti-Poverty Conference will never know what hit it, Fahad thought acerbically.

Cobbling together the one-kiloton terrorist nuke had been no mean feat. Four months ago, he'd arranged to acquire a seven-foot Civil War cannon barrel from the estate of an old-time arms collector on the brink of insolvency. He had then had Haddad haul it to the shop. There, his assistants had elevated the seven-foot smooth-bore steel tube up on a hydraulic lift, and with cut-dies and a high-tech screw machine, they had threaded the two barrel ends. After screwing a steel tamp into one end, he'd then dual-laser-welded it into the barrel. After the tamp-end of the barrel had cooled off, he had pushed the extra-high-explosive (EHX) through the length of the barrel until it rested flush against the tamp. The EHX was pre-embedded with a detonator, into which he would later transmit a radio signal that would set off the EHX.

Into the barrel's open mouth, Fahad then inserted an ultrathin aluminum canister, pushing it through the cannon until it was flush against the EHX. The drum contained ten near-circular disks of bomb-grade 90 percent highly enriched uranium (HEU). Each of the disks was firmly fixed inside the canister and close to its adjacent disks, but none was touching. Those disks constituted the A-bomb's bullet. The end of the canister, which faced the target, was wide open and had no lid.

He then jammed the bullet's tight-fitting target—a comparably thin, open-ended aluminum container filled with the same kind of disks, also packed close together but not touching. That canister's curving cylindrical surface was covered with a thick heat-absorbing asbestos coating.

Then came the tricky part. As he'd done initially with the propellant/bullet end of the barrel, he screwed in the tamp. On its interior face, he'd glued a piece of circular firebrick, protecting the disks from excessive thermal energy. He'd then dual-laser-welded the tamp to the barrel until, like the tamp at the howitzer's propellant/bullet end, it was inextricably bonded to the barrel. The entire howitzer barrel was now effectively a single seamless unit, one unbreachable piece of steel.

He had required the help of his two Saudi assistants. They were good boys, but they were willing to die for their religious principles, while Fahad wasn't. Instead of the jihad, he had forty million reasons for incinerating the UN—i.e., $40 million. Those boys worked for nothing, for expenses.

Those boys were fools.

He didn't care how loyal and discreet they were. He did not trust people who willingly exposed themselves to certain death out of ridiculously irrational religious convictions. He refused to put his life and the fate of this highly complex operation into the hands of two demented morons. He was professional.

So they'd had to go. They were now shot dead and encased in two 55-gallon steel drums, whose tops he'd welded in place with an acetylene torch. His driver was in the third barrel. The delivery man was in the fourth. He'd used the newly purchased chain saws to cut off the men's limbs, so he could fit them into those barrels. He'd performed the operations on the plastic tarp, which he'd disposed of in a fourth drum with the driver. All four barrels were weighted down with lead bars and loaded onto the back of his truck with the forklift. Late that night he would drive them to the Hudson River, roll them onto a trawler and take them out to the river's middle. After puncturing holes in the drums with a hammer and a cold chisel—so that the bodies' decomposition gases could escape—he would sink the drums in the middle of that massive waterway.

He would then deliver the nuke to his paymasters at the New Jersey helipad. He would forklift it onto the chopper, help them fly the helicopter to the UN and roll the nuke onto the roof of the UN's Secretariat Building. After taking off, he would detonate it for them after they were at a safe distance from the blast wave.

At that point, he would see that his pay was deposited in his clandestine offshore account and land the chopper at a remote Jersey farm. After driving off, he would go to ground and disappear forever to a life of peace, ease and luxurious comfort.

3

We can either have democracy in this country or we can have great wealth concentrated in the hands of a few, but we can't have both.

—Supreme Court Justice Louis Brandeis (1856–1941)

Secretary General Jean Paul Renault stood before the UN General Assembly and stared out over the 800 ambassadors and translators. He had just finished introducing and thanking the various UN officials, and now that august body sat before him as if they were a vast theater audience, which in a sense they were. They were even more on edge than he was. The world's democracies were up in arms against what they claimed was "an income-inequality plague," and at the UN the demand for reallocation of assets had finally reached the tipping point. Something had to break. Jean Paul was indeed about to deliver the speech of a lifetime. He was about to make the case justifying the confiscation of one-third of all illicit funds currently secreted in foreign black-hole accounts by the world's superwealthy tax cheats. A new UN agency would then redistribute the money to those around the world who were less advantaged. If victims of genuine exploitation could prove their case in court, they would receive an even greater share.

The Secretary General glanced at his image in a side monitor. He had deliberately down-dressed. His black three-piece suit looked as if it had been custom-tailored for him even though he had bought it off a rack at a nearby Walmart. But then he was easy to buy suits for. Clothes often fit him with no alterations whatsoever. Reporters often commented on his tall, regally slim physique. He was frequently told that his thick, meticulously coiffed white hair and mustache made him look distinguished, and he was glad he'd taken his wife's advice and gone to his hairdresser. This speech would live forever on YouTube. He wanted to look good, not out of personal vanity, but because the seriousness of the issues at hand demanded that he make a good impression.

"For the last thirty-five years, we have watched as more and more wealth has been concentrated in fewer and fewer hands. As we speak, the net assets of a single Wall Street investment firm, BlackRock, are 50 percent greater than the entire GDP of Germany, the third wealthiest nation in the world. BlackRock handles other assets, however, besides its own, so the total value of all BlackRock assets are valued at over $14 trillion—which tops China's GDP. Given BlackRock's rate of growth, their assets might well exceed America's GDP in a few years. Currently, there is no way for BlackRock's top executives—nor any top executives, for that matter—to be held to account for the management of these holdings. Whereas government officials can be defeated in elections, the transnational superfirms, their top executives and America's Mega-Rich Plutocrats are, in effect, nations unto themselves and untouchable. Most of today's J. P. Morgans and John D. Rockefellers are virtually beyond the law. That the Justice Department refused to seriously investigate, let alone prosecute, any top Wall Street executives for wrongdoing after those people melted down the global economy in 2008 is living proof of Super-Money's ability to avoid serious legal or political reprisals. As then-Attorney General Eric Holder confessed, Wall Streets moguls were 'too big to jail.'

"The trillions of dollars the Super-Firms and Über-Rich garner each year in government subsidies also bear ample witness to their political omnipotence. For instance, the fossil fuel energy and financial sectors garner more than $6 trillion a year in subsidies from global governments. Those subsidies sap over 8 percent of the planet's total GDP—so much that the World Bank has asked specifically for an end to all energy subsidies everywhere. According to another study, the U.S. has spent more money protecting Mideast oil for J. T. Tower and his fellow energy oligarchs than it did fighting Soviet/Chinese Communism during the Cold War.

"Over a century ago Theodore Roosevelt broke up the Rockefeller oil refinery monopoly for being too large and powerful, but our situation is graver than anything that that president faced. Today's corporate welfare enriches the financial elites on a scale that the 19th-century robber barons never dreamed of. Nor has the planet ever known a breed of plutocrats as unproductive as those sucking up most of the world's wealth. At least Rockefeller produced oil, a valuable commodity that fueled that century's Industrial Revolution, and Henry Ford revolutionized transportation. But as the financial journalist Jules Meredith has written: 'Unlike the robber barons of the 19th century, Tower's billionaires produce almost nothing that is useful or socially redeeming: Wall Street money-making-money-off-money scams, internet hype enterprises, fiscally destructive mergers—yes, 80 percent of mergers line the coffers of the key players but impoverish everyone else—predatory casinos, and, of course, debt-derivatives, which Warren Buffett called 'financial weapons of mass destruction.' The majority of today's robber barons enrich themselves off greed, vanity and folly; that is all. They produce nothing of value.

"The corporate profits of the world's financial sectors are especially obscene. In the United States alone, for example, the financial community sucks up 50 percent of that country's nonfarm corporate profits, and around the world that industry is equally voracious.

"The situation has gotten so bad that in the U.S. the top one tenth of 1 percent of the population possesses more money than the bottom 90 percent.

"No good can come out of so much avarice. John Maynard Keynes once described the money motive—the accumulation of wealth solely for wealth's sake—as intrinsically pathological. By that standard, the financial machinations of today's oligarchs and plutocrats are 'intrinsically pathological'—so much so that the world financial community now resembles not a global banking complex as much as a gigantic vampire bat with its wings wrapped around the people of the earth, its fangs sucking out the last dregs of their hearts' blood.

"As some of you might know," Secretary General Renault continued, "Oxfam—in conjunction with *Forbes* and Credit Suisse—has published a rigorously researched and painstakingly documented study that proves that eight men, six of whom are Americans, now possess more wealth than one-half of the world's population. These figures probably understate our fiscal crisis. Some economists now argue that the top seven oligarchs are richer than that half of the planet's populace.

"As our resolution painstakingly documents, these oligarchs and their transnational corporations have deliberately created and are exacerbating these economic disparities. Their strategy is to impoverish workers in the developed world by outsourcing their jobs to the world's most economically depressed countries and then paying even those workers only the lowest possible Third World wages. Their other monopolistic tactics include underpaying their suppliers and contractors. At the same time, their expenditures on their businesses' upgrades and infrastructure shrink. Through such strategies, these corporations have for over four decades grossly suppressed wages for employees everywhere and depleted their own companies. Then they merge, merge, merge their firms, until today's plutocrats are tomorrow's oligarchs.

"The predatory rich—and the corporations they represent—exhibit no allegiance to the countries in which they reside and which have helped them to prosper. Their only loyalty is to that nation that grants them the lowest taxes, allows them to pay the lowest wages and permits them to poison the planet with the greatest possible impunity. Consequently, they end up paying in taxes a smaller percentage of their revenues than they pay their cleaning staff and their secretaries. In fact, their tax rates often approach zero percent. These exploitative elites then hide their filthy lucre in labyrinthine networks of secret offshore tax havens. As their wealth explodes and their power to buy politicians soars, the gap between the ultra-rich and the rest of the world will, of necessity, increase astronomically.

"For thirty-five years, these politically ambitious and obscenely powerful magnates have conducted a gradual but persistent financial takeover of the planet. They have been particularly eager to turn the U.S. into an oligarchy. As Jules Meredith reports in her book, *Filthy Lucre*:

> In the United States, the Oligarch Movement is headed by President J. T. Tower. The heart and soul of that movement are his 200 megadonors. He has organized them into a clandestine, rigorously disciplined political group, which he has nicknamed at various times "Murder, Inc." and his "Killer Elite." Tightly coordinated at the grassroots level, this group is dedicated to steamrolling its opposition in state and local elections and radically gerrymandering congressional districts in their favor. Active at the topmost levels of government as well, where it peddles influence and strong-arms legislators with primary threats, it is infinitely more powerful than any other group around—arguably more powerful than any U.S. political group in history.

"Time was that society condemned avarice. Asking for excessive interest on a loan damned the usurer to hellfire everlasting. Christ Himself could not have been more adamant about the evils of financial predation. The Lord's Prayer's literal translation says nothing about 'trespasses.' In the original Greek, as well as in Hebrew and Aramaic, the word is 'debts'—monetary debts. The supplicant is strongly advised to forgive his or her debtors—*all debtors*. Near the Lord's Prayer's close, Christ says that God will treat us the way we treat those who owe us money. If you're hard on them, God will be hard on you. Christ exemplifies His hatred of greed when He flogs the money changers out of the temple. He believes they are committing the sin of avarice because they are charging people fees for the privilege of purchasing a special kind of currency—church-blessed money. In other words, the priests were making money off money, and Christ drives them from their house of worship.

"Paul famously tells us: 'The love of money is the root of all evil,' and the serpent tells us why in the Garden of Eden. He convinces Eve to bite the apple, telling her that if she and Adam 'eat the fruit of the tree thereof, then ye shall be as Gods.' That is the siren song of riches and profligacy: If you have enough money and material possessions, you can live as a god on earth and do anything you want. Money lust is the implicit overreaching of God; it's hubris incarnate.

"In chapter thirteen of *Revelation*—which chronologically ought to be the book's first chapter—greed provokes Armageddon, leading us to the End of Days. John of Patmos has an angel explain in that chapter why God will visit this apocalypse on us and then kill and torture in perpetuity over one-third of humankind: The angel announces to the world that God wants us to either reject avarice—and stop trafficking financially with the Anti-Christ—or God will sentence us eternally to hellfire and brimstone. You can have Paradise, the angel says, or money, which will be promptly followed by hellfire everlasting. One-third of humanity says, 'We'll take the money.' Humanity is, of course, destroyed, and the greedy ones go straight to hell.

"In the New Testament love of money is far and away the deadliest of all the deadly sins. It tells us that greed will destroy human beings by the billions and will in the end rid the earth of humanity's shadow.

"The time to stop this oligarchic take over is *now*. The hard truth is that oligarchy and democracy are mutually incompatible. If this financial exploitation of our planet and its people does not stop today, if the UN's resolution mandating the mass expropriation and redistribution of a full third of the über-rich's illegal assets is not passed, we will witness the end of freedom and democracy throughout the globe. The world will enter a new Dark Age, and global totalitarianism will inevitably follow, just as it did in Putilov's Russia. So we are out of time, and we must act today. There is no room left for compromise."

There were five, stunned, uncomprehending seconds of silence, then the General Assembly rose up in a single monstrous protracted roar—sudden, spontaneous and elemental—a tsunami of approbation.

Glancing at a panel of side monitors, the Secretary General saw multiscreen footage of massive crowds all over the world—in Beijing and Buenos

Aires, in London and Mumbai, in New York and New Dehli—thundering for the bill's passage.

Mon Dieu, Secretary General Jean Paul Renault thought to himself. *This bill will pass! Nothing can stop it—nothing short of an asteroid strike on the UN.*

4

"Fuck Tower," Kamal said. **"He's an idiot."**

Raza, Marika, Fahad and Tariq stood in the closed hangar of the helipad in rural New Jersey. A friendly New York City police officer, whom Fahad had handpicked months ago, had borrowed an NYPD chopper for them, and Raza would pilot it. All four wore the dark blue uniforms of New York's Finest—complete with gun belts, sidearms and gear.

The craft before them was an Airbus AS365, featuring a cruise speed of over 175 miles per hour, a range of over 500 miles and air-endurance of nearly five hours. Most important, with its two Turbomeca Arriel 2C, turboshaft engines and heavily reinforced, customized cargo deck, it could easily handle three tons of payload. Given the howitzer-barrel nuke in its cargo bay, it would need that kind of power and structural reinforcement.

Raza, Marika and Tariq watched Fahad forklift load the bomb into the chopper's fuselage, and then watched him strap the bomb down.

"Time to check in with our employers?" Raza asked Marika and Tariq.

"I expect so," Tariq said.

They entered a nearby office and shut the door behind them. It had three gray metal office chairs, a gray metal desk, two filing cabinets, a desk phone and an open booted-up laptop computer. Raza sat down and punched in the Skype number for Kamal ad-Din, their financial backer. He came on and immediately linked in Prince Waheed. Both Kamal and Ambassador Waheed were dressed in long white *thawb* robes and keffiyehs.

God, Raza thought, *Kamal does look like a "Muslim Moby Dick,"* to quote one of McMahon's more blistering witticisms.

Raza, Marika and Tariq closed ranks in front of the computer so they could all see each other.

"So how is it going?" Ambassador Waheed asked. On the computer's Skype screen, he was smiling broadly.

"The cargo's on the chopper," Raza said, "and we're ready to rock."

"Splendid job, Fahad," Kamal said, joining Waheed on the computer screen. *"The number you did on Jowett was outstanding. Because you imme-*

diately leaked that in-flagrante-delicto footage, it's already out there on the web. We were able to watch Jowett's final hours."

"Those Wall Street derivative assholes will think twice about fomenting Middle Eastern famines from now on!" Waheed said.

"The networks even ran the footage," Fahad said.

"With Jowett's genitals obscured, of course," Prince Waheed said, *"but still the impact was overpowering. The West has to know now that the New United Islamist Front can get to anyone."*

"Did he suffer much?" Kamal asked, his mouth twitching in anticipation.

"We actually have a summary of a medical report," Marika said, "that was leaked to the papers and posted on the internet just a few minutes ago. The report's summary reads:

> *The coroner's report says that Jowett was found with "his penis in a condition of extreme tumescence and black with gangrene. Seeping green pus, the penis was exuding a foul-smelling gas from the orifice." The autopsy also noted "retrograde infection with massive swelling of the inguinal lymph nodes. The scrotum," the report said, "looked like a fully inflated soccer ball." Jowett's eyes were described as "glazed, the subject's mouth thick from heavy respiration due to his attempts to expel the acid load created by the body's sepsis. Since sepsis is highly catabolic and capable of causing the subject to burn up to 6000 calories a day, the subject appears to have sustained weight loss."*

"So," Fahad asked, "how's that for sheer unmitigated agony? Did Jowett go through as much hell as you people had wanted?"

"That sonofabitch got what he deserved," Kamal said, his computer-screen grin even wider and brighter than before. *"He personally orchestrated famines throughout the Mideast, then bragged about it afterward—all for the sake of making a few quick dirty bucks."*

"Who knows how many people he starved to death?" Marika said.

"Millions," Raza said, agreeing.

"There was one minor mishap," Fahad said. "I couldn't get a clear shot at Jules Meredith."

Fahad did not tell them why. That failure was too humiliating.

"We know," Kamal said, *"and Putilov is furious. He was not only mad at her himself, he'd promised President Tower personally that you'd take her out."*

"Gentlemen," Raza said, attempting to placate Kamal, "it will happen. I guarantee it. There just wasn't time to do everything."

"*That's too bad,*" Ambassador Waheed said. "*I wanted the bitch dead as well.*"

"Gentlemen," Fahad said. "We're under no time pressure to kill her. We can do it any Monday morning."

"*Still Putilov is hopping mad,*" Ambassador Waheed said. "*Tower won't be happy either.*"

"Fuck Tower," Kamal said. "*He's an idiot.*"

"Agreed," Fahad said. "Also perhaps you might remind Putilov how long it took for his hero, Stalin, to kill Trotsky, so Meredith's time will come. I plan on seeing her again. Personally. Meredith isn't going anywhere."

Fahad was lying. He was taking off when this was over, disappearing like smoke and never seeing any of them again.

"*We'll tell both of them that,*" Waheed said.

"I'll offer my services as well," Marika said.

"Moi aussi," Raza said. *Me, too.*

"*That should appease them,*" Kamal said.

"*Not if they decide to attend that UN Anti-Inequality Conference,*" Waheed said.

His comment provoked gales of laughter.

"Speaking of which," Raza said, "we have to get going. We have a conference to attend to."

The men were still laughing when Raza switched off the Skype call, and the four of them walked out of the office toward the chopper.

5

Please, just let us get through this alive, one more time, Elena silently prayed to the God in Whom she'd never believed, *and I promise I won't allow any of us to do anything this goddamn stupid again.*

Elena sat strapped into the chopper's jump seat, alone with her thoughts. What was happening? What had she done? She'd always been destined to end up doing something utterly disastrous, something as insane and fucked up as this. She could see it all so clearly now.

She recalled her childhood, growing up in the West Texas desert country. Her father had been a former biker, who cooked crystal meth for the Hells Angels, until he blew himself and his cook shack to Kingdom Come, leaving Elena an orphan. By coincidence, however, she'd recently met Jules, a fellow El Paso ninth-grader, and Elena had saved her from getting stomped by an outlaw girls' gang. Jules and her family immediately took Elena in and raised her as one of their own.

Her first year of college she'd dated a guy who'd turned out to be a bona fide Mideast terrorist. He'd returned to Pakistan, but her obsession with him had led to her join the Agency. She'd blazed through their training school—"The Farm"—with flying colors. Testing high on linguistic skills, she had excelled in the field. After becoming the Agency's foremost undercover agent in Pakistan, she'd met Jamie there. He was running black ops for the Special Forces on the Afghan–Pakistan border, and they'd fallen in love. Eventually, she had taken over the CIA's Pakistani desk. For a time, she'd been the world's foremost expert on Saudi–Pakistani terrorism. But then the Company had turned on her, Jules and Jamie, putting out shoot-to-kill orders on them all. They had had to flee the country.

Eventually they'd been cleared, but they'd all sworn they'd never return to the States. Something had happened to America. The whole nation had gone wrong. None of them had wanted any part of the U.S. ever again.

But then this shit happened, and none of them could turn their backs on it—Jules in particular. She had dug up stuff on Tower and the Saudis that they just couldn't ignore.

Still Elena knew in her soul that she, Jamie and Jules never should have come back and gotten involved. She should have somehow stopped them. She should have stood up, put her foot down.

Well it was too late for recriminations. Hell was coming to the Homeland, and once again, she, Jules, Jamie and her friends would be in the thick of it. And if the U.S. caught them, Tower would see to it that they spent the rest of their lives in some Guantanamo-style hellhole.

Or Kamal's crew would kill them.

If she could just keep them all alive, if she could get them all out of this in one piece, she swore she would drag them all back to Sweden by their throats, crotches and the scruffs of their necks. She would never let any of them return to the U.S. ever. She would never let any of them get involved in this crazy shit again. America and rest of the world were just too fucking crazy.

Please, just let us get through this alive, one more time, Elena silently prayed to the God in Whom she'd never believed, *and I promise I won't allow any of us to do anything this goddamn stupid again.*

She stared out of the chopper's windscreen and watched the skyscrapers of the Big Apple growing larger and larger.

6

Who would have dreamed it? Raza Jabarti—a heartless murdering terrorist with more blood on her hands than any hundred
men in the movement—was smitten with a foul-mouthed American comic-satirist and had moved heaven and earth to bring
McMahon to Pakistan so she could be with him.

Raza sat in the big police chopper, alone with her thoughts. No one was
saying much. They all had a lot on their minds. She was piloting them
toward the UN's imposing, flat-roofed skyscraper—its Secretariat Building. It would make an excellent bomb site. At that height, the blast and fire
damage would be much greater than it would be at ground level. The New
United Islamist Front physicists had calculated that the explosion would
easily obliterate the entire UN complex.

"Let those UN assholes try to confiscate our offshore trillions after we *nuke
them off the face of the earth*." Ambassador Waheed had laughed when she'd
first told him of her plan.

Her mind wandered. She could not stop thinking of Danny McMahon.
She'd told him about growing up as a Saudi girl, then a young woman, and
how miserable her existence had been. She'd joined the jihad for the simple
reason that two of her group's stronger men, Fahad and Kamal, had thought
that if women fought and died like men, they should have the same rights
and privileges as men. Fahad and Kamal had looked out for her, protected
her from the clerics and fanatics. She'd known freedom for the first time in
her life.

Still she'd hungered after more. Given her high position in the movement,
she'd had access to Western books and DVDs. Fahad and Kamal believed
in Sun Tzu's dictum, "Know your enemy," and so they'd encouraged her to
learn the ways of the West.

She would never forget the evening she stumbled on McMahon's DVD
documentary on the insanity of organized religion. Entitled *Relig-Idiots* it
reduced all faiths, most notably Islam, to sheer, babbling lunacy. She'd
watched it hundreds of times, could recite every line of it and was haunted
by it even to this day.

She began reading his books, watching his monologues and TV shows as-siduously, recording copies of every one of them. In plain fact, she'd become obsessed with him. He had truly liberated her, lifted the scales from her eyes and shown her the Light.

All religions—Islam most of all—were pure fucking madness.

So she'd organized McMahon's kidnapping. She'd argued they should abduct him, because he was the biggest, high-value, anti-Islamist critic on earth. By capturing and transporting him from New York to Pakistan, they would prove for once and for all that no one in the world was beyond their reach—not even America's superstar entertainers.

She'd argued the publicity value was incalculable, the ransom money astronomical and furthermore it would be . . . *fun*. For the rest of their lives, they would laugh their asses off over his kidnapping and the excruciating tortures which they would inflict on him.

But in truth, his kidnapping had merely been a very complicated way of getting to meet and know her idol.

Who would have dreamed it? Raza Jabarti—a heartless murdering terrorist with more blood on her hands than any hundred men in the movement—was smitten with a foul-mouthed American comic-satirist and had moved heaven and earth to bring McMahon to Pakistan so she could be with him.

She wondered what he thought of her. She'd terrified, beaten and tortured him halfway to death. She had also given him the wildest fuck of his entire life. Even more amazing and more unbelievable, while she'd had sex with legions of lovers, she'd never come close to experiencing an orgasm with any of them—not ever. She hated men—and life, for that matter—so obsessively she feared that her fury had robbed her of some simple essential erotic . . . *feeling*. In fact, she had been so indifferent to her lovers' myriad ministrations that she'd wondered if she would ever come.

Well McMahon had cured her of that problem once and for all. He'd rocked her world like Ragnarok, Götterdämmerung and Armageddon. All she had to do was think of him, and she was detonating with desire.

But what did he think of her?

Whatever he thought, he thought wrong.

Raza would prove him wrong.

Do not understand me too quickly, Danny McMahon, she'd told him. *Think not I am the thing I seem.*

PART XIX

"Raza-girl, we're going to bridge the inequality gap the old-fashioned way—by vaporizing those 500 billionaire cocksuckers! That's what I call a good start!"

—Raza Jabarti

1

President J. T. Tower sat in his private New York office at the top of the Excelsior Hotel. The furniture was all polished oak, the couches and armchairs upholstered in burgundy-hued raw silk. Portraits of the world's great warlords, Alexander and Caesar, Washington and Napoléon, MacArthur and Patton, hung on the walls.

But Tower was oblivious to all of it.

The only thing he could do was stare at his 96-inch wall-mounted flatscreen monitor and scowl. The damn UN bill was going to pass.

Suddenly, miraculously, Putilov returned the call that Tower had placed less than ten minutes prior. It usually took days for Tower to reach him, but Putilov must have been nervous about the vote as well.

"What the fuck is happening, Comrade?" Tower shouted into the phone.

Putilov hated it when Tower addressed him as "Comrade." He'd had men flogged, incarcerated, even killed for less offensive remarks. Still he had to humor this imbecile—for at least a while longer.

"Never fear, old friend," Putilov said unctuously. "This was all to be expected, and I shall soon extirpate the UN expropriation movement, root and branch."

"You can still stop them?" Tower asked, astonished.

Tower had been clearly unnerved by the UN speech and the enthusiastic reaction it was receiving across the globe.

"As you Americans sometimes say: 'I might have been born at night but not last night.' Of course I can."

"But people are agitating around the world to seize our offshore revenues," Tower said, "and this is just the beginning."

"So?" Putilov asked, his tone mocking.

"But how can you stop them?" Tower asked, his voice trembling with panic and terror.

Putilov suddenly lost it. Consumed with rage at the imbecile at the other end of the Skype call, he roared:

"By turning UN Plaza into a levitating nuclear fireball and annihilating every living soul in it! That's how we deal with our enemies over here. Understand me now, you pathetic fucking moron???"

Putilov was thundering at the top of his lungs, his face working in rage, his anger at Tower all but blinding him. Utterly beside himself, Putilov was no longer capable of placating or finessing or bullshitting the ridiculous born-rich fool any longer. Pulling a 9mm Makarov semi-automatic pistol from out of his middle desk drawer, he racked the slide in full view of Tower's hysterically screaming, jaw-gaping face and emptied the entire magazine into the Skype camera, his computer screen and Tower's confused face, which was staring back at him, bawling and sobbing in twitching, pissing horror.

His chief bodyguard entered the room instantly, his gun drawn.

"What's wrong?" the tall strapping uniformed Captain of the Guard, Dmitri Pavlov, asked, clearly distraught.

"Nothing, old friend," Putilov said, suddenly smiling for the first time in weeks. "Just something I've been wanting to do ever since I first spoke to the guy on the other end of the phone."

Putilov raised the smoking gun and studied it for a long moment.

"Can I help you in any way, Mr. President?" Dmitri asked.

"Everything's fine," the smiling Putilov said, motioning the man toward the leather and mahogany chair in front of his desk. "Here, sit down. Goddamn, I feel good. In fact, for the first time in years, I really feel really . . . *at peace.*"

"I couldn't be more pleased for you, sir," the captain said, hesitantly, uncertain how to respond.

"Reminds me of the early '90s, Captain," Putilov said, "when we were just coming into our own, when we were getting our first taste of power. Damn, we killed a lot of people back then. I just plain lost count."

"You had men killed, Mr. President?" Captain Dmitri asked—still not sure what else to say.

"Does the Pope shit in the woods?" Putilov shouted, slapping his thighs and laughing like a lunatic.

Christ, Putilov must have lost fifty pounds, Dmitri thought in stunned horror. He had been on vacation, hadn't gotten a good look at the president in several weeks, and now saw Putilov was a mess. His white shirt fit him like a loose sack. His cheeks were drawn and sunken; his parchment-skin hung on him like a shroud. He was utterly emaciated, and his face was twitching uncontrollably.

"Those sound like wild times, Mr. President," the captain said uneasily.

"You don't know the half of it," Putilov muttered. "Wyatt Earp and Bill Hickok had nothing on us."

Putilov slowly began to scratch his arms, then his face and neck, then his thighs and ankles. Taking the krok syringe out of his right-hand desk drawer, he at last stopped scratching and began to rub the syringe with an almost sensual intimacy.

"Most of all, I loved the fliers," Putilov said in a low whisper, as if imparting a discreet secret.

"Fliers, sir?" the captain asked.

"Those were the suspects," Putilov said, "that we'd take to a high window, maybe to the twenty-fifth floor or, say, to the top of the Ivan the Great Bell Tower on Red Square. A couple of us would hang the man upside down by the ankles. I'd say to the fellow, often a man we'd been close to for years, even decades, a man who thought we were his friends: 'You think you're so smart. You think you're better than us. You think you can do anything, don't you? I'll bet you think you can . . . *fly*? Here, show us.' Then we'd let go. But none of them could fly. Instead, they dropped, like lead bricks—except these lead bricks screamed and thrashed their arms all the way down, as if their limbs were wings."

Sitting down, Putilov threw his head back and laughed like a loon.

"You did this a lot?" the shocked captain asked.

"More times than I can count," Putilov said, wiping his eyes and smiling happily as he reflected on his past. "But those were hard times. Anyone who even looked like they could double-cross us had to go. We did give them a chance, of course, to prove their innocence. Nikolay Kruchina, Georgy Palov and Dmitriy Lisovolik—none of them had to die. They all had their chance . . . *to fly—or die*."

Again, Putilov exploded with hilarity.

"Then there was Mikhail Khodorkovsky," Putilov said, struggling hard to pull himself together but having to wait for his laughs to subside. "He got rich like the rest of us, but then he decided he was a *reformer*! So I seized his oil company and gave him a chance to reform *our Gulag Archipelago from the inside*. For nine years—in two of the toughest and coldest of our hard-labor camps—he learned what happens to those who turn 'reformer' on me!" Putilov then whispered conspiratorially to the captain. "I paid guards and inmates to 'reform' Khodorkovsky—that is, to beat the piss out of him and freeze him half to death in ice-cold isolation cells every day and night of those nine years. 'Reform those guys, bitch!' I always wanted to howl at him!"

Once more, Putilov's laughter rang and reverberated like the very bells of hell. In fact, Putilov was now laughing so loud and so hard that, once again, tears came to his eyes.

Reaching into his side drawer, Putilov pulled out a huge diamond-studded gold ring. Waving at at Dmitri, he slipped it onto his wedding finger.

"Did I ever tell you how I got this U.S. Super Bowl ring?" Putilov asked. "George Abbott, owner of the St. Petersburg Pythons NFL football team, came to visit me. He showed me the ring, and I said I wanted to look at it more closely. He took it off, handed it to me, I put it on my finger and walked away. I then refused to speak to him or any of his people for the rest of the night. Nor did I respond to any of his requests to return it, saying only that 'a gift was gift.' *Sorry, buddy. No returns, no refunds.* He even went to his old friend, for whom he'd raised scores of millions in campaign donations, George W. 'I-Saw-Putilov's-Soul' Bush, and had him call me to ask for it back. I told Georgie: 'I'll only give him the ring if you let me sell Iran a nuclear weapons manufacturing plant!'"

Putilov's whole body was racked so hard by convulsive guffaws that he almost fell off his chair. It took him a full minute to compose himself and continue the story.

"That nitwit Bush," Putilov said, "actually told his friend that his ring had become a national security issue and that Abbott should say publicly that he wanted me to have it."

Putilov then stared at the captain, his grin now twitching uncontrollably.

"So the man hadn't given you the ring?" Dmitri asked, still not knowing what to say or think.

"Of course not," Putilov said. "If the man had given me the trinket, it wouldn't have meant anything to me. I'd have thrown it in the Moscow River. I have baubles a thousand times more precious than his fucking ring. What makes it priceless to me is that I *stole* it from him. Abbott loves that ring more than his children, more than his testicles, more than life itself, and every time he glances at his ring finger, he remembers me, my superior smile, my utter contempt for him and how I robbed him of the thing he held most dear in his life, how I humiliated him on the world stage, and how, when he sent George W. Bush to me to get it back, I humiliated him, too, the President of the United States. I manipulated the U.S. president—the man who claimed to see into "my soul"—into making that NFL owner apologize to me in public for asking me for 'the gift's' return. I love that ring because I took it off its rightful owner and now he shakes with rage, fear and pain every time he thinks of me."

Again, Putilov exploded in an orgy of racketing laughter that shook his office and frightened Dmitri to his soul.

"Thank God," Putilov said, choking back his maniacal mirth, "I discovered polonium-210. The problem with 'fly or die' was it was over too fast, and so it really didn't hurt all that much. With polonium-210 poisoning though, the people experienced pure agony. They took days, even weeks to die, and all the time their guts felt like they were in flames. And now, I have something even more horrifying, as Benjamin Jowett learned the hard way. That's a pun, Captain—'hard way.' Get it? I killed that bastard Jowett *with a hard-on that wouldn't go down!*"

Now Putilov's hideous horselaughs were approaching apocalyptic proportions, and they only began to subside when he started to rub his arms, legs and neck again. Muttering to himself and grinning maniacally—even as he struggled to catch his breath—he said:

"Did I ever tell you about how I hunted and killed apartment rats as a small boy? I was so obsessed with the little bastards that after I'd clubbed one to death, I'd dissect it. Flies too. When I captured one alive, I'd hold it down with a pair of tweezers and try to figure out what made it buzz. I'd grab a second pair of tweezers and study it in detail. I'd rip off one wing, then the other. Then I'd tear off its feelers, next its legs. I'd remove its eyes one at a time, then open up its belly, scrutinizing it as closely as I could, examining its remains under a magnifying glass."

Then Putilov drifted off, humming some unidentifiable tune, his eyes distant and unfocused, a ghoulish grin twisting the left corner of his mouth upward.

"Did you ever find out where the buzzing noise came from?" Captain Dmitri asked, hoping to bring Putilov back to some semblance of reality.

"No, I never did," Putilov said, suddenly grinning brightly and looking Captain Dmitri straight in the eye. "But, on the other hand, those flies . . . *they didn't get around so good anymore!*"

Giggling like a deranged ape, he was, once more, rubbing his arms, legs, head and neck feverishly. The scratchings and ululations went on and on and on, and just when Dmitri thought they would never stop, to his surprise, they suddenly did. Putilov froze in place, sitting at his desk, still as a statue, staring fixedly, mindlessly at something unseeable and far away—something that seemed to be thousands of yards in the imperceivable distance. Spittle bubbled and burbled out of the right corner of his mouth. The froth oozed slowly down his jaw and after a long moment began to drip off his chin.

Oh, my God, Dmitri thought suddenly, *Tower must be the incarnation of evil. Just conversing with him on the phone has turned Mikhail Ivanovich Putilov, the strongest, most disciplined man I've ever known, into a raving, mouth-foaming, drug-addled* idiot.

Finally, Putilov stopped his staring, reached into his desk drawer and took out his aspirin bottle filled with krokodil tablets. Holding it close to his chest, he began rubbing it intently, almost orgiastically, rocking back and forth and softly humming and singing "The Volga Boatman."

Yo, heave ho!
Yo, heave ho!
Volga, Volga is our pride,
Mighty stream so deep and wide . . .

Returning to his right-hand top desk drawer, Putilov took out a bottle of Everclear, a small squeeze can of ether, a flask of gasoline, two spoons and a razor blade.

"I'm going to celebrate," Putilov said, smiling moronically at the captain, "with a little taste of the krok."

Putilov began grinding and chopping up the pills. Dmitri noted that the Russian president's desk was now crisscrossed with razor blade cuts and eroded from dried-up Everclear, ether and gasoline spills. Furthermore, as Putilov chopped away, he sliced his finger with the razor blade, and blood flowed heavily onto the whitish powder. Putilov, however, was oblivious to the bleeding. When he was done chopping, he poured the powder—blood and all—into the Pyrex bong, added Everclear, a long squirt of ether, a dash of gasoline, and applied heat. It quickly came to a boil. Turning off the lighter, Putilov hiked his sleeve all the way up to his armpit and tied it off just below the elbow with his belt. He drew the syringe-full of liquid out of the bong—without even waiting for it to cool—squirted out a few drops and then tapped the needle just to make sure there was no air in it.

"That stuff must be really good," the captain said in an attempt to make small talk and not appear critical of Putilov's drug habit. Still Dmitri could not help nervously eyeing the grotesque galaxy of needle tracks garishly scarring Putilov's fish-white forearm.

"Good?" Putilov said, grinning. "If God had anything better, He kept it for *Himself.*" He gave the captain a wicked, conspiratorial wink.

Putilov smoothly, knowingly inserted the needle into a hard-used wrist vein—the only visible and viable conduit on the entire arm—and pushed the krokodil home. His hands instantly dropped to his lap, his right index finger continuing to pump blood, unabated, onto his leg. His head then snapped back. Eyes rolling into his head, his jaw fell wide open, hammering his sternum like a blackjack, and he pitched forward.

More spittle spumed and seethed out of the dictator's mouth. Running down his chin, the translucent slaver relentlessly smacked and splattered Putilov's desk. The large round globules slowly merged into a small, noxious but steadily expanding pool of drool.

2

Raza's laughter soared through the night.

Raza piloted the chopper along the East River toward the roof of the UN's thirty-nine-story Secretariat Building—the highest skyscraper at UN Plaza. Turning on everyone's voice-mikes, she announced to her team:

"I'm going to set down in a few minutes, so prepare the ramp."

Marika, Tariq, and Fahad got up from their jump seats and walked over to the far edge of the ramp. As Raza hovered over the roof, they prepared to hydraulically lower the heavy-gauge, ten-foot-long and eight-foot-wide ramp over the edge of the hatch. She would then push the hoist button that raised and rolled the cannon-barrel bomb down the ramp.

"Everyone ready?" Raza shouted.

"Roger that!" Fahad shouted.

Marika and Tariq nodded.

With her left hand fixed on the controls, Raza took an MP5 machine pistol out of her canvas ordnance bag and fired quick bursts into each of them, center-mass first, then their heads.

"Well played," Raza said softly to herself. "Now let's head this crate over to its rightful destination—J. T.'s Needle Tower of Power. Its flat roof will make a perfect 'Tower-of-Power' landing zone."

Heading the chopper north, the tall slender Needle Tower quickly swung into view.

"And now billionaire assholes everywhere," Raza said to herself with droll amusement, "can stare into their TV screens and watch what real power looks like. Raza-girl, we're going to bridge the inequality gap the old-fashioned way—by vaporizing those 500 billionaire cocksuckers! That's what I call a good start!"

And with that her chopper roared up and over the East River toward the J. T. Tower of Power.

Raza's laughter soared through the night.

3

"What do you think I am? A terrorist?"
—Raza Jabarti

Jamie piloted Jules's news chopper south over the Central Park Reservoir en route to the UN. Banking southeast toward the East River, he spotted a police helicopter, a half mile away, heading north up Second Avenue.

"Hey, Elena," Jamie shouted to her, "something's weird about that chopper. Its hatch is open, and it's slowing down over J. T.'s Needle Tower. See if you can a get a look inside."

Elena had a pair of Monarch HG 10X42 binoculars strung around her neck. At that distance, the inside of the chopper would appear less than eighty yards away through the binoculars.

"What's bothering you?" Jules asked Jamie.

"Tower has hundreds of federal agents and half the U.S. Army inside that skyscraper," Jamie said. "Why would a police chopper be over there? It can't do anything for them. It should be covering UN Plaza. That place is huge, spread out and impossibly difficult to protect. It would take Patton's Third Army to properly secure it. The UN needs the NYPD choppers, not that building."

"Oh, my God," Elena screamed, focusing the binoculars on the interior of the police helicopter through the open hatch, "is that who I think it is? Danny, is that her?"

McMahon took Elena's binoculars and fixed them on the police chopper.

"As I live and no longer want to breathe," he shouted. "It's Raza, and the chopper's cabin has some bodies on its deck. Someone shot them to pieces, and one of them looks like Marika."

Elena relieved him of the binoculars and refocused them. "Fahad's dead too," Elena yelled. "Jules, zoom that nose camera in on that open hatch. Jamie, move in closer."

Jules was still strapped into her jump seat, her open laptop camera controls resting on her knees. She moved the joystick around until the camera was focused on Elena's open door. On her monitor and on the video assist, mounted above the chopper's control panel, the police helicopter came into view. Jules zoomed in for a close-up. Now Jamie, Elena and their team could also see into the chopper.

The cabin clearly had three bloody bodies in cop uniforms on its deck, and weapons were scattered all around them. Only Raza, who had just slipped out of her police uniform, was left alive. Decked out in a black tank top, matching panties and sunglasses, an MP5 straddling her lap, she lowered the helicopter onto the roof of the Needle Tower of Power on 59th Street.

Elena's own chopper was now less than a quarter mile away from Raza's, and in the camera monitor, Elena saw Raza studying her through a pair of field glasses. The MP5 braced on her hip, Raza lowered her binoculars but continued to stare Elena down, looking her dead in the eye, giving her the evilest grin Elena had ever seen—and would ever see.

Elena also saw that on the cabin's deck was a hydraulically powered ramp which would lock on the open hatch. Just behind the far side of the ramp was what appeared to be . . . a . . . a . . .

A cannon barrel!

"Holy shit!" Elena screamed. "Raza has the fucking nuke!"

The chopper was now on the Needle Tower's roof. When two rooftop guards in black suits and sunglasses approached the open hatch, she raised the silenced MP5 machine gun and stitched them each across their faces with short, rapid bursts.

She then pushed a button, lowering the ramp onto the building's roof. It hooked automatically on to the edge of the open hatch. The hydraulic lift eased the old cannon barrel onto the ramp, and it began rolling down the ramp onto the Needle Tower's roof.

Elena and her team wore headsets, so Elena said to Jamie:

"They're probably on a police frequency. See if you can reach them. Danny, you know her. Try to talk her out of this."

"In the meantime, swing around," Rashid yelled. He was holding the Barrett-M83 anti-transport sniper rifle by the barrel. "I ought to have a shot."

"Swing it around," Elena yelled to Jamie. "Let him take it. Danny, you talk to Raza."

Meanwhile, Rashid eased himself down on the chopper's deck. He lowered the Barrett's bipod. He laid himself belly-down, propping the rifle's muzzle on the edge of the open hatch. He began adjusting the scope for distance and windage.

"Hi guys," Raza's voice was on their radio. *"Who all's there?"*

"Rashid and I, for openers," McMahon said.

What the fuck? Elena thought, stunned.

"Ask her what's going on!" Rashid shouted. "That's not a terrorist nuke, is it?"

"*Is a pig's pussy pork?*" Raza thundered in their headsets, clearly having heard his question. "But don't worry. It's only one kiloton—probably less. It won't destroy your sacred Big Apple, but it's going to incinerate the holy shit out of J. T.'s 59th Street Needle Tower of Power—to say nothing of those mega-rich motherfuckers inside. You know, the ones plotting a hostile take-over of Planet Earth?"

"Almost ready," Rashid said.

"I thought you were going to nuke the UN," McMahon said to Raza.

"*And kill all those caring, hardworking, innocent people?*" Raza asked. "*What do you think I am? A terrorist?*"

Her insolent laughter filled their headsets.

"Instead," McMahon yelled, "you're going to nuke Tower's oligarchs?"

"Of course I am," Raza said.

Again, her malicious laughter rang in their ears.

"I don't get it." McMahon said.

"*And you never will,*" Raza said. "*Remember what I always told you, Danny?*"

"Not to understand you too quickly," McMahon recited numbly.

"*Because,*" Raza said, "*you can never understand us—our world, our women, our lives.*"

Suddenly, Raza was back at the controls, and her police chopper was lifting off, then banking south away from the Tower of Power, as fast as it could.

Rashid's big Barrett roared, but the shot missed, as did the second.

"*Don't chase me,*" Raza yelled at them. "*You'll head straight into the fireball. Bank north as fast as you know how.*"

Jamie instantly wheeled the chopper around and headed straight for the park.

"*Goodbye, Danny,*" Raza shouted, laughing maniacally. "*Don't think of me too harshly. In my own way I almost . . . love you.*"

Elena and her crew were back over Central Park, Raza's hilarious howls still bombarding their eardrums like the baying of bloodhounds after tree-ing a prey. Rocketing over the zoo, they were coming in fast and low over the Central Park Reservoir, then—

They were too close to the bomb to hear the blast, which at that distance produced decibels far beyond their hearing range. Against the windscreen, however, they glimpsed a dimly reflected flash of the bomb's thermal flare, and the reservoir water below replicated the blaze as well. They felt the shuddering, shattering, earthquake power of the shock wave. Knocking them sideways, it sent them spinning toward the drink. Crashing into the water, the blades smashing and thrashing against the surface, the chopper rolled twice. The aircraft finally came to rest upside down in about five feet of water, which quickly extinguished the engine's flames.

Unbuckling their harnesses, they dropped down onto the cabin ceiling, which was now underneath them. One by one, they eased themselves out of the hatch into the middle of the reservoir.

To the south, an incandescently brilliant, ever-expanding, red-yellow fireball slowly rose above the city. It was too blindingly bright to observe with the naked eye, but Elena could note its progress, which was mirrored in the reservoir's H2O. Only when roiling billows of dark, dense smoke enveloped it did she turn to watch. Levitating upward, the rising fire and dark, billowing smoke slowly, incrementally began to dissipate with infinite lassitude.

As the dense, fiery clouds languidly and lazily dispersed, Elena turned to survey the extent of the destruction. Through the drifting haze and to her eternal dismay, Elena saw that J. T.'s Needle Tower of Power was no more.

EPILOGUE

The evil that men do lives after them;
The good is oft interred with their bones.
                    —*Julius Caesar*, III, ii

By attempting to nuke the UN, Tower, Putilov, and their Saudi allies had obviously conspired to commit a crime of almost unimaginable horror. This was clearly one of the most important stories in history, and Jules's book publisher nagged Jules to write a book.

She was uniquely positioned to tell that story and was the most logical person to tell it. Many of the participants offered to help. Elena said she would give Jules the inside story of Danny and Rashid's rescue, and Elena was convinced she could talk both Rashid and McMahon into telling Jules theirs and Raza's story. The two men owed Elena and Jamie their lives and would be honor-bound to assist. And, of course, Jules still had all of Brenda Tower's tapes.

Furthermore, Elena was convinced that if Jules didn't write it, the true story might never be told. Putilov, the Saudis, Tower and their allies were already flooding the airwaves and internet with cleverly crafted disinformation, preposterous conspiracy theories and outrageous lies. Elena told Jules she owed it to history to set the record straight. Her account would have an authority and authenticity that the other reports could never possess.

For a long time, Jules resisted, saying she wasn't up to it. She was too close to everything that had happened and frankly found what she and her friends had gone through to be intensely depressing. In the end, however, she understood that the story was too historically significant not to be told and that, like it or not, she was the only writer capable of obtaining all the facts.

And luckily, as awful as the bomb attack had been, the blast's aftermath wasn't hopelessly unmanageable. It could have been much worse. While the casualties would eventually number in the thousands, and the property damage was exorbitantly expensive and devastating in the extreme, the city itself was not rendered uninhabitable—not even in part. Fahad's bomb had been a partial fizzle—barely half a kiloton—and so it achieved only three percent of the Hiroshima yield. Also, since it had been detonated from a height of one thousand feet, the city experienced far less fallout than it would have suffered had the bomb been exploded at ground level. As a result, its destruction was focused and localized: It eradicated J. T.'s Tower of Power, but not entire blocks of buildings.

Still the cleanup posed a massive challenge, requiring the combined efforts of FEMA, the U.S. Army Corps of Engineers as well as legions of private contractors. Toxicity tests had to be run throughout much of the city, followed by months upon months of arduous decontamination.

While many New Yorkers relocated, most duct-taped their windows and sheltered in place, leaving their homes only for food and other necessities. Within two months the bulk of those who'd been displaced were back in their homes and returning to work. New Yorkers had, once again, been resilient, indefatigable, and the city was soon recovering with impressive celerity.

Within a year, most of the cleanup had been completed.

Tower and his sister had been meeting with the mayor in downtown New York at the time of the blast, and Putilov had been in the Kremlin; hence, they survived. Their reputations, however, would not fare as well. Rashid had worked with Raza, Marika and Kamal ad-Din on the plot, and since they did not know at that time that Rashid was a double agent, they had told him everything. His testimony implicated Putilov and the Saudis' U.S. Ambassador, Prince Waheed, in New York's nuking. Rashid also testified that while Putilov and Kamal had not trusted Tower with all the details, Tower, however, knew that something horrendously catastrophic was about to happen at the UN—a terrorist act so cataclysmic it was guaranteed to derail the UN's Expropriation Resolution—and by dint of that knowledge Tower had tacitly acquiesced.

Shortly before her death from cancer, Brenda Tower confirmed her brother's complicity under oath.

Even so, the principal players—Putilov, Kamal and Waheed—proved to be beyond the reach of international law. Russia and the Saudis refused to extradite them to The Hague for prosecution. Nor did the FBI build an indictable case against Tower. His plausible deniability proved too steep a hill to climb, and the Bureau's former director, Jonathan Conley, had a long and notorious history as a Tower stooge. He'd spent several years assiduously covering up Tower's misdeeds. But while Tower might have avoided prison, he seemed destined to spend the rest of his life as a political pariah, universally reviled, with law enforcement agencies worldwide investigating every sordid detail of his financial and political life, past, present, future. Moreover, impeachment was always a possibility. While those proceedings had turned partisan and were, for the time being, stalled in the House, expulsion from office was still a possible outcome for Tower.

As for Raza, she had clearly committed an unpardonable crime against humanity. While many people—perhaps even the majority of the world—despised the billionaire oligarchs for their predatory greed and exploitative monopolistic business practices, no one condoned nuking them into fiery oblivion. Jules denounced Raza's attack in her book as an unspeakable act of barbarism. Among other things, the nuke killed untold thousands of innocent bystanders. Among the blast's many victims were the Tower of Power's employees—everyone from janitorial help to waitstaff to security personnel. Furthermore, many nearby residents succumbed from or would eventually die from the explosion, its fallout and the combined aftereffects.

Jules and her friends condemned the strike categorically.

Still Jules was also aware that with a single nuclear strike, Raza had stopped the oligarchical takeover of the world's democracies dead in its tracks. It was a historic achievement to say the least—that much was undeniable—but one Jules honestly couldn't get her head around. In an act of inconceivable destruction, Raza—it seemed to Jules—had come to symbolize the species' most aggravating paradox. The human heart was indeed a marriage of heaven and hell, and her bomb blast had proven Raza capable of incomprehensible evil and at the same time . . . *redemption*. Because of Raza, the forces of global freedom would live to fight another day.

Jules wondered how history, hundreds of years from now, would come to view Raza—or any of them for that matter. She honestly did not know. She wasn't even sure what she thought of Raza. Hoping Shakespeare might illuminate the conundrum, Jules took her book's title from Mark Antony's funeral oration in *Julius Caesar*.

> *The evil that men do lives after them;*
> *The good is oft interred with their bones.*

Jules titled her book *The Evil That Men Do*.

Ironically, much of the planet, at least for the time being, romanticized the wickedness inherent in Raza's act. A so-called "Cult of Raza" rose up across the globe, honoring her for her epochal, frighteningly violent, world-changing feat.

Furthermore, Jules had pulled from her camera footage a truly electrifying photo of Raza in the chopper. Having taken off her cop's uniform, she was decked out in a black tank top, panties, the police hat tilted back on her head. Her long ebony hair was flung over one shoulder and down her chest.

The wire stock of her MP5 was braced against one hip. She had removed her wraparound aviator sunglasses and was staring fearlessly into Jules's camera—and by extention into the hearts and souls of people around the world. Her glinting eyes were evil as sin, lewd as Lucifer; the right corner of her mouth was hooked into a supercilious yet startling sensuous sneer. She seemed to be telling everyone everywhere to "go fuck themselves." For decades to come, that shot would appear on TV screens and magazine covers around the world and was reproduced on hundreds of millions of posters and T-shirts. Raza graffiti and slogans sprang up on walls and buildings across the globe, featuring rallying cries such as:

"Raza lives!"
"Raza for President!"
"I Love Raza!"
"Go Raza!"

Despite the carnage her nuke had wreaked, she was celebrated everywhere as a living legend and a transcendent hero. Billions of people worldwide admired her beyond reason or measure.

Nor did Raza's war on the planet's financial elites end with the nuking of the Tower. Not only was the UN's Anti-Inequality Expropriation Bill passed by acclamation, Jowett's assassination and Raza's annihilation of the top five hundred global oligarchs inspired the explosive emergence of clandestine vigilante groups across the globe. Many of these organizations called themselves "Soldiers of Raza" and were soon attacking the super-rich wherever they could find them. Their admirers called them, "freedom fighters," while their critics naturally branded them terrorists. Whatever they were, they made the lives of the world's wealthiest plutocrats a living hell. Many of these tycoons retired from the business world to armed compounds, leaving their worlds of commerce and living out their days in paranoid isolation, in private fortresses, surrounded by security forces and armed to the teeth.

But while the world struggled with what Raza had done, Jules still had a book to write. She had reams of material on Tower—she'd already written exposés of his financial criminality for over a decade, and of course, she had his late sister's tapes—but while Putilov's and Kamal's histories of predation were well-known and extensively reported on in the West, Raza was a mystery unto herself.

Jules was able to establish that Raza had been born to a wealthy Wahhabist family who lived in a large compound outside of Medina. She learned Raza's father had been strict and severe in his enforcement of his Wahhabist faith and that she had eventually left home and joined a cadre of militants who, among other things, granted equal rights to women warriors. Quickly, Raza had risen through the ranks.

Jules, however, felt that she did not understand the woman. She saw Raza as the key to understanding everything, particularly Danny's experiences. Something had happened between Raza and him. It was common knowledge they'd had sex. The evidence of their dalliance was glaringly apparent to Elena's team from the moment they broke into the torture chamber . . . everything from black, lacy, semen-stained panties wrapped around McMahon's hard-used gonads to bright crimson lipstick streaks garishly emblazoning the insides of his upper thighs and his crotch.

McMahon, however, was silent as the grave on the subject of Raza and made it clear their story was off-limits. Jules felt stymied.

But it wasn't McMahon's silence about Raza that bothered her. In the end, she didn't care as much about the story as about Danny. In her private life, Jules was guarded and did not make close friends easily. Next to her sister, Elena and Jamie, Danny was the best friend she'd ever had. Now he was in trouble, refused all attempts at contact, and she didn't know what to do.

It was also clear to her that his sojourn in the beast's belly—in that Pakistani hellhole—had damaged him far more than he was willing to discuss or would admit. Jules believed that his memories of physical and psychological pain not only tormented his mind, they tortured his soul. That he refused to discuss what had happened or how he felt only made matters worse. He now suffered from a black despondency that seemed to know no bottom. Jules believed he'd lost something back in that safe house, and if something was not done quickly, he might well snap. She feared he would kill himself.

Among other things, he no longer performed; he never went out in public and never laughed. He never even smiled. He'd lost his sense of humor. He stayed home alone, refused to see friends, drank and smoked dope.

When Jules learned how bad off he was, she immediately flew to L.A., and against Danny's avid and reiterated orders, drove straight from LAX to his home in the Hollywood Hills even though it was after 10:00 P.M. Getting out of her rented car, she caught a glimpse of herself in the side mirror. Dressed in a tastefully tailored black three-piece power suit and matching heels, she looked to be the personification of respectability. Good. She wanted him to feel he could rely on her. She needed his trust if she was going to help him.

She then turned to take in his house. She'd visited Danny here whenever they were both in L.A. but hadn't been back for at least two years. It was even more impressive than she'd remembered. A four-level white stone mansion, its front was dominated by a picture window so huge and all-enveloping it appeared to be almost a wall of glass. Perched on the edge of a high cliff, it looked out over L.A. from an imposingly Olympian height.

She started up the sixty steep brick steps to the front porch. Looped over her shoulder was a black canvas book bag containing a first edition of her new book on J. T. Tower, *Filthy Lucre: J. T.'s Tower of Financial Power*. She had affectionately inscribed it to her old friend. She also brought four bottles of his favorite Bordeaux as well as assorted cheeses, black olives, jars of mustard and baguettes. She feared Danny would resent her intrusion, and she hoped, if necessary, to bribe her way into his home and confidence with food and wine. Nonetheless, she struggled to steel herself against his wrath. He'd made it clear on the phone she was unwelcome.

Reaching the big oak door, she stood on the glisteningly white, Corinthian-pillared porch and knocked gently. When nothing happened, she knocked harder. When that failed to rouse him, she hammered on the door as hard as she knew how with the bottom of a Bordeaux bottle.

"Danny, I know you're in there," Jules screamed, "and if you don't let me in, I'm going to smash three bottles of super-expensive Bordeaux all over your pristine, pure-alabaster porch. You'll never get the stains out. Then I'll throw the last bottle through your embarrassingly ostentatious picture window. I'll write columns about you saying that Raza turned you into a fucking S/M freak. I'll announce you're coming out of the hard-trade kinky-deviate closet. You better let me in or I'll write that you—"

Finally, the door swung open, and McMahon was standing there in a black fluffy terry-cloth bathrobe, his face puffy, his eyes bloodshot and haggard.

"Here," she said, extending the black book bag filled with goodies, and when he reached out to grab them, she put a shoulder into him, knocked him off balance and bulldozed her way into his vestibule, then into the living room.

The front room was immense, taking up half the house's main floor. Its carpeting and furniture—particularly the big semicircular couch and over-stuffed armchairs—were all upholstered in white silk. On the matching walls hung exquisite Matisse, Monet, and Manet prints. On one side wall hung a 100-inch flat-screen TV, and on the other was a Bose sound system. In the far corner was a grand piano which Danny actually played rather well.

But the wall-length picture window with the panoramic view of Los Angeles was what got to everyone and still continued to take her breath away.

That big front room seemed to just out over the edge of the world. It was night, and the lights of the city blazed in the valley below like a million-trillion scintillating stars, each one proffering a universe of its own.

Turning to face him, she grabbed a pre-opened liter bottle of Bordeaux, yanked out the cork with her teeth, and took a deep drink. She handed Danny the bottle and emptied the cheeses, black olives, crackers and signed book onto the big glass oval-shaped coffee table.

"Jules, why the fuck have you flown here all the way from L.A.? It wasn't to give me wine, cheese and a book, was it?"

"I want to find out what's wrong with you. Why you're such a hateful prick, why you don't see or even talk to your old friends anymore. Why have you stopped performing? I want to know what the hell's going on, and I'm not leaving till I get some answers."

"And I don't give a fuck what you want to know."

"Danny, it's me, Jules. We go way back, and we're going to talk."

He stared at her a long moment, his eyes expressionless, void of any feeling.

"Talk to me, Danny."

"Oh, fuck you, Jules," he finally said. "Why should I see people I don't want to see? Why should I work if I don't want to? Nothing's fun anymore. I got plenty of money. I hate all of it, and I don't need the stress."

"You can't turn your back on your friends."

"My so-called friends can all bite me. They're all just a bunch of moochers, ass-kissers and starfuckers."

"Say that about Elena and Jamie, I'll buttkick your sorry ass through that window and straight over that cliff."

"I'd never say that about Elena and Jamie. They rescued me from hell."

Jules let out a deep sigh and shook her head slowly. "I hope you aren't feeling sorry for yourself. I mean about what happened back in Pakistan, in that compound? I know it had to be bad, but it can't be undone. It's nothing you can't get past. Do you want to talk about it?"

"No."

"I understand Raza did something to you. Maybe she even took something from you—some pride, some dignity, some belief in yourself."

"Jules, what fucking business is it of yours?"

"It's my business because I'm pissed. You haven't hit on me once," Jules said, fighting to keep her voice from cracking. "You aren't smiling, smirking, giving me all those cute little Danny McMahon looks. You aren't coming on to me, and it's hurting my feelings."

"It's not you, Jules. To tell the truth, I never want to look at another woman again for the rest of my life."

"What in hell did Raza do to you? I know you two were getting it on."

"It was more a rape on her part, and, yeah, we had sex—sex from hell— and with a little luck it'll be the last sex I ever have."

"In that case," Jules said, getting up, "fuck the wine. Let's do some serious drinking."

She walked into his kitchen. He could hear her banging around in his pantry where he kept most of his wine, liquor and his beer refrigerator.

"Hey," she shouted out to him, "I found a seventy-five-year-old unopened bottle of Macallan's single malt. I didn't know they even made seventy-five-year-old single malt. Let's drink it, okay? The whole bottle."

"Why the fuck not?" McMahon shouted back at her. "Let's put it out of its misery."

"But I warn you, Danny," she yelled back, "I'm not letting this shit slide. We're getting to the bottom of all this tonight, even if I have to kill you."

He heard her bang around some more, collecting glasses, Lord knows what. Then there was silence.

He turned to study the lights of L.A.

Get to the bottom of it, huh? Jules was as good a friend as he'd ever had, but he couldn't tell her what was really going on. How could he tell her about hours of uncontrollable crying jags or the endless nights spent laying in his bed late with the muzzle of a .300 bolt-action Weatherby rifle between his teeth, jiggling the trigger's last bit of tension with his big toe, working that infinitesimal amount of play, teasing that final micro-ounce of slack before the spring snapped and the round detonated—lying there late into the night balanced between life, the trigger's engagement, the hammer's fall and the Final Gift of . . . Death?

But then he also heard that still, small voice, whispering to him:

"Not yet."

And then his own voice also whispering, arguing in response:

"Why the fuck not?"

How could he tell Jules that Raza was right—that life was a pile of shit, not worth the living, a ghoulish practical joke played on the pathetic human race by that sick sadistic psychopath otherwise known as God—or Allah or Odin or Whoever the Fuck He Was—and if he, Danny McMahon, had his way, he wouldn't have stopped with vaporizing J. T.'s Tower of Power, he would have nuked the whole fucking universe, beginning to end—the Big Bang, the Big

Rip, the Big Crunch, the Almighty included—so that when he was done, the whole thing never would have been.

Yes, Raza had taught him to understand her world.

How could he tell Jules that she was right, that Raza and that horrific torture-hell had broken him, destroyed him, had taken everything from him? That all he wanted now was to stop the terror, end the nightmares and erase the pain? How could he tell anyone about that kind of horror—show what his heart had become—especially someone he cared about and who cared about him? How could he tell Jules that he was finally beaten, whipped to the bone and that all he was looking for was the first good place to die.

Fuck it. The Hollywood Hills was just as good as any other place.

"Danny," Jules yelled from the pantry, interrupting his thoughts, "I'm talking to you!"

He had to say something.

"I don't know what I'm going to do," he said loudly, directing his voice toward the pantry. "I've been thinking about moving to where I can be by myself, maybe find a place out in the Mojave Desert, some place desolate, hard to get to, some place where I can be alone. What I'd really like is a redoubt surrounded by attack-trained dogs and electrified chain-link fences, no visitors allowed."

Then he looked up and Jules was standing in front of him. Her suit was gone, and she was only wearing her black high heels and her matching bra and lace panties.

Shit, they looked like Raza's panties.

Goddamn, she was wearing Raza's black lacy panties.

She handed him a rock glass filled to the brim with seventy-five-year-old Macallan's single malt.

"Fuck you and that paper asshole you've grown and that pussy you now have where your cock and balls used to be," Jules said, taking a long, slow, savoring pull, then swirling it slowly around her mouth before swallowing it. She then put her empty glass down on the coffee table, swung a long leg over his lap and sat down, straddling his crotch.

"Bottom's up," she said, smiling.

He slowly savored and drank the ancient scotch.

"Now Danny," Jules said, "let's get down to business. You told me once that you liked me with bright scarlet lipstick and that you'd love to watch me put it on. You said watching women put on bright scarlet lipstick turned you on. Well here it is."

She took a gold lipstick tube out of her bra, formed her mouth into a large sensuous O and began coating her full generous lips with layer upon layer of crimson, all the while her eyes glinting with wicked wanton lust.

She began rotating her hips on his groin, moaning softly:

"Come on, baby, come to Jules. We'll work through this. Stay with me, Danny. Jules can fix it. Jules can fix anything."

He turned his head and looked away, unable to make eye contact with her.

"Don't you look away." She grabbed his chin and turned his head, forcing him to stare at her. "Come on, baby, keep your eyes on me. Tell Jules. You can tell me anything. I'm not leaving till we take care of this. You think Raza took your strength, your heart, that she broke you? Well Jules is here now, and Jules is putting Humpty back together again."

He looked up at her, and she was still giving him that slow, soft smile, the eyes still glitteringly playfully but also filled with mean mischief.

Suddenly, for the first time in months, he found himself getting aroused—uncontrollably aroused.

"Oh, my, and here you said you weren't interested in the feminine gender, but that's not true. You *are* the rampant male tonight, aren't you? All that talk about not wanting women—I hope that wasn't a ruse to get Jules between your sheets."

His brain was so thick with lust he couldn't speak, and his vision was starting to twitch.

Taking his head in her hands, she bent down and kissed him—a long, probing, languorous kiss. When she pulled away, he was breathless.

"Danny," she whispered in his ear, "it's going to be okay. Everything's going to be all right."

She began rotating her hips against his crotch again, harder and harder with infinite inexorable indolence, all the while smiling that sly omniscient this-is-just-for-you smile, her eyes locked unblinkingly on his.

"And here you said you weren't interested in women," she whispered again to him, her breath hot and sweet, her tongue darting in and out of his ear, then returning to his mouth, lazy arduous kisses, her tongue lively and licentious. "I think you're interested. At least something down there thinks he is."

She lifted his legs onto the couch and undid the belt of his short black robe.

Then she was lowering herself onto him, kissing him all the while, lewdly now, luridly, making her way down his stomach with her lips and tongue, taking her time, caressing him with her mouth, eternally, languidly meticulous in its myriad ministrations, whispering over and over:

"It's going to be all right, Danny. Jules promises it will be all right, and Jules is never wrong. Jules will make everything all right."

He lay his head back, his eyes locked on Jules's.

"That's right, Danny. Keep your eyes on me. Keep them on Jules. Don't look away. It's going to be just fine. I promise Jules will fix everything. Jules always makes everything . . . *fine*. Jules always makes everything . . . *all right*."

Yes, he believed it now. Jules would do it. It was going to be all right. Jules was here, and Jules would make it all right.

Yes, Jules would always make everything . . . all right.

AFTERWORD

"There is no present or future—only the past endlessly repeating itself..."

—Eugene O'Neill

1

Back in the early 1980s, I wrote a series of thick, heavily researched westerns that featured a dozen or so actual historical figures. My main character, outlaw Torn Slater, was fictional, however, and throughout the five books he went through his own horrendous version of *The Odyssey.*

The West's quintessential desperado, Slater had the perfect résumé for his profession. Adopted and raised by the legendary Apache war chief Cochise, by age fifteen Slater was a genuine virtuoso in the fine arts of raiding and killing. At the age of sixteen he'd fought for the South at Shiloh and then teamed up with Quantrill, Bloody Bill and the James–Younger Gang in Kansas, where he further refined his warrior/bandit skills. After the Civil War, he returned to the West, but in a sense, he never stopped refighting his earlier conflicts. Refusing to rob individuals, he focused on holding up banks and trains. Slater was no Robin Hood—quite the contrary—but his war was with Big Money, not ordinary men and women. He was happy to leave the mass of humanity alone—as long as they left him alone.

For the second Slater novel, *Savage Blood*, I created a couple of larger-than-life villains who continued through the rest of the series. One was the real-life dictator of Mexico for over thirty years, Porfirio Díaz. Brutal beyond belief, he was the Josef Stalin of our neighbor to the south. He exterminated or subjugated its indigenous Indian population—far more ruthlessly than Generals Sherman and Sheridan ever dreamed of doing in the U.S.—driving most of them into early graves or hacienda slavery. At the same time, unlike Slater, Díaz pandered to the super-rich. At one point, it was estimated that less than 1 percent of the population owned 85 percent of the land.

Still Díaz's apologists argue that he convinced his oligarchic backers to build railroads, a profitable mining industry, big banks and spectacular, if oppressive, haciendas. To that extent he did drag Mexico, kicking and screaming, into the 20th century. Díaz ran much of the country on forced labor, however, with most of the citizenry living in abject poverty.

In my novels, Díaz is obsessed with hunting Slater down, not to kill or imprison him but to convince him to rob U.S. banks and trains for Díaz. In return, in *Savage Blood*, he offers Slater sanctuary in Mexico, his personal protection from all law enforcement on both sides of the border and lots of money. Slater naturally declines his offer. He is not without his principles.

The series's other chief villain was James Sutherland, a highly eccentric English billionaire. He is also obsessed with Slater, and when *Savage Blood* begins, he is leading a team of bounty hunters through the scorchingly hot Sonoran canyonlands in an attempt to track Slater down. Here is a description of Sutherland as seen through the eyes of the hard-bitten trail hand John Henry Deacon, who is ramrodding the expedition:

> *Sutherland—the dapper limey in the crimson bowler with the silver and turquoise hatband. The rich bastard was putting on a fresh, ruffled white silk shirt, tucking the tails into his red whipcord jodhpurs. The dandified riding pants bloomed outrageously around the thighs, then tapered tightly against the knees. They were tucked into black riding boots of imported calfskin, which were heeled with sterling silver buzz-saw rowels. He carried a British swagger stick under his arm. He was smoking his black, ubiquitous, fruity-smelling, tailor-made cigarettes, and his eyes glittered maniacally. They always glittered maniacally. He made Deacon sick. He made Deacon sorry he'd ever signed on.*

While Sutherland loves making money—lots and lots of money—his primary ambition in these novels is more dramatic than that. Sutherland's plan is to kill the outlaw in a most outrageously horrifying way for the most outrageously avaricious of reasons. As Sutherland explains to James Deacon, the grizzled old trail hand:

> *"Mr. Deacon, I've shot game for hides, for food and for the trophies. I'm killing Slater for the trophy. You see that hogshead of water? After I kill Torn Slater—the most wanted marauder in thirteen states and territories—I'm cutting off his head, bleeding it like a stuck pig, putting it in the barrel and then mixing a large flask of concentrated formaldehyde with the water."*

"Why?" Deacon asked in stunned disbelief.

"Sir, I shall put Torn Slater's head in my Wild West Show and take it across the country in a clear glass crock. I shall build my show around that head, and around my live-on-stage reenactment of how I impaled the outlaw with my compound bow and my quiver full of tribladed broadheads. I shall perform for millions, make tens of millions, hundreds of millions, and be even richer than I am now. All of you—who will, of course, be actors in my Wild West Extravaganza— will be rich. We'll be bigger than Halley's Comet."

Such sadistic greed and malignant hubris will not go unpunished.

In the sequel, *Hangman's Whip*, I let Díaz capture Slater and incarcerate him in a slave-labor silver mine. The Spaniards dug thousands of such mines throughout Mexico as soon as they discovered in the early 16th century that the country was one vast mother lode of silver. They mined that ore with a savagery that knew no bounds; to be consigned to one of those hellholes was a death sentence. Ironically, all the silver and gold that the Spaniards ripped so violently out of the earth and at so much cost in human life never even went back to Spain. It went straight to their Dutch bankers. Even then, bankers were the real powers behind the throne and the preeminent profiteers.

Since I've always believed that the relentless pursuit of wealth for wealth's sake was inherently wicked, I made Slater's prison mine truly miserable. I wanted to show where uncontrollable greed ultimately leads: straight to hell. Here is how I described Slater's prison mine in *Hangman's Whip*:

Monte de Riqueza, the Mount of Riches—a tremendous treasure trove of a hill, filled with enough gold, silver, oil, copper, iron, nickel, lead, zinc, magnesium, coal, sulphur, potassium nitrate and methane gas to make half the adult population of Mexico millionaires.

For untold centuries Mayan and Aztec slaves mined its dark depths. Equipped with pick-axes, driven by the cuarta's lash, these dumb engines of flesh honeycombed its vast interior from one end to the other, trailing the veins and drifts and mother lodes like rockchewing moles.

Monte De Riqueza is a living hell. For the subterranean fires, whose upwelling countless eons past, thrust forth this massive mountain, bake its rocky bowels like a kiln. And the deeper the descent, the hotter hell becomes. The air temperature rises two degrees for every hundred feet, until at three thousand feet down, water does not drip from the facings but hisses, pops and detonates, as steam clouds blind the eyes.

Yes, for Slater, Monte de Riqueza is an inferno of methane gas, falling rocks, cracking timbers and raging cataracts. But the worst nightmare is fire.

Spontaneous flash fires fed by dust, endless gas detonations and blazing coal seams and runaway oil fires combine to create howling conflagrations that scream through the interconnected timberwork of the tunnels, caving in the walls, bringing down the overhead rock, sucking the air out of the tunnelworks like pressure whooshing out of a bursting air hose.

Slater, however, is sentenced to a very special inferno, a uniquely hideous hell-of-hells, where the chances of surviving more than a month approach nullity. Defying the odds, however, Slater has survived two years. He mines sulphur in the so-called Sonoran Pit.

Eventually he busts out, and in his wake Slater blows up and incinerates the entire labyrinth of mine shafts, costing its co-owners, his nemeses James Sutherland and Porfirio Díaz, countless billions.

After barely escaping the mine fires, Slater ends up on a narrow mountain ledge, 500 feet up from the canyon floor. From that vantage point he witnesses what he has wrought:

Suddenly, Slater heard the noise. He looked up at the towering slope looming 8,000 feet above him. What he saw was a mountain in its final throes, a million-throated thing, screaming of darkness and bloody death, bursting into flames, going mad with feral suffering.

Monte de Riqueza, with hellfire in her belly, was making known the presence of all her age-old tunnels. Thousands of apertures, opening up out of nowhere up and down the mountainside, spat great spurts of red-orange flame and long twisting ropes of inky-black smoke.

The firestorm inside, thirsting for oxygen, had ferreted out every crack and fissure for the air to feed the flaming timbers and dust, the coal and oil, gas and shale.

The winds swept through the tunnels with hurricane force. The super-heated fire-breathing cyclones now converged with a flood of flaming oil, both of them crashing through the intricate maze of tunnels, igniting forever the vast seams of coal and shale, exploding infernos fueled by the bottomless pit of methane gas pouring up out of the hell-sump below.

The prisoners were lost in their entirety.

Slater had killed every one of them.

Standing on the eroding ledge, however, he felt no guilt. Instead, he could suddenly see it all, wrenching his awareness wildly, seizing his very soul with a violent shudder of vile delight, as he realized the sheer immensity of what he'd done.

Men died—that was true—but his war was not with them. He knew that, they knew that. Monte de Riqueza was what counted. She, the hateful harlot of illimitable riches, had been his goal all along.

The mountain herself was now transcending the world of smoke and flames. The throat of the fire sucking breath through her tunnels, the din of torrential winds, the dense coils of black smoke rushing out of every throbbing orifice of her groaning body—her roar had now grown elemental. The mountain was no longer simply in flames, she was standing up and screaming, finally revealing herself for who she was: the back-arching whore of avaricious wealth, balanced in agony on the hard, sharp spasms of her last hell-heat. And when Slater looked up and saw the great ball of fire, floating slowly over the mountain's top, blown up from the depths through the abysmal maw of the vertical main shaft itself, rising gracefully, angelically, with incandescent brilliance toward the wispy clouds, now tethered to the snow-capped summit, he thought with shocking clarity that maybe, just maybe, this was the moment he'd been born for.

Which is a long way of saying that I've always believed that malignant greed—the lust for financial power—warrants its reputation as second-worst of the Seven Deadly Sins, topped only by pride, which is the seed sin, the motivating force behind all other evils. Malignant greed alone leads humanity into the worst forms of radical evil—infernal enterprises such as slave-labor mines and the retailing of nuclear weapons technology. None of the other Seven Deadly Sins is capable of forcing otherwise sane people to commit acts of such unspeakable horror.

Why, you may ask, is malignant greed so uniquely disastrous? Because the other deadly sins are finite and ephemeral in their wickedness. Rage, for example, may cause you to kill a person, but the rage ends with your victim's death. Lust may drive you to seduce your neighbor's wife, but it ends with her possession. Greed, on the other hand, knows no satiety. The rapacity of men like Díaz and Sutherland can never be extinguished. Furthermore, money lust can very well lead you to commit every other sin in the book, and even then, it will never be satisfied. There will always be something else to steal and someone else to rip off.

As we shall see, in the New Testament greed is ultimately apocalyptic, annihilating the entire human race—in fact, all life on earth.

2

Time was that society condemned avarice. Asking for excessive interest on a loan damned the usurer to hellfire everlasting. Christ Himself could not have been more adamant about the evils of financial predation. The Lord's Prayer's literal translation says nothing about "trespasses." In the original Greek, as well as in Hebrew and Aramaic, the word is "debts"—monetary debts. The supplicant is strongly advised to forgive his or her debtors—*all debtors*. Near the Lord's Prayer's close, Christ says that God will treat us the way we treat those who owe us money. If you're hard on them, God will be hard on you. Christ exemplifies his hatred of greed when he flogs the money changers out of the temple. He believes they are committing the sin of avarice because they are charging people fees for the privilege of purchasing a special kind of currency—church-blessed money. In other words, the priests were making money off money, and Christ drives them out of their house of worship.

Paul famously tells us: "The love of money is the root of all evil," and the serpent tells us why in the Garden of Eden. He convinces Eve to bite the apple, telling her that if she and Adam "eat the fruit of the tree thereof, then ye shall be as Gods." That is the siren song of riches and covetousness: If you have enough of money and material possesssions, you can live as a god on earth and do anything you want. Money lust is the implicit overreaching of God; it is hubris incarnate.

In chapter thirteen of *Revelation*—which chronologically ought to be the book's first chapter—greed provokes Armageddon, leading us to the End of Days. John of Patmos has an angel explain in that chapter why God will kill and torture in perpetuity over one-third of humankind: the angel announces to the world that God wants humanity to either reject avarice—and stop trafficking financially with the Anti-Christ—or God will sentence us eternally in fire and brimstone. In other words, the angel tells us, we can have Paradise, or money, which will be promptly followed by hellfire everlasting. One-third of humanity says, "We'll take the money." And of course, the earth is destroyed, and those of us who are consumed by greed, go straight to hell.

In the New Testament love of money is far and away the deadliest of all the deadly sins. Greed destroys human beings by the billions and, once and for all, rids the earth of humanity's shadow.

So how and when, to quote Oliver Stone, did greed become "good"?

3

Supreme Court Justice Louis Brandeis wrote: "We can either have democracy in this country or we can have great wealth concentrated in the hands of a few, but we can't have both." Most reasonable people would hold that statement to be self-evident. The superwealthy buy politicians the way the rest of us purchase chewing gum. If political contributions continue to be unregulated, financial might will inevitably lead to political power. After all, power begets power, and money begets money. Thus wealth concentrates into fewer and fewer hands, and eventually a handful of über-rich oligarchs will gain control of a country.

Which is now happening in the U.S. To say otherwise is in flagrant opposition to the facts. As I point out in *The Evil That Men Do*, eight people are now wealthier than one-half the world's population, and six of them are Americans. The American financial sector—that is, the kinds of people who make money off money and whom Christ flogged out of the temple—now annually sucks up over one-half of non-farm corporate profit in the U.S. Today, the world's ultra-rich hide one-third of the planet's annual GDP in offshore black-money accounts and pay no taxes on it. One hundred plutocrats spend more money financing America's dominant political party than all other contributors put together. In Russia, 111 people possess a full 19 percent of the country's wealth.

To say that oligarchy is compatible with democracy also is diametrically opposed to the facts. The tsunami of political donations triggered by Citizens United bears witness to the willingness of the rich to spend billions in their efforts to deregulate their avarice. Plutocrats spend fortunes each year trying to circumvent the law, most notably tax laws. In a very real sense, the rich hate the rule of law . . . at least any laws that restrict their financial predations.

G. K. Chesterton once said of the rich: "The poor have sometimes objected to being governed badly. The rich have always objected to being governed at all."

It was not always thus. When I was a boy, the U.S. had anti-usury laws, and

Wall Street was a modestly profitable industry, not the financial behemoth it has become. When did Wall Street commence sucking up 50 percent of all non-farm corporate profits in the U.S.? When did this Revolution of the Rich first begin? When did the Great Oligarchy Movement begin?

4

During the early '80s under Ronald Reagan, America witnessed the deregulation of Wall Street, which, through tax incentives and the weakening of anti-trust restrictions, gave the big banks financial incentives to conduct corporate mergers. Such mergers have always been costly and risky. To finance a merger, the participating companies have to borrow tremendous sums, and to cover those debts, they must fire employees en masse. After the merger is completed, both companies are mired in debt and lack the personnel to grow their companies properly. The restructuring also leads to disorganization and confusion. The surviving employees tend to be frightened and overworked.

Almost all merger studies conclude that in the long run, about 80 percent of mergers are manifest failures that impoverish both workers and stockholders. A *Harvard Business Review* analysis concluded that the failure rate could be as high as 90 percent.

I live in New York City and have known lots of Wall Street executives, including mergers and acquisitions (M&A) lawyers and investment bankers. Most of them are quite blunt about the havoc mergers wreak.

Over the years, I've asked a number of them why they do it, given the mergers' history of destructiveness, and they say quite openly that a handful of CEOs, investment bankers and M&A lawyers—people such as themselves—profit excessively off the mergers even though they do so at the expense of stockholders, employees and the nation. In short, they ply their trade because a relatively small number of people make money at the expense of everyone else involved.

I told one of these people that I'd heard that plastic-encased trophies are given to the people who conduct these mergers.

"You mean tombstones," the man said.

"Why do you call them tombstones?" I asked him.

"They're given to us for the companies we just killed," he said, smiling wryly.

I asked one M&A specialist if a corporation can expect to gain any advantage at all from a merger. He said mergers usually lead to the weakening or obliteration of one of the merged companies, so they are a way of liquidating competition. At the time he made that statement, such takeovers were a violation of the anti-trust statutes.

Over my forty-nine-year career in the book publishing industry, I have seen firsthand how mergers have merged countless publishing companies out of existence. When I started out, there were scores upon scores of book publishing houses. Now five houses are responsible for over 80 percent of book sales, and they are all owned by non-American companies. The paperback industry, which a half century ago produced 80 to 90 percent of book industry profits, has seen its once-myriad book distributors wiped out by mergers. Consequently, today's paperback industry barely breaks even.

Over the last thirty-five years mergers have shrunk the number of companies in most major industries—the oil, airline, pharmaceutical, communications and banking sectors just to name a few. Increased monopolization within major industries is precisely how oligarchies are created.

5

Back in the early '80s, when I was writing *Savage Blood* and *Hangman's Whip*, another Wall Street revolution was in its infancy, and a friend of mine got in on the ground floor. He had doctorates in both math and physiology, and a top investment bank had recruited him to work in New York, developing something called "derivatives."

He did his best to explain derivatives to me, saying that they were arcane, complicated financial instruments that allowed investors to hedge their bets in much the same way that a bookie lays off bets, thus limiting his risks. The problem was, he said, that his department was "securitizing them." Derivatives, however, weren't like regular stocks. Traditional securities were collateralized by the companies that issued the stocks. Derivatives, on the other hand, were pure intrinsic uncollateralized debt.

"Why do people buy them?" I asked.

"Largely because none of our customers understand what they are," he said. "The dirty little secret on Wall Street is that the bulk of the big stock customers know very little about the securities they purchase. For instance, if you're a firefighters' pension-fund manager in some big city and you're hired to invest the money in the fund, you're competing against maybe four other guys in that city who are also investing the fund's money. At the end of the year, the person who comes in number five gets fired—or doesn't get a big raise and a handsome bonus. So you're under a lot of pressure to perform.

"In reality, you're looking at thousands of investment opportunities every year, and you don't have time to study and understand them. They're just blips on a computer screen to you. Now you may know that some hotshot company or superstar investment banker, whose name is always on the front page of *The Wall Street Journal,* is backing one of those offerings. If that's the case, then you know the guy and the bank are ultra-famous and successful. Also you see the prices on their offering are starting to rise on your computer screen. The offering is taking off, and if you don't buy in fast, your competition at your firefighters' fund will, and at the end of the year, you may be out of a job. All you know is you better get on board fast.

"So in the Land of the Blind, being an inherently incomprehensible security is not a bad thing. It can be a virtue, and I create incomprehensible securities for a living. No one understands them, so I'm always being called in to explain my derivatives to potential customers. Our sales people sell them but can't explain them. I can't either, but I sound more knowledgeable than the sales people do."

My friend said derivatives were the Wrath of God, and he predicted that they would spread across the planet like a pandemic, one day bankrupting the global economy. He hoped he'd be retired when that happened. Last time I talked to him, he was retired and was keeping most of his money in cash.

And what happened to the derivative market? True to his prediction, the total value of global derivatives is now over $1.5 quadrillion. Derivatives—which, to repeat, are pure intrinsic uncollateralized debt that almost no one understands—sank Enron at the beginning of the 21st century and would have sunk the U.S. banking industry in 2008 without a U.S. government bailout.

These bank crashes come with disturbing regularity. It's worth remembering that in the late 1980s, merger mania almost destroyed the U.S. banking system, which had lent most of the money for those failed takeovers. The savings and loan banks were largely wiped out. President George H. W. Bush and Alan Greenspan bailed out the commercial banks through the issuance of thirty-year bonds at 8 and 9 percent interest. The bonds were so profitable that the commercial banks became healthy enough to absorb all the losses they sustained when they financed bad mergers.

By the end of the 1980s, mergers had more than tripled corporate debt in the U.S. and had transmogrified Wall Street from an industry that financed corporate expansion to one that created and securitized debt—as well as proliferated mergers that also proliferated debt. Instead of a financial industry, the big Wall Street banks had become a debt-finance industry. Today the world's financial sector has fabricated and sold, to repeat, over $1.5 quadrillion worth of global derivative debt.

6

When did leading plutocrats and oligarchs in the U.S. become so successful at buying up our politicians? Obviously the wealthy have attempted to suborn politicians' votes as long as there have been politics. In her book *Dark Money,* however, Jane Mayer described a more disturbing trend. She described a group of approximately 200 radically rich donors who have organized to such a degree that their combined GOP contributions are greater than all other contributions put together.

Furthermore, the political plutocrats are nothing like the great American tycoons at the beginning of the 20th century—Henry Ford, Andrew Carnegie, John D. Rockefeller and Edward Harriman. Those men, while capable of great ruthlessness, were pioneers in industrializing America and helped to turn the U.S. into a global superpower. Jane Mayer pointed out that today's Radical Rich were typically men of a different stripe. Many of them made their fortunes off Wall Street hedge funds—which bankrolled the mass production and securitization of debt—and lobbied hard to shrink the antitrust division and the power SEC; they were casino tycoons who promoted gambling, hardly a socially redemptive avocation; they were petrochemical magnates who fought tooth-and-claw to abolish the EPA and saw the wholesale polluting of America and the acceleration of global warming regardless of the consequences as their God-given right; or they were munitions manufacturers, beer barons or defense contractors.

But most of them were derivatives moguls.

And many of these billionaire donors were extremists. Some of them had parents and grandparents who had trafficked with Adolf Hitler and Josef Stalin. Some had believed Eisenhower to be a paid agent of the Soviet Union. A few of them dismissed Ronald Reagan as a pseudoconservative and a sellout for not fighting hard enough to abolish Social Security and Medicare.

Mayer described in detail the New Oligarchs and the hold they eventually acquired on the GOP. *Forbes* called them "the invisible rich," and at first they worked in secrecy and in the dark—so covertly that when Barack Obama first took office he was only vaguely aware of their existence. The invisible rich seemed to come out of nowhere, and Obama's people complained that these groups blocked and attacked them so fast and so furiously they did not know what had hit them.

The hard right's first major successes were at the statehouse level, where they swept election after election after election. Once in control of the governorships and statehouses, they could gerrymander voting districts and expand voter-suppression laws, making it prohibitively difficult for minorities, college students, the working class, the disabled and the elderly—the base of the Democratic Party—to cast ballots. They quickly commandeered the House of Representatives and marginalized the Democratic Party almost out of existence.

After that, the Radical Rich were in position to take over the Supreme Court, where they pushed through Citizens United, which allowed the rich to donate almost unlimited sums to political parties of their choosing. At that point, they were effectively able to purchase any legislation that increased their wealth and power. They were even able to channel many of those donations through foundations, which allowed them to take charitable deductions, inspiring Warren Buffett to dub their movement the "Charitable-Industrial Complex."

Their political ideology? It came down to money and power, pure and simple. They all wanted to keep the IRS's carried-interest loophole, which kept the majority of their taxes below 20 percent. The petrochemical barons wanted to castrate the EPA and eliminate pollution restrictions. The Wall Street tycoons wanted to abolish Dodd–Frank and defang the SEC so they could do high-stakes deals unimpeded, then get taxpayer bailouts when their gambles went south—as they did during the debt-derivative debacle of 2008. There were no "ethical principles" involved in their political movement. It was a zero-sum, winner-take-all, war-to-the-knife, upper-one-percent, "I'll-leave-you-bleeding-from-the-rectum" business philosophy. Mitt Romney summarized their attitude perfectly when he said 47 percent of the country was "moochers and takers" and it was us, the Upper One Percent, against them. They wanted a country run by the unelected rich who were answerable to no one.

7

The U.S. has a vast and heterogeneous transnational economy based on free markets and free trading. For super-rich corporate moguls to turn America's political-economic system into an oligarchy would be an ambitious—but not an impossible—undertaking. Thanks to decades of highly destructive mergers that have shrunk the number of leading companies in most of the top U.S. industries over the last four decades, we have seen corporate power concentrated into a rapidly shrinking number of hands. Jane Mayer points out that since the oil industry is dominated by only a half dozen mega-firms, it is arguably an oligarchy. The airline industry is dominated by four companies and is, by definition, an oligarchy. Today in the U.S. we also see increasing monopolization within individual cities and regions, particularly in health care services.

So what would an American oligarchy be like?

One of the many problems with oligarchy regards erosion of political rights. Since the oligarchs are able to buy the legislators, presidents and judges, they exert undue control over the political/judicial systems, and their rights perforce trump the rights of ordinary people. The political/judicial system then exists to advance their interests. Increasingly, they force the legislature to nationalize their business risks and privatize their economic rewards.

Since the oligarchs face little if any competition within their various industries, they have immense control over their employees' wages and working conditions. Consequently, the oligarchs share, if not control, the massive power of the state, and they are subject to relatively few checks and balances. Might makes right, and given the erosion of the legislature's and the judiciary's authority, all that is required for a tyrant to assume absolute power is a coup. Caesar Augustus, Napoléon, Lenin, Hitler, and some say Vladimir Putin came to power through coups d'état.

Russia is very clearly an oligarchy run by an extremely powerful strongman, Vladimir Putin, and while I write about Russia in my novel, my character is not Russia's current president. I do, however, accurately describe the state of Russia's economy, that nation's essential demography, and my statistics are accurate. It is not a pretty picture. One of my characters, the journalist Jules Meredith, writes a newspaper piece summarizing the damage that the tyrant Mikhail Ivanovich Putilov and his oligarchy had done for the Russian people:

> *What has Putilov's oligarchy done for him, and what has he done for his fellow citizens? In the late 1980s, he'd been thrown out of the KGB, and he was a nobody—just a busted-out intelligence agent who had drifted into politics. He had never been a lawyer, doctor, teacher, scientist or scholar—a manufacturer, a financier or any kind of businessman. He was merely a KGB functionary who had created nothing of financial worth or socially redeeming value. Yet twenty-five years after entering politics, Putilov owned twenty official residences with*

24/7 round-the-clock staffing. One of them—"Putilov's Palace"—cost his oligarchical supporters $1 billion. He was the proud possessor of four yachts—one of them worth $50 million—fifty-eight airplanes and almost $1 million worth of watches. One of his favorites was his $60,000 white-gold Patek Philippe Perpetual Calendar.

Worth over $200 billion, Putilov was easily the wealthiest man on earth, with two and a half times as much money as the second-biggest billionaire, the legitimate businessman Bill Gates.

How had he acquired such prodigious riches?

In the 1970s the USSR had kept tens of millions of dollars' worth of foreign currency in secret accounts concealed in other countries—partly to fund operations abroad. Intelligence agencies worldwide had abundant evidence that Putilov and his brigands stole almost all of it. He then arranged for the theft of over 500 tons of bullion purloined from the old USSR's gold reserves. He and his crew also mastered the arcane minutiae of asset-stripping, the privatization of government properties, extortion of legitimate businessmen, outright thievery and the simple art of murdering anyone who got in their way. And of course, they exacted bribes on an almost cosmic scale. Even today, a simple meeting with President Putilov costs a Russian businessman $10 million. Some Russian businessmen privately grumble that the cost of doing major deals in Putilov's Russia is a 35 percent bribe to the new Czar.

A Spanish prosecutor who had successfully wiretapped many of Putilov's business partners while they were in Spain—building illicit villas with conscripted Russian military personnel and running various black-market enterprises—said the transcripts proved that Russia's mafiosi were an integral part of those and many other of Putilov's operations. In fact, over the decades Putilov, his ex-KGB associates and his coterie of oligarchs had found the Russian mafia to be invaluable allies. They routinely employed them for targeted beatings, killings and other acts of calculated terror, which assured the Putilov clique's total domination of Russian politics and economic markets. All the while, he and his junta reaped hundreds of billions of dollars.

Putilov even managed to plunder his fellow plunderers. Setting himself up as the ultimate crime boss, his economic system became known as Putilovism—a tribute system in which all the players bowed to his absolute authority. In exchange Putilov bestowed on them the right to pillage those around them on a historically unprecedented *level—he has granted them utter immunity from legal punishment. As part of his protection racket, Putilov awards diplomatic counselorships to his most loyal followers, freeing them of domestic and foreign prosecution and most forms of intrusive surveillance.*

The West assists Putilov and his people at every turn. After Putilov and his pirate crew lawlessly loot their own land, the Western world—with its strict adherence to law and order—sees to it that these freebooters' ill-gotten gains are safely and secretly secured. Under the aegis of these democratic privacy laws, Putilov has constructed for himself and his cronies a seemingly impenetrable underground labyrinth of thousands upon thousands of hidden accounts.

To put the sum total of Putilov's thefts into perspective, consider that the U.S. GDP is $18 trillion and U.S. tax-free offshore accounts contain $2.1 trillion, or 12 percent of its GDP. The world's GDP is around $75 trillion, and the total amount of global black money buried abroad is around $26 trillion, or about 32 perent of the planet's GDP. As obscene as those percentages might be, they pale before those of Putilov's Russia. The $1.3 trillion that Putilov and his cronies have locked away in Western banks is more than 100 percent of Russia's GDP, which is only $1.26 trillion. In other words, Putilov and his wolf pack have devoured the equivalent of Russia's entire annual GDP!

So we know what Putilovism has done for Putilov and his billionaire partners. It's made them all unimaginably rich, but what has it done to the Russian people? Theirs is a story of unremitting poverty and brutal exploitation. Despite one statistically aberrant population spurt, that nation now faces a long-term population implosion—not explosion. According to the Brookings Institution by the century's end, Russia could well see its number of citizens drop from 143.5 million to 100 million people, its 1950 census level.

Why the contraction?

Putilov's oligarchy has stretched his people to the breaking point. Instead of upgrading Russia's collapsing health care system, he has plundered those programs remorselessly and funneled the money into the pockets of himself and his wealthy friends. Consequently, the depressed and oppressed Russian people labor under some of the highest rates of alcoholism, tobacco abuse and drug addiction on the face of the earth. Deaths from HIV/AIDS are rampant as are loss of life from heart disease, air/water pollution and suicide. Consequently, male longevity in Putilov's Russia is fifteen years lower than that of men in Germany, Italy and Sweden. The life expectancy of a fifteen-year-old boy in Russia is three years lower than that of a Haitian fifteen-year-old boy. Polish women live an average of six years longer than Russian women. In fact, each year, Russian men kill more women in their families than the Afghans killed Russian soldiers during that entire conflict.

Such long-term depopulation trends also spell economic disaster. A Yale University study says Russia has entered a "demographic perfect storm." In thirty-five years, persons of worker-age in Russia will constitute less than 14 percent of the population. Moreover, the country is witnessing a rapid decline in the educational and skill levels of its workers. All of these stressors will put profound pressure on the pension plans and health care providers servicing Russia's rapidly aging population.

Unsurprisingly, foreign firms are not eager to set up businesses and invest in Putilov's Russia. Among advanced nations, Russia under Putilov ranks number one for corruption and bribery; it rates last in legal, financial and political transparency. Moreover, doing business in Russia can be highly dangerous if you are not part of Putilov's in-group. In the last ten years Putilov's supporters in the business community have bribed cops, judges and prosecutors to imprison their competitors, putting over 300,000 innocent businesspeople behind bars. According to one estimate, such individuals represent 15 percent of Russia's prison population.

Putilov even refuses to build the minimal infrastructure businesspeople need to conduct business. While China during the last decade has built almost 4,500 miles of roadways, Putilov has yet to construct a single transnational highway. Because of corruption, pipelines in Russia cost 300 percent more than they do in the EU. Of the $50 billion Russia spent on the Sochi Olympics, over $25 billion went into the coffers of Putilov and his partners.

Each year, bribery, kickbacks and extortion under Putilov are estimated to drain 33 percent from its $1.26 trillion GDP.

The sad truth is that Putilov and his supporters are less interested in running their businesses efficiently than they are in robbing the country's economic sector and hiding the money overseas. Among the world's nations, Russia now has, far and away, the highest percentage of its GDP secreted in clandestine foreign bank accounts—many of them in the West. As we mentioned earlier, Putilov and his cadre *of crooks have hidden over 100 percent of Russia's annual GDP abroad.*

The effect that all this corruption has on the financial well-being of individual Russians is devastating. Credit Suisse estimates the median wealth of adults in Russian households to be $871. In other words, half of Russian adults have a total household wealth of under $871. Under Putilov, median household wealth for a Russian adult was 85 percent of that for his or her counterpart in India, where that person was worth $1,040. In Brazil, median wealth is is $5,117; in China it is $8,023.

According to Credit Suisse, in the Land of Putilov, 111 people control 19 percent of that country's entire wealth, and the upper 10 percent possess 85 percent of the money.

While the Russian people under Communist rule historically had a long tradition of literacy and academic achievement, and while they are still relatively well-educated in math and science, there are limited job opportunities for their best-educated people, many of whom are brilliant, creative, ambitious and highly trained in these disciplines. The country produces shockingly little technological innovation or development. The state of Alabama produces more patents each year than Russia. Austria develops thirty-five times as many. Employment opportunities are so dismal that one poll indicated that almost two-thirds of the Russian population seriously considers emigration.

Under Yeltsin, Russia had financial problems, but people and businesses enjoyed relative personal and financial freedom. Putilovism changed all that. Russia's expanding free market system was turned into an economic dictatorship with all major business decisions dependent on the whims of a single ruler. To achieve this position of total power, Putilov had to pauperize and subjugate the entirety of the Russian people and rip successful Russian companies apart piecemeal. As Karen Dawisha has written: "Massive companies that had previously flourished in the private sector, like Mikhail Khodorkovsky's [oil company] Yukos, were raided and taken over by Kremlin insiders."

Such tactics have driven most investors out of Russia. U.S. hedge fund magnate William Browder is a classic case. He'd invested heavily in Russia and had done well—until he rebelled against Russia's corruption and its lack of business transparency. Putilov responded by arresting Browder's lawyer–auditor, Sergey Magnitskiy, and jail-

ing him. Savagely beaten in prison, Magnitskiy was also starved, subjected to freezing cold and denied medical care. He subsequently died.

The United States under Barack Obama did fight back. Obama put those responsible for Magnitskiy's death and for the illegal expropriation of Browder's assets on a visa-denial list and refused them entrance into the U.S. Russia responded to these actions by trying Browder in absentia and Magnitskiy posthumously—both for tax evasion. After sentencing Browder, who by that time was living overseas, to a long prison term, Russia seized and gutted his Russian companies, funneling hundreds of millions of dollars into Putilov's private bank account and those of his jackal pack.

It was also the first time in history a legal system had tried a corpse.

Meanwhile, Russia's economy continues to fall apart. Not only has their leader's ferocity frightened away foreign investors, it has scared Russian businessmen into leaving Russia. Over 300,000 such businesspeople have moved to London, hoping to find a safer environment for themselves and their families. With macabre irony, some of these émigrés have continued to work for their government, ransacking the Russian economic sector. At the same time, however, they and their families rely on law-abiding Londoners and that nation's respect-for-the-law political system to provide peace and security for themselves and their loved ones. The hard painful truth is that the Western banking system has acted as Putilov's willful enablers and fraudulent financiers.

As I said, my character Putilov is fictional, but I accurately describe the statistical effects of oligarchy on Russia's citizenry. Rule by a handful of super-rich autocrats has typically led to the commandeering of the legislative and judicial branches of government, resulting in state racketeering on a massive scale. In the case of Russia, the compete takeover of Russia's news media was also predictable, and it, consequently, became a propaganda arm of the state and of that nation's oligarchs.

Russia is not the only oligarchic tyranny in recent memory. In *The Arms of Krupp,* William Manchester describes a scene in which Germany's top industrialists ask themselves whether they should support Hitler in his campaign for the chancellorship even though he has made it quite clear that he plans on making himself dictator for life. They decide to back him, in large part because he has offered to rid them of their union problems—a promise he would ruthlessly keep. They, consequently, shower massive political contributions on him. Their decision to bankroll an indisputably evil monster is based almost solely on greed.

Manchester goes on to describe in shocking detail how, after Hitler conquered foreign nations, these same oligarchs would assist him in commandeering the foreign factories, plants, mills, mines and oil operations. Sometimes they and the Reich would simply strip out the heavy industrial equipment and take it back to the Fatherland, where the materials would be refit for use in the oligarchs' plants. They would bring back hordes of slave laborers to work in their plants as well. One industrialist became so rich and powerful off these "hostile takeovers" that, Manchester wrote, his company's "smokestacks stained the sky over almost every continental country, from Belgium to Bulgaria, from Norway to Italy." That firm owned thousands of ore pits and coal mines in foreign lands as well—even in Russia.

In another blood-chilling scene, a group of these preeminent plutocrats pore over a European map and a list of all the nations in that region that Hitler has recently conquered. They begin chopping up these countries' industrial sectors like gangsters carving up 1920s Chicago, dividing up factories, plants, refineries and mills among themselves. Throughout the book, Manchester depicts these moguls swelling with pride as their bottom lines swell with black ink generated by Hitler's conquests.

The Arms of Krupp dramatically demonstrates what happens to a country when a small clique whose main ambition is to accumulate illimitable wealth seizes power. Totalitarian tyranny cannot be far behind.

Americans should not think the kind of behavior we have just described is relegated solely to foreign cultures or worlds in crisis. The U.S. has had its own version of American oligarchs staring at a map of another country and contemplating what to do with that nation's most lucrative industries.

Many experts believe that Iraq's untested oil reserves are among the most valuable on the planet. In early 2001, Vice President Dick Cheney met with a number of top U.S. oil executives. He showed them a map featuring Iraq's oil fields and facilities. (The map is available online.) He also listed for them the firms to which Saddam Hussein had promised those oil sites. No U.S. firms were on that list.

It was clear to all present that they would not gain control of that oil unless the U.S. took those facilities from Saddam, and two years later the Bush team invaded Iraq. There is ample evidence to support the contention that the Bush team wanted to expropriate Iraq's oil. To argue otherwise is fundamentally naïve.

Nor has America's propensity for predatory avarice diminished. As I pointed out in the novel, Donald Trump's former national security adviser,

Michael Flynn, attempted to sell the Saudis and a number of their Arab neighbors forty nuclear power plants. (*Politico* reports that Flynn made such a pitch to the king of Jordan in the presence of two other top Trump officials.) Such plants bring the possessor nation dangerously close to developing a nuclear weapons program. The next few steps are strictly low-tech and shockingly simple to execute. Furthermore, the Saudis have a long history of bankrolling ISIS/al Qaeda-style terrorism, are drenched in sun, rich in oil and have no need for nuclear power plants—unless they view them as a starter kit for a nuclear weapons program. Solar power plants would be far more cost-effective for them.

8

Of course, such oligarchic coups d'état require control of the electoral process as well as the economic takeovers of major industries. Still such electoral coups are easier to achieve than most people realize, and, once more, Russia is a master of those dark arts. The evidence that Russia engages in all sorts of electoral meddling is overwhelming, and so I tried hard to keep those parts of the book authoritative.

In researching electoral sabotage, I owe an inestimable debt to Sue Halpern's reportage on voter hacking in *The New York Review of Books* and to Bev Harris's marvelous documentary, *Hacking Democracy,* as well as to her website www.BlackBoxVoting.org. *The New York Times, Politico* and *Wired* also covered the subject in great detail. I am likewise obliged to the *Times* for its excellent coverage of the bot-wars Putin waged against Hillary Clinton.

So in the novel when Putilov describes how, through his cyber-hacking, he threw the election to J. T. Tower, I tried to show how Putilov could have actually accomplished that feat. I attempted to base all of Putilov's assertions on demonstrable fact:

> . . . *Putilov had many reasons for despising democracies. First and foremost, it was too damn easy for men like himself to overturn their democratic elections. The stupid Americans had proven that point at a Las Vegas computer convention. At one exhibition, U.S. cyber-experts changed the voter tabulations on thirty different voting machines, turning thirty mock-election losers into winners. The experts changed those election outcomes in mere minutes. Furthermore, they left no trace, no evidence of their criminal manipulations.*
> *Putilov had, of course, done the same thing during America's last*

presidential election. Unfortunately, Putilov's hackers weren't as good as the Vegas cyber-experts, and U.S. investigators were able to confirm that Russia had fooled with America's voting systems. To counter those charges, Putilov immediately launched a disinformation campaign. He ordered one of his stooges—that country's idiotic FBI director, Jonathan Conley—to issue a statement claiming that the U.S. voting system was too spread out, too diffuse and too diverse for hacking to succeed. That statement was of course a flagrant lie. The voting machines' software could be compromised in a heartbeat—as the Vegas conference had proved—and, anyway, the main tabulators, which counted the votes, were connected to the internet. The average smartphone had more anti-hacking protection in it than your typical voting machine, and the cyber-tools necessary for stealing elections— especially those needed to purge voter registration lists and to falsify absentee ballot requests—were readily available online. Consequently, Putilov could hack into the U.S. voting system at will and with a vengeance. Likewise, the systems' manufacturers and support technicians could plant vote-altering malware any time they wanted. Nor were the manufacturers interested in stopping Putilov's election hacking. When the Princeton Group began testing voting machines, one manufacturer threatened them with a lawsuit, and when, in the documentary Hacking Democracy, *cyber-expert Bev Harris proved how vulnerable they were, the machines' manufacturers—instead of thanking her for tracking down the flaws in their equipment—had threatened to sue her.*

You got off lucky, bitch, *Putilov thought to himself.* In my country, I'd have had you jailed, killed—or both!

God, Putilov hated that documentary. He was sure that after it came out the Americans would build a cybersecurity firewall around their voting systems. In that documentary and on her website, www.BlackBoxVoting.org, Harris had described defect after defect after defect in America's voting systems. For instance, she showed how touch screens could be programmed to register one's vote for the opposite candidate. She laid out how incredibly simple it was to flip absentee and mail-in ballots and make them register as votes for a candidate's rival. She pointed out how in one district votes for Al Gore in Florida had been subtracted from Gore's final tally instead of being added to it. She demonstrated how—after voting systems had been hacked and the vote tabulations changed to elect the loser— forensic investigators lacked the technological means to detect and prove the system had been hacked and the outcome reversed . . . the same thing the Vegas experts had proved. She laid out for the world how hackable U.S. elections were.

But the moronic Americans did . . . nothing.

So Putilov had waged an all-out cyber-attack on America's last political race, and after more than twenty years of hacking elections— both in his country and in those of his neighbors—there was nothing Putilov and his experts did not know about rigging a country's electronic voting systems. So they penetrated and plundered every aspect of America's state, local, and national elections, and those vote thefts had been as easy for them as stealing milk bottles from sick babies. In fact, they had faced no obstacles at all. The voting machine vendors refused to work with the anti-hacking experts, because they knew that they could be held liable, when their voting equipment was proven faulty and that their stock price could very well plunge precipitously. The states, who had absolute control over all elections within their borders, also refused to let the Department of Homeland Security help them insure the integrity of their elections. They had stonewalled them when they offered to help prevent election hacking. Many of those states were already in the business of rigging elections through voter suppression laws and voter registration purges, and they did not want the feds looking over their shoulders. The state politicians also feared that their ineptitude in the face of proven cyber-attacks would become a political issue. In the coming elections, their opponents would accuse them of gross incompetence, and their opponents would, of course, be right. Thus, the states, like the private firms, ignored almost all outside cyber-security help. Putilov recalled how The New York Times *had described in painful detail the states' refusal to cooperate with these federal anti-hacking experts. The* Times *reported that the states would not allow the cyber-cops—both from within and without the U.S. government—to sort through voter databases, searching for vulnerabilities or attempts to phony up voter data, even though such intrusions had already been spotted in elections in over twenty-one states. Instead the states and the private companies rebuffed offers of almost all in-depth forensic investigations into their blatantly hacked elections. They had made sure that government couldn't probe and monitor U.S. elections and that there was almost no way to audit the vote tabulations afterward. Only two out of America's fifty states created systems that allowed for accurate vote recounts. Putilov and his allies could even kill many of their opponents' votes in the cradle before their ballots could be cast. Putilov and his U.S. allies could purge any and all voters who were ex-felons, who had the same names as other voters in the registry or who had failed to vote in recent elections.*

Putilov allowed himself a small, malicious smile, as he recalled how he and his military spy agency, the GRU, had pillaged the providers of electronic election equipment and services and the anachronistic voting machines themselves as well as how he had exploited the states' laughably ludicrous recount procedures. Putilov and his henchmen had raided the private vendors and state-run voting systems in almost half of the country and reversed the nation's election results with breathtaking facility.

Of course, the GRU's manipulations did not go utterly undiscovered, but it did not matter. When cyber-irregularities were occasionally detected, Putilov's good buddies, J. T. Tower and Jonathan Conley, saw to it that his electoral sabotage was quickly debunked and deflected. Even before the election, when the FBI caught Putilov's people hacking into the Democratic National Committee (DNC), Conley saw to it that the Bureau bungled and delayed informing the DNC of the cyber-attacks. Consequently, Putilov had every file and email that he needed—with which to discredit the Democratic Party and its candidates—long before the DNC realized the seriousness of the breach.

Putilov's hackers now knew how to overturn any and all U.S. elections at the state, local and national level with impunity. There was nothing America could do about it. As Wired *magazine had titled one of its articles, "America's Electronic Voting Machines Are Scarily Easy to Target."*

The memory of those cyber-assaults forced the Russian dictator to laugh out loud. When North Korea had hacked the electronics/media firm, Sony, the U.S. had done more the punish the Hermit Kingdom than that country had done to Putilov, and he had overturned many of their last state, local and national elections. He had even made J. T. Tower the American president.

And now with the help of J. T. Tower and their Saudi allies, he and an elite cadre of global oligarchs were poised to purge the earth of all its so-called democracies. The pernicious plague of "one person, one vote" would be flung down the planet's "memory hole" for all time to come.

You can't help but love capitalism, can you? *Putilov thought, grinning. It had made him the richest man in the world, and now the Old Free Enterprise System was about to help him wipe all those reprehensible representative democracies off the face of the earth.*

Putilov couldn't wait to hack America's coming election. He would be even better at it next time. After that election his band of merry cyber-thieves would leave no evidence whatsoever . . .

And last but not least, I am indebted to *The Daily Beast* for their marvelous work on Donald J. Trump and his profiteering off the Russian birth-tourism business in Miami.

9

The problem of malignant greed has haunted humanity since the invention of hard currency. Avarice was a menace then, and it's a menace today. In describing the cause of the Peloponnesian War, the cataclysmic conflict that destroyed the world's first and arguably greatest democracy, Thucydides writes: "But as the power of Hellas grew, and the acquisition of wealth became more an objective, the revenues of the states increasing, tyrannies were established almost everywhere [throughout that nation]. . . ." Thucydides also informs us that "war is a matter not so much of arms as of money." When Athens demands tribute from the Melians—which they simply do not have and cannot pay—the Athenian emissary explains that if they don't pay, the Athenian soldiers will kill every man and enslave every woman in their land. When asked why, the emissary explains: "The strong will do what they can do, and the weak will suffer as they must."

Thucydides believed that financial rapacity eventually destroyed Athens—arguably the greatest democracy in world history.

Plato wrote 2,500 years ago in *The Laws:* "[T]here should exist among the citizens neither extreme poverty nor, again, excessive wealth, for both are productive of great evil." He wrote again in *The Republic:* "Any city, however small, is in fact divided into two, one the city of the poor, the other of the rich; these are at war with one another."

Plato's student, Aristotle, informed us: "Poverty is the parent of revolution and crime."

Jesus tells His disciples that while the rich may reign on earth, in His Heavenly City: "The last shall be first and the first shall be last."

The Apostle Paul writes: "Love of money is the root of all evil."

In *Revelation,* John of Patmos warned that human greed leads to Armageddon and the destruction of the planet.

Plutarch warned us over a hundred years after Christ: "An imbalance between rich and poor is the oldest and most fatal ailment of all republics."

Gibbon explained that two of the top causes of Rome's fall were a "widening disparity between very rich and very poor" and a passion for "displaying affluence."

Dante told us that the problem with greedy people is that they "are ill-givers and ill-takers."

Shakespeare speaks out on income inequality in *King Lear*, saying: "So distribution should undo excess, and each man have enough."

Thomas Jefferson warned Americans: "Banking institutions are more dangerous to our liberties than standing armies."

Oliver Goldsmith believed: "Ill fares the land, to hastening ills a prey, / Where wealth accumulates, and men decay."

Balzac told us: "Behind every great fortune is a crime."

And as I quoted at this book's beginning, Keynes predicted: "The love of money as a possession—as distinguished from the love of money as a means to the enjoyments and realities of life—will [one day] be recognized for what it is, a somewhat disgusting morbidity, one of those semi-criminal, semi-pathological propensities which one hands over with a shudder to the specialists in mental disease."

The great 20th-century historian A. J. P. Taylor feared avarice like hell itself, believing it was even the primary cause of that greatest of all human evils, war, saying:

"No matter what political reasons are given for war, the underlying reason is always economic."

And as Nicholas Kristof said:

"Since the end of the 1970s, something has gone profoundly wrong in America. Inequality has soared. Educational progress slowed. Incarceration rates quintupled. Family breakdown accelerated. Median household income stagnated."

I wrote in another book:

"In *The Decline of the West*, Oswald Spengler tried to make some sense of all this financial destruction. He prophesied that Western democracy would not escape the curse of greed. It too would devolve into 'a dictatorship of money' and go the way of both democratic Athens and republican Rome. Nor did he believe 'the dictatorship of money' would go gentle. At the close of his book, Spengler wrote, 'Money is overthrown and abolished only by blood.'"

In his *A Study of History*, Sir Arnold Toynbee discovered a pattern in all this economic predation. He analyzed the rise and fall of twenty-two civilizations, and found their demise always followed the same basic paradigm. While these great realms were all eventually invaded, what the barbarians found was Oz—a hollow shell. Through economic exploitation of their people at home and through imperialist wars abroad—all of which were designed to line the coffers of the monied classes—their rulers had bled their once grand and glorious civilization white. Toynbee said these great empires had died through "suicidal statecraft" and that he was "a coroner-historian."

Perhaps worst of all, Toynbee felt that the U.S. was headed into the same downward spiral as the twenty-two previous civilizations, which had, as he put it, "passed through the door of death." Back in the 20th century, Toynbee explained where America was at in its stage of development:

"Of the twenty-two civilizations that have appeared in history, nineteen of them collapsed when they reached the moral state the United States is in now."

10

On the other hand, Toynbee, unlike his contemporary historian Oswald Spengler, believed that civilizations always had choices. They did not have to end up on the ash heap of history. He also believed, however, that the choices were ethical ones. Suppose Toynbee is right, and our world does not have to pass through Toynbee's "door of death." What choices will we make?

. . . Why must we leave our bounty to the dead?
   Shall blood fail?
Or shall it come to be the blood of paradise?

—adapted from Wallace Stevens's
"Sunday Morning"